THE THRONE
OF BONES

About the Author

Brian McNaughton was born in Red Bank, New Jersey, and attended Harvard. He worked for ten years as a reporter for the *Newark Evening News* and has since held all sorts of other jobs while publishing some 200 stories in a variety of magazines and books. *The Throne of Bones* won the World Fantasy and the International Horror Guild awards in 1998 for best collection.

THE THRONE OF BONES

Brian McNaughton

WILDSIDE PRESS

Berkeley Heights, New Jersey

The Throne of Bones
A publication of
Wildside Press
P.O. Box 45
Gillette, NJ 07933-0045

www.wildsidepress.com

SECOND EDITION

For Gene DeWeese,
W. Paul Ganley, and Robert E. Briney,
who know where the portals lie.

Table of Contents

Brian McNaughton
and the Stories that
Compelled Him
Rich, Phantasmic, Creepy as Sin

The first I ever heard or saw of Brian McNaughton was when Rick Hautala addressed him as though he were a ghost come back to type among the living.

This happened in one of those computer network-places where the horror writers congregate. The person who kept the gate posted a note that he was letting Brian in, and Rick Hautala wrote, "Son of a bitch! It's Brian McNaughton!" I know Rick pretty well, and as he typed that I could just imagine his eyes wide and his mouth hanging open, and I wondered who the heck this *Brian McNaughton* was.

So I asked around a little bit. Only the old timers — folks who'd been writing and reading horror since before the last big bust — had even heard of him.

This doesn't reflect on Brian so much as it reflects on the nature of the market for horror fiction. The horror business ebbs and flows regularly, and radically; the low tide goes *so* low that it drives most all horror writers out of business — and out of memory, too.

A thought experiment, for knowledgeable readers: off the cuff, how many major horror writers can you recall who were writing in 1965?

Let me assure you: there was commercial horror fiction in distribution in 1965. There were writers writing the stuff, there were readers reading the stuff; we don't reside here in a context that bursts already in full bloom from the brow of Stephen King.

I can think of a couple, very quickly: Sarban and Robert Bloch.

Compare this with, say, SF: how many minor SF writers can you recall who were writing in 1965?

I could name a dozen without really trying. (But will refrain: most of them are still around, still working, and would bludgeon me for describing them as minor SF writers from the 1960s.) It's not hard to remember well-known SF writers from the thirties, even the twenties.

The horror business eats writers alive.

Brian got hit hard in the horror bust of the early eighties. And almost at the end of it he threw up his hands and wandered away to labor in a steel mill in New Jersey, or a printing plant in Maine, or a shoe factory in Rhode Island — some dreary place or other; I hate remembering which.

I hate to think how long it was before he started writing again, too. Two years? Three? Five at most. And then he found a used typewriter someplace, and started writing — almost against his will.

You hold in your hands a book of stories that forced Brian McNaughton back to work. They're rich, fascinating stuff — creepy and unsettling and phantasmic. They'll make the same demands on you that they made on Brian: they will demand and compel you, and fill you full of terrible wonder. When you've finished them you'll find yourself wanting more.

*

These aren't horror stories, exactly — but they aren't entirely innocent of horror, either.

These stories take place in a world . . . hmmm. Imagine what Tolkien's *Lord of the Rings* would have been if Tolkien had tried to tell that story sympathetically from the point of view of the human denizens of Mordor.

That's the book you hold in your hands. It's special stuff.

When I said this to Brian he took issue with me. "Tolkien and the Tolkienites," he said, "have never been my cup of tea . . . my world is certainly not unique in its darkness, no darker than Robert E. Howard's world or any of several created by Tanith Lee. Compared to Clark Ashton Smith's Zothique, it is Carnival in Rio all the time.

"And my memory may not serve me over the vast gulf of time that has intervened since I read it, but I think E. R. Eddison's *The Worm Ouroboros* was set in a pretty ghastly milieu. And then there's William Hope Hodgson's *Night Land* or the Dreamland of H.P. Lovecraft, as in *Dream-Quest of Unknown Kadath*."

And certainly he's right, so far as that goes. But all those things he names come from the wide thick root of traditional literary fantasy — a root that manifests nowadays mostly as horror fiction. Modern commercial fantasy, where it grows out of traditional literary forms at all, grows almost exclusively out of Tolkien's work. What Brian's done here is something very interesting: he's grafted this rich, phantasmic, traditional, and *dark* material back onto the monochromatic trunk of the modern genre.

Make no mistake about that: despite Brian's denial, the work of Tolkien and the Tolkienites clearly informs his fantasy. This is modern fantasy, the sort of fantasy that attracts broad modern audiences — because Brian, whatever his deliberate literary influences, is as much a captive to his context as any of us are.

Delightfully so. Fascinatingly so. You and I are very lucky to have this book to read. The things that compelled Brian to return to the career he'd abandoned are powerful things indeed.

*

Which brings us back to Brian's life and his lifework.

When I finished reading the manuscript for this collection, I asked Brian where I could find copies of his older books.

He waved me away.

Back in the seventies, he said in a letter a few weeks ago, he used to write books with *Satan* in their titles. He's doing something very different now; none of that work really matters.

My foot, I said.

But there was no arguing with him: He wouldn't tell me anything more.

He's equally shy with his biography. Here and there in the five years or so I've known him, I've heard Brian mention old fannish horror types in whose youthful company he committed fanzines — but when I asked him point-blank about fan-ac he responded very coyly. "None of my bio seems terribly important or interesting," he said, "except for the literary influences cited above. Smith, whom I discovered around 12, was my foremost influence, one that I certainly hope I have outgrown — as a direct influence, that is, not my taste for his work, which is still strong — and absorbed."

"But I was born in Red Bank, NJ, in 1935, went to school there and to Harvard, where I dropped out after a couple years. At the time I thought of myself as a poet, but *that* ambition never got very far and I became a newspaperman instead." He smiled sardonically. "When the paper (the Newark *Evening News*) folded around 1970 — having given me an education in politics and other areas of human depravity that I have since profitably converted into fiction — I set out to make my living as a writer of fiction. Most of this stuff, mostly for men's mags and under a variety of pseudonyms as well as my own name, is pretty reprehensible and forgettable. I think even all those novels with *Satan* in the title are best forgotten that I wrote in the 70s and early 80s."

So far as I can tell, those books are out of print and unfindable, completely lost in time. I would like to see those books. I suspect that we'd all be richer if we could find them.

— Alan Rodgers

Ringard and Dendra

The most extravagant rumors of the stranger's ugliness had been nothing but plain truth. A further rumor had yet to be investigated, that he was a fiend whose mother had made a fool of herself with a snake. I dismounted and walked towards him, my hand resting on the hilt of the manqueller that hung by my saddle.

As if we had been chatting all day, he asked, "This used to be the slope of a hill, didn't it?"

That was obvious. The Sons of Cludd had sheered it right off, leaving the cliff of bare earth that towered above us. I assumed they had planned to build a retaining wall, for destabilizing gullies already scored the cliff, but they had abandoned the picks and shovels that lay rusting about us and run off to hunt witches.

I tried to restart our conversation on a formal basis: "I am Lord Fariel."

"Of the House of Sleith," he stated, and I managed not to flinch when he swung his eyes at me. "You didn't lay your own land waste, did you?"

Except for their extraordinary sadness, his eyes were those of an ordinary old man. It was their setting that had upset everyone, tattoos like the patterned skin of a reptile. Not even his eyelids and his lips had escaped the needle. The scaly effect was accidental, because the details depicted nothing more sinister than exotic flowers and fungi.

However odd, a human garden was pleasanter than a human snake, and I answered him less stiffly: "The Empress wanted the Cluddites out of her hair, so she sent them to fortify the border. They tell me this will be a supply road."

He nodded absently as he scanned the pines at the top of the cliff, then turned and pondered the hardwood forest on the interrupted slope. He seemed to be looking for lost landmarks.

I said, "You don't come from here, do you?"

"I do. My wife may have been your kinswoman. Dendra Sleith?"

I gaped as I would at a confessed elf, for he was a creature found only in fireside tales and songs. My Aunt Dendra had long ago been kidnapped on her wedding-night by a woodcutter's son named: "Ringard?"

"The same."

My father would have killed him on the spot. Less impetuous relatives would have deferred his death, the better to savor it, but I felt only curiosity about a man whose stature in our provincial gossip was mythic. Disfigurement aside, he was bald and bent and ordinary as an old boot. He looked hard and lean, but so does the oaf who slops out my stables, and nobody would ever sing rousing ballads about *him*.

He stared at me with the dignity of a hound too weary to fawn or cringe. If I'd struck him, I don't think he would have been impressed. He had been struck before.

Contrary to his expectations, I was concerned for his safety. "You had better come with me," I said. "The Cluddites are in the grip of a witch-craze, they've misused some of my people already, and your appearance. . . ."

His smile was an angry twitch. "Like many others who served with Lord Azaxiel, I was shipwrecked on the coast of Tampoontam, where the savages gave me the choice of joining their tribe by either adoption or ingestion. You might say that I earned these decorations in the service of our late Emperor."

The Cluddites wouldn't say that. They would assume that old Ringard had dined and worshipped in the fashion of his adoptive brothers. Burning an idolatrous cannibal might strike them as a diverting respite from burning witches. While I considered how to warn him tactfully, he asked, "What set them off?"

"One of their preachers, of course. An owl hooted, a wolf howled, the wind sighed among the trees—they don't like any of that. They're mostly from Zaxann, this bunch, swineherds and ploughboys, but they seem afraid of the woods."

"The gulf between a woodsman and a farmer is as great as that between a grand lord like yourself and a common sailor." He gestured at the raw gap the Holy Soldiers had cut through the hill. "Farmers hate trees."

While we talked he had led me toward a pile of felled trees, tall as the cliff, that the Cluddites had pushed aside. He circled the heap, climbed it easily as a monkey, peered into it as if searching. Once or twice he called softly, though I could not hear the words.

"Have you lost a dog?"

"No." He gave no explanation, but he caught the hint that his behavior was odd. He scrambled down and accepted my offer of food and shelter.

*

My household had cheered me for riding forth alone to confront the infamous Snake Man who had scared them even more than the witch-hunt. Their enthusiasm cooled when I brought him home for dinner. My wife and sisters absented themselves from the table and banished the children to the nursery.

The servants who attended him at trembling arm's length averted their eyes from his fantastic decoration, so I was kept hopping to spare him from being scalded or carved. He was, after all, my long-lost uncle, for kidnapping is an acceptable form of marriage in our part of the world. The social gulf in the couple and Aunt Dendra's status as someone else's bride suggested quibbles, but I was no lawyer. He hardly noticed my efforts as he attacked his food in the style of a woodcutter turned sailor and adopted by cannibals. Some of my more legitimate uncles had worse manners.

Finished, unselfconsciously stuffing bread and imperfectly stripped bones into his pockets, he asked, "Do you remember Dendra?"

I had often asked myself that. I think my memory of the fair-haired girl with the sly smile who had joined me in romping with the hounds or making mud-castles, when she should have been practicing the lute or counting her jewels, derived from stories I had been told, and from a portrait I found in a storeroom. I did remember a sudden lack in my life, a moment beyond which my childhood no longer seemed so happy. That, I think, was my only true memory of Dendra.

I wanted to let him talk, so I said merely, "I don't think so."

"If you remembered her, you would know," he stated. "She was . . . entirely herself. Her hair was the color of rain when the sun shines."

While his eyes turned inward, I noticed that the children had defied their mother's order and were peeking at my fabulous guest from a shadowed gallery. I pretended not to see them. Later, when I should have chased them to bed with assurances that he was only telling a story, I had forgotten them, so I was blamed for their nightmares; and for their fear, not yet overcome, of the woods around our home.

When his silence had continued for some time, I prompted, "Was?"

"Oh, yes. I assume she's dead. I certainly hope so, for the alternatives are unthinkable." He treated me again to that angry twitch he used for a smile. "I searched in Crotalorn, but the palace of Dwelphorn Thooz has been eradicated. Even Amorartis Street is gone, buried under the mosaic paving of a spacious new square."

I called for more wine and suggested, to my everlasting regret, that he begin his story at the beginning.

*

Even as a child (Ringard said), I loved trees and grieved that my father chopped them down so that louts like us could suck hot soup. I would often sneak outdoors at night to avoid sharing the fire. In the hisses and crackles so comforting to everyone else, I heard tiny shrieks of agony.

Each tree was different, even each oak or larm or hemlock from the others of its kind, and I believed that certain trees spoke to me. I followed my father to work each day: not as other small boys would, to play at woodcutter, but to watch with grave disapproval and make sure he left my special friends standing.

It was no use beating this nonsense out of my head, though he tried often enough. He was finally persuaded by one of our neighbors, a woman whose wisdom was ordinarily viewed with suspicion, that I was favored by the godlings who lived in trees. Even my stolid father used charms to fend off the snits of dryads his work might discommode, so the wise woman's explanation, though not welcome, was accepted. My mother imagined I would grow up to be a priest, and I encouraged her delusion.

As it does to us all, time callused my finer senses. I grew deaf to the voices of trees. I couldn't bring myself to chop one down, but I would guide the oxen that hauled it out of the forest. I even overcame my qualms about splitting and stacking wood, although that would once have been as distasteful to me as cording human corpses.

One day I was chopping kindling in our yard when I noticed a piece that looked like a wolf—no, not exactly: as if a wolf were trapped in the wood, and I could free it by knocking off the irrelevant parts. It was a very poor likeness that I carved, but my father recognized it. My mother displayed it over the hearth, refusing my pleas to replace it with any of the better figures I was soon making.

In every stick I saw hidden shapes, and I became obsessed with revealing them. My father fretted that I meant to ruin him by turning his valuable firewood into whimsies. I perversely maintained that my carvings had more worth than kindling, that they even justified the sacrifice of living trees. Those captive owls and trout were really there. Why would the gods let me see them, if not to set me the challenge of liberating them?

No one ever thought of selling the results, and my parents began to suspect that my lunacy had returned in a new form. I tried to explain, but talk of freeing wooden captives dismayed them. My mother removed the wolf from its place of honor on the mantel.

I discovered an abandoned hut in the forest where I could steal away to work in peace. Before long the figures had crowded me out, but I squatted at the entrance and liberated still more birds and beasts, demons and men. I was mustering an army to protect me from the demands of the world, and I felt an urgent need to make it ever larger as those demands grew clamorous. A plan was afoot to send me to the Pollian monks in year or so. Loving shapes and patterns as I did, no future held less appeal than adoring the Sun God until he should blind me.

Totally absorbed in my work one day, I was startled out of my wits by a girl's voice: "Oh, *ugh!* Why are you making such a filthy beast?"

The wood that came to hand was full of turtles lately, not filthy beasts but well-armored philosophers. I tried to tell her that my subjects chose me, but I was unused to wedging my thoughts into words. As I mumbled and stammered, she roamed through my array of defenders, gawking and disarranging.

"What grotesque rubbish!" she said. "You ought to make only nice things, like this bird, this horse. What's this?"

"It's a troll."

"I thought it was my brother. If you painted them, it might be easier to tell. Wouldn't they all look nicer if they were painted?"

"No," I said automatically, but it was an idea that had never entered my head.

"I'll bring paints tomorrow. You'll see."

And she was gone, before I had determined who or quite what she was, apart from one more intolerable intrusion of the world. I thought of gathering my friends together and moving on to a less frequented part of the forest, but that would have taken enormous effort. I should have chased her away, and I angrily honed the sharp words I would speak tomorrow.

She wouldn't be back, though. She was a mooncalf who had slipped her leash. Paints, indeed! Priests and lords might have paints to splash on their toys, but the people I knew, scrabbling for wood or hides, were lucky to get whitewash for their hovels.

Why should I regret that she was crazy, or that I probably wouldn't see her again? Because, I told myself, I would never be able to throw insults and rocks at her. Nevertheless I entertained visions of my friends dressed up in pretty paints. I saw her working beside me with her brush, pausing to gaze admiringly at my carving. She would admire me even more when a bear or a wolf came upon us and I scared it off. A girl, I had thought, was only an inferior sort of boy, but now I grew bemused with the differences. The biggest difference was her ability to ruin a whole day's work with so little effort. No boy had ever done that.

She spoiled my next morning, too, by failing to return. I could only whittle aimlessly. Some of the pieces I found held her face, but I had no talent for exact likenesses of individuals. Her memory changed more the closer I examined it, until I hardly remembered her face at all.

Convinced at last that she wouldn't come, I had just submerged into my work when she dropped beside me from nowhere. I could have carved myself a more eloquent tongue than the one knotted behind my teeth, but she chattered for both of us as she painted the troll that had recalled her brother: yes, painted, to my astonishment, in the yellow and blue livery of the House of Sleith. The colors of that Tribe were repeated in her untidy clothes and the ribbons of her braids. I guessed she was a thieving servant from the castle.

Some days later she told me a story in which her distracted nurse called for her as "Lady Dendra," but I shrugged that off. One of the few things I knew about great ladies was that they didn't run loose in the woods with bare feet and dirty faces. She was even queerer than I was thought to be, but I didn't hold it against her, for she was my first non-wooden friend.

I carved, she painted my carvings and gave them life. She brought me books with pictures of tigers, griffins, men with black skins and suchlike mythical creatures, all of which I later found hiding in my wood. We made up histories for the figures and played elaborate games with them whose rules evolved daily. She gave me a set of knives that glimmered like the morning star, that cut the toughest oak as if it were fungus. She talked about our living together in the castle of the Sleiths when we were married, where we should have more than enough room to keep my creations out of the rain.

To part with my friends pained me, but I could work such magic in her face with a simple gift that I would often give her figures she liked. When she let it drop that her fourteenth birthday was near, I labored in secret on a family of gnomes I had detected in the stump of a festiron. I freed them perfectly, and when I presented them to her on the eve of her birthday, she was transported. She gave me in return a hug and a kiss, two wonders entirely new. My cheeks burned, my brain floated away like a cloud, to specify only two of the bizarre effects, but she was so dazzled by her gift that she failed to see that I was fatally stricken. She ran off and left me to perish of fever and delirium.

She didn't appear the next day, nor the next. Her absences had always hurt, but this one was torture. I had so much to tell her, so much to ask her, so much to learn. Would she kiss me again?

On the evening of the third day I was returning home from the forest when I saw that men in leather and iron were roaring in my father's face while buffeting him about the head, kicking him in the behind and dunking him in the horse trough. Their trappings were yellow and blue, and their questions concerned me and *Lady Dendra*.

Bawling with outrage, blind with tears, I dashed forth to patter bare fists and feet against iron backs. To my astonishment it was my father who met my attack, and who practiced on me the interviewing techniques he had just learned. My mother ran screaming from the hut—not to rescue me, as my leaping heart believed, but to add the weight of her big red fists to the beating. She screamed questions, alternately incomprehensible or shocking, while the laughter of the castle bullies rattled in my ringing ears.

After the men rode off, my mother said that I would one day thank her for the beating, as it had probably spared me from gelding and garroting, the punishment for "mongrels who sniff at fancy bitches," but I never did.

When I felt well enough to walk to my private place, it seemed pointless. *Lady* Dendra wouldn't be there, only a rabble of dummies. They could all rot, the captives could stay locked in the wood, nothing mattered. But my beautiful knives were there, her gift, and I might fittingly use one to cut my throat. That would certainly show everybody.

When I returned by night she was, incredibly, waiting. She'd run here every time she could elude her new keepers. The gnomes had been our undoing. She had prized them above all her birthday gifts of stallions and silver and silk, and innocently praised my artistry to men who would bellow for their battleaxes when anyone spoke of art. We talked, we wept, we embraced, and this led us to the secrets we had suffered in advance for discovering. My friends stood guard around us in a haze of moonlight that grew brighter than any noon.

We two fools assumed that life would go on as before, and we promised to meet the next day; but when I came home at dawn, soldiers from the castle clattered around our cottage like wasps. Unable to find me, they were inflicting the prescribed punishment on my father, while my mother called down curses on my head. This time I declined to intervene.

I crept back to my hut by a devious route, but the soldiers had stormed straight to it. The grass where I had lain with Dendra was a scorched waste, trampled by hoofs and boots. My faithful friends had stood their ground and diverted the enemy's wrath. Not one of them remained, no fragment could I recognize in the ashes.

I ran where the woods were too thick and the crags too steep for horses, the legends too frightful for men. I renewed my conversations with the trees, although I did all the talking. With no one to teach me shaving or sewing, my beard sprouted and my clothing burst its seams. The simple folk who glimpsed me screamed and ran away.

The creatures I freed now were weird. I would sometimes leave carvings in exchange when I slithered near the homes of men to steal a pig or a chicken, for Dendra had told me my work had value, but my gifts were mistaken for fetishes of dreadful virulence. At the farms where I left my works, tributes of food and wine would thereafter be placed outside the tightly secured gates with scrawled pleas that I spare the household from further tokens of demonic wrath.

One night I awoke staring, closer than I am to you, into the yellow eyes of a wolf. It stared back for a moment, then fled in terror. I examined myself, my gnarled and battered limbs, my burr-snarled hair, my twisted mind. I had no liking for the creature I had carved from my own being. I had freed a real troll.

In the morning I scrubbed myself with sand and water, hacked away a year's worth of hair and whiskers, and draped my body in the hides of the spotty cats who had controverted my claim to their kills. I passed among the farms and villages as a solitary hunter, odder perhaps than most of an odd breed, but not implausibly so.

The whirl and clamor of a carnival drew everyone from the countryside, and me with them. Only when I stood beneath the snapping banners of yellow and blue, shielding one ear against drums and horns to hear the shouted answers to my questions, did I understand that the gods had led me to this very seat of the Sleiths on the day of Dendra's wedding.

I resisted the impulse to dash headlong against stone walls and steel, for the wilderness had taught me patience. No one wanted the friends I had freed during my Savage Period, some would have paid me to put them back in my bag, but many desired the skins I scarcely valued. In an afternoon of bored haggling, I collected more silver than my unlucky father had seen in his whole lifetime. I bought fine clothing and a handsome horse. (At least I thought them fine and handsome, but Dendra later sniggered at both.) Then I waited.

When the last drunken sentry had tumbled into the moat, I strode boldly into the castle and picked my way through a tangle of snoring Sleiths on the elegant stairway. I breasted a wave of fruits and flowers until it burst against the door of the bridal chamber. Inside, a naked man chased Dendra around the blossom-smothered bed. He was so fat and clumsy that he might have pursued her all night if I hadn't snatched up his traditional bridegroom's scepter and broken his head with it.

I planned to escape to the wild crags and sunless glens, but Dendra would have none of that. "Let's go to the city," she said. "It's noisy and crowded and not as pretty as the woods, but at least we'll have bread. And music. And plumbing."

It was a happy thought. I'm sure our pursuers displaced every boulder and uprooted every bush in the west country, never suspecting that a rogue bumpkin would make for Crotalorn. It wasn't the imperial capital then, just a provincial city that had been decaying for centuries in the shadow of the mountains, but it was grand enough to awe me. Gazing up at the dome of Ashtareeta's temple, I lost my balance and sat down heavily on the pavement, to the amusement of all the pinched and foul-mouthed midgets who had been jostling us.

Never having felt its need, Dendra knew even less about money than I did. We used ours to take a fine apartment near Ashclamith Square, where we dined on Lomar melons and worrells' eggs. I planned to carve and she to paint, until we had earned such wealth and fame that her kinsmen would beg us to forgive them, but we divided our time between making love and gadding about the theaters and fighting-pits. Although we gave our landlord a handsome sum, only a month passed before he surprised us by demanding a second payment. The bailiffs who heaved our things out the window assured us that his was the common practice of the greedy city.

We had nothing but my knives and her paints. Thieves had snatched our clothing, our bedding, even our pots and pans before they hit the street; but, being young, we welcomed our new adventure. We failed to see our future in the wretches who begged for coppers and fought dogs over garbage. It was their hard luck not to be Ringard and Dendra, but we suffered no such handicap.

We debated our prospects, but they shrank when she forbade me to become a hero of the pits and I denied her a career as temple nymph. I could always skin more spotty cats, but the forests they prowled were a long way away. Hugging each other to keep from falling down laughing, we competed to invent grisly details for a ransom note we might send her father.

"We could sell apples," she said.

"Where would we get apples?"

She pointed. We had wandered into Amorartis Street, where mansions crumbled among gardens run wild. Above our seat at the base of a wall stretched a bough from the orchard within, bent with the weight of fat and glossy apples. Why had the beggars who disputed husks and scraps in the lower town not come and picked them? Because they lacked brains and enterprise, obviously, or they wouldn't have been beggars. No people, no dogs, no life at all disturbed the street that twisted between leaning walls. We persuaded ourselves that the orchard had been abandoned.

After tramping all five hills of the city without an apricot or a lark's wing to share, we were more interested in eating the fruit than selling it. I couldn't reach the apples, so I lifted her to the top of the wall, where she sat and tossed them down to me. Between bites, she twittered of her plan to occupy one of these vacant houses and make money by playing the lute on street-corners.

"Do you know what a lute costs?"

"You could carve one from apple-wood, and—" Her words ended in a shriek as she fell backwards over the wall.

I was set to laugh, for she had fallen as suddenly and comically as if jerked by an unseen hand, but when I heard nothing more, when she failed to answer my shout, I flew up the face of the wall. In the garden below, a disgusting old man, his hand clamped to Dendra's mouth, was dragging her into the bushes.

"Oh," he said, with a grin so false they would have hooted him off the stage of the cheapest theater, "is this lady with you, young fellow?"

Though soiled and tarnished, his robes and ornaments were those of a nobleman, and my father's fate at the hands of the ruling class was still vivid in my memory, but rage hurled me at him with no second thought. I was the lad who had fought panthers in the mountains, and a snake could have counted on its fingers the heartbeats left to this doddering lecher, but he slipped aside and left me to imprint the ground with my face.

"What an unfortunate fall!" he said, helping me up while I was too dazed to remember my homicidal intent. "Are you all right? I'm so sorry, that wall is so old and neglected it was bound to give way. You won't sue me, will you?"

Dendra was free, but she didn't run; my strength had returned, but I didn't break his neck. I wondered why I had first thought his silver beard tangled and filthy, his kindly smile oily. Fluttering light and shadow among the leaves must have deceived me. We had been deceived, too, in thinking this garden abandoned. Unlike its neighbors, it had been lovingly tended inside its neglected walls. I was dazzled by the strange shapes and colors that rioted around me, dizzied by an almost forceful exhalation of unfamiliar perfumes.

"We should apologize," Dendra said with the contrite condescension that only a great lady can bring off, "for stealing your apples."

"Why, then, you must be hungry!" cried Dwelphorn Thooz. "Come, apples are for horses, come inside and eat a proper meal."

Later it struck me that he'd been stealing my wife, never mind the apples, but she assured me that my fall had rattled my brain. She had fallen, he was helping her, it should have been obvious. She convinced me, for I could hardly believe that such a gracious old gentleman would drag her into the bushes, even though I'd seen him trying.

He led us indoors, where the garden pursued us through rooms capped with bubbles of sweating glass. Dendra trilled over the bizarre surprises around every turn, but I fretted and twitched at the clusters of horse-heads no bigger than my thumbnail, with flossy manes and perfect little teeth, or the vines that stirred restlessly at our approach and erected purple pricks. The sweetness of the blooms was cloying, but it muffled all but the hint of an underlying, fishy odor that might have been nauseous in its unmasked form.

Such misgivings seemed no more urgent than doubts whether I had found ten gold coins or only nine. Our host called for a meal of a dozen exotic dishes, served by oddly listless and abstracted slaves. He could barely contain his outrage that artists like us should be homeless and poor, and he promised us the use of a garden-house that would have been called a palace back home. He praised our work before we had done any.

"How could two young persons, so beautiful, so intelligent, so sympathetic, fail to create anything less than masterpieces?" he demanded, as if I had insulted him by doubting his faith in us.

His own situation was lamentable, he disclosed as we picked our way among the claws and tentacles of sea-creatures and the spikes of vegetables whose flesh was so difficult of access that I feared I was trying, given my ignorance of social graces, to eat table ornaments. He told us he came from Sythiphore, which we had never heard of, but whose natives are victims of slanders on their customs and religion. Had he not denied that his people were descended from sharks, I might have overlooked how widely his eyes bulged in his flat face, or what thin lips he partly masked with his beard.

"You wouldn't believe the lies my neighbors whispered about me, just because I spend my time reading books and pottering in my garden—"

"Where are they all?" Dendra asked.

"They died, I suppose, or left. We seldom spoke, as I cared nothing for their japes and follies."

"And why do you read books and potter in your garden?"

"Why, young man, because I'm a passionate botanist! It took study, as well as hard work, to produce the apples that tempted you, and can you deny they were delicious? Do you know of any other gardener who can grow sarcophage or selenotropes in Crotalorn? Have you ever before seen necrophiliums blooming so gloriously any farther north than Fandragord?"

I had to answer no to all these questions, and so did Dendra, who even seemed to understand them.

Only once during the meal did his jollity falter, and I sensed a threat as he said, "I must implore you to spare my beloved trees for your masterpieces, especially those in the Bower by the south wall. The gardens of my absent neighbors can provide you with all the wood you'll need."

*

Wandering in his garden the next day, I was amazed by my ignorance. Trees were like members of my family, and yet I could hardly identify one out of every five I saw. The strange ones were indeed strange, like sculptures that called for no further attention from my knives, but they were twisted as if in bondage and torment. Despite the vivid blooms that burst around us, despite the bright sunshine that dappled through unquiet branches, I was oppressed by the feeling that I was straying in darkness through an unknown forest. These trees might have said much to the boy who had understood their language, but I was no longer that boy.

Dendra shared none of my disquiet. She laughed and exclaimed over the beauty of the garden, distinguishing the roses from the pavonias for me, who had never paid much mind to flowers.

"And what's that?" I asked.

"It's a tree, silly! What a question!"

We had come to the Bower that Dwelphorn Thooz had spoken of, a ring of graceful trees whose branches intertwined above a pool. I was reluctant to enter. The trees disturbed me, the smooth-skinned trees that neither she nor I could name. Whether I was upset by their unfamiliarity, or by some curiosity of their shapes or proportions or arrangement, I couldn't say. I felt like a dog I once owned, who would gleefully charge a bear but sometimes tremble at the shadow of a passing cloud.

Dendra felt nothing of this. She romped forward through the grass, thick and green despite the gloom of overarching limbs, and dropped to her knees at the edge of the pool. I wanted to call her back, but I wanted even less to evoke the look of sorely-tried noblesse oblige she put on whenever I hinted of omens or intuitions.

She leaned forward to admire her reflection in the pool, and her beauty caught my breath. Clear eyes sparkling in the water-light, pink lips parted, she could have been the naiad who haunted the glade. In the next instant she screamed, and no omen or intuition could have kept me from dashing to her side.

"What is it?"

"Oh—I thought—" She seemed confused, like one roused from a dream. "I thought I saw something in the well."

I looked. It was in fact a well, perfectly circular and lined with pink stones, its water clearer than the air around us in a shaft of sunlight that pierced the Bower directly overhead. I felt at first that I might reach in and touch the pebbles lying at the bottom. In the next instant I saw intervening shimmers that hinted of fearful depth. The pebbles were boulders. Dizzied by the shift in perspective, I stumbled and almost fell, or—as it seemed then—was almost sucked in.

"No!" I cried when she scooped up the water in her palm, but I was too late to keep her from drinking.

"You're mad!" she laughed, splashing me.

I thought she might have been right. Swiftly as one of that dog's dreaded clouds, my vapor had passed. What if the trees did look like men and women stretched on some wizard's rack that denied the limitations of flesh? I was familiar with such fancies: they were visible only to an artist's eye. A plain man would have seen only trees.

Several shipboard floggings later curbed the tendency, but in those days I invariably did whatever I was told not to do. I always thought I had a good reason for defying my betters. In this case, I felt a craftsman's need to test an unfamiliar wood.

"Oh, Ringard!" Dendra sighed when I drew my knife, knowing my ways too well to say more.

The boughs were too high above me, and there were no windfalls in this well-kept garden, so I slipped the knife into the bole of a tree, into what might have been the tormented muscles of a woman's calf. I recoiled instantly, not just from the sickly feel of the tree's flesh and the flow of pinkish sap, but from the shrieking in my head. My inner deafness had been suddenly, horribly cured, and I was denounced and importuned by a choir of wailing voices.

"Forgive me!" I cried. The pain of those phantom screams was more than I could bear. The Bower darkened, the tall shapes spun around me like demoniac dancers in a constricting ring.

"Are you ill? Ringard?" Dendra's voice restored me. I turned into her arms and gripped her. The other voices fell still as leaves in a faltering breeze.

"Let's go," I said. "We can find somewhere else to live."

"Don't be silly. We can go elsewhere when you've sold some of your carvings, if that's what you really want."

"At least let's avoid this Bower. It's—"

"But I love it! It's so weird. I think a god must live here."

"Something must." I knew better than to argue with her. She could be no less contrary than I.

*

While Dendra happily played at housewife, I sought wood for my work. No sooner had I dropped over the wall to a neighboring garden than I felt a jolting realignment of my senses, like one emerged from the enthrallment of a dark puppet-theater to mix with real people in a daylit street.

It was a jungle floored with sodden leaves, but it grew only normal plants. No fruits or flowers shocked me with their shape or coloring. I breathed in the honest mold and damp as if I had been denied air for a day and a night. If Dendra hadn't remained behind, I might have kept on walking to the farthest end of the city.

Fallen branches lay everywhere, I had brought an ax to cut them to manageable lengths, and without even trying I saw a hundred shapes —friendly, healthy shapes—begging to be freed. I ignored them and pushed through the undergrowth to the house. It was no airy fantasy of spires and bubbles, but a forthright home of solid timbers. Walking through an open door to find myself among elegant furniture, I feared that the householder would presently seize me for a thief. Then I noticed all the dust, the rain-streaked carpet, the leaves that crackled under my feet.

The inhabitants must have fled without closing the windows or finishing a meal whose desiccated relics cluttered a table. Animals had trooped through to gnaw and claw and defecate, and even as I considered this evidence I was startled by a scurrying rat. Snatching up a handy bit of litter to throw, I dropped it with an oath. It was a human skull.

My first thought was that a derelict had crawled in here to die, but that seemed less likely when I considered the childish proportions of the skull; and when I noticed the other old bones and once-splendid garments that lay near the five chairs around the dining table. Although animals and the weather had disordered it, the picture of diners arrested by death in mid-bite was easy to reconstruct.

Similar sights awaited me in other mansions: a chamber-pot holding the bones of its last user; two lovers twined in an embrace whose moisture and warmth had been anciently sucked into the unloving sky; a child's hand, melted to an inartistic stain on the half-drawn picture of a tree.

I could stand no more horrors. I ran back, scrambling over walls, stumbling in ditches, remembering only at the last minute to lop off some of the wood that had caught my eye. Death had snatched all these unfortunates with a plague, I told myself, or with poisoned water. That his neighbors had earned the enmity of our host might be purest coincidence, but I nevertheless resolved to quit his hospitality as quickly and politely as I could.

No sooner had I climbed into his garden and breathed its perfumed air than urgency faded. I had no desire to linger here, but I no longer itched to run. A sense of peace beguiled me as I walked the winding path to our fine new house.

That peace vanished when I found that Dendra had gone to bed, where she lay pale and drawn.

"It was that water you drank," I said. "If ever I saw a well haunted by an evil spirit, that was it. We must leave this place at once. We—"

I saw that she was giggling at me as I paced and fumed. She said, "I didn't get this way from drinking water."

"What way?"

"Pregnant."

I was stunned. I sat and gaped. I had wanted to pour out my adventures in the street of the dead, but now I could not. It was bad enough that our child might be marked by a fish-faced wizard and his demon plants without filling her head with images of rats and skeletons. I pasted a grin on my face, kissed her and made much of her, but for the first time I resisted when she tried to draw me into bed. I told her she looked ill, that she should rest, and this was true, but I wanted to start on the work that would free us.

I labored for hours, fascinated but appalled by the creatures that begged for release. I thought I'd seen a shy rabbit in the wood I had brought home, a dancer from Lilaret, a hound biting its paw. What emerged were a snarling rat, a demon capering on a skull, a ghoul gnawing a bone.

I was surprised to see that Dendra had joined me to paint my demon. She looked well enough, but her glances at me were apprehensive. I had no idea how to explain the work I was doing, so I pretended to be absorbed in it, and soon that was true.

When I next looked up, she had retired. Stretching my fingers, I nearly screamed from the pain. Without noticing, I had worked beyond the limits of flesh. The world outside was gray, stung by the flashes of brilliant blossoms.

She painted while I slept, so that my wares were ready for the public when I rose at noon to breakfast on bananas and figs.

"I wasn't sure what color to paint that . . . thing," she said, indicating my ghoul.

"Green looks right."

"You don't like this place at all, do you?"

Careful not to sound like the grumpy bear she sometimes called me, I said, "I'd be happier if we weren't beholden to a patron. And you must admit that we're far from the center of things. Just getting to the theater—"

"I think I need peace and quiet now," she said. "And this lovely garden—wouldn't it be so much nicer for a child than a noisy street full of whores and cutthroats, with musicians over our head and opium-eaters next door?"

This was not an entirely unfair picture of our former home, but she'd once praised its urban diversions. I restrained myself from telling her what I knew and suggesting that even our old neighbors on Ashclamith Square would have been preferable to plague-stricken corpses. Though I was horrified by the length of the stay her words implied, I said mildly, "You don't want to put down roots here."

She laughed. "That's exactly what I feel like doing!"

It seemed wiser to get the money we needed to move before we argued about moving. Her lips tasted oddly bitter when I kissed her, like privet leaves. I had heard that pregnant women ate curious things.

Heading for the gate with my armload of carvings, I met Dwelphorn Thooz.

"But what have I done," he said when I told him where I was going, "that you should deny me the first chance of buying your creations?"

"After all your kindness, I can't ask you to buy my work."

"You mean, my kindness has denied me a right enjoyed by the first wretch you meet? Would you oblige me if I were a monster of cruelty? Why then, trolls lusting to couple with infants and posthumes gorged on virgins' blood will tremble at the whisper of my deeds! Should *Dwelphorn Thooz* be written on the earth and the word *kindness* inscribed on the remotest star, the universe will crumple with shame for holding so inapt a juxtaposition."

I believed he was joking, but how could I know? Reading a Sythiphoran face is impossible, I have since learned, even for the owner of another one. I arranged my pieces on the grass, resigned to the necessity of offering a gift. He seized on the ghoul and scrutinized it from every angle.

"Have you been perambulating our necropolis at midnight, young man?" He studied me even more intently than he had my sculpture. "Where, then, have you seen a ghoul?"

"In the wood," I said, and explained how I worked.

Excepting Dendra, no one had ever heard me out with such alert interest and apparent comprehension. "Extraordinary," he said. "And it's an extraordinary likeness, although the color is wrong. They're gray, you know." While I again debated whether he was making fun of me, he said, "Some day we must have a serious talk about your future. Your talent is perhaps greater than I supposed. I had thought of taking on an apprentice. . . ."

"An apprentice botanist?"

"Yes." He laughed. "Something like that."

I gave him the ghoul, but then he insisted on buying the other pieces for a sum that staggered me. It so staggered me that I failed to notice that no money changed hands. Instead of real silver from the market, I was left with promised gold from my host. But how could I press him for payment while I accepted his free room and board?

These thoughts crushed me only later, and I was still grinning as he said, "I would highly recommend the water from the Bower to your wife. Strength, grace, stature and long life are the least of the gifts it imparts."

I blurted, "I hate that place!"

"I thought you might, and so I must warn you to stay away from it. Trees are sensitive, too, you know, and I wouldn't want my darlings upset by your hostility." I blushed with guilt for the test I had made with my knife. I think he knew about it. "But I'm sure they would welcome your charming wife. Women are different." He pinched my arm playfully before scurrying off with the work that had cost me a sleepless night and the strength of my hands.

*

Dendra scoffed at my suspicion that our host had taken my work to keep us from leaving. She scorned my suggestion that he meant us no good.

"You're just not used to dealing with the upper classes," she said with an infuriating sniff.

"Polliel spare me from the upper classes, and may Sleithreethra tear out their ribs for needles to knit their shrouds!"

This group included her and all her relatives, and she lectured at length on the proper handling of bumptious churls. I stamped about and grumbled, then attacked my work with a vengeance. My mood soured further when I realized that I was acting just like my father, who would chop trees with especial vigor after quarreling with my mother. I took a perverse pleasure in the pain I inflicted on my cramped hands.

I freed a botched creature like a cross between a man and a shark. Dendra criticized it with slapdash painting, and we both laughed at the absurd result. We ended by embracing tenderly, but I knew that our argument had only been put aside. I had to convince her that this place was unhealthy. Perhaps it was only the light diffused through the plants crowding our windows, but I thought her skin was taking on a greenish tinge.

I worked through the night again. Before dawn I gathered those pieces that Dendra had already painted into a bag and lowered it over the wall into Amorartis Street, where I doubted that any sane footpad would lurk. If our patron again relieved me of my creations on my way to the gate, I would at least have those figures to sell.

As I returned home stealthily, a pale form shimmered from the Bower. I froze, imagining things worse than a human intruder. It was nothing but a man, however, whom I failed at first to recognize in his pasty nakedness as Dwelphorn Thooz. His halting gait was bringing him directly towards me, and I withdrew into the shelter of a plant whose red mouths parted slackly as the darkness faded. Perhaps I could have fled unnoticed, but I was curious to see if his body displayed fishy anomalies.

He looked normal enough, but as he passed close by me I saw that his skin was scored with fresh scratches and welts. A gleam lit his eyes, and a smile flickered on his bruised lips as he muttered a litany of female names. In those days, on the rare occasions when I gave any thought to the topic, the amorous practices of the old amused me; but at that moment my impression that he was stumbling home from an orgy gave me a chill. I stayed in hiding until the sun was fairly risen, desiring a glimpse of the ladies who had frolicked with the ancient lecher, but no one else walked away from the slim and swaying trees of the Bower.

*

I don't remember if I kissed Dendra goodbye, or what words we said. I was preoccupied with the details of my escape, as I saw it: which pieces I would offer our host if he stopped me, how I would word my refusal if he asked to buy them all. As it happened, I never saw him, and I walked through the gate like a free man. My other bag of sculptures lay undisturbed outside the wall. I slung it over my shoulder and began to whistle as I tramped to the lower town.

My whistle soon dried in the plaza fronting the Temple of Polliel, a notable marketplace for handicrafts. Not just the permanent stalls, but pillars of the surrounding colonnade had been claimed by the craftsmen's ancestors and passed down to them, or so they maintained with words, fists and feet. Trying to do business here, I was told by a priest whose sanctity cowed my attackers, was like barging into a stranger's home and sitting down to his place at the table. For a fee, he said, the Temple would assign me a space, but I calculated that the rights to the darkest shadow of the remotest column would cost me more than I would earn if I lived forever.

The gods took note of the priest's rebuke and heaped my shoulders with a massive weight of dead, hot air that stretched to the very top of their pitiless dome. I wandered into streets undisturbed by merchants and buyers alike, a desert of brick and stone with not one cool tree for shade and no undisputed place to sit down, where householders practiced art criticism with dogs, cudgels and slop-buckets. My carvings seemed hammered from iron, as did my shoes. When the morning crawled into the furnace of afternoon, bloated clouds piled themselves to phantasmagorical heights and blackened the green slopes beyond the city.

Darkness fell long before sunset. Hot air gusted randomly. I knew that a storm was coming, but I clung to my purpose. Even though I managed to sell a few things, I was engaged in folly, for how long could I carve all night and walk all day?

I spoke that question aloud, and I was answered by a crack of thunder that scrambled my bones inside my skin, by rain like a mountain torrent, by chunks of ice that rebounded from the cobblestones to the highest eaves. Bolts of lightning fell as thickly as the hail, and just as close, while I cowered in a doorway and babbled absurd promises to whatever god might protect me.

I had lived through many storms in the open air, and they hadn't much frightened me; but in the forest, I would know to avoid the oaks and festirons that heaven loves to blast and shelter under a depsad or a beech. In this stone wilderness I knew nothing, I was just a naked target on a battlefield where light and noise fought the final war. The door I clung to gave me no more shelter than a raft on a wild ocean, but I glued my body to its deaf and unyielding panels. Except for continuous shaking, I could no more move than one of my sculptures.

I kept telling myself that storms like this pass quickly, but I was wrong. During those lulls when it gathered its strength for an even wilder assault, the wailing of a distant multitude rose from every direction, led by crazed shrieks from nearer houses. It was no comfort that every other soul in Crotalorn shared my belief that the Last Day had come. The wind ripped slates from the roofs and bricks from the walls to shatter in the street, then tired of finicking vandalism and flung down the building next door. The rain pressed down so hard that the dust from this disaster shot out horizontally to batter me as a blast of gritty mud. I couldn't hear my own screams, much less any that might have come from the steaming rubble that towered before me.

Whether I fainted or was knocked senseless, I don't know, but I woke to comparative silence and darkness. The men working on the fallen building were bellowing orders to one another, their picks and shovels clattered and rang, but the noise was thin and unconvincing. They were only a few steps away, but they might have been gnomes laboring on a far mountain.

I watched them dully for a while before I thought of lending a hand. Then I thought of Dendra, and I ran all the way to Amorartis Street through bewildered multitudes who milled in a light drizzle of rain.

*

I knew that our home was empty when I crossed the threshold and felt its ghastly silence, long before I had called through every room and run outside to bellow in the dripping garden.

"Ringard, Ringard, find all your courage, for you have need of it," said a soft voice at my shoulder.

"What have you done with her?" I screamed at Dwelphorn Thooz.

"I?" Like an enigmatic messenger in a dream, he held up Dendra's tiny green shoes before my eyes. "Not I, poor boy, the gods! They envied us her company. They snatched her away."

"Damn you, foul wizard, what are you babbling about?"

"The storm. Didn't you notice it?" He thrust the shoes at me, and I seized them. The velvet was singed, the silver filigree fused. "She was gathering despodines when the bolt struck." He burst into convulsive sobs and tore at his hair as he managed to finish: "Those pretty little shoes were all we found."

His show of grief seemed genuine to me, who had never seen any man but an actor on the stage shed tears. I gripped his hands to keep him from tearing out more of his beard. But my voice was still harsh as I said, "I saw the storm. It blew houses down, but not one petal of your garden is disarranged."

"We were spared its full fury," he said, "as sometimes happens. A shower of rain, that one stroke of lightning—and dear Dendra was no more."

"Take me to her."

"Haven't you heard me? Of course you haven't, forgive me! No human ear can hold such horror. She was totally consumed, or if you wish, assumed bodily into the eternal happiness of Mother Ashtareeta's arms. Count yourself blessed that no charred bone remains—"

Screaming to blot out such words, I shoved him aside and dashed to the parterre where Dendra had once clapped her hands and exclaimed over the glory of the despodines. I battered them under my feet, I ripped them from their stalks, worthless weeds that still existed while she could not. I roared her name until my throat tore. At last I fell exhausted to my knees in a bare patch. In the darkness I felt only stubble about me, which crumbled to ashes under my hands. I had found the spot where lightning had struck; but only that.

*

The old man gave me a room in his palace, where I stared out a window and ignored the food his slaves brought. He became a familiar object, like a chair whose absence I wouldn't have noticed. He talked to me at length, he read from books that might have been inspirational, but it was all just words, words, when the only word was *Dendra*, and that word meant *nothing*.

One night a storm broke overhead. I was driven to run outside and leap crazily through the garden, shaking my fists at the gods and daring them to take me, too. In the midst of these antics I woke from my long trance and sobbed while the storm thundered and flashed past.

Another man might have fled the scenes that recalled his lost love, but that happy man could have buried all hope with a palpable corpse. This decisive act was denied me. I had only my host's testimony that he had observed a thunderbolt and found a pair of shoes. Dendra might spring from a flowery thicket at any moment, laughing at the trick she had played. Perhaps the bolt had erased her memory, and she had wandered off, but would return here when she came to her senses. She still lived in my dreams, but they might not follow me among strange scenes and foreign faces. I was chained to the place.

Wood whose captives I had meant to free was brought to me from the garden-house. What captives, I couldn't remember as I turned the pieces this way and that. I saw nothing but sticks. My knife could only cut big pieces into little ones.

I went out among the gardens of the dead to look for better wood, but nothing in the jumble of lines and curves spoke to me. The only shapes and textures that mattered had been stolen from the universe, leaving chaos.

No trees had ever spoken to me so loudly as those in the Bower. They knew what had happened to Dendra, and I would sooner trust them than my host. I ignored his warning and went there, struggling to hear. I remembered my panic as one remembers a childish game that no longer compels. I sat beside the well, which was only a well, and meditated on the trees, which were only trees.

I looked for the one I had wounded, but I couldn't find it. I would swear it had been removed, but no gap marred the perfect ring, and I was doubtful where it had stood. If it had been replaced, it had been replaced by a fully grown specimen without disturbing the ancient moss of the surrounding earth.

Its replacement might have been one tree that differed from the others, its lines disfigured by a swelling of the bole probably due to disease or insects. This was curious, for elsewhere in the garden there was no worm in the apple or canker on the rose. I stroked the deformity, thumped it, learned nothing. Inchoate feelings stirred as elusively as tatters of a dream, and I thought for a moment that they signalled the return of my lost hearing, but they were soon still, and I was alone among silent trees.

*

My inability to work shamed me, but my patron never mentioned it. At mealtimes he lectured of plants and their marvelous properties to heal or harm, not seeming to care that I wouldn't have understood even if I had listened. I watched him, though.

I was most alert when he guided me through his indoor jungles, less to the names and peculiarities of his gorgeous monsters than to the layout of the palace. No one interfered with my prying whenever his duties took him from home, for his dull slaves tended to drowse in his absence, and I was free to explore everything from his fishy kitchens to his fishier bedroom. A priest might have clucked over his queerly illustrated books, but my only concern was for traces of Dendra, and I found none.

Behind the kitchens lay cages of small animals and a pen for goats. Although none of them figured in our menu, the stock was regularly thinned and restored. I learned the reason for this one morning when I assisted the botanist in feeding cats and rabbits to some of his livelier horrors.

"My boy, you're a marvel! Other prospective apprentices may have shown more aptitude for study, but none of them could abide the glory of nature unveiled. Botany is no field for the squeamish."

The sight of a shrieking cat gripped by the claws of something whose appearance partook of the orchid and the octopus might have disturbed me in my previous life, but now I merely watched. When I shivered, it was from the question that I spoke as soon as it pierced my mind: "Could one of your specimens eat a human being?"

"What a question! My plants are finer creatures, almost human themselves."

We had used a noose on a pole to extend the cat to this "finer creature," but now I leaned into the great tub where it sprawled and thrust my hand among its unoccupied claws. They closed on my wrist, but I was almost disappointed when they released it.

"That's right, test every assertion for yourself," he said, thumping me on the back. "You have the makings, sir, of a scientist."

*

I grew fond of the swollen tree in the Bower, whose deformity subtly altered and enlarged from week to week. It said nothing to me, but I felt almost at peace when I sat leaning against its trunk and listening to the meaningless prattle of its branches.

I came and went stealthily, a trick I knew well. Wizard or not, my host never surprised me, though he once came close.

Sitting against the tree, lost in some reverie of Dendra, I felt a sudden tingle, and I couldn't say whether the skin of my back or the bark had crawled. Whatever its source, the sensation alarmed me. Not a leaf stirred, and I was struck by the fancy that the trees had fallen still with anticipation. At the same time I glimpsed movement, frighteningly close, a flash of color that I recognized as my host's robe.

I withdrew into the hedge outside the ring. Just then Dwelphorn Thooz entered with a group of slaves bearing barrels that slopped and gurgled. He muttered endearments as he ladled out portions of raw meat and entrails at the base of each tree.

Although the fate of the cats and rabbits hadn't disturbed me, I was sickened to see him feeding raw meat to these trees. I had come to love them in spite of my first impression, because Dendra had loved them. I wormed my way backward as quickly and silently as I could.

"You must keep your strength up, my dear," I heard him saying as I slipped free of the hedge. "You can't just think of yourself now, you know."

I cast a last look at the Bower as I skulked off, and saw that the trees, so unaccountably still a moment before, were tossing their heads in the windless air and bending their limbs low as if to feast.

*

The moon glared pitilessly through my window that night, commanding me to be up and doing. When I covered my head with the bedclothes and clenched my eyes, its imprint on my eyelids became the face of Dendra. Springing up and pacing the day-bright room did no good. I felt her breath and smelled her sweetness in the warm breeze from the restless garden. She was near.

Why had he spoken to the tree in just those words, urging it to eat: "You can't just think of yourself. . . ?" Had that fearful storm taken Dendra, or had it expressed the outrage of the gods at a gross breach of their laws?

I thought I heard a cry. It was a cat, perhaps, a rutting cat, but it would have been the first such cry I had heard from the enchanted garden. No animals ventured there, no birds, not even the insects that my host had told me were so essential to the propagation of plants. I threw on my clothes and thrust my stoutest knife through my belt.

I didn't dare strike a light as I crept through the palace, but the carnivores stirred all around me. I jumped at shadows, cringed from phantom caresses. I imagined the footsteps of my host in every click and slither from the tubs where the monsters grew, but I took heart from the thought that these loathsome noises masked my own footfalls.

Outside I heard again the screaming I had mistaken for a cat, and ran straight to the Bower. A white thing writhed at the foot of my favorite tree, no longer swollen. I recognized it as a newborn infant, I guessed its origin, but the shock of this blasphemous miracle was driven from my mind by a greater wonder. My talent had returned. Within the tree, pleading for release, I saw Dendra.

Perhaps I should have roused the sorcerer and begged him to reverse the spell. Perhaps I should have sought help from another wizard. Such possibilities occurred to me only later. At the moment I saw nothing but a challenge that I had met thousands of times before, to liberate a captive from wood. I drew my knife and attacked the tree that bound her.

It began to go wrong from the start. The grain of the wood was erratic, its density unfamiliar. I cut too deep, and sap flowed black in the moonlight. Not fluidly, as a human expression would evolve, but as a jolting succession of static images, Dendra's look changed from elation to horror. I had no way to stop her bleeding until I had freed a human body whose wounds I could bind, so I hacked more desperately, but I only cut her more.

She might know something about the conditions of her enchantment. If she could speak, she might help me free her. I concentrated on her mouth. I shaved and pared with an intensity of concentration and a steadiness of hand that I had never known before as I tried to free her lips, her teeth, her tongue.

As I said, my talent never ran to likenesses of individuals. In this case the pattern lay before me, her very face was visible under my knife and my fingers, and I don't know where I could have gone wrong, but I did.

From the ragged caricature I had made of her mouth, a scream burst forth, a scream strangled by the blood that sprayed over me. In a sudden burst of anger and despair whose onset gave no warning, I drove the heavy blade between her eyes. Sometimes I can delude myself that I did it to cut short her suffering, but it was my own pain that impelled the knife into the wood.

Unable to look at her, I turned my attention to the baby, a perfectly formed boy. I cut the cord and tied it, I washed him in the water of the cursed well, I wrapped him in my shirt and rocked him, but he wouldn't stop crying. I suspected he was hungry. I turned to his mother. Now I saw nothing but a tree, a dead tree whose drooping branches trailed silky leaves on the moss.

"Oh, you wretched man!" screamed a voice beside me. "You miserable fool! What have you done to my finest creation?"

I didn't care that I had been discovered, that I had enraged the wizard or that his hulking slaves stood near at hand. I watched the old man's frothing, stamping rage with curious detachment, and I hardly heard his threats as I noticed that his body held images begging to be freed. The shapes that I saw were those of bones, muscles and entrails, and I seized him in order to liberate each and every one of those images with my knife.

I succeeded brilliantly.

When I came to my senses, I wondered why the slaves had not defended him. They seemed to be lying dead or stunned, but when I examined them, I found that the things I had mistaken for fallen men were nothing but heaps of rotting vegetation. I snatched up the baby and fled, not liking the way the branches thrashed and clawed the face of the moon. As I ran from the Bower, I saw the trees bending as if to feed.

All but one.

*

I left Crotalorn that night, taking only a milk-goat from the wizard's menagerie to provide for my son. It was my intention to bring him to this castle and claim for him the status of a Sleith, whatever it might cost me.

It was an unfortunate journey. Perhaps goat's milk disagreed with him, or perhaps my clumsiness and ignorance did, but the baby fretted when he wasn't screaming. Busybodies pestered me until I found that I could discourage them by explaining, between suppressed coughs, that the poor child's mother had died of the plague.

He seemed to calm when we came into the forested hills of your domain. I believed that he sensed he was coming home and would soon be in the better care of his maternal relatives. He gurgled and cooed at the trees.

Near the place where you found me today, I paused to collect my thoughts and rehearse the speech that would introduce Dendrard to his grandparents. I bathed him at a spring and set him naked on soft moss while I washed myself. When I returned to pick him up, I found that I could not. The earth gripped him.

I didn't know what to think. An animal, a snake, something held him to the ground. I pulled, and he screamed more loudly than ever before. I babbled at him, fussed over him and managed to calm him, but at the same time I very gently rolled him to one side to determine how he was caught, and by what.

My knife was out, for I didn't know what I would see, and I'm glad—I suppose I'm glad—that I refrained from striking at once, for my first sight suggested that the foul tentacle of some underworld creature gripped my child at the base of his spine. What stayed my hand, I think, was Dendrard's apparent contentment. Not even my screaming changed his look of pure happiness.

Though my hand cringed, I forced it to explore the thing that held my son. I expected a texture of scales, a chill of slime, but the reality was worse. What I felt was the firm pliancy of young wood. No creature had seized my son from the earth. It was he, Dendrard, who gripped the earth with the root sprouting from his backbone.

I stumbled backward, cursing and praying with equal futility. My eyes remained fixed on him, on his calm, empty gaze as he stared up at the blue sky, opening his little fists and spreading his fingers like branches.

I ran. Roots tripped me, branches raked me, trunks battered me. I fought my way free of the angry forest, but the first men I met on the open road were a press-gang from the Lord Admiral's fleet, wandering far inland in their desperation for recruits. They thought I was mad, but they told me lunacy was no impediment for an oarsman on a trireme, nor were they much impressed by my assumed cough. They had seen real plague, they said, as I would.

I vowed to go back and find Dendrard one day. I never imagined that thirty years would pass. I hadn't remembered that your lands contained so many hills, so many springs, so many trees. Nor had I foreseen that Cluddites would rearrange the landscape.

*

Ringard's tale was ended, and so was the wine. The servants had long since gone to bed, but I took him up to the room they had prepared. The candles had burned out; it surprised me to see that the glowing sky made them unnecessary. The forest beyond the window nevertheless looked very dark.

"If you find him," I said, "what do you propose to do?"

"Listen to his voice—although it's been a very long time since I last heard the voices of trees, I may have an ear for that of my own son." He flashed his unpleasant smile. "If not, perhaps I'll merely sit for a while in his shade."

I left him, and in the morning he was gone.

*

Several days later I heard that the Snake Man had fallen afoul of the Sons of Cludd. Anyone with a good word to say for an accused witch becomes a suspect, but I felt that the man had a claim on me. And I was curious to learn if any trees had spoken to him.

The smell of burning wood, burning flesh and righteously unbathed bodies led me inerrantly to the Holy Soldiers' encampment. Easing my horse through a mob draped in white robes and droning dissonant hymns, I bitterly regretted the good old days when my father would set the hounds on Cluddite preachers. Now they were more numerous than those hounds' fleas, and not even a lord of the House of Sleith would dare to throw one down the stairs if he came calling.

They had transported much of the forest to their camp, stripped the trees of branches, set them in rigid ranks, and decorated each with an unlucky victim. Some were already choking on the smoke of their feet as it rose to their nostrils, but I was not too late. The pyre around the distinctive figure of Ringard lay unlighted.

"Take heart!" I called to him when I came near enough to be heard. "Your nephew is here, Lord Fariel."

They hadn't quelled his wit. "I wouldn't boast of our connection in this company, if I were you."

Before leaving to seek someone in authority, I asked, "Did you find him? Dendrard?"

"No, fortunately. They would have liked him even less than his father."

Talking to the victims was forbidden, I learned from the men who rushed up to unhorse me and hustle me before their captain. He was in a good mood—he didn't smile, of course, they consider that a sin, but he didn't tie me to a stake—but that was all I could gather from his barbarous accent and Zaxoin turns of phrase, some of which, I believe, he made up as he went along to confuse an unbelieving outlander like me. I did pick the words "talk" and "tree" out of his rapturous gabble, but even if he speaks perfect Frothen, it's hard to concentrate on the words of a man whose sleeves are decorated with the dried tongues of blasphemers and ears of heretics.

"Wroken word on writhen tree spoken, burn on broken tree witch writhen!" he bawled, winding up his spittle-spraying harangue in fine Cluddite style and gesturing toward the stake where Ringard hung.

I cursed, I wept, I took it less nobly than Ringard himself when the torch dipped and his pyre blossomed up to contain him like a crystal cup. His head twisted, probably to deny these zealots the sight of one more tortured face, but it seemed to me that he was pressing his ear to the stake in an effort to hear a last message from the medium he had loved so much.

Then he turned back toward us, and that face, crawling with unknown flora, held an expression of such torment that it must have gratified even the most jaded of the Holy Soldiers. Yet his words, when they rang across the distance and over the roar of the bonfire, were absurd: "Not the stake! No, no, not the stake!"

It was over quickly enough, although the victim's sense of time may have differed from mine. The black stake bore a black gnarl, and it was all so much indistinguishable charcoal. The sudden reports that made me cry out were only the eruptions of boiling sap, or marrow.

His last words had puzzled me. He was no imbecile, he had been alert to the end, he had known what they meant to do, so why had he protested against the stake? Trying not just to examine my memory but to relive the moment just past, to catch the words still ringing in my ears, I convinced myself that I had misunderstood him.

A prudent man would have made his exit, but I was so distraught that I seized the chief fanatic and demanded, "What was it he said? Did you hear the man's last words?"

"'Deafen your ears to the words of wisdom, and to fine phrases be as stone,'" the captain quoted quite clearly from *The Book of Cludd*, and the import of his hard stare was even clearer.

There was much I would have asked him, but I had outworn my welcome. They kept my horse, my weapons and my clothing to further their good works, and I was forced to pick my cold and painful way through the sighing and creaking forest far longer after dark than I would have liked. Countryman though I am, I had never noticed that the riffle of leaves and clitter of loose bark can sound exactly like human conversations, whispered with earnest intensity. I paused often to listen, but I could identify no single, coherent word, with the doubtful but disturbing exception of my Tribal name: *Sleith*.

In the days that followed I noticed, too, that certain leaves, when they flashed their pale sides to the bright sun, could suggest hair the color of rain; and that the slim grace of some trees, the firm molding of others, the quality that I can only describe as the joyful nature of still others, stirred memories of a girl who had once romped with me and the hounds when she should have been counting her jewels. If Ringard had been mad, his madness had been metaphorically apt.

And he had surely been mad. The Cluddites had felled hundreds of trees and burned hundreds of victims. Coincidence can be stretched only so far. Yet I had convinced myself that his last words, after he had listened to a cry from the tree they had randomly chosen for him, had not been, "Not the stake!," but, "Not *this* stake!"

The Throne of Bones

"Several faces I recognized; though I should have known them better
had they been shriveled or eaten away by death and decomposition."
                                        —H.P.Lovecraft: "The Tomb."

I
Lord Glyphtard's Tale

You're moving good,
But you just fell down;
You're moving good,
But you're thrashing round;
You're moving good,
But you're spewing gore;
You're moving good,
But not no more.

                                        —"Song of the Graveyard
                                          Watchmen"

As a child I was told not to gather souvenirs from the cemetery, but it
was hard to determine where our overgrown garden blended with the
overgrown fringe of Dreamers' Hill. I had found skulls that clearly lay on
our property. If Mother permitted me to collect them, although she would
shudder and urge me to find a healthier pastime, why shouldn't I pick
up skulls that lay in plain sight a few steps farther on? If it was right to
uncover relics with the toe of my boot when I glimpsed them protruding
from the earth, why was it wrong to seek them out actively with shovel
and crowbar? The inability to make such fine distinctions has forever been
my undoing.

I once believed that my graveyard rambles were the first steps to a career
in science. Our home lay under the massive cliff of the Anatomical
Institute on River Avenue, where scholars were not only encouraged to

give the closest scrutiny to such beguilements as skeletons and naked bodies, but were also held in the highest respect for doing it by everyone but Mother, who called them lechers and necrophiliacs.

The students of art and medicine were a more than usually high-spirited bunch, it's true, and it's true that they sometimes trespassed through our property with suspicious bundles or vomited on our front steps, but Mother, as she did against so many things, had a special grievance against the Institute. The building that blocked our sunlight until midday and disgorged rowdy trespassers at all hours was formerly the palace of the Glyphts, and she was a Glypht.

Unless you come from Crotalorn you have probably never heard of that tribe, but whenever I mentioned my name to a stranger in my native city, it provoked a look of thwarted recognition, usually succeeded by one of embarrassment. Nobody said, "Oh, you're the fellow whose family was massacred by an unknown intruder when you were a baby, aren't you? As I recall, only you and your mother were spared, unless she was the one who did it. I myself am inclined to think your father was guilty, for who but a moron would believe that his body was carried off by the killer?" Gossip, even more than the crime itself, may have caused Mother's mild unhingement.

I am called Glyphtard Fand, my late or absent father having been associated with a much-decayed branch of that truly Great House, but Mother was correct when introducing me, to my embarrassment, as Lord Glyphtard. The title derived from her great-grandfather, who was governor of Orocrondel, a post that in those days meant being a broker for pirates. It was he who built the palace, but his son gave it away, and we lived in what was formerly the gardener's lodge. Although a queer statue of her grandfather dominated the lobby of the Institute, the students surely remembered his philanthropy far less often in their prayers than Mother did in her daily maledictions. To hear her talk, you'd think he had left his heirs naked in a thatched hut, but the gardener of the original estate had been an important man, marshaling an army of slaves and artisans, and he had lived in fine style in a mansion with twenty spacious rooms. Real lords from the Houses of Crondren or Vogg, dwelth teammates whom I have brought home from time to time, have seemed impressed by the magnificence of our *lodge.*

It was a faded magnificence. The roof leaked all the way down through four floors to the cellar. Opening any one of the thousands of volumes from our library, you would find inside the covers a wet wadding like cheese curds. The smell of rotting carpets and soggy wood filled the house, for we couldn't afford to repair the chimneys and burn off the damp. The half-dozen or so servants who remained were really pensioners: if one of them spent a full day doddering through a dimly remembered pantomime of household chores, Mother would have to spend the next week nursing her.

I learned at an early age that we had little money, but money was a subject discussed only by the sort of louts who came around to bang on our door and demand it. I thought my fortune lay in science, not realizing then that it was just a pastime for unworldly cranks. If knowledge was power, as the cranks maintained, and if power was money, which was self-evident, then knowledge should bring money. The gentlemanly education I enjoyed, parsing classics and stressing penults with a series of cheap tutors, hadn't equipped me to untangle that syllogism.

So I collected skulls, delighting especially in those that were malformed in odd ways or had been pierced by weapons, measuring them and labeling them and entering jejune speculations on them in notebooks. Rarest of all were perfect specimens, since almost all that I found had been gnawed by animals, as my tutors said, or by ghouls, as Mother and the servants insisted.

"I won't have that thing in my house," Mother said when she saw one that had been furrowed especially deeply by fangs. "What if the ghoul that gnawed it developed a taste for it? What if he comes back looking for it? 'Where's my skull?'" she creaked in a singularly hideous whisper, "'Where's the boy that stole my nice, tasty *skulllll?*'"

Mother could be fun when she wasn't lamenting all her grievances, but she was quite put out when I laughed at her performance. She didn't realize that she had succeeded in scaring me, but that I enjoyed being scared. I didn't laugh from disrespect, but from delight in my fear and from appreciation of her talent. Unfortunately I didn't have the words to explain that when I was twelve, and my reaction enraged her. My entire collection was shoveled into the trash; whence I retrieved it and transferred it secretly to the loft of a disused stable. She would never have entered such a dark, cobweb-draped refuge, and it was far beyond the range of our most robust servant's totter.

I had seen plenty of rats and dogs on my expeditions, and I carried a stout stick for protection against them on my tours of the necropolis, but I longed to see ghouls. I took to haunting the most desolate and ominous sections, even sneaking out at night to do so, without finding a trace of one — with the possible exception of a broken tusk that, according to one of the scientists at the Institute to whom I excitedly brought it, came from a wild boar. He was not impressed by my argument that some few people had claimed to see ghouls, but no one had ever claimed to see a wild boar within the city limits of Crotalorn.

"You want to talk to Dr. Porfat," he said with a dismissive contempt that convinced me Porfat probably knew more about it than he did, but I was never able to find that scholar in his office.

*

Necropolis, city of the dead, is not too fancy a word for Dreamers' Hill.

Thousands upon thousands have been buried there, and its upper slopes are very like a city. Elaborately rendered in miniature, palaces and temples line streets that would take days to explore and years to appreciate.

Even if those buildings were not cubicles for moldering corpses, if they carried no morbid associations whatever, but had been erected through artistic whim, their effect would be disquieting. The place is like a bad dream, in that it is so like real life but so arbitrarily different. Space has been compressed, the distance we expect between one house and another is missing, for the dead have no need to take the sun in their gardens, they have no use for privies or stables or servants' quarters or any of the other clutter that surrounds a home.

At night, when I took to wandering those streets, there were no idle strollers, either, and few human sounds but my own footsteps among the still little buildings. I heard strange noises that I ascribed to night birds, to contentious cats or curiously articulate dogs, and some that I could ascribe to nothing on earth, but what frightened me more than any sound was the unnatural scale of the houses and the insane perspective of every vista. Surrounded by so much unreality, how could I believe in a real world to which I might return?

Under the circumstances it was ironic that I should sometimes have been jerked back from the brink of panic by the tramping of the watchmen and their raucous bawling of tasteless songs:

Got a bone for a head, got a bone for a dick,
Got worms in my bed, and I'm feeling damned sick,
I'm dead.

Under the circumstances, I say, because I had become one of those for whom the watchmen watched; or, more accurately, whom they tried to scare off with their noise. My passion for collecting had expanded to include desiccated corpses in their entirety, those which struck my fancy either through freakishness, through some dim hint of former beauty, or through mad contortions suggesting the horror of untimely entombment. Now that my collection numbered more than five hundred specimens, I was very particular in my selection; and if I found no human relic worth taking, I would justify my time and trouble by gathering up a necklace or a few rings. By the age of eighteen, I, Lord Glyphtard, had become a grave-robber.

Mother encouraged me, but it would be unfair to say that she meant to. She had once been beautiful, or so she often told me, the child of her middle years, and she was still absurdly vain. She gadded about in outfits that would have been thought frivolous or immodest on a woman thirty years younger. She was childishly fond of jewelry, and her delight in any cheap trinket I gave her could transfigure her for a day. Since giving her such gifts seemed to be the only way I could please her, I regretted that I could do it so seldom.

So my first harvests of the tombs went to Mother: gold rings, a ruby brooch, a silver necklace, all in a heavy, antique style that appealed equally to her love of glitter and her sense of whimsy. I would tell her I'd found them, and although she never questioned this, the explanation sounded increasingly thin to my own ears. I began selling gold plates and silver statuettes to sly shops near Ashclamith Square, where no questions were asked. There I would pick up anklets and amulets of porphyry and chrysoprase for Mother, telling her I had won bets on dwelth matches.

I never needed a better lie, not even when I had the roof fixed and the chimneys swept, or bought a fine horse and some pretty slaves, for she knew that I played dwelth with people who wagered enormous sums. She had fretted over my playing, fearing broken bones and even death, but I had sung back her favorite song to her, the one about "doing something healthier than moping in the graveyard and playing with skulls," and what could be healthier than dashing around a field all day in the open air, kicking other young noblemen and bashing them with a club?

We believe whatever suits us, and it suited her to believe in my unlikely luck in order to pursue one of her obsessions with a clear conscience. Even more than the house we lived in, she wanted to prettify her father's tomb. It was one of the mansions on the upper slopes, weirder to me than most of them because it was an exact miniature of the Institute I saw every day from our windows. My grandparents were the only occupants, earlier ancestors having been buried in a crypt beneath the real palace, and it more than met their needs, but Mother had always lamented that it held none of the luxuries that the fashionable corpse requires. Hardly a week passed that she didn't ask for a staggering sum to buy the sort of gold toothpicks or toenail-clippers that I was busily stealing from other people's tombs. It would have been more economical to take her shopping-list with me to the cemetery, but such mean calculation would have made me feel like a thief, and I lacked the honesty to admit to myself that I was one. I preferred giving her the money and posing as a sporting genius.

I was curious how she was spending my money, so one night I entered the miniature Institute. I no longer needed a crowbar. I had taken a few sample locks home for a scientific study of their mechanisms, and now I could open almost any door without a key. I shut this one firmly behind me: of a piece with other nonsense about the afterlife, it was meant to open from the inside.

Entering the miniature palace and lighting a lamp, I found not a tiny lobby dominated by a figurine of my great grandfather, as some warped edge of my mind expected, but a parlor of cozy but normal proportions. Only the marble panels in the wall where windows might have been suggested that I was not intruding on a richly furnished home. In anyone else's tomb I would have rejoiced in the dyed garments out of Lesdom, the ivory elbow-scrapers inlaid with lapis lazuli, but here I could only grumble at the extravagance. My grandparents watched me disapprovingly, two of those realistic funeral busts that follow you everywhere with their eyes of polished gemstone. Grandfather, with his thrusting chin and craggy brow, looked even odder than his own father in the statue at the Institute, but I had to admit that I shared his vaguely canine cast of features.

I looked handsome, however, in the portrait that Mother had put up for the edification of the stone heads: rather like a poet of the gloomy and self-indulgent sort with my pale skin, long black hair and the somber clothing I favored. Mother looked downright beautiful, and at least forty years younger; she might have been my little sister. The dual portrait had obviously been painted from earlier pictures; but with sardonic anachronism, she wore one of the antique necklaces I had stolen from a neighboring tomb. For all eternity, or until the painting rotted, my grandparents would be forced to gaze on evidence of my misconduct.

I was chuckling over this when I hoisted the panel that concealed Grandfather's sarcophagus and rolled out the shelf that held it. Corpses that had met with violent ends intrigued me, and none more than his, a victim of the massacre in my own home. It wasn't my intention to steal his skull, merely to have a look at it. Perhaps I meant to compare it with my own, to see if I was less handsome than I hoped.

When I had at last succeeded in pushing the ponderous lid aside, I stared for a minute into the black void, then went and got the lamp to confirm what I knew. I still couldn't believe my eyes, and I reached inside for some evidence that the coffin wasn't completely empty, but I found none. He was gone.

I'm sure this tomb had never heard such laughter, and I was grateful the walls were thick and solid, for I couldn't restrain it. My laughter was often inappropriate by others' lights, and now it had nothing to do with mirth. Another would have wept or roared with fury, but this was my only available response to the ironic perfection of the outrage. If I could have put my hands on him at that moment, I'm sure I would have kept laughing while I tore the malefactor limb from limb.

Poor, silly Mother, from reverence for her beloved parents, and perhaps from uneasiness at the good progress she herself was making toward the afterlife, had spent a few days out of every week making this little home comfortable for a tenant who was long gone and would never return. She didn't know, certainly; she would never have committed the sacrilege of having the stone lid removed for a peek at the old corpse.

I knew whom to blame: henchmen of the hated Anatomical Institute, as a way of spitting on our family. Her father's bones now decorated a classroom, if they hadn't been jumbled into a bin or thrown out with the garbage. Perhaps the learned men still got a snigger out of their secret insult when Mother came to complain about the noises, sights and smells their students inflicted on us.

I put back the empty coffin with more reverence than I'd taken it out and opened the panel that held Grandmother. Here I made a stranger discovery. The lid appeared to have been undisturbed, it fit seamlessly; the sarcophagus had been carved from a single block of stone without fissures: yet Grandmother's incomplete skeleton was disordered, the remaining bones had been gnawed and broken. No matter how badly her killer had used her, her remains wouldn't have been dumped into the coffin any old way. Rats may be smart, but they don't take the lid off a sarcophagus, eat the corpse, and replace the lid.

After resealing Grandmother's remains, I collapsed into a sandalwood chair and stared at the busts. Were the people of the previous age more stern and righteous than we are, or did their artists merely make them look that way? This pair would never have laughed at the atrocity. They wouldn't have found my own activities amusing, either. Grandfather looked like the sort of dutiful tyrant who would have held me down, however regretfully, while the executioner performed his long task.

My eyes kept straying to the panels behind which Mother and I would lie. I had always been impatient with superstition. If I ever met a god I would apologize for disbelieving in him, but not until then. For all I cared some use could be made of tainted meat by feeding me to the dogs when I died.

Or so I had always believed that I believed. However irrationally, I shuddered to think that some larval physician would one day rummage through my corpse and try to match my liver and spleen against a diagram; and I wept for my poor, stern fool of a grandfather, who had already suffered that indignity.

I felt that some ringing declaration was in order, but all I could do was mutter, "Vengeance," with my eyes averted from Grandfather's fixed stare. Vengeance, indeed! If I took revenge, if I made an accusation, even if I asked a few clever questions with the utmost tact, people would talk, Mother would hear, and the truth would destroy her.

*

Odd, how fresh air and open space can clear the mind in an instant. Once I was strolling downhill beneath the stars, I had the answer to the puzzle, hardly a puzzle at all. A pair of oafs had been dispatched from the Institute to collect my grandparents. The two of them had carried Grandfather off, imprudently leaving the door ajar and the second sarcophagus uncovered. After delivering the first body, lingering for a good laugh with their fellow students and perhaps a few toasts to the corpse, they had staggered back up the hill to find that some animal had beaten them to Grandmother's remains. Having routed the dogs, the panther, whatever, they had found that Grandmother no longer met their standards of anatomical coherence, so they had resealed her coffin and the tomb behind them and gone home. No supernatural agency was needed to read the riddle, and certainly no ghouls.

It was about then that I tripped over the ghoul's jaw.

I didn't know what it was, of course, only an inconvenient object that had tangled my foot and sent me tumbling with a horrifyingly loud clatter of tools. I lay absolutely still for a time, my ear pressed to the ground for any hint of hurrying footsteps, before I dared rise on hands and knees to find what had tripped me.

There was no moon, but I could have counted the hairs on my hand by the radiance of Filloweela in her guise as morning star, and I instantly spotted the white bone jutting from the earth. It was half a jaw, with most of the teeth attached, and one of these was a curved lower canine as big as my thumb. It was exactly like the tusk I had taken to the Institute a few years earlier. The jaw was more massive and elongated, the huge molars looked fit for grinding stones, and there was still that bizarre fang to be accounted for: but the jaw and its dentition were like those of a man. No scientist could have mistaken it for a wild boar.

Forgetting the watchmen and the impending dawn, I took my pick from my bag and swung it with a will against the hard soil. I broke up the chunks and sifted them through my fingers, I dug to the depth of my knees in a circle wide as I was tall, but I found not so much as another tooth or sliver of bone.

Although it was by then fully light, I recklessly walked up the hill for anyone to see, for this was an open field of raised sarcophagi below the more fashionable streets of mausoleums. I gave this no thought at all as I searched for a likely spot where the jaw might originally have lain. I was poking my shovel around the base of a stone coffin when a voice said at my ear, "Have you lost something, sir?"

I didn't mark until later the heavy sarcasm. I forgot that he was a watchman and I was a grave-robber whose conviction could mean public dismemberment. In my single-minded excitement I acted guiltless, even with a bag of questionable tools slung over my shoulder and a shovel in my hand, and my manner disarmed him completely.

"Have you ever seen anything like this?" I demanded, thrusting the jawbone under his nose.

"Cludd!" he cried, backing away. "That's a ghoul. Leave it, sir, put it down! To touch one of them — you don't know what it might do."

I laughed. "There are no ghouls," I said, mocking the wisdom of the Anatomical Institute.

He shook his head violently. He was a big, red-faced brute, but he looked as if he might weep or faint. "You don't know, sir, you don't know!" Still backing away, he waved a weighty arm in the direction of my grandparents' tomb. "I heard one of them laughing just last night."

*

Last night I had briefly seen myself taking a battle-ax down from the wall and giving the Anatomical Institute the housecleaning it deserved. As judges are more apt to be lords than scholars, I probably would have suffered nothing worse than banishment from the city for a few years, and would have returned to enjoy a piquant notoriety. In my absence the students would have thought twice about puking on our steps.

Such roaring deeds were alien to my nature, however, and my strange discovery jolted me back to my true self. Next day, instead of going to the Institute to bathe in the blood of scholars, I trotted up the steps to consult them politely about the jawbone wrapped under my arm.

I paused before my great-grandfather's statue, letting the scholarly swarm find paths around me while I studied it attentively for the first time. I had remembered it as being odd beyond its depiction of a wise old head with the body of a young athlete, for that was a convention of public sculpture. My memory suggested that he sat on a bench, but now I saw that his seat was a coffin with the lid suggestively shoved aside. He examined a skull in his hand, surely a fit occupation for the patron of the Institute, but his expression was queerly unscientific. With great subtlety the artist had hinted that he was not so much meditating on the skull as leering at it. If the statue had come to life, he might in the next instant have kissed it, or gnawed it.

I dismissed these fancies and began my search for Dr. Porfat's office. The other scholar's contempt had raised him in my esteem; and if derision were a good gauge, he rose higher each time I asked the way. I wondered if the name were not some comic catchword, not only from the smirks or giggles, but also from the imaginative directions it evoked. After climbing marble stairs, then wooden ones, then a metal ladder or two, and at one point creeping across a precipitously sloped roof of loose slates, I found my way to a door under the cobwebbed eaves of the remotest tower, where the hieroglyph for Porfat had been burned into the wood many years ago. The door was locked, and no amount of knocking produced a response, so I opened it.

Except for more dust than any tomb, and for towers of books and bones and papers, some of them seeming to support the high ceiling and others wavering ominously to my steps on the uneven floor, the room was empty. One of the windows was not entirely blocked by heaped manuscripts, and one grimy pane commanded a misguided toymaker's view of the necropolis. I lingered there a long time, picking out likely tombs I had not entered and marking concealed pockets and byways of the rumpled terrain whose existence not even I had suspected. I took some notes on the back of a handy paper.

"Dr. Por— oh!"

I kept writing as I glanced up with feigned annoyance. It grew harder to feign as I noted eyes the odd, dark blue of plums, slack and sensuous lips, breasts that were rather small but rose at a presumptuous angle. Although she wore the egalitarian motley of a student, the shadowy, tiger-stripe tattooing of her neck and cheeks proclaimed her the grandest sort of Vendren.

"He's not here," I said. "I was leaving a note."

Her initial fright gone, she stared suspiciously. "May I help you?"

A thief or scholarly spy wouldn't have carried a ghoul's jaw, and I unwrapped it to show her. "I wanted his opinion of this."

From the watchmen's reaction and hers, I was almost ready to grant the bone magical properties, for she cast down her burden of books and papers to snatch it from me. She turned it hurriedly this way and that, staring more avidly than my great-grandfather at his skull. It gave me the chance to stare at her in similar style.

"Sleithreethra," she whispered with appalling reverence, and I made the appropriate protective sign against that Goddess. I regretted this superstitious lapse, for it earned me a glance of disdain.

"Where did you get this?"

Her tone said that I had shrunk from menacing intruder to halfwit errand-boy. "In the refectory, where else?" I said, but I gestured out the window.

My joke earned me only a grimace of impatience. "Will you show me?"

"If you like. It's a ghoul, isn't it?"

She turned to search among the papers she had dropped, some of them probably lost forever among Dr. Porfat's rubbish, and she returned with some scrolls that she gave me to unwind. When I made no move to roll them out, she came close beside me, as I had hoped she would, to do it herself.

When I tore my eyes from a close study of her curly, auburn hair, I saw that they were pen and ink sketches, and they were ludicrous: not from lack of skill, for she was an accomplished draftsman, but from her preposterous notion of ghouls. Those creatures, gorging on carrion, burrowing through graves, haunting the night and fleeing the sun in dank tunnels, were lower vermin than their closest associates, the rats and worms; for if the legends had any truth, they were humans who had rejected their humanity.

In her vision, the lank and distorted limbs were graceful, the brutish heads with their fanged muzzles noble as those of fine dogs. I never would have imagined that a female with tusks jutting up to her nostril-pits could have enticed me, but one nude freak draped languidly on a tomb hardened me even further than the artist had. Most of the images were less sexual than absurdly romantic, of ghouls as outsized elves who spent the enchanted midnight gazing at the moon with bright globes of eyes that echoed its beauty.

"Have you seen them?" I asked.

"As a child, I thought. . . . Well, I heard them, I'm sure of that, and I've never forgotten it. It was Dr. Porfat who described them for me when I brought him my first drawings, and I wanted to see if these were more accurate."

I studied the jaw without comment. Comparing it with her artwork was like comparing tales of chivalry with the iron weight of a spike-headed flail.

She surprised me by saying, "I'd like to draw you."

"Why? Do I look like a ghoul?"

She gave that question more thought than I believed it warranted before she said, "No, not really, but you do look unusual. It's mostly your body that interests me." She shocked me, but didn't displease me, by squeezing my arms with her tiny hands and tracing the contours of my chest. She batted my hands aside when I tried to reciprocate.

"You're better than most of the models we get."

"I play dwelth."

"That's the sort we get, and you're not like that at all. It takes hard, repetitive labor to develop your sort of muscles. Are you a soldier? I know! You're a gravedigger, aren't you? That's how you found the jaw."

You may imagine how little I cared for this deduction. "I am called Lord Glyphtard," I said, as I very seldom did. "I amuse myself by gardening."

"How amusing that must be!" It was clear she believed me not at all. "When will you show me where you found the jaw?"

"Now?"

"Don't be silly. You don't look for ghouls by daylight. Tonight?"

As I closed the door behind us, I'm sure she heard the firm click of the lock. She said, "You forgot to leave your note for Dr. Porfat."

"I'll wait until I see him."

Umbra Vendren was too observant, she was too smart, and she was even more eccentric than Mother. "Eccentric" might be less than apt. Her ancient Tribe was notorious for cruelty, depravity and madness, even if they all weren't, as so many believed, witches. I saw no harm in guiding her through the cemetery, though, and perhaps distracting her from ghouls long enough to satisfy my taste for her.

If nothing else, my way of stumbling into my career as a grave-robber should have taught me that one thing always leads to another.

*

She wore black, but Vendrens always do, a garment that fit her like a shadow under her silk cape, and her hair was hidden by a slouch hat with a raven's feather. You would have spotted her immediately as a grave-robber if she had walked onto a stage; or into a cemetery.

"Planning on a bit of gardening?" she asked.

We were a matched pair: I had brought my pick and shovel and crowbar only from force of habit, but I explained, "I thought you wanted to dig up ghoul-bones."

"He wasn't buried. They eat their own dead, too, and the bone you found must have rolled away unnoticed. But I want to see where you found it."

Walking through my damp garden into the cemetery, she said, "Porfat thinks ghouls are sick people, that they have a disease you can get from breathing graveyard air. Or," she added maliciously, "from contact with ghouls, such as playing with their bones."

That was nonsense. If graveyard air made you a ghoul, I would have been ten of them. "You handled it."

"Do you have it?"

My find had so delighted me that I carried it like a child's favorite toy of the moment, and I pulled it from my cloak. She held it up and licked it along its length, and I thought then that *sensuous* was less the word to describe her mouth than *depraved.* She eyed me slyly as she tongued the place where its lips might have been.

"I want to be a ghoul," she said. "Don't you?

She could make me feel less sophisticated than our oldest and silliest servant, and I had to struggle against making the sort of sign that had earned her contempt. "Not really."

"Oh, but it would be *fun*! All these pigs, these fools with their absurd pretensions, their preposterous vanity, their cowardly wish to spin out their empty, stupid, greedy lives forever — " she paused to spit on a handy sarcophagus " — it would show them what they're good for, living or dead, to *eat* them!" She kicked another moss-grown coffin hard enough to hurt herself, but she was a typical Vendren, I feared, and pain was beneath her notice. "What do you expect from pigs? Pork, that's all, *pork*, and if I were a ghoul I wouldn't care that it was rancid. I want to tear them up and strew them around, and then I want some great, beautiful monster to drag me down among the mud and the worms and the rot and fuck me!"

She had raved her way into the subject that really interested me, and I reached out for her, but she shrugged my hand off and raced deeper into the field of the dead. She stopped, picking a coffin at random, and tried to shove off its lid. She spat furious curses when she failed to budge it.

She was screaming louder than ever, urging me to come and use my tools. I was tempted to fade into the shadows and leave her to the watchmen. Even if they weren't cowed by her status, they surely wouldn't take her seriously enough to arrest her. Instead I hurried to help her and told her to be quiet.

"I'm sorry," she said meekly. "I have strong feelings on the subject."

"You'll have strong feelings when they put you on the scaffold and use one your severed legs as a spool to reel out your intestines," I whispered, but her bright attentiveness suggested a child hearing plans for a jolly outing.

Once the lid was off, she clambered up to peer inside. "It's empty!" She began cursing again.

"It would be, this close to the Institute."

"Nonsense. A ghoul could move that lid more easily than you did. That's why they're empty." She adjusted her hat to a more determined angle and scanned the terrain, her eyes resting at last on the higher slopes of the necropolis. "Could we get into one of those mausoleums?"

"I suppose we could try," I said, "but only if you promise to be quiet."

While we were creeping up the hill, crouching behind sarcophagi and taking advantage of all the hedges and trees I knew, she muttered, "He wants *me* to keep quiet?" She didn't explain this, but after a while she said, "You have a wonderful laugh, do you know?"

"When did I laugh?"

"When I was telling you how I wanted to be a ghoul." I didn't remember laughing, but it would have been my likely reaction to the alarm I had felt. She added, "I think your laugh was what attracted me to you."

This was the first encouraging word she had spoken to me, and I tried again to detain her, but she hurried on to the streets of tombs.

I wanted to choose the tomb, a relatively secluded one that I knew I could open, but she stopped at a miniature temple of Polliel. "This one," she said, slapping the door. "I hate this bastard God with his great, ugly, peering, prying eye, like a slimy fried egg you get every morning whether you like it or not."

I had thought I was getting used to her blasphemy, but I winced. While she puzzled over the seams of the door, I took tools of my own design from my cloak and opened the lock as if I had the key.

"I knew what you were," she said, smiling up at me. "That attracted me, too."

She had forced me to see that I was a slave to the same superstitions as Mother, and no more so than now: for I had never violated a priest's tomb, and I realized that I had been irrationally avoiding the wealthiest ones of all. The jeweled vestments and gold chalices and censers and asperges that dazzled me in my first glance, when I had lit a lamp, were worth the loot of twenty ordinary tombs, and my second glance raised that estimate to fifty.

She went straight to the panel that concealed the priest, higher and more embellished than those of acolytes and temple virgins, and gestured impatiently for my help. When I had opened the coffin I staggered back, gasping and retching, for his had been a fairly recent burial.

Perhaps she already was a ghoul. She inhaled the stinking fog of decay as if it were perfume before leaning into the coffin and spitting in the corpse's face. "False priest!" she hissed. "Sleithreethra will destroy your god, night will prevail, darkness will rule forever and ever." And then I made a protective sign whole-heartedly as she mocked him with the motto of the Goddess's foul cult: "Joy always!"

She began hoisting him out of the coffin, cursing when a rotten arm fell off and laughing when a long-trapped pocket of gas erupted like a fatally explosive fart, but with an infinitely fouler odor, a stench that forced me to fling open the door with no thought of caution and vomit on the street outside.

"Don't be such a baby," she said as I sucked gulps of clean air and fought to retain consciousness. "Help me find him one of his cute boys to warm him up."

The coffin she chose contained a temple virgin, but she decided to make do with this. It was a much older corpse, the skin browned and drawn tight as a drumskin over the bones, with hair of the unnatural, reddish hue that comes to some of the dead. She stripped off the holy woman's gown and arranged her head-to-crotch with the priest, snarling when bits of them snapped or sloughed off.

I tried to accept her frightfulness as a natural albeit extreme extension of girlish doll-play while I chose the best items to steal. It would have been foolish to try selling the cloth-of-gold vestments or other religious paraphernalia, but I cut loose the largest of the emeralds, sapphires and rubies from the robes and dropped them in my bag. They could have come from anywhere, they could be sold anywhere, and just one of them would maintain my household in style for a year.

"Well?" she said, reminding me that I was not alone with my account-books. "I thought you wanted me."

I turned to see that she had shed her clothes and was lounging in the priest's coffin, her chin propped on her hand, her head angled winsomely. The pose and expression suggested a mischievous child playing at seductress in a bathtub. I saw that she was younger than I'd thought, but that didn't make her less insane; nor did it make me less eager to have her.

In some ways it was a vile experience. Leakage from the corpse had permeated the porous stone, and the coffin trapped the odor, so that it was barely possible for me to breathe whenever I lowered my face to kiss her. I had no idea how she was able to lie in the bottom with a smile, but she did. To cup her buttocks with my hands, I had to work my fingers through a film of slime that held unspeakable shreds, and some of them could move. All the while I made love to her, my stomach churned.

"Tell me when you're coming," she said, "so I can change back to a corpse."

"Don't," I gagged.

I hardly knew whether I meant, "Don't say it," or, "Don't do it," so different was she from any woman I'd known. She was pleased by my efforts, but oddly detached, and nothing I did could touch her deepest feelings. She kept making little jokes about what we were doing, so I shut her mouth with kisses and tried all the harder to touch her, but my best efforts earned me only a languid sigh, no more than the reaction you might get by scratching someone's back in the right place.

"Very nice," she said, working her way out from under me and leaving me to lie in the filth. Her pretty bottom was smeared with my handprints in human decay, and as she padded across the room a crushed maggot dropped loose from one flexing cheek.

She took up where she'd left off, scrawling obscene words on the walls with rare pigments from the priest's toilet. After watching her for a while I climbed out of the coffin and threw her over a table, taking her from the back without preliminaries, almost brutally, but she didn't especially mind; nor was she especially moved.

"That was nice," she said.

When I had filled my bag with loot and she had glutted her appetite for sacrilege, we scraped the filth from our bodies with the vestments and put on our clothes. I made to close the door behind us, but she stopped me.

"No," she said, "leave it open for the ghouls."

"And how will they know to come?"

If she meant to punish me for humoring her, she succeeded. Her shriek of laughter burrowed through my teeth and augured all the way down my spine. It was so reckless to make such a racket in these silent streets that I, too, laughed. For the first time she kissed me impulsively and with feeling.

*

With variations of danger and depravity, we played the same theme on succeeding nights. The servants of no god were safe from her, or me, except possibly those of the Joyful Goddess; but then her cult has no monuments on the Hill. By finding religion I earned far more in six nights than I had in six years of secular looting, but my success drove me out of business. It set the city writhing in convulsions of holy delirium. Mobs of maniacs surged back and forth through the streets, seeking rival sectarians to stamp flat, for Umbra's scrawled messages would give one god credit for the outrage to another. Sleithreethrans suffered most of all, but this delighted her, for her cult forever seeks to validate its nihilism.

Crowds came to the Hill at night with torches and bonfires to guard the tombs of their clergy, burn suspects, and continue their street-battles. It was no place for a quiet thief like me, but Umbra went there every night to scribble slogans, spread rumors and cheer on the factions.

These events convinced me beyond doubt that ghouls not only existed, but that they were numerous and active. In all the tombs we left open, the bodies were either missing or mutilated, even those in coffins we hadn't disturbed, whose covers could never have been lifted by animals. My skin crawled when I pictured the invisible entourage that must have trailed us every night, and I wondered if I could ever bring myself to return to the cemetery, even at noonday. Despite their superhuman stealth, I decided that they must be a species of ape, stupid by human standards.

"If they had any brains," I told Umbra, "they would shut the doors of the tombs behind them. Nobody would know that the priests' bodies had been stolen. They've spoiled a good thing for themselves."

She laughed in my face. "Do you think so? They're not only smarter than you, they have a better grasp of politics. Come see all the corpses from last night's riots. If any are left."

With the tombs beyond our reach, I pandered to her necrophilia by showing her my museum. She was wild about it; she moved into the loft. When not inciting riots, she spent hours sketching or playing with my curiosities. It amused her to be intimately stroked with a dead hand, to be mounted while she kissed a corpse, but she was no more than amused, and I could not touch her heart. My fascination with her grew each day. I was in love, but she wasn't.

After she had been living with me for a few weeks a delegation of Vendrens came to call, some of them in the terrifying regalia of Death's Darlings, all of them shadowed with tiger-stripes. I found myself engaged to be married.

Mother disdained the class from which I might normally have drawn a bride, and Umbra was far above our station, but that carried no weight at all. Her nose was too big, her lips too full, her eyes too far apart, her teeth crooked, she walked with a stoop; her feet were too big, her legs too skinny, her hips too wide; she probably dyed her hair, she probably had Ignudo blood, her drawings were obscene, she talked like a washerwoman and ate like a pig. Put all Mother's offhand sparks together in a sustained flame, and the beautiful, high-born and sometimes well-mannered girl I loved would have stood revealed as a freak escaped from an exhibition. Like a bird's, Mother's voice was pleasant enough when you disregarded the nonsense it twittered.

*

Despite my efforts to coax her out after we were married, my bride stayed in the loft. She liked living with my collection and expanded it into more pungent bywaters than I ever might have charted.

The riots ended when a detachment of Never-Vanquished, a crack regiment with a non-sectarian tradition, was posted near the Hill to break heads impartially. Umbra again grew eager to violate tombs. She promised we would do it discreetly this time, she indulging her passion for playing with the dead, I filching their trinkets. Unfortunately, after our few nights of looting the clergy, I no longer needed to rob graves. Instead of giving me time to do whatever I wanted, wealth burdened me with obligations. My new in-laws took me up, putting me on to brokers and merchants. I found myself underwriting cargos of emeralds, apes and opium, and getting richer by the day.

By the day, in fact, for now I had to stay awake while Umbra slept, and afterward I had no taste for creeping among the tombs all night. I didn't want her to go scavenging alone, at the mercy of watchmen and grave-robbers and those religious fanatics who might still linger after the disturbances, but I would have had to chain her to the bed to stop her.

Parroting the prattle of our servants, I warned her that ghouls notori-ously lust for human women.

"It isn't true." Her tone of dejection wounded me.

I brooded my way into the certainty that she would deceive me. She never denied me when our schedules allowed us time to make love, but she would lie inert with a languid smile, probably dreaming she was dead. Her whimpers over a well-cooked dish seemed more heartfelt than any I could evoke. Touching her heart had been a challenge, but a challenge remains a pleasure only while hope lives that it can be met. She was like a riddle posed by a demon, whose answer changed each time I cried, "I know it!"

After weeks of unsuccessful searching, I began to find fresh bruises and scratches each time she bared her body. She laughed them off as the results of diving into a prickly hedge to avoid the watch or falling into a concealed crypt. I knew that she had found someone more to her taste, a medical student who could do clever things with corpses, or some lusty grave-robber of the lowest type, perhaps a whole gang of them.

"I thought I was escaping all my dull, daylight relatives when I married you," she said, not troubling to deny a thing when I accused her, "and you've turned out duller than any of them."

*

I lurked behind a clump of adomphadendrons where I could watch the stable. Its flinty walls were silvered by the kind of moon she favored in her art, a vast and perfect globe that floated low on the horizon, tinged with blood and mottled with blue mold. It was a fit night for her elfin ghouls to romp, a night whose pull she couldn't resist, for I myself felt it drawing me to the Hill. I might have abandoned my purpose and gone ahead to prowl the graveyard on my own if she hadn't picked that moment to come out.

I bit my lip to hold back a cry, or perhaps a laugh, of pain; she wore nothing, and her beauty tore at my innards like a clawed hand. The moon had carved her from its own substance, and nothing existed but those two white fires, the one walking to rejoin the other. Her step was languid but purposeful. I could almost feel her nipples tightening, her nostrils flaring to savor the scents of honeysuckle and bloodstrange as the night worked its spell on her.

She was no less attainable than the moon itself. I could run up behind her and make myself known, I could kiss her and feel her and throw her on the grass, I could fuck her till I spent blood, and she would sigh and tell me it was "very nice." I ground my fists into my temples until the moon and her daughter blended in a lens of tears.

Taking control of myself, I crept forth to follow her, tiptoeing and dodging among the furred sarcophagi. I carried no tools tonight but a sword, and I had slung it over my back to avoid clangorous missteps.

She led me into the longest-neglected slum of the necropolis, a savage place of fallen slabs and flourishing brambles. If this was her nightly haunt, it explained the welts and scratches on her alabaster skin. To go without sandals at least among the thorns, among the concealed pits of splintered bones, was mad, but of course she was mad, it had always been part of her attraction. The least of her dangers was a fall or a pricked foot. She was at the mercy of any wild animal or twisted lurker. I should go with her always and protect her. I would give up my pretense of respectability and become the rogue she had mistaken me for. Even if I had to become a ghoul to do it, I would make her happy.

I was jolted from my warm bath of sanctimony by her shrill cry: "Exudimord!"

I had no idea what that meant, but the gladness in her voice chilled me, and I feared it was a name, an uncouth, foreign name. The fear grew as she called more loudly, "Exudimord Noxis, come to me! I am here!"

"To me, too, Exudimord Noxis," I muttered under my breath as I drew my broadsword.

She cried out happily and ran toward a once-splendid tomb that had been ravaged by the growth of an oak. She was as pretty a sight as anyone had ever seen, a woman clothed only in the warmth of her lust as she ran through the moonlight to meet her lover.

Then I saw my rival, and I sighed with exasperation. Nothing but a marble statue squatted on the portico, a white gargoyle mottled with fungus. The sculptor had viewed ghouls more rationally than she did, and he had rendered the beast in the full flower of its foulness. Indecorously by modern standards, he had given his creation an engorged phallus whose ridges and warts suggested an instrument of torture. The face, I thought, was a vicious caricature of some personage I knew from other sculpture, a hero or politician who had provoked the artist to wrath. I was about to rise from concealment to interrupt my mad wife's tryst with the statue when it moved.

My feelings were like a breaking wave that tumbled me end over end, turning the world upside down and back again, sweeping me I knew not where. Horror, yes, terror, of course, but wonder and scientific curiosity, too, and morbid curiosity, and prurient curiosity, and jealousy, oh, yes, excruciating jealousy, they were only a part of the witch's brew that boiled in my skull.

When my vision cleared, Umbra was on her knees with her mouth glued to the monster's most monstrous attribute, adoring it, mumbling muffled endearments and squeals of delight. Nothing could be more different from her languid, inattentive style with me. The stroking of its foul claws set her quivering like the strings of a lute. Her excitement erupted into a frenzy of passion when the ghoul tumbled her over and took her like a dog. She sobbed, she howled with ecstasy at each thrust, she clawed the earth and chewed the grass as she rammed alternating hindquarters back to slap his hipbones.

I didn't dash out and attack them by surprise, as I should have. I stood up and advanced with the deliberate steps of a sleepwalker. My feelings had coalesced into a rage so terrible that nothing could have stood against it, or so I believed. I walked with the invulnerability of the zealot on his way to the stake, for absolute justice guided my steps and righteous wrath powered my arm.

I raised the sword. The baleful, yellow eyes rolled round to glare at me. The white arm streaked with mold and dirt swept backward, bearing the back of a gigantic fist at its end. My face went suddenly numb. I remember being lifted into the air, but I don't remember landing.

*

I woke. I rolled onto my back. Seeing the moon helped me remember. It was large as before, and as low. No time had passed.

My enemy was upon me!

I jerked upright, flailing about for my sword, but I was in no danger. The moon now hung behind the city of the living. It had fully sailed its majestic course over my blind face.

The rank weeds lay trampled in a wide circle, as by a fight, or by inexhaustible lovers. A stench of rut and rot thickened the air I tried to breathe. My sword lay broken in three pieces, contemptuously, as if over the monster's knee. I pictured Umbra pleading for my life as I lay helpless, and I screamed at the shame of it.

An echo of my scream surprised me, and I turned to see that the door of the tomb yawned open on broken hinges. I mounted one, then two of the cracked steps for a closer look, but the interior was utterly black. For such an old tomb, one whose occupants had long gone to feed the bloated oak that had burst through its roof, the smell hanging at the black doorway was unaccountably vile.

"Umbra?" I called, and I heard the echo again. The flat emptiness of the tomb gave her name a sardonic edge. Retrieving the pieces of my sword, I wondered why this disused ground should be littered with so many fragments of relatively new bones. In case something watched me from the tomb, I refrained from picking them up for a closer look. I would return to this place with a light, and with an unbroken weapon.

As for Umbra, she could lie with the worms in hell, and I was well rid of her. Then why did tears roll down my cheeks? When I wiped them I felt crusted blood and winced at the pain of a split lip and probably broken nose. I laughed. Ghouls were real.

I didn't go to the stable in order to look for her. If she had not been spirited away to the underground, as a woman taken by the fairies of ballads, I assumed she would have the sense to avoid me by mundane means. I went there to clean out my museum. I would open the hayloft door and shove it all out to burn. But why bother? I would burn the stable with its contents. I felt the need of a grand gesture to shut my past behind me.

When I had climbed to the loft and lit the lamp, Umbra sat up in bed and stared at me. The duvet slipped from breasts abraded by coarse grass. Her lips were swollen from eager kisses, her arms bruised by clutching hands. Her eyes looked even darker than plums as she watched me.

I said, "If Dr. Porfat's theory is correct, you should be well on your way to full ghoulhood." My tone was mild, but as I spoke I was pulling down skulls from the shelves and stamping on them. They were hard to break.

"What do you want from me?" she screamed. "You're the ghoul, you! You want to devour me. You watch me with your great, knowing eyes, trying to crawl inside my head and paw my soul, like some nasty boy poking at a spider in a bottle."

"I wonder what you ever could have seen in me," I said, kicking a tormented mummy into yellow bones and powder.

"I thought you looked like a ghoul, I thought you laughed like one. Oh, was I ever wrong! You? You're a pig like all the rest of them, a squeamish, prissy pig, tiptoeing into tombs and out again with a girlish shudder. You're nothing but a sneak-thief too timid to steal from the living."

I guess her words hit home. Without forming the intention, I hurled a dried head. It struck her hard in the eye, but it didn't stop her shrieking tirade. "You aren't fit to infest the bristles on a ghoul's balls, you with your dry, pecky kisses and your pathetic little pecker! Why don't you go and stick it in your precious, filthy-minded old bitch of a mother, that's what you both probably want — "

I seized something to hit her. I didn't realize, until its point had slipped into one side of her neck and peeked from the other, that it was a baling-hook. I had to laugh at her goggling astonishment. When she tried to spout even more venom, her mouth gushed blood. She thrashed wildly as a gaffed fish and blubbered inarticulate words.

I wrenched the hook forward, tearing her throat out, and pounded her face with my fist until her struggles became a convulsion that bent her body upward in a jerking arc. The quilt slipped away, revealing the bruises on her legs and the inflammation of her overtaxed sex. I jammed the hook into it and ripped a hole more fit for a ghoul, though I then claimed it as my own. I regretted that she felt so little of this, for her eyes were dead as glass before I had finished.

"That was very nice," I said in her own, detached tone.

*

Mother put out the lamp when she entered a short while later, for morning outshone its light. The noise must have been terrible indeed to draw her into the dark tangle of junk that filled the lower floor.

"I heard you laughing," she said. "I knew something was wrong."

She studied the body. She surveyed the disordered collection of necrophiliac trophies, whose existence I doubt she had suspected. She said, "You've ruined a perfectly good duvet."

I said, "She deceived me with . . . someone else. I went mad."

"Better you than her. All the Vendrens are crazy, you know. It was only a matter of time before she murdered you in your bed, or before one of her inbred, degenerate brothers did it."

She arranged Umbra in a mockery of peace and tucked the quilt over her. "Whatever you do, don't add her to your collection," she said. "You must bury her as quickly as possible, then give out your story about her infidelity. That may satisfy the Vendrens, especially if we grant her the honor of proper burial in our family tomb. But we don't want them to see her body."

"You have some experience with this sort of thing," I said, referring to that which was never mentioned, the family massacre.

She tried to wither me with her displeasure and stare me down, but I was no longer the little boy who persisted in repeating a naughty word. She dropped her eyes first. She said as she made to leave, "I have to organize the servants to clean up your mess."

"It's time we spoke of this," I said, blocking her way to the ladder.

"It has nothing at all to do with you," she said. "Get out of my way!"

"*Nothing at all to do with me?* That my own grandparents and my father were taken from me, one way or another, by violence?"

"With this, I mean, with what you've done to your crazy whore of a wife. That's your only problem now. Keep your mind on *that*, why don't you?"

"And why should it have anything to do with this? Keep talking, Mother, you're telling me things. Did you imagine that I believed I killed Umbra because Grandfather happened to be a ghoul?"

That was no random shot. I had at last connected the face of Umbra's lover with the sculpted head it had caricatured: my grandfather's. I had no idea why, or how, but Mother could tell me some of it, that was plain from her dismay. She rolled her eyes with the wild stare of a panicked horse, looking for some other exit from the loft, but I gripped her frail shoulders.

"No!" she cried. "That's not true, that's vile to say that! He suffered from a . . . a growth disorder, that's all, his bones kept growing, he became grotesque, and his mind was affected. His own father had endowed the Institute in the hope they would find a cure for him, but he wanted no part of those mountebanks, he wanted his palace back, as I do, as you do. He was like you. He had a scientific turn of mind. He collected specimens from the graveyard, too, the bones of fellow-sufferers."

"A ghoul," I groaned, dropping my hands and turning away. "Sleithreethra!"

"No!" she shrieked, making the protective sign. "No, he wasn't!"

"He nevertheless murdered all the others, didn't he?"

Her escape route was clear now, but she didn't take it. She said, "We locked him up most of the time, toward the end, but he had his good days. He seemed entirely his old self on the night we had him down to dinner, but he complained about the food, especially the saddle of lamb. He would chew some and spit it out, making truly horrible faces, then chew some more and spit it out. . . . We could see he was working himself up to a violent state, and Mother was about to call the servants to take him back to his room, but. . . . He said, 'I'll show you what kind of meat I crave!', and he seized your father. There was nothing we could do. It was over before I could rise from my chair, and with those jaws of his, and those hideous hands — he tore your father apart before my eyes, and ate him.

"Mother tried to stop him, but he struck her just once and broke her neck. The servants, too, he fought them off and killed two of them without interrupting his . . . his meal.

"I had a dagger at my belt, a silver dagger that he himself had given me, and I plunged it into his back, but he clawed at it and pulled it out. And then he turned to me. I thought it was the end, I couldn't move, but he extended the dagger to me, hilt first, and said in his most charming way — it was ghastly, to recognize his normal, courtly self behind that face — he said, 'I appreciate your effort to help me, dear girl, but it won't do any good.' And he laughed.

"He had taught me to use the dagger, to stab upward for the heart, and that's what I did. He was no ghoul, just a mortal man. He fell down dead."

"You're sure you killed him?"

"Glyphtard, murdering one's father is not the same as locking a door or putting out a light. I'm sure."

"I'm sorry."

"You should be. Ghoul, indeed! The poor man was ill. No one would have believed that, though, from the condition of your father. They say that a madman has the strength of ten, and it must be true of the appetite, as well. We buried what little remained of him in the garden, and we told everyone that the intruder made off with his body."

"So that everyone thinks he was the murderer."

"Yes, but he was a Fand, don't you see? If people wanted to believe that, it was no stain on the honor of the Glyphts."

*

Organizing the servants was no simple task, for Mother chose only the oldest and presumably most trustworthy to bathe and anoint Umbra and sew her shroud. They doddered, wailed, gossiped, sent one of their number to fetch the water they had neglected to bring, went to find the woman who had gone to fetch the water, misplaced the holy oils, lunched, lost their needles, wandered off, napped, and had her ready for burial by sundown. In a fury of impatience by then, I nearly slipped by telling Mother I didn't need it when she gave me the key to the family tomb.

*

I dismissed the slaves, far younger men purchased with my new wealth, who had carried Umbra to the tomb and laid her in the vacant sarcophagus that had been meant for my father. I told them I would watch over her that night. One of them warned me to lock the door against ghouls. I think my laugh at this offended his sense of decency.

Alone, I stared at Grandfather, he at me. I had no doubt of it: howsoever bulged and extruded by a massive growth of bone and teeth, howsoever dehumanized by owls' orbs of glowing yellow, this was the face I had seen last night. The ghoul that Mother had killed had risen from his stone coffin, dined on the body of his wife, and gone off to join his kind. Grandfather's life as a human being had spanned more than six decades; but after two decades more as a ghoul he was still strong enough to bat me aside like a puppy, virile enough to satisfy my wife.

"Vengeance," I said, patting his stone cheek. "Vengeance, indeed!" I whipped off my cloak to veil his bust. After a moment I covered Grandmother's, too.

I cast aside the lid of Umbra's sarcophagus and tore open the shroud that had cost so much time and trouble. Even by the liberal standards for a corpse she was no longer lovely. Aside from the marks of my ripping and pounding, garishly but ineffectively cosmeticized, her flesh had gone puffy and yellow. As the servants had warned it would, deploring the way we rushed them, rigor mortis had seized her. Her knees were drawn up and her hands clawed as if to ward me off, her lips were lifted from her splintered teeth in a defiant snarl. I certainly knew what a dead body felt like, but I was shocked that these breasts should be so cold when I cupped them in my hands, that these nipples should not rise when I played with them.

I heard myself sigh, perhaps from regret, as I abandoned that diversion and opened the bag I had brought, not my usual tools, but a collection I had prepared while the servants were laying her out. I took a boning-knife

I had sharpened like a razor and cut between her breasts, then forced the flesh aside to bare her ribs. It was impossible to crack them open in the cramped quarters of the coffin. I rolled up one of Mother's extravagant carpets so as not to soil it and hauled Umbra out, dumping her on the tiled floor. Then I forced her ribcage wide and cut her heart loose from its tubing.

As a bitter joke, I kissed the heart I had been unable to move before setting it by, but I wasn't defiling her corpse just to amuse myself. An old wives' tale had it that a ghoul's body must be exposed to sunlight for a full day before it can be called truly dead. Having heard Mother's story of Grandfather's death, having seen him in the filth he now used for flesh, I was willing to credit that belief and anything else, no matter how bizarre, that I had ever heard about those vermin. According to an even less credible tale, a ghoul can for a time assume the identity of a corpse whose heart and brain it eats. I would take no chances. The ghouls had had enough fun with my wife, and she with them. I had brought a stone crock for her organs, and I would take them home with me to lock away in a safe place.

I cut a ring beneath her still-lovely auburn curls. Her scalp squeaked a protest when I ripped it off. I peeled her face down, no great loss now, to reveal the raw bone beneath. Sawing her skull was arduous work, as it was slippery and hard to hold, and I wanted my cut to be precise. I would leave no slightest morsel of her brain to amuse a ghoul.

My hands by now were smeared with clotted gore, and when I paused to rest I was horrified to catch myself absently licking them clean. I had never tasted human blood, or the congealed slime that was like Umbra's blood, and I wondered why it didn't sicken me. I deliberately licked my hand. Except for the idea of it, I found nothing to dislike.

I turned her over, revealing a huge bruise of pooled blood on her back. I had to stamp on her buttocks and crack some of her bones to compose her more comfortably for sawing the back of her head, but by then I was too weary to go on. In the hope of refreshing myself, I reached for the food I had put by.

I wish I could make my thoughts and feelings at that time clear, but they weren't clear then, nor are they now. I had seen the great love of my life — yes, she was — polluted by the foulest of fiends, I had been beaten senseless, I had murdered her that morning, I had heard and guessed more than enough about my heritage to drive anyone mad, and now I was violating her body in accord with a superstition I would have laughed at yesterday: it would be inadequate to say I was *overwrought.*

I may have been asleep for a moment without knowing it, because the final horror began just like a dream: I was eating something that I assumed I had brought with me, but I couldn't remember bringing anything, nor could I say what I was eating. Instead of looking in my hand, as any sane, waking man would have, I pondered the question while continuing to chew and swallow.

I put the food aside and resumed sawing, stopping every now and then for another bite. Only when I had sawed off the top of Umbra's skull did I know in a dim way that I had devoured her heart. I began to scoop out gobbets of her brain and eat them, too.

*

I had no idea why I was wearing my husband's clothes. The sleeves were too long, they got in the way of . . . what I was doing.

It couldn't be his stupid joke, as I thought when I came to myself and noticed the clothes, because I was the one doing it: I was the one eating this unknown woman's corpse. The mere fact didn't repel me. I had wanted to join Exudimord in his feasts. I had wanted to share his pleasures. But the things he offered me always stank and crawled with maggots, and my weak, human stomach would rebel. Not even his promise that I would become a ghoul if I acted like one had given me the strength to overcome my despised nature.

Why had he never given me fresh meat like this? It was delicious! He must have been testing me.

And I knew he must have arranged this treat. Had I passed his tests at last? "Exudimord?" I called. Sleithreethra! Just saying his name made me squirm inside, made me moist and ready for him.

He wasn't here. No one was, just me and the corpse, inside a little box I identified from murals celebrating their fatuousness as the tomb of the Glyphts. *Lord* Glyphtard! I had to laugh. If the lowest of Vendrens pissed on the highest of Glyphts, the stream would disperse to a golden dew before it fell far enough to touch him, and he would think he had been kissed by the fairies.

Living near the cemetery, collecting those amusing relics, he had duped me into believing him something more than human, but he was only a cheap tradesman, posing as a nobleman and playing at ghoul. I tore off his hateful clothes.

The clothes were his best, Fand-green silk and lace, that he might wear to a ball, but — I pulled off the hat and confirmed my suspicion, that it was one of those black things with a flat crown you wore to funerals. His mother? I spat out my mouthful. No, it wasn't she: I couldn't be absolutely sure, since the body had been ripped and disjointed and spread in a circle around me, but I believed this had been a much younger woman. At length I found confirmation of this, not one of the crone's calloused hoofs, but an intact foot almost as pretty as my own.

However hard it was not to, I shouldn't hate Glyphtard's mother. The bitch had unwittingly made my wildest dreams come true. Spying on me, as always, she had seen me coming home from the cemetery one morning and had implored me not to go near the oldest section at night, and especially nowhere near the tomb of the ancient pornographer, Chalcedor. A particularly vile ghoul, devoted to that writer's lubricities in his human life and now consumed by an itch for young women that he could seldom satisfy with living ones, was reputed to lurk beneath the tomb. One day, perhaps, I would tell her how right she'd been, and thank her.

The mystery of the corpse seemed impenetrable. The only young women in the household were slaves, but not even a Glypht would lay a slave in his family tomb, however much he might have doted on her; nor could I alone have eaten so much of her body. I called my lover again. He *must* be here! I tried to look inside the coffins, the only places Exudimord could be hiding, but their lids were too heavy to move.

How did I get here? My last memories made me cringe. I saw Glyphtard's leather coat coming at me like a falling wall. He had beaten me, but now there were no bruises nor even tender spots on my face or body.

I considered the obvious possibility, that I was dreaming. Whenever that thought crossed my mind in a dream, I would wake up, but now I didn't. Besides, I never dreamed such convincingly banal details as the chafing of my heels when I walked in my husband's boots, the annoyance of a shred of meat caught in my back teeth, the fluttery sound of the lamp as its oil ran low. Unlike the illegible symbols that puzzled me in dreams, the inscriptions on the sarcophagi made sense.

Other possibilities . . . but I hadn't the courage even to name them. The walls of the tomb drew closer, there was no air! I ran to the door, expecting the worst, but it opened. The night brushed my face with a feather of fine rain. Dripping eaves plashed and pattered. The breeze chilled me, but I could bear to stay in the tomb no longer with my unanswered questions.

I wobbled back in Glyphtard's boots to get his cloak. When I took it down, I screamed to find two Glyphts, uglier even than most of them, piercing me with bright eyes. My heart almost stopped before I saw that they were only sculpted heads of the dogs that had whelped the old bitch. That was an apt metaphor: Glyphtard's grandfather looked as if he should have been kept outside on a chain. And yet I found something in his brutal face that stirred me, a familiarity that was pleasant, but at the same time so disturbing that I turned away and blotted his features from my mind.

I went out in the dark street and called for my lover. How I wanted him! He had stirred me as no mere man ever had, he had woken me fully from a sleep that my husband had only been able to fret and ruffle, like a restless bedmate, and I always yearned for him, but now my want was close to madness. I screamed for him. I began running down the narrow street, although I had no idea where it would lead me.

I collided with what seemed a fixed obstacle, but it pinned me with thick arms.

"What's this?" the watchman demanded.

"Unwrap it and see," a second one laughed.

"Let me go! I am the chosen one of Exudimord Noxis, King of Ghouls!" I screamed.

"And I'm the Spring Queen, you addled baggage." He smelled bad enough from sour wine and sweat, but when he undid his coarse breeches, the stink of his unwashed privates gagged me. "Come dance around my pole."

"Oh, look at this!" the second watchman breathed with a lecher's reverence when he had torn away my cloak. He patted my buttocks, then hooked me unspeakably with a cruel finger. "We must have won the favor of Filloweela, Gorpho. How did we do it, do you suppose?"

"Don't question the gods," the first one said, blindly pushing his hard cock against my belly, "just take their gifts."

"Then take this one from Oreema!" I spat in his face as I thrust my knee up between his legs. Tender flesh jammed against unyielding bone. He bellowed and doubled over, releasing me, and I turned to run, but the second one hit me hard enough to make light explode before my eyes with the handle of his bill. I fell to my knees, and I had no strength to resist when he kicked me all the way down and rolled me over. He lay between my legs, and they were useless against him now, but I tried to claw his eyes. When he proved that he could hold both my wrists with one huge hand, I knew the fight was over even before his hurtful probe gouged into me.

The first one kicked him as he lay grunting and thrusting. "She's mine!" he bellowed. "She ran into my arms, didn't she?"

"You let her go, stupid. She'd be gone if I wasn't here. Use her mouth."

"That's what your father should have done with your whore of an Ignudo mother," Gorpho grumbled, but he dropped to his knees by my head.

"I'll bite you!" I cried. "If you do, I swear, I'll bite it off!"

"Yes, and I may have a sore prick for a week, but you'll be blind for life, bitch," he growled, and when he pressed his thumbs on my eyes I believed him. I opened my mouth to his foul-smelling penis.

I thought they might let me go after sating their desire of the moment, but their male itch to outdo each other burned in them more hotly even than honest lust. No more to them than a ball hurled back and forth in their disgusting contest, I was beaten and used for what seemed like all time.

They granted me a longer respite than usual. I tried to stop sobbing with shame and pain so I could hear their whispers.

" . . . cut her throat."

" . . . Vendren tattoos."

"Even if she is crazy, we can't let her live to tell."

"No!" I shrieked, trying to run. "Exudimord! Help me!"

My scream choked on blood as the first hook bit into my neck. The second caught me in those parts they had so cruelly used. I had thought I could feel no more pain there, but I was very wrong.

My last thought was an absurd one: that I had suffered these wounds, or ones very like them, before.

*

I, who have told my tale as Glyphtard Fand, have told you those things as Umbra. I saw them with her eyes, felt them with her body and knew them with her mind, even her second death.

When I woke, male that I was, I instantly clutched my male parts to make sure they hadn't been invaginated like a glove. To a touch made clumsy by my distracted state, those parts seemed not merely present but transformed to outrageous proportions, even though I still shivered and retched with loathing at the imprinted memory of phallic thrusts. I felt no pain from the wounds I — she — had suffered, but I remembered them, too. It seemed unlikely I would ever forget them.

How could such things be? A ghoul, not a man, adopts the identity of the corpse whose brain and heart it eats, or so the stories said, and I was a man. Then why had I eaten her? Perhaps I was the victim of a last prayer or curse mouthed by my wife to her foul Goddess.

The scum who had raped me in Umbra's guise had stolen my cloak and my boots and thrown me down a stairway to the sunken entrance of a tomb, there to be rained on all night. I was cold and wet, but the worst discomfort, oddly enough, came from the wan light of the damp day. It was like gritty dust on my eyeballs, and I squinted to the verge of blindness as I mounted to the street. Consequently, before I knew what I was doing, I blundered among mourners in solemn procession.

Now it's true that we provincials have a much less casual attitude about nudity than Frothirans, for instance, but the appearance of a naked man hardly called for such an ear-splitting chorus of horror and outrage.

"Good people, forgive me, I was robbed and beaten — I had no thought to desecrate your obsequies — "

Incomprehensibly, my mild words stirred only more anger and fear. "Keep it from Mother Ashtrella's coffin!" a voice shrieked beside me, and that cry was taken up by dozens of screamers. I took my hand from my eyes — more screams, as if I conducted a choir of lunatics — and saw the white gowns of Ashtareeta's clergy flapping and fluttering about me like pigeons harried by a dog.

"Good ladies — " I began, but a brick bounced off my skull, and I roared with fury. The cry drove them mad. The mob tried to escape the clogged street, but it could do so only over the bodies of its members. I watched in amazement as the holy women trampled their fallen sisters. The coffin fell. One woman flung her body over it to protect the corpse, whom she presently joined in death.

Obviously, the religious hysteria that Umbra started had only lain dormant, waiting for a jolt to revive it. Their terror-stricken, backward glances told me that they didn't see me as a man at all, but as some demon of their fantasies, newly risen from the underground. I played the role in which they cast me by fleering and gibbering, and I laughed like a true demon when that perfected their panic.

Armed watchmen were fighting their way toward me. I grimaced and shook my fists, laughing at the way they struck aside the women they rushed to defend. I tripped across the street on the heads of packed mourners, like one crossing a brook from stone to stone, and leaped from the last shrieking skull to the roof of a tomb.

I had no idea how I made such a leap, or what possessed me to know I could. I was an athlete, a fairly good one, and the tombs were not so tall as houses, but it was impossible that I should have done that with the ease of a cat springing onto a table. More flung bricks and slates distracted me. I leaped to another roof and dropped into the next street of the necropolis.

Given a moment, I raised a hand to my bruised head; and screamed at the sight of that hand. It was twice as broad as it should have been, and the fingers sprouted claws. My new, misshapen body was suited to the hand. Leaning against the wall of a tomb, I felt that my back was ridged and bristly as a hog's. My screams of horror became horrifying laughs.

However ugly, my feet were fast and sure, and I used their skill when the watchmen boiled out of an alley just then. I began to revel in my new agility. I danced away from the catching hooks and thrusting points of their bills as Umbra hadn't been able to, taunting them, playing out the game from street to street and rooftop to rooftop, jibing or farting at them whenever they seemed in danger of losing me.

If only the light didn't vex me so! I had to get home. I would lose them; they wouldn't have recognized me as Lord Glyphtard. I could hide in the stable and enjoy all that food I had prudently stored while deluding myself that I was assembling a scientific collection. Mother would help me hide. Mother. . . . She had known, when she warned my wife to beware of Chalcedor's tomb, that Umbra saw "keep out" signs as warm welcomes. She had known, when she told me that fairy tale about her father's death, that he was alive and well beneath the tomb. A cynic would say that Mother, for any number of unsavory reasons, had played procuress to her father with my wife; and few ghouls are not cynics. I needed to have a talk with her.

I escaped the narrow streets to the open slopes, where the light seemed even more intense and painful, though in my previous life I would have called this a dark day and ordered lamps to be lit. Lamps! I never wanted to see another lamp.

A shout answered my laugh. Ahead, a man pointed to me, guiding a mob. They were cleverer than I thought, these humans. They had spread the alarm beyond the necropolis and cut off my way home. The watchmen behind me had fanned out. I would soon be surrounded. I leaped onto a stone coffin, dancing from one foot to the other, waving my new, monstrous penis at them and blowing kisses, but coolly choosing an escape-route while I did it.

"Filth!" a man grunted, shockingly close, and my old reflexes would never have escaped his thrusting bill. It grazed me as I rolled off the sarcophagus. I laughed at his wit, though I'm sure he had none, when he said, "I'll teach you to eat corpses!"

He tried to hook me, but I evaded that by leaping toward him, back onto the coffin. He wore my cloak! My boots! I gripped him by the arm and screamed in his face, "That was very nice!"

He had no idea what I meant. His face was a mask of stupidity and terror, molded from suet. I wanted to explain it to him at leisure, I meant to drag him along with me and add to his considerable knowledge of perversion and cruelty, but I misjudged my new strength, and his arm tore free from his shoulder.

"I'll eat this later," I cried, flailing him about the head with the twitching arm, "and I'll be back tonight for the rest of you!"

Unhappily, I doubt that he understand this threat; his mind was preoccupied. And now the other watchmen were upon me.

By swarming in, they had opened a route to the oldest part of the cemetery. I leaped over their heads, over their raised hooks, and capered away, pausing to hold up the severed arm and make its hand wave good-bye to the screaming owner. I reveled in my new talent for outraging these silly creatures. They took things so seriously! I knew now why my laughter had seemed so *inappropriate* to others. "You think everything is a joke," people would so often complain, and even I hadn't known then that everything *was.* "Glyphtard Fand" had been nothing but a clever illusion, I understood at last, but I had finally cast it off like a drunkard's mask of sobriety.

I let them stay close behind me as I threaded surely through the briers and hidden slabs. The light was less obnoxious here, and I was unwilling to end the game. But I fear that I outsmarted myself. Right across my planned escape-route, but still concealed by tangled forest, I heard horses and clanking metal. Horses could run me down, armor could turn my claws, and the men who used such things, the troopers of Never-Vanquished who had quelled the riots, were no rabble of tanglefoot watchmen.

I kept moving forward, though, for I had let the pursuit come uncomfortably close, and my steps led me to a tomb I recognized by the tree growing from its roof. It was the spot where Exudimord had amused himself with Lord Glyphtard's wife. It was the tomb of Chalcedor, which concealed the lair of his admirer, my ancestor.

"Grandfather?" I called in a fair imitation of a human voice as I danced up the steps, wringing the watchmen's arm to make it give up its last drops of blood to the cracked and tilted flagstones. "It's Glyphtard, dear Grandfather. Come and talk to me. If you dare!"

Better than I had hoped, I heard the rumbles and growls of a disturbed sleeper just inside the vault. The old fool had grown too fat and careless to hide underground.

"King of Ghouls, indeed! King of fat groundhogs, king of worms, king of decrepit idiots! Come out and let me crown you with my foot!" I shouted, still in a manlike voice, but the voice that roared back from the tomb was pure ghoul.

The soldiers heard his roar, and I heard their quiet commands. The mob behind me had marked it, too. They blundered forward more hastily. I dropped the arm across the threshold and leaped to the top of the tomb, then into the tree.

From Glyphtard's memory, I scarcely recognized the wreck that tottered into the light and stared down at the severed arm. It was ludicrous that Glyphtard had found this slug so fearsome. The drowsy ghoul blinked and scratched and stared even more stupidly at the oncoming watchmen. Then he laughed and brandished his claws. It was clear that they, too, found him fearsome.

Encouraged by their fright, he snatched up the arm and shook it at them as he stalked forward. Being human and therefore blind to my many excellences, not one of them would have doubted that this was the same ghoul they pursued.

The soldiers now emerging from the rear of the tomb had crossbows, and three bolts tore into his back. He looked down at the steel heads protruding from his chest as if wondering, *Whatever can these be?* He turned to take five more of the missiles, one of them penetrating his skull. That one must have hurt, for he tried to wrench it loose with both hands as he lurched, roaring, in an erratic circle.

The watchmen found their courage. They dashed forward to hook his legs and pull them separate ways. He could still fight, breaking oak bills and heads left and right, but footsoldiers with two-hand swords moved in to chop him like firewood. When the horsemen had threaded their way through the brush, there was little left for them to do but skewer his pieces on their lances and jig them boldly aloft.

Waiting and watching from the corpse-fed oak, I pondered my life and my curious metamorphosis. I felt a poignant regret for Umbra. With her high spirits and her love of death, she might have made a better ghoul than I would, and a fit wife for me now. I hadn't appreciated her finer qualities. Then I realized that these thoughts must be those of Glyphtard Fand, perhaps his very last. I was a ghoul, who needed no wife, and my deepest regret for Umbra was that I had left so little of her to eat.

After the crowd marched off in triumph and a reasonable time elapsed, I climbed down to rearrange Grandfather's well-stocked larder, and to rest my eyes before introducing myself to the underground host as the new King of Ghouls. Even if I hadn't overthrown the old one, the title was surely deserved by a ghoul who knew how to pick locks.

II

The Lecher of the Apothegm

Quodomass Phuonsa prided himself on the variety of unlikely subjects his art had immortalized, and he sorely regretted that he had never practiced it upon a ghoul. The old saying, "He would fuck the ghoul that tried to eat his corpse," was often applied to him, and he itched to prove this as true as he could without actually dying.

A man who would ravish a ghoul faces three obstacles, Quodomass knew. The first of these is their ugliness. Tales abound of men driven mad by the sight of them. Insofar as the accounts of such eyewitnesses can be reconciled, their form is vaguely human, though grotesquely long and lank. Different stories add to this the jaws of a hyena, the claws of a sloth and the hump of a wild hog, crammed inside a skin whose color and texture evoke comparison with the foulest diseases and even with advanced stages of decay. Quodomass had followed his guiding genius into every sort of thing that he could penetrate, sometimes with the assistance of rough surgery and without regard to signs of life, and his only worry was that ghouls might not live up to a reputation so piquant.

Fear, the second obstacle, could be almost as easily dismissed. Quodomass doubted that ghouls could be anywhere near so savage as the mobs that had lusted to tear him in pieces for his least popular triumphs. He had often diverted himself by joining such mobs to rail against the creator of the masterpiece with more tears and curses than the grieving parent or spouse. Unlike most men, as he saw them, he had the courage to trust his luck.

The only true obstacle was finding a ghoul. So crafty and elusive are these creatures that advanced thinkers have denied their existence. This skepticism is not shared by those who frequent graveyards at night, and all such persons with whom Quodomass ingratiated himself had tales to tell. They had heard the laughter of ghouls, smelled their stench or stumbled upon the leftovers of their slovenly feasts. Although none had actually set eyes on a ghoul, reliable acquaintances of their most trustworthy friends had.

Persistence, he believed, shone brightest among his virtues. He would spend months stalking a human target; he could devote years to an inhuman one. On rainy days, when he found little work as a porter at Crotalorn's central market, he would wander among the grand tombs and open pits of Dreamers' Hill, studying the landscape that he began to haunt by night. He justified his nocturnal visits by running errands for the watchmen, and even walking their rounds for those too drunk to function. As he became a familiar figure, he earned bigger tips by carrying burdens for grave robbers. A hard judge of others, Quodomass was scandalized that these criminals should often be watchmen, too, but he hid his disapproval with smiles and an unflagging eagerness to make himself useful.

At such times he thanked the Gods who had fashioned him so cunningly for deception. His compact body belied his strength; his boyish looks took ten years off his age, if he covered his bald spot; his contempt for the frivolities in books masked a superior intellect; and his cheery demeanor hid the fact that his brain was gnawed by fiery maggots. The fear that they might leak out and be seen by others obsessed him, another reason why he always sported a rakish kerchief, and giving rise to his nervous compulsions to brush his shoulders or beat his head with hard objects.

His most generous employer was a pudgy young nobleman of minor degree called Weymael Vendren. A student of necromancy who collected the relics of ancient masters, Weymael knew a lot about ghouls, and Quodomass once boasted of the saying that was so often applied to him.

"Fuck the ghoul who tries to eat you, eh? That's not impossible, if you know how to rise from the dead," Weymael muttered as he plied his instruments on the complex lock of a bronze door. "I could show you how, I suppose, but rising from the dead is usually more trouble than it's worth."

"There'd be no physiological problem? I nearly . . . I mean, I heard of a fool who nearly did himself a serious injury by attempting to couple with a statue of our Princess."

"Stop banging your head with the lantern and hold it steady . . . yes, right there. No, they're quite compatible with mortals. Sexually, anyway. They used to be human, you know." Weymael paused to give him a thoughtful look. "They were people whose filthy habits provoked a monstrous transformation."

"Then you could kill one? Strangle her, for instance, or cut her in pieces, or take some lengths of heated wire and a pair of pliers — "

A flick of Weymael's ferrety eyes told Quodomass that he had revealed too much enthusiasm for an academic discussion, but the necromancer returned to his work without quizzing him.

"I suppose you could, but catching her and holding her down, that would be a big enough problem, unless you found one who enjoyed it. Enjoyed sex, I mean, not being strangled."

"Is that possible?"

"Why not? Male ghouls are supposedly wild about human women, which may be why you don't see many girls around here at night." A sound like steam hissing and clacking at the lid of a kettle, Weymael's aborted laughter, unnerved the porter. It suggested the notoriously mordant mirth of ghouls. "The offspring of such unions are always destroyed, and that's a pity. I might learn something from studying a demi-ghoul, or perhaps use its services when it grew up. Be sure to tell me if you find a complaisant ghouless, Quodo."

To abbreviate his name like that, which almost everyone did, was to drive a spike of rage between the eyes of Quodomass Phuonsa, but he concealed the pain with a broader than usual grin. Momentarily distracted, he had no chance to deny his intention of waylaying a ghoul before the lock gave up its secrets and the door swung open on a dank and fetid interior.

"After you," Weymael Vendren said, as he always did.

*

Reflecting at leisure, Quodomass believed that the necromancer might help him in his quest, but he found it impossible to break the lifelong secrecy that had spared him from the rack, the block and all the other apparatus of official art critics. Besides, he wanted to catch a ghoul so he could humiliate and torture it, while Weymael Vendren would want to keep it in a cage and take notes on it. But since their ambitions might not be entirely inconsistent, he returned casually to the subject of ghouls whenever they met.

"Nothing attracts them like a corpse," Weymael said, "which is why the wealthy go to such lengths to keep these stinking tombs sealed. I believe you'll not find that wine to your taste. It was sometimes poisoned to punish common thieves."

Quodomass sprayed it out, retching, and inwardly cursed Weymael for keeping silent when he had cracked the jar.

"If you can drink that — hand me the hacksaw, please, this bastard's neck is tough as wood — if you don't mind the taste of that, I can give you a potion that simulates death. I'll have you buried with a net and a hammer in your coffin, and when the ghoul rips it open to get her dinner. . . ."

"No, thank you." Though he was furious with his clever patron for divining his purpose, and perhaps even his secret nature, he had concluded that he need not fear him. Since adepts of the black arts are masters of delusion, judges at that time thought it pointless to try them. An accusation of witchcraft carried an automatic sentence of death.

"It wouldn't work, anyway," Weymael said. "Let me see that hatchet, I'll get this head off him yet! No, trying to attract just one ghoul to a corpse would be like dropping your pants in a swamp to catch one mosquito. You'd wake up with a hundred of the filthy things fighting over you."

Quodomass shivered less with fear than with a fearful excitement. He said, "A net would be good, you think?"

"Don't you go to the fighting-pits? If the netter knows how to use it, he beats the sworder almost every time, and a ghoul's claws are like swords." Panting from his exertions, the necromancer tossed him an unexpectedly heavy head, dried to stony hardness. "Put that in your bag and we'll be skipping along."

As they left the violated tomb behind them, Quodomass thought he heard a rustling in the bushes. He gripped Weymael's arm and gestured him to silence. More than one creature was furtively afoot, many more than one, a mass convergence on the unlocked tomb.

"Yes, there they go," the necromancer said, unperturbed. "Want to go back and check out the pretty ones?"

Quodomass stared hard at the tomb, but he could barely separate its decayed outline from the moonless darkness. He thought he saw a dim flickering at the door; he heard what might have been a shrill giggle and its hollow echo.

He was terrified, but not even his terror could preclude a sudden and urgent erection. Nevertheless he shouldered his bag and walked quickly away from the unholy swarming while Weymael followed, hissing and clacking to himself.

*

The porter was disappointed with his noble patron for even knowing about the fighting-pits, much less discussing them like a connoisseur. The pits were illegal in Crotalorn, and as Quodomass prided himself on his good citizenship in most respects, he avoided them. His work in the market had given him a wide circle of lax acquaintances, though, and it was easy enough to find someone willing to sell him a net made for trapping men.

"I'll throw in the trident for another two silver fillies," said the grim old man as he hefted that vicious weapon. "It has drunk deep."

So had he, to judge by his red eyes, and Quodomass deplored drunkenness. He also disapproved of the name "filly" for the coin bearing Princess Fillitrella's image, though even the Princess herself had been heard to use it. Buying the trident would lend credence to his guise as the sort of moron who would collect souvenirs of the pits, but he wanted to disoblige the disrespectful old sot, so he smiled and said, "No, thank you."

"What do you want the net for, catching girls?"

"No, of course not!" Quodomass caught himself brushing his shoulders vigorously, and he forced his hand down to clench his knee. He met the man's contemptuous stare with a grin as he said brightly, "These weapons were the ones you used?"

"I had thought such an ardent follower of the sport as yourself would call them *tackle*, not *weapons*. No, they belonged to a man called Fast

Fandard, who in the end proved not quite fast enough." At last he turned his pitiless gaze toward the window of his squalid hutch, permitting Quodomass to relax his grin before it could collapse in a flurry of twitches. "He was my son, and I need the money to bury him."

"Oh, I'm sorry." Quodomass looked suitably solemn, even though he felt like grinning now. He had a patron whose passion for anatomical studies was limited to athletic young men, and he would pay enough for this information to reimburse him for the "tackle." "When is the funeral?"

"As soon as I come up with six fillies for those flap-kneed Sons of Cludd. Until then they'll keep the poor fool's body in their temple and drone hymns over it. He was giving them his money from the pits so he could join the Order, did you ever hear anything so outrageous? Those bigots condemn pit-fighting, but they gladly took the money he earned there. If they had finally condescended to admit him, they would have made him repent his wicked occupation for the next thirty years." He again proved his perspicacity by adding, "But you don't want to hear this anymore than he did."

Quodomass was delighted. Cluddites were buried in shallow graves to facilitate their resurrections, and in a cheap section that was ignored by watchmen and robbers alike. The father wanted six fillies for the net and trident, but Quodomass invoked his talent for shedding tears at will and pressed eight on him, hoping to gain his trust and later learn the particulars of the funeral. The student of anatomy would pay him twice that, and digging up Fast Fandard would be no work at all.

The father was an ungrateful boor. He sneered into the porter's tearful face as he handed over the trident and said, "Watch you don't sit on it."

*

"Going fishing?" Weymael Vendren asked, laying a book aside when a slave ushered in Quodomass Phuonsa with his clumsily wrapped purchases.

The book, Quodomass saw, was no volume of monstrous spells, but a collection of tales by the pornographer Chalcedor. Not a single skull or dried bat ornamented the bright room, open to the scented airs of a garden, where Weymael lounged in a brocaded robe with a tray of cordials and tidbits at his elbow. It was the first time the porter had dared to call on him at his home, and his impersonation of a social parasite was flawless.

Quodomass waited pointedly for his host to dismiss the slave before answering. They waited, too, staring at him until he felt the prickle of thoughts creeping from his brain. He clamped a desperate hand to his head, and was on the verge of fleeing when he noted Weymael's encouraging nod and interpreted it correctly: he was expected to remove his kerchief. He pulled it off reluctantly. A surreptitious glance revealed only a few hairs, whose loss he could ill afford, clinging to the grease of continuous use. He refused to surrender it to the slave, however, and Weymael consulted the frescoes of the ceiling before waving her away.

Quodomass at last answered, "Yes, fishing for a ghoul. You say nothing attracts them like a corpse, right? And what better bait for a female ghoul than the corpse of a handsome young athlete?"

Asking about Fast Fandard in the Market, he had learned that the fighter was better known for his looks than his skill. If he had not been treating the gallery to a display of his heroic profile, everyone said, he might have noticed that his last opponent had revived and was swinging an ax at his spine. Struck by inspiration, Quodomass had decided to give up the money he might get from the anatomist and use the body to obtain his heart's desire.

Until now, their conversations about ghouls had been held on the fanciful level of drinking companions who joke about robbing a palace. Quodomass now revealed his artistic credentials, citing several unsolved crimes and a few that had been considered solved by everyone but the wretches whom the public executioner had deprived of progressively more essential organs.

He had never imagined that anyone could make Weymael Vendren shiver, and it pleased him that he had. "I don't doubt that you're a monster, Quodo, but you don't realize: ghouls are even more loathsome than you are."

"That's the point, lord! Sex with a ghoul would disgust me as not even a human being can anymore, and I'd want to smash it and tear it — " He cut this outburst short when he noticed how the other's jaw hung slack. Wrenching his flicking hand away from his shoulder, he said with his most engaging grin, "It would be a challenge, don't you see, to my artistic professionalism?"

"Yes, I believe I do see. But what have I to do with your refreshingly original perversion?"

"You are surely the wisest man I know, and — "

"I wonder about the other wise men you know, if you think I'll swallow such gabble. What is it you want, Quo?"

The spike of anger at this further diminution of his name nearly blinded him, and he let it show as he snapped, "You know about ghouls. I think you even *know* ghouls. And I know you'd rather help me than help fuel a bonfire."

Quodomass could hardly credit the stupidity, the uncharacteristic stupidity, of his own words. They had betrayed his lifelong labor to make everyone love him. He would often give his victims a reassuring pat and remark what nice hair or eyes they had just before striking the final blow, and those who persisted to the end in calling him vile names had no idea that he would forever after cringe from the memory of their hatred. But Weymael Vendren, who numbered ghouls among his acquaintances and was on speaking terms with dead wizards, could find means more hurtful than name-calling to vent his spleen.

Dreading an eruption of the gnawing creatures he had stirred up, he jammed his kerchief back on his head as he groveled on the floor before the necromancer and babbled of the demon that had seized control of his tongue. Hearing an inhuman hissing and snorting through the thudding of his forehead against the parquetry, he feared that his patron had summoned such a being, but when he dared to look up he saw that Weymael himself was making the noise as he writhed in the throes of his queer laugh.

"You want me to pimp for a ghoul? Thank you, Quodomass Phuonsa! You've done more to cheer me on a dreary day than a whole troupe of clowns ever could. Very well, I'll help you. If you'll help me."

"Beloved master, my life is yours — "

"That goes without saying," Weymael interrupted. "Forget about smashing it and strangling it and all that other depraved lunacy. Just amuse yourself with the wretched thing, and then bring it here. And don't use that damned fish-fork on it, either."

"Oh, this? It came with the tackle. I planned on using a cudgel to subdue her."

"You'll need an iron bar, and don't hesitate to use all your strength, or you'll regret it. Better still, I'll give you a needle dipped in a certain potion. Just prick her, and she'll sleep almost as soundly as your bait."

"I want her awake, or nearly so."

"Then use it afterwards, or you'll never be able to drag her here. Would you trust that butterfly-net to hold a tiger?"

When Quodomass left, Weymael escorted him to the door. This courtesy flattered the porter until it struck him that he was no longer trusted to be alone with the slaves, most of them young and female, who attended the fat man.

*

Waymael's warnings haunted Quodomass like the aftertaste of tainted food as he clutched his frayed net in the ditch where he had been hiding since sunset. The Cluddite graveyard lay so far down Dreamers' Hill as to be almost part of the swamp beneath it, and Weymael had told him it was seldom visited by ghouls, who preferred to stay close to their hidden trapdoors and burrows on the farther slope. News of a corpse that had been permitted to ripen above ground would lure them almost anywhere, however, and the necromancer had promised to whisper that news into the hound-like ear of a ghoul called Gluttoria. Her fondest wish, he said, was to enjoy a quiet meal by herself.

"They all spy on one another and try to follow any ghoul suspected of knowing something they don't," he had said. "So should you see, should you even suspect the presence of a second ghoul, you'll soon have them on you like lice. Don't kiss her good-bye, don't bother to pull up your drawers, just put your trust in Cludd and run for his temple."

Before sunset, he had watched the tiny figures of the celibate warriors bustling in and out of that squat building or marching like animated toys on the adjacent parade ground. They might have seen him, too, if he had raised his head above the level of the grass, and he had frequently cursed the god and his inconvenient temple on his long and painful crawl to a drainage ditch that lay near the newest grave. But as darkness fell and a milky fog breathed from the swamp, he began to regret its distance. The guards at the door might hear his loudest cry, but by the time they determined where he was and what he wanted, he could have been distributed into a hundred greedy gullets.

It was more than fully dark, now that the fog had crept up the slope, and he checked his equipment again, but there was little to check beyond a net and an iron bar.

"The skull undergoes a drastic transformation," Weymael had said, "making it fit to butt aside rocks, and to support the muscles of the lower jaw, so don't worry about breaking it. If you want to stun her, you'll have to swing as if you mean to send her head flying. Take my advice and use the needle, first thing."

He examined the needle now, sheathed in fine leather, before stowing it in his shoulder-bag and sealing it away. He had no intention of furthering Weymael Vendren's obscene research. The necromancer was helping him, he suspected, in the hope that he would impregnate the beast. The thought of success, of his unnatural offspring raised by that snickering, corpse-filching, upper-class fop, sickened him even more than the worst fantasies generated by his own brain-worms.

"I'm sorry, lord, I followed your instructions, but it would seem that I'm stronger than you thought," he would say, explaining why he had pounded the thing's skull to porridge after raping it. If that failed, he had a final piece of tackle that he now pulled from its protective sheath: the late pit-fighter's trident. If the necromancer wants a baby, he thought, let him get his own ghoul.

He had lowered his eyes to the equipment for no more than a minute or so. He had heard nothing. But when he raised his head over the rim of the ditch, his nerves shrieked like wires stretched to the snapping-point. Almost close enough to touch, a pale form stood over the grave.

He thought that it might be a woman, no matter how tall, thin and poorly proportioned; but in the next instant, when it squatted and sent dirt flying back between its legs with paws like shovel-blades, he knew what he was looking at. The urge to cower in the ditch and try not to give himself away by whimpering almost overpowered him, until he was distracted by the rippling muscularity of the creature's buttocks, the sway of its heavy breasts. He was not only capable of raping a ghoul, he realized, he was eager to do it, and a familiar surge swept him up into that heaven where he ruled as an implacable god.

He had practiced indifferently with the lead-weighted net, for he knew that nothing ever went wrong when he surrendered himself to the guiding genius of his art, and as he rose he cast it with probably more skill than Fast Fandard had ever shown. He drew the running-lines tight to form a bag that shrouded the ghoul down to her knees. He leaped forward and dealt a blow to the head that would have felled a horse, but the only discernable effect was a slight bend in the iron bar.

Such had been his confidence that he had left both the trident and the needle in the ditch behind him, but he was not ready to panic. He stood astride the ghoul and raised the bar in both hands in preparation for a stroke that would have awed even Fand or Venda of the epics. It never fell, for he was shocked rigid by a sound.

He had heard some very peculiar noises while lurking at night in the graveyard. Not entirely to his satisfaction, he had explained them as the creaking of old trees, the scuttle of dead leaves across the portico of a tomb, perhaps the distant scrape of a shovel on stone or the baying of a hound; but what he now heard partook of all those sounds and threw his memories into a new alignment that dizzied him with its implications. He knew he would never again mistake the voice of a ghoul for anything else on earth, or under it.

"Weymael?" it said. "Is that you?"

To read intent or emotion from such a voice was impossible, but the language of her body was clear as she presented her splotched and bristly rump with an inviting wriggle. Dropping to his knees and fumbling his breeches down, he thrust through an interstice of the net and into her before he answered, "No, you bitch, it's Quodomass Phuonsa, who would fuck the ghoul that tried to eat his corpse!"

Expecting an eruption of resistance, he dealt her another fearful blow, but she unleashed a giggle that would have chilled a wretch burning at the stake as she battered his belly with her buttocks. Like nothing he had ever penetrated, she was tough and gristly, her clasp abrasive as sand. He thought at first he was rubbing against the fibrous hemp of the net, but his fumbling fingers confirmed that their organs were joined.

Ignoring the near-pain of the friction, he twisted and thrust like one trying to stab all the way to her heart. He cursed her and cuffed her and twisted her breasts, firm as melons but disconcertingly slimy, while hammering her skull with the bar. Infuriatingly, she urged him to be less shy and gentle.

"Quodo!" she grated, and she pounded a further triad of spikes into his brain: "Oh, Quo! Quo! Quo!"

The muscles of his right arm shrieked for mercy, and he dropped the bent bar from numb fingers as he sagged against her back and tried to suck air through the ammoniac reek of her hide. As she stifled her shriek of completion in the dirt of the grave, he was forced to admit that it was he who had been mastered.

He backed away cautiously on his knees. He would take no chance with the trident, not until she was unconscious. He pictured the location of his bag. He rehearsed in his mind the action of flipping open the clasp and getting the necromancer's needle. He knew he could do it in no time at all. She had not yet stirred from her sighing repose.

Glancing back at last, he was startled by a line of shadows at the rim of the ditch. He supposed that their frenzied copulation had turned him the wrong way, and that he no longer faced the ditch, but he paused to puzzle over those objects. They could have been a row of misshapen cabbages, unlikely as that seemed in a graveyard. He was about to reach out and touch one when the dim luminance of the fog gleamed on its suddenly bared fangs.

Then all the ghouls rose from the ditch.

Put your trust in Cludd, the necromancer had told him — and unless one happened to be a Son of Cludd, that was a sardonic catch-phrase for abandoning all hope — and run for the temple. So desperate was his desire to follow this advice that he believed he was doing it. He heard the racket of someone running in the swamp. That could have been no one but himself. The pale forms that blocked his escape as they shambled toward him were only hallucinations. How could he be kneeling here, waiting to be torn to pieces, when he heard himself running?

Impossibly, the sound of his splashing steps receded. He caught a glimpse of the running figure before the fog swallowed it completely: a fat man with a robe hiked inelegantly to his knees, a man nothing like himself but very much indeed like Weymael Vendren, who had apparently felt obliged to observe the first stage of his experiment. Quodomass screamed his name, but the footsteps never faltered. What was more bitterly disappointing, not one of the ghouls took this hint to pursue the fleeing scientist.

Ransacking his recollection of love-songs and romantic tales for words he had never used, Quodomass scrambled back to fling himself on the mercy of Gluttoria. She rose and parted the fighter's net as easily as a bride would part her veil. "Please!" he cried as he stumbled to his feet and embraced the filthy creature. "I love you — I want you — be mine forever! Yes, we come from different worlds, but love conquers all. Doesn't it? Tell them!"

As she drew him to her breast with claws that slipped through to his ribs, Quodomass tried to unleash a scream that would leave the distant temple guards in no doubt whatever of his location or his desire, but her lipless mouth darted forward as if for a kiss. He found it impossible to scream without his tongue or lower jaw, which she began to chew before his eyes.

*

Before the underground host could fling itself on the flailing body of the rapist, Vomikron Noxis, King of Ghouls, decreed that they save his virile member for last to see if he could live up to his reputation. Gluttoria claimed it as her prize when it became obvious that Quodomass Phuonsa's proudest boast had been an empty one.

III
The Ghoul's Child

Even if they were not immediately eaten by their mothers, the offspring of ghouls would be short-lived, for they are typically formless things that seem less the product of parturition than pathology. It therefore roused great envy among the mining community when one of their number gave birth to a perfectly formed baby boy; who would have looked rosy, had anyone been so perverse as to light a lamp in the dank niche where he was born.

"Kill it," said Vomikron Noxis, King of Ghouls.

"No," said the mother, Gluttoria.

"Let me kill it, then. We'll store it till it's ripe, when the flesh begins to drip sweetly from the translucent bones — "

Not even a ghoul can stand the full-throated shriek of another one in their narrow tunnels. The King wriggled backward, clutching his blasted ears.

New mothers, he recalled, have whims, and he assumed Gluttoria would come to her senses. After a time he peeked in on her with what he believed to be his most charming grin.

"That's smart, letting it grow a bit," he said. "There'll be more meat, perhaps even some to share with your old lover — "

He closed his eyes against shrieks even more piercing, and was thus unprepared for the whirlwind of fangs and claws that ravaged his face. He abandoned his dignity and ran, screaming for mercy.

"Slut!" he roared, when he believed he was safe. "Virago!" And to his sniggering subjects he muttered, "Whoever kills us that aberration will have the key to our larder."

Some ghouls tried to snatch the child away, losing eyes, ears or hands for their trouble. Though she was big and strong, Gluttoria couldn't stay awake forever; nor could she survive on a diet of eyes, ears and hands while nursing the child. She stole away with her baby to an area of Dreamers' Hill where her kind seldom venture.

*

Gluttoria had no idea if Vomikron Noxis had been her lover, since ghouls usually ignore such trivia. She knew he hadn't sired the child. Most unusually, she remembered her encounter with the father, and that was partly to blame for her odd behavior.

He had been a human being named Quodo, who said he was overcome by love, an emotion most un-ghoulish. It was unthinkable that a man would want to lie with a ghoul, but Quodo had. So deranged had he been by desire that the puny human had actually believed he was raping her.

Gluttoria had dim memories of love from her human life. The first man to make tender advances to her had been an uncle, when she was of an unseemly age. She had tripped him on the stairs in a spirit of fun that seemed to suit his jolly groping, but the fall broke his back.

She had thought that giving up love was no loss until Quodo offered it to her in her new and infinitely less lovable guise. Her feelings had so confused her that she tore the poor man to pieces. Ghouls do not weep, but she sometimes did when she recalled that unthinking moment.

Had the child been an ordinary ghoul, or even an ordinary boy, her fond regrets might have provoked nothing more than a heartfelt sigh between the two bites needed to wolf him down. But to her the baby was a prodigy that outshone the boasts of the most addled parent. Poignant music was insipid beside his screams, rapturous poetry was bombast to his gurgles. His hair was yellower than her eyes, his eyes bluer than her vestigial lips. He reminded her of the confectionery images of the infant Polliel that are eaten on that God's birthday, except by little girls like Gluttoria, who had thought them too pretty and would burst into tears to see other children eat them.

She named the baby Polliard, seldom speaking this presumption above a whisper for fear of offending the ghouls, who hated the Sun God, or the God, who was believed to feel the same about ghouls.

*

Gluttoria fled with her baby to the summit of Dreamers' Hill, where the tombs of the Great Houses gleam among spacious gardens. Behind a very old tomb of the Fands, less well tended than others, she found a derelict charnel for the remains of servants. Her comrades had never discovered it, even though the lock had been broken long ago by a grave-robber seeking only gems and gold. It was packed with a wealth of dried food, though, and Gluttoria abode there for many months, reveling in the leisure to play with her son and guide his first steps.

She discovered that mummified flesh could be restored to a semblance of freshness by soaking it for a day or so in the blood of animals or, better still, stray children. She weaned Polliard on pre-chewed scraps of such food, while he found all the toys a boy could wish for among the litter of skulls and bones.

One skull he called "Dada," his first word, and this never failed to get a laugh from his mother; but she was a ghoul, and almost nothing failed to get a laugh from her. Polliard early developed a similar sense of humor.

Reminders of Quodo, however, turned her thoughts to a pressing need that wasn't at all funny. Ghouls are neither solitary nor chaste by nature, and she had long ago reached the limit of satisfaction she could get from faded memories of dalliance imprinted in the old meat she ate.

*

After a long evening at the Willing Lepress in Hound Square, Picote Phrein would often cut across Dreamers' Hill to his room in Bloodstone Close, where he wrote poetry and, with more success, begging letters to relatives. He claimed to have witnessed weird scenes inside the graveyard, but he claimed to have seen marvels everywhere else, too, so his tales aroused as little interest as his poems.

In fact he skulked through the cemetery in hopes of seeing one special sight that he never spoke of, though he wrote poems about it. He would describe it as the struggle of an eight-limbed, two-headed monstrosity, with much rhythmical grunting and writhing, to split itself into separate human beings. He depicted its fission in triumphant terms, for he shrank from physical contact. His own pleasures were solitary; versifying aroused him more than the sights that inspired it.

He could usually find something worth seeing near the watchmen's lodge, but the watchmen were fat and their sweethearts tended to be stringy whores. Less often, but more to his aesthetic taste, he would descry troopers of Never-Vanquished with elegant young ladies in the weeds near the oldest tomb of the Fands, and that was where his unsteady steps led him this night.

He found nothing in the usual bowers. Worse, he strayed too near some carcass left to rot unburied. The smell so sickened him that all the wine he had drunk on credit blew forth to feed the azaleas.

Having wiped his lips with his kerchief, he waved it vigorously before his face to flap away the nauseous odor, but it clung as persistently as if he'd stepped in its source. Trying to sniff his sandals, he lost his balance and sat down heavily. The odor grew stronger by the minute. He ascribed this to a change in the wind until he realized that the wind was still.

He admitted that he was lost, a condition not unfamiliar to the night-prowling poet. He normally would have slept where he sat and found his way home by daylight, but an invisible tangle of briers oppressed him and a nearly palpable fog of decay threatened to poison him. Even if he grew used to breathing the stench, he would be tormented all night by images of worms boring through the heap of carrion, rats gnawing it while lice and fleas sucked their blood. At this minute a cosmos of vermin might be turning infinitesimal footsteps his way.

He sprang to his feet, beating his clothes and suppressing screams that nevertheless slipped through his teeth as squeaks of panic. The phantasmal tickles that multiplied to vex his whole skin could be nothing but the strutting and preening of corpse-gorged flies. That thought shattered him like a mirrored image of a man. He hurled himself into hopeless battle with the whips and claws of the bushes.

"Please!" he screamed when he fetched up against a solid figure. Rebounding off bones and hard muscles, he cried, "My name is Phrein, I mean no harm!" He grasped that the person was naked and female, but whatever assurance this gave him was offset by her looming height and stony solidity. "I wasn't spying. I lost my way, that's all."

Picote's attraction to women was neutralized by a distaste for all creatures, himself not excluded. Not even the comeliest parcel of skin could wipe away an image of the tubes and sacs of feces, urine and blood it secreted, the ghastly bones and slimy organs it held, the foul gases and sweats it exuded. The prettiest belly was forever at work grinding dead flesh to muck. He tried to minimize the nastiness of life by eating only vegetable food. This diet confirmed his prejudice by making his own functions even more disgusting.

But he could sometimes overcome his revulsion for others in total darkness, and it wasn't difficult with a well-built young woman who never spoke a word. She was not unlike one of his solitary fantasies. By pretending that she was, he began to enjoy her embrace.

She seemed friendly, although her intentions were as dark as her appearance. She was young, and her breasts were large and firm as those of a sculpted goddess. How drunk was he? He stroked her belly; his fingers ventured into the coarse hair beneath it. He hadn't been deluded by a statue.

"No!" he cried, for she apparently had a knife, and she used it to slit his breeches and free his thickening member. As if in apology, she dropped to her knees before him. Her tongue — but could that be a tongue? It was dry, it was grittier than his cat's, it very nearly hurt. He touched hair whose greasy snarls distressed him, but before he could explore her face with his fingers and verify that she was using her tongue, she batted his hand aside with appalling force. He tried to stifle unmanly whimpers as he speculated on the nature of an overgrown woman who would assault him with a knife in a graveyard and force him to accept the most intimate kiss. The lunatic asylum was but a short sprint from here.

The encounter had distracted him from the nauseous odor, but now that gagged him. It seemed to rise directly into his nostrils from the kneeling woman. He sniffed the fingers that had fondled her. They smelled as if he had slipped them into the core of all foulness.

His hand shot to her face before she could anticipate the move, and he learned that it was nothing like a human face. The mouth that caressed him, however tenderly at the moment, was a trap of fangs.

"Ghoul!" he screamed, and her bloodcurdling laugh avowed it.

"Speak kindly to me, man. Tell me how you love me." Her voice put him in mind of a large dog, growling as it pushed against a door with rusty hinges.

"I love you as I love my life!" Picote cried fervently, but he tried to pull away.

It was futile. Her hands held his buttocks, and when her claws dug in, he realized that she had needed no knife to cut his clothes. She flung him flat on his back and mounted him with brutal efficiency. He felt himself clutched in a tube even grittier than her tongue. Black against the sparkling dust of the galaxy, her lank body and malformed head made a sight to match her smell.

"You're not hard anymore," she rasped. "You don't love me!"

Picote couldn't refute the evidence she held. He had disdained human women for polluting their innards with lamb or veal, and he lay in the grip of a creature that supped on maggoty men. Her loathsomeness had not just withered his erection, it had killed it, and he might as profitably have spent his prayers and wishes on compelling a noodle to stand tall.

"Yes, that might — please, try," he said when she writhed down and lowered the iron gate of her muzzle to his chilled genitals, for he thought she meant to kiss them again; but that was by no means her intention.

*

With the corpse of the poet slung over her spinal ridge, Gluttoria stamped homeward in a fury. Her timid tender of love had been spurned. Worse, her hope of retrieving the ingrate's souvenirs of lubricity by eating his male parts had been mocked by a dull dream of a flailing hand that had nearly beaten her into a stupor.

"Where's your duster, you idle shitabed?" Polliard roared when she stooped to enter their home. "Has no one cleaned this chamber since the hounds' banquet? What mean all these whoreson bones and liches?"

She laughed, her rage swept away on a wave of delight in her child. He had been gnawing on a servant, and he spoke with the booming voice of a butler to the Fands, dead these two hundred years. In the next instant he was laughing like a normal two-year-old, or like one who had learned to laugh from a ghoul.

"Eyes!" he cried in his proper voice, spotting a rare delicacy and stretching up to grip the poet's nose. "Eyes!"

She dumped her burden and popped out one of the treats for him, watching fondly as he sucked and savored it the way she would have. She had almost dreaded the dreary sights those eyes must hold, but she grew curious when Polliard's face glowed with wonder.

"No, dearest, this one's for mother," she said firmly when he tried to snatch the second eye.

"People fighting," he said incorrectly, and she sighed as she chewed and beheld the moonlit interwreathings of undulant bodies that had so fascinated the dead man. His eyes had more zest than his testicles, and she wished now that she had kept both of the former for herself. But even that would have been no substitute. She knew that she had to go once more among the ghouls.

*

Gluttoria braved the light of day to spy upon the living. She lurked behind bushes and squirmed through ditches to trail processions bearing the smallest coffins. She watched the grieving mothers for any false note in their wailing, any lack of conviction in their pitiful gestures. More rigorous than an unbought critic, she rejected them all as adoptive parents for Polliard.

She studied mothers with living children, noting each blow, each harsh word, each lapse of attention. She recalled her own childhood with its overfond uncle, spiteful mother, absent father and tiresome brothers. The necropolis was the only place to raise her son, and she was his only fit mother. She had no choice but to bring him with her to the tunnels of the underground host.

*

"Promise!" she commanded.

"Yes, yes, yes!" Vomikron grunted.

"Promise, damn you! Say it!"

"Yes, yes, yes!"

Gluttoria wrenched free from the King of Ghouls and kicked him in the snout when he tried to splice their interrupted conjunction.

"What is it you want, you impossible creature? We missed you, we love you, we desire you more than any other, haven't we said what you want? Lie down, before our royal balls burst!"

"My son," she said.

"Oh, that. Why do you insist — oh, never mind, very well, we'll honor your whim. We won't hurt him. We won't let anyone hurt him. You have our word as King."

His word meant no more than his title, Gluttoria knew, for she, too, was a ghoul. And because she was, she couldn't deny him, or herself.

"Oh yes, Vomikron! Yes, my King!"

*

It was true that Vomikron desired her above all others, but as she had been: the jolliest of ghouls, a star shining among some very dim wicks indeed. Ghouls love pranks, but few had the old Gluttoria's genius for conceiving them; and in playing them, none matched her boldness and dash.

He recalled how they had invaded the Temple of Death to steal the body of a despised sergeant of the watch named Gorpho. They had filled his coffin with an equal weight of ghoul-droppings, which were next morning enshrined with full municipal honors in an impregnable tomb. With phenomenal self-restraint, the two ghouls had rationed his pieces between them for months in order to keep satirizing the oaf.

One night the adventurous Gluttoria ate just enough of Gorpho's heart and brain to fool his old comrades themselves, and she stormed into their lodge bawling orders at malingerers. One watchman was trampled in the rush to escape the revenant, and his corpse, too, was carried below.

But that was before she had excreted that blond tumor, that warm-blooded maggot, that pudgy bundle of snivels and giggles and gawks that dared to play *horsey* with *him*, but only when the conniving mollycoddle knew that his shrew of a mother was near. Bearing the monster had driven her mad, and her wits would return only when the changeling was gone.

Even had the King not desired his favorite's recovery, the child would have been like a gallstone stuck in his teeth. Vomikron had once been beautiful, he had been precocious, the Sun God had shone from his radiant face on the dullest day, and a mother had trumpeted his unique genius when he had remembered to wipe his nose. Now he dwelt in filth and scavenged among the dead.

Gluttoria had lately taken to going aboveground by day with the child, saying the fresh air and sunshine would do him good. Vomikron's own mother would say the same when he spent too many hours dreaming over the scientific collection he had gathered from the graveyard. Why had he never listened? Polliard — the obscene *name* made him scream whenever he thought it! — listened. He would grow up to be a man, a man who knew too much about the Lower Kingdom.

He wouldn't have to hurt the little horror, not necessarily, to get him out of the way. If he could be made to stray, some mortal would collect him, most likely a childcatcher gathering slaves. His beauty would earn him a place as a pampered catamite, and when it lost its first blush he would get enough fresh air, sunshine and exercise to satisfy the most demanding mother by pulling a galley's oar.

But the boy was too smart, and he had been treasonably warned against his own King. The problem seemed insoluble until just before dawn one morning when Vomikron was prowling a paupers' pit and someone unwittingly dumped the fresh body of a young woman on top of him.

*

Alphea's feet ached with cold. The pain jolted her from a nightmare where a toothless witch prodded her and forced her to drink vile potions. She tried to rearrange the bedclothes until she realized that there were none, nor clothes of any kind.

She dropped to a crouch before she even dared look for prying eyes. It was a familiar dream, walking naked in the open, but this was no dream. Her feet were so cold because they were soaked with dew. At least there was no one to see her, but neither was there anyone to help her get home.

She knew that she was on Dreamers' Hill, surrounded by sarcophagi whose cracks and mossy stains spoke of great age. That was no more helpful than knowing she was in Crotalorn, for the cemetery was a city in itself. She believed she had heard that the sun rose in the east, but when she tried to correlate that notion with the real sun, and with her recollection of the city's layout, she only gave herself a headache.

If she walked downhill, she would leave the hill: that made sense. But something inside her insisted that she walk uphill. This made no sense, but the feeling was too strong to fight — until she glimpsed a scrap of white cloth behind a bush. The need to cover her nakedness was so strong that Alphea ignored the inner voice and ran downhill to see if that cloth would serve.

She nearly tumbled into a pit of shrouded corpses. A raucous storm of crows exploded in her face from the white cloth at the rim of the pit. It was another shroud, one that had been torn open. The body inside had been torn open, too, its skull cracked and its ribs pried apart. Its hair was black as her own, but that was one of the few details she noted before she ran. Her inner voice told her sternly to stop screaming and stop fretting about clothes.

It was most unlike the inner voice she was used to. That voice had told her not to lie with Crondard, the handsome stableboy. It had told her not to seek out the old woman on Plum Street, but to confess her shame to her parents and endure their displeasure. That voice had been easy to ignore. The new one was like a savage dog barking in her head, drowning out her proper thoughts.

The witch in Plum Street. . . . Alphea stopped short and inspected herself. The mound that had been so obvious to her, but that not even her prying sister had noticed, was gone; her belly was positively flat. But she felt no pain, no unpleasant sensation at all. No one had suggested the witch was *that* good! She laughed, but her laugh rang hollow, and with her next breath she tasted tears that had rolled to her quivering lip. She wished — she didn't know what she wished, only that she were home in bed, preferably fast asleep.

"You're a woman, aren't you?" piped a voice from the air.

Alphea's arms jumped to shield her breasts. She searched wildly for an invisible imp until she discovered a small boy perched above her on the roof of a tomb. He wore only a shawl fit for the burial of an ancient prince, worked with gold threads and fringed with opals set in silver.

"Of course we are!" she cried, and was distracted from her curious slip of the tongue by a burning flush. He should have been too young to embarrass her, but his gaze was impudent beyond his years. She dropped one hand to shield her crotch.

"I've never seen one walk," he said, and slid off the tomb to land at her side like a cat. While she was still marveling at his agility, he pinched her thigh. "You feel different, too — *Mama!*"

She had slapped his hand and was considering further retaliation when he let out that hideous shriek. "Where is your mother?" she demanded.

"We'll have her teach you manners, you little monster!"

"She went to find strawberries. She says they're *good* for me." No other child had ever made a face of disgust that could chill her. He said, "I much prefer liver."

Alphea screamed: neither at his inhuman grimace nor his strange words, but at the horror bounding toward them from a thicket. She thought it was a wolf, then a wild hog, then a human freak, but she took no time to sort out these mad impressions, for quite plainly it was death itself, and it was coming for her. She snatched up the child and ran, not daring to look back.

The boy screamed, too, screamed for his mother. He foolishly tried to wriggle from her grasp, biting her neck viciously, but she ignored the pain and gripped him tighter. The thing screamed behind them, but her inner voice screamed loudest of all. It urged her to run until her heart burst and keep on running.

Shouts answered her. A serpent of mourners writhed into segments, some running from her and others hurrying forward. The snarls and shrieks at her back were impossibly close. Help was too far away. She wrenched forth an extra burst of speed, but a claw raked her shoulder.

Something erupted in her head, as if that tiny inner voice were a boil that suddenly swelled and burst to deluge all the corridors of her mind with its noxious fluids. With strength she hadn't known she possessed, with ruthlessness she knew she didn't possess, she gripped the child by his ankles and slung him ahead in a high arc. The mourners shrieked with dismay, and some charged faster in an attempt to catch the whirling boy before his brains could be dashed out.

By the time she cut to the left, knowing that Gluttoria would stay in pursuit of the boy, the part that called itself *Alphea* was a whisper from a fading dream. The soul of Vomikron Noxis impelled the running form, which ran faster but grew less human with every step. It pained him to see Gluttoria race headlong into a mob of men whose swords and daggers were flashing out; but at least it proved that she was hopelessly mad, and that he was better off without her.

*

Dodont often told his few regular patrons at the Willing Lepress that the things of this world were as shadows to the pious, but he was known as a sour man, and skeptics ascribed this to his signal lack of shadows. Most unlike himself, he whistled as he buffed the bust of the late and neglected poet, Picote Phrein.

"Why are you happy?" demanded a Fomorian Guardsman who drank here every morning because the innkeeper's normal mood suited him.

"You saw the new sign, the Plume and Parchment?"

"If you want to honor Picote, you should call it Ferret-Face's Dog-Oil Shed, as he did."

"When he wasn't begging for credit." Dodont spat on the bust, paused for a moment, then resumed polishing. "Nothing's so good for business as a dead poet, and I picked him for a winner."

"Better than when he was farting and puking and telling us all what rotten guts we have. Ar's crabs!" The barbarian shuddered to recall the poet's ways.

"Why do you think I put up with him? Now the mayor is coming here today, Lord Vendrard, and a dozen of our currently immortal poets to dedicate — "

"They make enough noise, don't they?"

It was too early, certainly. The fowls and joints and the suckling pig for the banquet to honor Picote weren't in the oven yet. But the guardsman was right: a mob had burst tumultuously into Hound Square.

"Ar's botch! Is that our mayor they're hoisting to the lamppost?"

*

The mayor never came. He had recently made a sarcastic riposte to critics who had faulted him for ignoring a rumored plague of ghouls. He saw no need to verify his conviction that the creature hung up on display that morning was only a monstrous hyena. His presence in Hound Square would confuse the superstitious, he said, in excusing himself from the poet's memorial feast.

By noon, word of the marvel had bounced back and forth across the Miraga and up and down Crotalorn's five hills. A solid mass of human beings jammed the square and the streets leading into it. None of the other dignitaries felt that the effort of fighting through that mob was justified by either a dead poet or a dying ghoul.

Those who came for a free show were disinclined to pay for drinks; nor did many who had viewed the speared, gaffed and imperfectly disjointed horror as it rotted before their eyes want to sample Dodont's banquet, even at reduced prices. As the day wore on, closed doors and windows could not keep the smell of the thing from the inn.

"The more it steams away, the more it looks like an ordinary girl," the Fomor said. "Are they playing a joke?"

If his only customer had much more to drink he would believe that Picote's bust was an ordinary girl, too, but Dodont poured more wine and said, "A girl wouldn't be alive. See how it watches the sun."

The innkeeper ground his teeth as he said this, for the thing's apparent devotion to Polliel mocked his religion. It would die, said the watchmen who hung it there and refused to remove it, if it spent the full day in the sun; but the abomination seemed entranced by the deadly sight.

When he could tolerate such blasphemy no longer, Dodont went out and fought his way through the crowd to the ring of watchmen. "It keeps mouthing the God's name," he protested. "Can't you stop it?"

"*Polliard,*" a watchman said. "That was the name of the boy it would have killed, if some woman hadn't saved him. She ran off before anyone could thank her."

"And the boy?"

"To be sold, unless someone claims him. Besides *her.*" He jerked his thumb at the dangling ghoul and laughed.

"Look at that! Look! It's saying *Polliel,* I tell you!"

"Polliard," the watchman sighed, and looked away.

In fact Dodont was right. Staring at the sun, Gluttoria was thinking of those gilded candies she had been too tender-hearted to eat as a girl. She might have stared all day in wonder at the beautiful sun if the innkeeper, enraged by her sacrilege and his lost business, had not snatched the inattentive watchman's bill and poked her eyes out.

IV
The Doctor's Tale

I took some satisfaction from slamming the door of my office behind me with all my strength. I would have been better satisfied if the head of the odious dilettante who had thwarted me at the auction had been peeking through it.

Apart from his status as a minor specimen of the Vendren Tribe, I knew nothing about the man, but a reflexive dislike had seized me from the moment I first noticed him loitering at the Anatomical Institute. The sound of his laughter, a staccato wheeze, was merely distasteful, but the sight of it, with its attendant twitches and tics, was nauseous. He could have been a student or even an instructor, but I suspected he was one of those who prowl the fringes of schools for unsavory purposes. I often saw him in the company of a boy whose striking beauty was marred by an air of precocious depravity. Just the sight of those two typically lurking in a shadowy corner, with a group of admiring students hanging on their words, could put me out of sorts for the rest of the day.

My dislike had been unreasonable, perhaps, but today it found a reason.

I am an enthusiast for the work of Chalcedor, an unappreciated genius who flourished two centuries ago. Critics dismiss his vision as provincial, which it was, and pornographic, which it also was; but he gives us a picture of life in Crotalorn as real people lived it in his day, a day more to my taste than the bumptious, tawdry, jostling present. I find his rare manuscripts especially enthralling, since he would doodle in the margins while waiting for inspiration to strike. Often naughty, sometimes whimsical, his sketches let me glimpse the mind of a long-dead man who seems to have been not much different from myself.

Studying an auctioneer's catalog a week ago, I noticed an unsorted lot of books and papers from the estate of Magister Meinaries, whose name no one but a student of Chalcedor would know, who had lent money to the writer when, as often happened, he fell on hard times. The lot was most likely nothing but law-books and ledgers, but I persuaded myself that it must hold at least one of several lost manuscripts, and I foolishly expanded on this notion aloud while perambulating the quadrangle with an associate.

I did not observe that Vendren person skulking nearby while I babbled, but he must have overheard, for the detestable man came to the auction, and came with much more money than I brought. He paid an absurdly high sum for a box that was, on the face of it, nothing but rubbish, confirming my suspicion that he had filched my intuition.

I stormed out of the auction-house in high dudgeon. I think I would have crossed the street to kick a stray dog or beggar, but fortunately none presented themselves on my way to the Institute. I stamped up the many and tortuous stairs to my office and, as noted, derived some satisfaction from slamming the door.

Even this small relief was short-lived, for the impact of the door loosened some rickety shelving overloaded with books and osteological specimens. These fell against a towering heap of crates filled with notes and correspondence that, in turn, fell against a second, similar heap, and a disastrous avalanche would have ensued if I hadn't reacted with more agility than I thought I commanded. I blocked the collapse, flinging out my hands and somehow finding just the right spots to support. It was one of those rare moments when I am pleased to be almost abnormally tall and wide.

But the issue was still in doubt. My footing was slippery as I leaned across the door, the piles were enormous, and my arms began to tremble from the strain of supporting the mass. A cloud of dust had been stirred up, and I struggled painfully to suppress a sneezing-fit that would have provoked a catastrophe.

An uninformed person might say that my office was a mess. My dear sister has gone so far as to say that my true life's work has been to construct a wonderfully complex playground for rats and cockroaches. But I knew precisely where everything was in this apparent disorder. I could put my hand in an instant on any book, manuscript or specimen I might require. It took care and luck to retrieve them, of course, but I knew where they were, and I would have lost them forever if my sister sent in her servants to "tidy up," as she sometimes threatened.

Now I was in danger of losing this system to a fit of my own ill temper, and this knowledge did nothing at all to improve it.

Having for a moment mastered the urge to sneeze, I began analyzing the unbalanced mountain. Moving with great care and deliberation, I just might be able to disassemble it a piece at a time to prevent total collapse. I stretched as far as I could, reaching to the very top of the pile that loomed above me.

Using the head of a stick or a sword in an irksomely officious way, someone rapped sharply on the door.

"Wait!" I cried. "Don't open the door, whatever —"

"Eh? Eh! Porfat, good, you're hiding in there!"

Since my imbecile brother-in-law was a prince, he didn't just open doors and walk in, he hurled them open to reveal himself, though perhaps it would be more accurate to say, "since my princely brother-in-law was an imbecile." The door knocked my feet out from under me, the foremost pile fell on top of me, the other heaps collapsed. Previously unaffected mountains of boxes and shelves and books and scrolls in remote parts of the office were sucked into the universal disaster, though I didn't witness their ruinous fall. Buried in papers as I was, I could only groan at the din that raged throughout the scrupulously maintained order of my files.

"You need to have someone in here to tidy up this mess," Prince Fandiel said, after he had shoved enough debris aside to haul me to my feet. "Nyssa mentioned that she wanted to lend you some servants, but I really didn't imagine. . . ." He surveyed the chaos with distaste. I think he believed that my office had always looked like this, even though loose papers still wafted lazily in mid-fall from the crash he had provoked.

I might have assaulted any other intruder, but even if the prince hadn't been owed the consideration due Nyssa's husband, he always managed to put me off balance. His heroic figure and impeccable turnout would have accentuated the squalor of my office on its best day. I normally thought of myself as middle-aged, overweight and unstylish, whenever I bothered to think about such superficialities at all, but in the presence of this warlike demigod I was no more than old, fat and slovenly. I imagine he had a similar effect on everyone. I could almost hear his military superiors muttering to one another, as they promoted him to posts of ever-higher responsibility, "You don't suppose he *really* can be an imbecile . . . do you?"

"Ghouls, Porfat," he said, perfecting the devastation by shoving the contents of my desktop to the floor so he could perch on it. "Ghouls."

"Indeed," I sighed. "I know something about them."

"Well, then, where do I catch one?"

"I've been trying to do just that for forty years. I may once have come close, but. . . . Why do you want one?"

"The thief known as Squirmodon. You've not heard of him? Amazing! He murdered and robbed any number of wealthy people, and now that we've caught him, he refuses to tell us where he hid his loot, despite the most relentless interrogation. He is to *spite* what what's-his-name, you know, that martyr fellow, was to . . . whatever it was he died for."

Since the Empress had moved her court to Crotalorn, the regiment known as Never-Vanquished had taken over the maintenance of order in the city, and Prince Fandiel was its commander. I had assumed he confined his police work to politically motivated slogan-painters when he wasn't engaged in more congenial functions, such as laying out parade-routes to cause the greatest inconvenience to the public. The image of my brother-in-law as a thief-catcher bemused me.

"And what has this thief got to do with ghouls?" I said.

"Among the lower orders, the belief is common that a ghoul can discover a man's secrets by eating part of him."

"This is nothing new," I said. "Superstitions of all sorts gather around these creatures. In the absence of any evidence —"

"Ah, but this is new! A cult that worships a so-called King of the Ghouls has sprung up in the city. Like all cults, its true object of devotion is cold cash. You can chop off the ear of your partner in crime, feed it to the King, and for a price he will tell you how grossly you were cheated on your last robbery."

"You know more about this than I do. Why haven't you found them?"

"They don't want to be found, at least not by the authorities. But everyone I've spoken to knows someone who knows someone else who's actually witnessed one of their obscene ceremonies. Everyone believes it. Take Squirmodon. The wretch has been broken on the wheel and deprived of all but his most essential parts. He scarcely seems to notice anymore when the Lord Collector of Tears visits his cell with the hot pincers. But when I suggested to him that the King of the Ghouls might be enlisted to discover his secrets, he flew — or rolled, actually — into a paroxysm of rage and terror. If he still had his teeth, I might have suffered a serious wound to the ankle."

"Superstition," I repeated. "Students of madness have described a mental ailment called Fornikon's mania, the morbid fear that a ghoul will eat your corpse and personate you to your loved ones. This would seem to be a universal outbreak of that delusion, probably caused by overcrowding, high prices, and the decline of manners in our sorry age."

"Doctor, they can't all be crazy, not every single sneak-thief and cutthroat in Crotalorn. But they all believe it. And from what I've heard, I'm forced to believe in the existence of the cult, though I'll reserve judgment on its usefulness until we've found it. And found a part of Squirmodon remaining that we can safely cut off. But if anyone can track them down, it's surely you."

I had to laugh, although the prince was not used to being laughed at and obviously liked it not one bit. "Do you know what that is?" I asked, gesturing toward a corner of the office.

"A pile of rubbish," he snapped, and I had to admit he was right. Grumbling, I trudged over to remove the weight of disordered papers he had dumped on the prize of my collection.

"No, look here," I said, when I had uncovered an oblong box and pushed its lid aside. "After years of haunting graveyards, exhuming bones and questioning witnesses, this is the closest I've yet come to a ghoul."

"A skeleton," he said, peering over my shoulder. "Rather a large one, but it appears to be female."

"A *human* skeleton," I amended, and he agreed. "But according to the testimony of a score of witnesses who saw it while it lived, and of hundreds more who saw it hanging from a lamp-post in Hound Square, it was a ghoul. A few believed it was an ape or hyena, or even a cross between them, but not one witness averred that these human bones came from a human woman." I picked up the skull and the lower jaw, drawing his attention to teeth that were white and regular. "I suspect she may even have been beautiful, but a mob crazed by drink and blood-lust deluded themselves into believing her a monster."

"Two explanations readily suggest themselves, Doctor. Either someone gave you the wrong bones, or else she changed back to her human form when she died. Ghouls were once human beings, weren't they?"

"Such is my theory, but it has no room for miraculous reversions. Ghoulism is a natural disease, and you could no more reverse its effects than you could regenerate a missing limb. When you eventually get around to burying Squirmodon, do you suppose his body will be whole?"

"No, of course not," said the prince, "but he's not a ghoul."

You can't argue with logic like that.

*

I thought about restoring order after the prince left, but the task was so overwhelming that the most I could do was shuffle through the mess, sighing and making despairing gestures. I couldn't decide where to begin. My surroundings were an apt metaphor for my long efforts to become an expert on ghouls.

I sat on the edge of the "ghoul's" coffin and stared gloomily at her pretty skull, which mocked me in the time-honored tradition of skulls. Could the prince be right, that someone had given me the wrong bones? I forgot exactly how I had come by them, although the written details of the acquisition were . . . somewhere in this mess.

To my best recollection, the ghoul had been chasing a woman and child across Dreamers' Hill in broad daylight. The woman had sought to save the child by throwing it to a crowd of mourners. Ignoring the woman, the ghoul pursued the child and ran headlong into a flurry of swords. The many wounds she suffered were still evident in these bones, and they suggested she had died instantly, but witnesses insisted she clung to life long after her body was hoisted on public display.

I wished now I had investigated the incident more rigorously. As far as I knew, no one had ever come forward to claim or identify the remains. What became of the woman she attacked? And the child? After the passage of twelve years or so, it was unlikely that answers could be found to even the simplest questions raised by this unlikely story.

A scroll that I failed to recognize had fallen among the woman's ribs, and I withdrew and unrolled it. I soon wished I had not.

A few years before this mass hallucination, I had conceived a passion for an art student called Umbra Vendren. She led me on cruelly, and I could regale you with endless illustrations of my heartsick buffoonery, but you all know stories of mature men enslaved by fickle girls and can supply your own jokes.

Shortly after dropping me, Umbra married the notorious Lord Glyphtard. I took no comfort at all from her subsequent murder at his hands. If he had survived her by more than a day, I would have surely sought him out and —yes, time for another "old fool" joke — challenged him.

Like most Vendrens, Umbra was preoccupied with morbid fantasies. She was obsessed with ghouls. But whereas I sought to study the malady known as ghoulism for the advancement of science, she glorified the sufferers in her art. The scroll I now held was one of her pictures —ludicrous, wrong-headed, uninformed — I caught myself sobbing as I thrust it angrily aside.

Struggling to master my emotions, I paced to the north window of my study, the last place I should have gone. Thanks to my brother-in-law, a heap of books and bones no longer obstructed its view of Dreamers' Hill and, in the foreground, the woebegone mansion where Lord Glyphtard had lived.

Odd, the similarity of the young lord's fate to that of the woman in the box. After slaughtering Umbra, he had run mad through the necropolis and metamorphosed into a ravening ghoul. Evidence for the truth of this story was persuasive, however: he had left a welter of dead men in his wake, torn limb from limb in a way no ordinary mortal, no matter how maniacally energized, could have done. Armed soldiers ran him to ground and treated him in the same style. None of his relics, unhappily, survived; they had been burned by stupid priests.

To pay my condolences — and to investigate, as tactfully as I could, the history of this peculiar young man — I had visited his mother, Lady Glypht. Admittedly, my mind was much disordered by grief and bitterness then, but I was struck by the unwholesomeness of a dank and gloomy house that seemed to exude a thicker miasma than the graveyard around it. The lady had surrounded herself with the scum of the Institute and its neighboring gutters in her hour of mourning, morbid scribblers and daubers, reputed witches and necromancers, proselytes of pernicious theories and followers of properly outlawed sects. Some time ago a colleague had made up a mocking name for my special field of study, *ghoulology,* and few words can irk me more, but this mob fawned on me and pelted me with respectful but foolish questions when Lady Glypht introduced me as "the celebrated ghoulologist." Given his home and his mother, it would have been a wonder if young Glyphtard hadn't grown up to become a ghoul.

It was all Umbra's fault, according to Lady Glypht. She had led her son astray, perverted his *scientific* investigations of the cemetery, perhaps even bewitched him with a Vendrenesque spell. She had seemed almost amused by this account of her son's death as she clutched my hands to her bosom and batted her eyelashes at me. I recalled that her husband and her father had been murdered years ago under circumstances never plausibly explained. I took my leave abruptly, having learned nothing.

*

I had grudgingly promised Prince Fandiel that I would try to find his ghoul-cult for him. If it existed, its membership would surely be represented among the necrophiles who fluttered moth-like around the dark flame of Lady Glypht. Gossip had it that she still befriended amateurs of the macabre.

But when I approached her home on the following evening I saw that things had changed since my last visit. Lights had burned everywhere then. Misfits had infested the house, spilling over into the gardens and the neighboring graveyard. Now the windows were shuttered and barred, and only a few dim lights glowed in a downstairs room. I chuckled at my ironic observation: it looked as if someone had died.

"*Like unto him that lieth with himself, he that laugheth with himself shall slay himself,*" quoted an alarming apparition that suddenly clanked to life in my path.

"See here, Sir! When and where I choose to laugh or lie or die are none of your damned business. Doesn't it say somewhere in your Book that he who jumpeth up in front of people in dark places might getteth his empty head broken?"

"I know not that," the Cluddite said. "Know you those words, Cluddrod?"

Even more alarmingly, he was answered by a second one at my shoulder: "Those words are not. He is a mocker, Zornard, and a scoffer."

"And a blasphemer. Tell us your name, that we may ask our reverend lord commander to write it down against the day when you are called forth to answer."

"My name is my own, Sir. Stand aside, or I'll have Lady Glypht set her dogs on you."

Most oddly, my threat placated the fanatic confronting me. Behind me I heard a source of retroactive terror, a sword scraping back into its scabbard.

"Your name is your own, but your face is in my eye, blasphemer," Zornard said. "If you have business with the witch, pass and be damned."

Losing my temper at the outset had given me more confidence than I had any right to feel, and now I wanted only to escape these homicidal rustics. For some strange reason of their own, the Sons of Cludd adored

Empress Fillitrella, and more and more of them were cluttering our streets and haranguing passersby every day. I was baffled by their presence here, but I had no wish to prolong a discussion with men so heavily armed and lightly civilized. I hurried forward, trying to make my abject flight seem like impatience to be on my way, as one of them quoted loudly, "*A fat man is but a shortcut between the pigsty and the graveyard.*"

"Dr. Porfat!" Lady Glypht cried with delight when a servant ushered me into a large and ill-lighted room. "Why have you neglected us for so long?"

Some idle gallantry was required, but I was too upset to attempt it. "Do you know that Cluddites are out there, screening your callers?"

"Why, yes, I hired them. The poor boys need something to keep them occupied, and one can't be too careful nowadays."

"They —" Whatever I meant to say drained from my mind as I saw that her door-keepers had let her down badly. That person who had outbid me at the auction watched me from the shadows. His unsavory young companion lurked by him, staring with what might have been called insolence in any normal boy, but that in this one conveyed the reptilian disdain of a grand and ancient lord.

"Doctor, have you met Weymael Vendren?" I believed I had heard the name in some unpleasant connection, never associating it with this man, but I was boggled by the next introduction: "And my grandson, Polliard?"

Could this be Umbra's child, and Glyphtard's? No, of course not, he was too young.

"I had thought —"

"Yes, that Lord Glyphtard was my only son. He had a brother, though, whose very name has been banished from this house. When Polliard's mother, a common person called Zara, died rather inconveniently, I put the boy in Weymael's care."

I wanted to say that I would not trust Weymael Vendren to mind a dog overnight, much less raise a child, and the wretched result seemed to justify this opinion. At a loss for any suitable alternative to such words, I stood silent as I endured Weymael's effusive greeting. The man actually embraced me.

"Dr. Porfat and I share a scholarly passion," he said. "I hadn't believed that anyone in Crotalorn knew enough about Chalcedor to connect him with Magister Meinaries, but the Doctor did, and very nearly stole a treasure from under my nose."

"*Chalcedor!*" Lady Glypht cried, leaning against me as if in need of support. "Doctor, I had no idea that our foremost ghoulologist hid such a naughty side."

I muttered some inanity about his value as a social historian while the lady giggled and Weymael twitched and wheezed.

Lady Glypht made no move to withdraw from our intimate contact, and I grew aware of an anomaly that had gone unnoticed in the shadowy room. She must have been at least sixty, but the body pressing my side felt no more than half that age. Having adopted the Frothiran fashions that arrived with the Empress, fashions more suited to the torrid climate and tepid decency of the former capital, she left me in no doubt that her skin was taut, her breasts high and firm. She had seemed unnaturally young at our last meeting; the intervening years had left her seeming even younger.

I disengaged myself as tactfully as possible, although she pouted, and took a few steps back from both of them lest Weymael should attempt to hug me again.

"When we last met, you were surrounded by some rather exotic admirers," I said. "Have you dropped them all?"

"*Exotic?*"

"It pleases the lady to patronize Crotalorn's most advanced artists and intellectuals," Weymael said, "but she fears that their habits and conversation might be unsuitable for one of tender years. She never receives guests of that sort when her grandson visits."

"Of course, you're an exception, Doctor. I promise to receive you eagerly anytime you might wish to enter my . . . home."

She said this with a perfectly straight face and Weymael simpered dutifully. Neither one of them seemed to notice that Polliard guffawed at the innuendo. Being mocked by all three of them was a sore trial of my temper, and I hurried to the point of my visit: "Some of those *advanced intellectuals* were obsessed with ghoulism. I had hoped to question them about a ghoul-cult that, some say, practices its rites in our city."

"How bizarre!" the lady cried. "Have you ever heard of ghouls worshipping anything, Weymael?"

"Their food," the ineffable Polliard suggested.

"No, this cult is made up of human beings," I said.

They listened with no more than polite interest as I expanded on this, but when I mentioned my brother-in-law's plans for the thief, Squirmodon, Lady Glypht said, "They have him in custody? Last week the government confessed that he'd slipped away to Bebros with all his spoils. An assistant minister took the blame and committed suicide."

I hardly knew how to respond. The imbecile prince had failed to warn me that I knew a dirty state-secret, and I had just handed it to persons whose connection to the slimy underbelly of the city may have been intimate.

"If I were a ghoul, I'd just eat him and keep the treasure for myself," Polliard said.

"I hope all this disgusting talk hasn't spoiled your appetite, Doctor. You will stay for a bit of supper, won't you?" My excuses were half-hearted, and the lady tipped the balance by pointing out that it had started to rain.

While she went to instruct the servants, Weymael Vendren launched a monologue on the last subject I wanted to hear him discuss, his enthusiasm for Chalcedor. I fumed and fidgeted until it dawned on me that, allowing for the stupidity of certain literary judgments, he knew what he was talking about. I had never even aspired to his grasp of Chalcedoriana, although he admitted that family traditions and private documents had given him a head start; for he was a collateral descendant of Princess Liame, obscurely nicknamed the "Amorous Cadaver" by her contemporaries, who had rescued the writer's bones from a pauper's pit and installed them in a fine tomb.

He had obviously not needed to overhear my guess about the contents of the lawyer's box to draw him to the auction, and I quietly rejoiced that I hadn't made an ass of myself by accusing him.

"I hope it proved to be worth what you paid for it. I was only guessing —"

"Worth it! Doctor, the box contained a manuscript of *Nights in the Gardens of Sythiphore*, including the five 'lost' tales that no bookseller would touch."

I was stunned. I had hoped to acquire some odds and ends for my own very minor collection, but I had almost —if not for Weymael Vendren — gained a fortune. A manuscript that rare, so rare that no one had even suspected its existence, would have bought me a luxurious retirement. I suppose it does me credit that this was not my first thought; although it was surely my second.

I blurted out my first: "May I see it?"

"Of course, Doctor. Please call on me tomorrow night at about this time —"

I had been aware for a while of a growing commotion in the background involving Lady Glypht and her servants, but I had paid it no mind at all. Now she thrust herself between us and demanded of Weymael, "Where is Polliard?"

We were both at a loss. The boy was gone, obviously, but we had been so absorbed in bookish arcana that neither one of us had the slightest notion when he had slipped out.

"You *idiot!*" she shrieked, and she struck him. No mere slap, she dealt him an open-handed blow that staggered him. "You let him leave the house. Go find him!"

"It's raining! My lungs . . . the graveyard, the night air —" I can't be sure of this, but I think he babbled something about "the King" before she silenced him with the back of her hand, this time drawing blood with her heavy, antique ring.

She turned on me, and I found myself involuntarily jittering backward after this display of savagery, but she transformed herself into a helpless female in distress as she gripped my shirt and wailed, "Help me, Doctor! The servants are old and even more useless than this creature, and the Cluddites are stupid brutes. Help me find my grandson."

I had barely agreed before she all but dragged me into the soggy garden and propelled me through it to the adjoining necropolis. I filled my lungs to call out, "Polliard!", but the name was garbled by an oath as she viciously pinched my lip.

"No, he'll only hide from us, the scamp," she whispered urgently. "Whatever you do, don't call his name."

The bizarreness of this adventure struck me only now. If any normal boy had romped off into the rain, a normal grandparent would have waited for him to get wet enough to come to his senses and return. One might call out threats or promises from the comfort of a dry house, not stalk him in silence and darkness as if he were an escaped animal. It seemed likely to me that the terrible fate of Lord Glyphtard had deranged his mother in certain areas. The thought of her grandson exploring a graveyard had provoked an onset of madness. The wetter I got, the more bitterly I berated myself for essaying the role of second lunatic.

I noted rain-smudged lights moving here and there on the hillside above us, and the occasional hoots and whistles that accompanied them were typically those of Zaxoin hillmen. At least a score of Cluddites must have been guarding her house, and the whole platoon had been sent out to find one wayward boy.

As first step in a plan to escape this circus and go home, I said, "It might be better if we separate."

"My own impulse, Doctor, is exactly opposite," she said and she seized me in her arms.

Mad or not, she was a remarkably beautiful woman who had been doing her best to stir me up since I walked into her house, and I wanted her even more than I had known. My mind ceased to function, except on the puzzle of the single hook that suspended her Frothiran wisp of a gown, and that was really no puzzle at all. I felt her kicking it away from her ankles as I cupped her bare buttocks in both hands and returned her hungry kisses.

Just before this lightning of passion struck, I thought I had heard an odd, scraping noise nearby. I had dismissed it as an effect of the pattering rain, or perhaps a branch scuffing against a tombstone, but now I noted it again, somewhat louder, and it had a metallic ring. I tried to pull back to listen, but she would have none of that. She moaned loudly as she kissed me, alternately hissing lecherous enticements, while dragging me down to the wet grass. It seemed almost as if she were trying to muffle the other sound.

I would have liked to proceed at a mature and civilized pace, but her impatience was nothing less than furious. It was she who saw to my undressing, and she had bared little more than the only part she required before gripping it and plunging it inside her with less tenderness than a suicide might wield a dagger. I cried out. Despite all her apparent ardor, she was physically unprepared, and it hurt.

"Yes, Porfat, yes, this is how I like it!" she insisted, and her voice rose to a scream as she urged, over and over again, "Deeper! Faster! Harder! Yes, hurt me, I love it!", interspersed with the sort of expletives that might have brought a blush to the cheek of Chalcedor himself.

I told her to shut up. She was putting our lives in peril. The Empress suffered the Sons of Cludd to station two regiments in the capital on the condition that they curb their impulse to chastise wicked civilians, but one should never tempt them. As rigid celibates, they reserved their most frenzied transports of condemnation for fornicators. Her cries might draw them down to hack us in pieces.

She ignored my command. I thought about withdrawing and running away from the madwoman, but at this point none of my thoughts carried much weight. I labored more vigorously in the hope of getting it over with quickly, but fear and distraction retarded me. When I pressed my hand over her mouth, she bit it, then redoubled her lecherous screams.

Her noise was overwhelmed by a roar that not even a scandalized Cluddite could have delivered. In fact it was not human. No tiger had been seen near Crotalorn in living memory; I could think of no other beast that might produce such a volume of angry noise. But when I turned my head, it was to see a pale shape that was more like a man than any beast.

My impressions are imperfect, because the thing instantly struck me with paralyzing force and lifted me by the shoulders as easily as I might lift an empty shirt. I remember an intolerable smell, but I remember nothing else.

*

I woke up in a blaze of lanterns lancing off naked swords and brass buckles.

"Zornard!" I cried, actually glad to see the wretched zealot.

"I am he, blasphemer. The Lord Cludd on High sent a ghoul to rebuke you for mocking the Scripture, but it fled from our honest iron."

"The lady. . . ?"

"The ghoul shrieked all manner of foulness in a woman's voice, and it drew us here. As," he added with heavy disapproval, "it must have lured you. We saw no lady."

I could barely contain myself as I staggered to my feet. After forty years of futile effort, I had finally come face to face with a ghoul, but my face was not the part I had presented. I had glimpsed it for only an instant over my shoulder. I ransacked my dizzy brain for details, but the most I could retrieve was an image of a large, pale form that might have been a man. That it was not a man I knew by its voice, its strength, and the nauseous smell that lingered in the air.

I called for the Cluddites to bring their lanterns closer as I scrabbled in the wet grass for footprints or other evidence, but I found nothing. I sensed that my rescuers were growing agitated, never a good sign, and at last one of them ordered, "Hide your shame, sinner!", reminding me to do up my breeches.

Quizzing these witnesses was equally useless. The ghoul had been a manifestation of evil, in their view, and to dwell on the details of any such manifestation would be sinful. They had accidentally stumbled upon the object of my long ambition, to see a real ghoul, and their one desire was to put it completely out of their minds. When my questions began to irritate them seriously, I gave up and left them to say their prayers.

They let me borrow a lantern, and I threaded my way through the tombstones to investigate the odd noise I had heard just before Lady Glypht launched her distracting performance. The ghoul had attacked me from the left, and that noise had come from my right. Some twenty paces in that direction I came upon a corpse that had been pulled from a partially opened grave. Its lower half was still buried, so that it seemed to be taking its ease in the hole. Something had been chewing on its head.

I failed to restrain a most sinful oath when Zornard said at my elbow, "The ghoul was feeding when you disturbed it."

"Perhaps," I said. "Why did Lady Glypht hire you?"

"She says a foul ghoul plots to abduct her grandson. We stand guard when the boy visits, for all evil things fear our righteousness."

"And your iron weapons," I said.

He agreed to this, but it puzzled me further. He had not noticed the shovel lying near the despoiled grave. No ghoul would need a shovel, nor would one use — and I checked this after Zornard had reclaimed his lantern and returned to his companions — an iron shovel.

*

At the Institute next day, I wasted an unconscionable amount of time peeking from the corner of the window that overlooked the Glypht home. I saw neither the lady nor her grandson, and no Cluddites were visible. Callers occasionally came and went, but it was beyond my powers of deduction to determine whether they were tradesmen, policemen, acquaintances, or ghouls personating human beings.

Sometimes a servant would dodder outside and stand for a while in puzzlement until a less senile specimen would dodder out and lead her back in. I repressed the fancy that these had only last week been healthy young girls, their vitality leeched to feed the unnatural lithesomeness of the witch.

I itched to know what had happened to her, and to her grandson. I could easily have sent her a bland note thanking her for her hospitality and inquiring about her health, but I had resolved to stay clear of her. Even if she was only what she seemed to be, I had no wish to admit an eccentric wanton into the constrained but comfortable life that I had, after a long and painful series of missteps, defined for myself.

But I suspected that she was much more than she seemed to be, and that disorder and inconvenience were the very least of the ills in her train. She had not wanted me last night, she had wanted only to distract me from some dark doings in the graveyard. She had known that the ghoul would be abroad, for she had hired Cluddites to keep him from the boy. Her cries of feigned passion had summoned it. Whether it killed me or not was all the same to her.

Speculating on her secrets was unpleasant, but I preferred that to thinking about Polliard. Someone had been opening a grave when we approached. Someone had begun to eat the corpse. Her son had been a ghoul, and perhaps her grandson had determined to honor the family tradition.

Who had his father been? The story of a second son whose name could not be mentioned in her home, when she had no qualms about mentioning the unspeakable Glyphtard, was so feeble that she must have thought me an idiot. The real question might be, Who had his mother been? Taken from a beloved wood-nymph, "Zara" was the commonest of female names, just the one she might have chosen for a hasty lie. The lady herself might be Polliard's mother.

My speculations were interrupted by a servant in unmatched castoffs of Vendren livery, who rather loftily introduced himself as Phylphot Phuonsa. I would have advised him that I had no wish to clutter my head with the names of errand-boys, especially not one so inharmonious and silly that it would probably persist like a mnemonic radish to my dying day, but he distracted me with a bow and a flourish that brushed the edge of sarcasm as he presented a weighty envelope. He picked his nose and toured my office with brazen inquisitiveness while I studied the message. It was addressed in the sort of fanciful, old-fashioned calligraphy that is favored by people I detest.

I hoped this message from Weymael Vendren would at least tell me if the lady and her grandson still lived, but he wrote as if none of last night's alarming events had occurred. It was no more than a graciously worded renewal of his invitation to visit him that evening and view his manuscript.

By now I had remembered hearing the name Weymael Vendren as that of a reputed necromancer, and this seemed not unlikely, given the man and his associates, but I could not refuse the chance to examine his find. I turned to instruct the servant when I saw to my astonishment that he was leaning half out of a window, apparently studying the overhang of the roof.

"You, there! What do you think you're doing?"

He made a show of refastening the window before dusting off his hands, excavating an ear with a fingertip, and examining the results. Then he said, "Bats, Sir. I hate bats."

"And did you find any?"

"Not a one, Sir, you're very lucky, but you really should have someone come and tidy up the mess in here. It attracts them."

*

Weymael Vendren lived, oddly enough, on Vendren Hill, a stronghold of that Tribe long ago, which had since passed into the hands of people with no names at all, or none they wanted known. The rickety tenements stacked onto its steep slope, until they should tumble into the Miraga and float out to sea, held every sort of failure: blind painters, tone-deaf musicians, illiterate writers, generous whores, squeamish cutthroats and honest lawyers. Weymael's deference to Lady Glypht made him seem a timid Vendren, a fit match for such neighbors.

An exasperatingly indirect course took me up stepped alleys and down misleading lanes to the top of the hill and over it, where it dropped off sheerly beyond a parapet. Dreamers' Hill loomed across a wild and twisting ravine. I tried to discourage the fancy that this wasteland separating the defeated from the dead would be a likely place for ghouls to congregate; the absence of night-prowlers on this side of Vendren Hill suddenly seemed less reassuring. I held my staff at the ready as I puzzled my way to Lunule Street.

A palace was the last thing I expected to find off that crooked alley, but when I had picked my way over the rusted bars of a fallen gate and into a forest that had once been a garden, I was confronted by a marble fantasy in the baroque style of the Late Kingdom, when Chalcedor himself had lived. Fallen and dismembered statues testified to the vivid history that had intervened.

The palace looked less grand up close. Roofs had collapsed, one wing had been gutted by fire, and little of the building seemed inhabited or even inhabitable. A broken bedstead, a wheel-less chariot and some seatless chairs sprawled among the junk clogging my way on the portico where Vendren lords and ladies had once strolled in elegance and wickedness.

I could understand why the crazy servant might grow obsessed with bats in such a place. It was he who, at long last, answered my knocking.

"Lord Weymael was called away," he said, "but he said you should make yourself at home."

He ignored my ill-mannered laughter and led me with upraised lantern through a once-magnificent hall, now a repository for more bedraggled furniture, battered weapons and the mouldy heads of beasts. I asked, "And what about his son?"

"He's gone, too. His ward."

I was relieved to learn that I would not be alone with that strange creature in this strange house, but it told me nothing about last night. Had he found a more suitable home among the ghouls?

"Did Polliard return here last night?" I pressed.

He made no immediate answer, and I expected he would remind me, quite justly, that no gentleman would quiz a servant about his masters. But at last he replied, in a tone bordering on despair, "He always returns." He added: "He went out with Lord Weymael tonight." After a further pause, as if straining his memory or imagination, he said: "To help the boy's mother, who can't get about on her own anymore."

Either he was lying or, hardly unlikely, Lady Glypht was, and I had small hope of learning anything worthwhile, but I asked: "Zara?"

He did not so much scratch his head as submit his scalp to an exhaustive entomological census, and we had threaded several dark corridors and arrived at a lighted room before he answered: "I believe I heard another name in connection with that lady, but you may very well be right, Doctor. Should you require anything at all, please ring."

His vagueness suggested he might be telling the truth, but when I turned to question him further he was picking his nose again, so I gladly let him close the door behind me and quit my sight.

After my tour of the ruined palace, the clean and well-furnished room was a surprise. It seemed the retreat of a thoughtful, bookish man who was far better organized and much wealthier than I. No volumes of wizardly lore lined the shelves, only copies of the standard classics. I saw not a single stuffed owl, human skull or figurine of Sleithreethra, but with the Cluddites so active lately, a genuine necromancer might regretfully dispose of his traditional paraphernalia.

A fire burned cheerily on the hearth, driving back the oppressive dampness of the other rooms, and I was distracted from my uneasiness by a sideboard laden with enough delicacies for a dinner-party. My desire for food vanished, however, when I noticed the scroll on top of a desk between two thoughtfully positioned lamps. This could only be the fabulous manuscript that had lured me here. I took a bottle of a rare Bebrosian vintage and a glass to the desk, where I planted myself and prepared to be awed.

And indeed I was. Those who condemn Chalcedor and all his works are especially incensed by the published version of *Nights in the Gardens of Sythiphore.* Unconstrained by facts, he created a world of infinite possibilities and pleasures that seems more vibrantly real than the reality, and Sythiphorians revere his memory more highly than any of their own artists. A reportedly shocking statue of the writer entangled with a cluster of nymphs dominates Chalcedor Plaza, and visitors are guided on tours of all the sites he would have frequented if he had ever actually visited that city.

What had been excised from the published version, oddly, were not the elaborately metaphorical descriptions of body-parts and their conjunctions, but a myriad nuances of character and motivation, along with disturbing but wittily phrased speculations on the sexual wellsprings of all human endeavor. I suppose prudes can grudgingly tolerate the antics of stock puppets, however lubricious, in works without artistic skill; when the puppets come to life on the page to feel improper emotions and think subversive thoughts, the shock is intolerable.

I hurried to the long-lost tales, "Animadversions on the Mystagogue," "The Obtuse Princess," "The Debility of Globbriel Thooz," and the others that can now be obtained, if only under the counter and disguised as something else, from any broad-minded bookseller.

I was disappointed — not by the stories themselves, for they are masterly, but by my inability to fall through the parchment and into the gardens of Chalcedor's fabulous city. I could not forget that I was only the second person who had seen these tales for two centuries, and an obligation to feel suitably humbled distracted my concentration. It was further distracted by my awareness of the person who had seen them first; for no matter how welcome I had been made to feel, this comfortable room lay in the depths of that man's weird home.

I am by no means high-strung, nor am I given to sensing the activities of ghosts, but I started more than once at noises of indeterminate origin. The fire on the hearth, the settling of the foundations, the servant's distant activities or perhaps even those of his bats: they were probably responsible for most of these sounds, but some scrapes and sighs and flutters were less easily dismissed. A faint, recurrent clicking was especially disturbing. I could not imagine what it was, and I began almost to dread its recurrence.

Restless, I got up and prowled to the casements at the end of the room, where I noted wind-blown branches whipping the face of the waning moon, but none of these tapped the panes. The imagined chill of the night outside, perhaps, made me shiver.

Pouring wine from a second bottle, and nibbling on some of the sausages and cheeses from the sideboard, I gave the room a more detailed scrutiny. My first impression of neatness, I was gratified to note, had been wrong. Books and papers, loose clothes, even some used plates and cups had been shoved behind or under any chair or table that might conceal them. When I trod on a lump in the rug and lifted its edge to investigate, my suspicion was verified: the servant had swept dust and scraps under it.

Prosperella, never at a loss for unpleasant tricks to play on me, must have been at my shoulder and nudged me to take a longer look. When I did, I noticed the ideogram for "Meinaries" on a crumpled ball of paper at my feet. Of course this was none of my business, but the thought of finding proof that Weymael had overheard my speculations about the auction and made a note of them was an irresistible temptation. I picked it up and partly unwadded it.

"Meinaries says he stored the Chalcedor materials in boxes marked C-100 to 105 at the Orocrondel Company's number two warehouse." Nothing odd there: Meinaries, though defunct, could "say" that in a letter or ledger that had come Weymael's way. The next sentence, however, alarmed me: "He insists he did not reclaim these before his death."

I hesitated before smoothing out the rest of the sheet. Did I really want to know more? But of course, unhappily, I did.

A different pen and a more agitated calligraphy had been used for the rest of the page, which may have been torn from a record of the necromancer's research: "M. persists in denying knowledge of those boxes after he stored them. He may be telling the truth, but Emerald Street is hopelessly dangerous. I should give him to P., the brute, who may learn more, and who lusts to eat his head. He believes Lady G.'s malicious lies and would acquire legal knowledge for his claim to the G. fortune, ha ha ha."

Though I detested even to touch this note, I put it in my pocket for later study. "P" could only be Polliard, and his desire to "acquire legal knowledge" by dining on a dead lawyer raised disturbing questions. I had never heard of a ghoul who could go about consistently in human form, but I doubted this would be the only shock awaiting anyone who delved into the secrets of the Glyphts.

Chalcedor or not, I had no wish to remain here any further, but my curiosity got the better of me. Unless he was a madman, Weymael Vendren was a necromancer, who could raise the dead to extract their secrets; and although I had seen several persons executed for this hateful crime, I had never seen one whose guilt was clear. It seemed odd indeed that his private library should be furnished with nothing more sinister than the epics of Pesquidor, the dramas of Fronnard Vogg and the vertiginous cosmology of Trisophrodes the Lesdomite.

The most suspect work was that of Morphyrion, the mad poet, in seven volumes. I discovered that these were not books at all, only their spines, concealing a panel that opened with a little pushing and prodding.

Behind it lay a box filled with the scrolls used by an earlier age — a far earlier age, indeed, by the look of them. I am no expert, but they appeared to be written in the language of the shadowy civilization that once flourished in the Cephalune Hills beyond Fandragord.

When I went to replace the box, I saw that something lay hidden behind it: a sort of bird-cage, although more strongly built. The lock that held its two halves together had been broken open, and it was empty.

The volumes of Trisophrodes were no more than they seemed to be, but the works of Fronnard Vogg concealed another secret compartment and another box of scrolls. These were ancient, but written in plain Frothen, and the first began with such a horrendous invocation to Sleithreethra that I rolled it quickly shut.

A cage lay in the depths of this one, too, but it was occupied: by a human head.

It was very old, little more than a skull with the hair and parchment-like skin adhering. A much stronger lock had been used to secure its cage, but this lock had been twisted and scratched by determined efforts to force it. I replaced everything as I had found it.

Much time had passed, and I feared that Weymael and his wretched ward might return at any moment, but I was arrested by the sight of some thick books on the highest shelf that purported to be the writings of Magister Meinaries. These proved to be another disguised panel. By stretching on tiptoe, I was able to pull out the box it concealed.

Unlike the others, this was packed with loose sheets, most of them scribbled with Weymael's hasty shorthand. One was a letter from the house that had auctioned Meinaries' box, telling Weymael that it had come from an innkeeper named Gourdfoot, of Emerald Street.

Unwilling to study most of these sheets, which appeared to be further records of a blasphemous interrogation, I let myself be diverted by a much older document on parchment. This was a detailed map of the section known as Blackberry Bank: quite useless, since the orderly streets had been destroyed in a great fire. The section was now a notorious slum whose existing tangle was partly depicted with black lines designated as streets in Weymael's hand: Algol's Close, Burntwitch Alley and *Emerald Street.* The latter cut through the corner of a large square that the original map-maker had identified as the number two warehouse of the Orocrondel Company.

Weymael had added a second group of lines in red that ended at the river and would probably have converged on Dreamers' Hill if that had appeared in the map. Three of them twisted through the site of the former warehouse and were here and there labelled with the ideogram for an entrance. One of these lay at the intersection of a red line with Emerald Street. I clicked my teeth together, as I sometimes do when lost in thought.

The habit is so old and deeply ingrained that I never notice when I indulge in it unless someone – usually Nyssa, with annoyance – calls it to my attention. You might say that someone called my attention to it now and had, in fact, been trying to call my attention to it all evening. The clicking that had unsettled me earlier was repeated, far more loudly, and in time to my own tooth-clicking.

It was louder, obviously, because the secret compartment behind the false books of Meinaries hung open.

I wanted, as I have wanted few things in my life, to fling the box back into the compartment, slam the panel shut and flee the palace with no delay. I was reasonably sure that I already knew what waited for me in the hidden compartment. But curiosity overcame me. By shoving a chair into position and standing on it, I could look directly into the secret place.

It was a severed head in a cage, as I knew it would be. Although eyeless and noseless, although dead for two centuries, it could still click its teeth. And although it had no lungs, it could squeeze a faint breath of fetid air past its leathery lips to whisper: "Bury me."

I astounded myself by saying, "Yes. Of course, Sir," and perhaps to explain to myself why I should plunge deeper into this nightmare, I added: "Thank you for lending money to Chalcedor when he needed it."

The head was silent. Had I dreamed or imagined − no, in an even flimsier whisper, it repeated: "Bury me."

My hand shook when I seized the cage and jerked it out. The head thumped appallingly against the bars from my haste and clumsiness, but I could not bear to look at it. Nor could I bear to hear it, and the first thing I did was to muffle it thoroughly in the cloak I had thrown over a chair.

To delay discovery and the threat of an immediate pursuit, I restored the box of notes to the compartment and closed the panel behind it. I had barely finished congratulating myself on my cleverness when I saw that I had left the map out on a table. Rather than take the time to move the chair and open the panel again, I stuffed it inside my shirt.

My eye fell on the lost manuscript of Chalcedor. I was already stealing from the necromancer, was I not? That was rightfully *my* manuscript, was it not, since I had traced it without resorting to diabolical means? Although I hated to do it, I left it where it lay.

I hurried out without taking a lamp, trying hard to restrain my oaths when my toes or shins collided with invisible junk. I heard nothing from Phylphot Phuonsa, but he was not my worst fear. I conceived the notion that Weymael and his ward had returned quietly, and that Polliard was watching me with his ghoul's eyes from the blackness. The skin crawled between my shoulders, where I fully expected a dagger to fall at any moment.

I reached the portico safely, and I had just begun to take what would have been my first breath for a very long time when I heard the creak and rustle of a cart over rough ground, a sedate clopping of hoofs. It was coming up the path toward me.

Despite the intervening cloak and cage, I was loath to clutch the head against my chest, but I fought down my rising gorge and did so as I hurried to the end of the porch and picked my way into the weeds and brambles of the garden. I felt reasonably safe when I was crouching behind the rim of a stagnant pool where broken nymphs cavorted.

I soon spied Weymael Vendren and his ward perched on the seat of a thoroughly prosaic cart, drawn by a mule, like a pair of farmers coming to market; but of course it was no load of yams they had just dug out of the earth. After dismounting, they hauled an oblong box from the bed of the cart. From the way they managed it, it seemed unusually light for a coffin, but of course a ghoul would be far stronger than a normal boy.

Polliard seemed to be fretting, urging more care, and at last Weymael cried: "Damn you, it's not a sacred relic of Filloweela, you know! And after all the ill treatment it's had already. . . ."

Polliard spoke quietly, and Weymael cried, "But what if the cursed thing decides to eat me?" Unfairly, since he was making most of the noise, he added: "And be quiet, can't you? That fatuous, posturing, overstuffed humbug is probably still here, swilling my wine and masturbating over my manuscript."

They disappeared into the palace before I could hear more.

I supposed Magister Meinaries would want his head to be buried with his body, but that was a far nobler deed than I had any intention of doing. I would have had to bring it home while I researched the location of his tomb. As a professor of anatomy, I could have explained its presence easily enough, but only if the thing kept still. I had no wish to lecture it on the need for caution, to hide it under my bed, nor even to keep it with me for one instant longer than absolutely necessary to keep my promise. I hurried toward the ravine.

The street at the edge of the cliff was deserted. I felt safe in reclaiming my cloak and setting the cage on the parapet. Unless I found a direct way of getting across the gap to the necropolis, where I intended to do whatever I could for Meinaries, I would have to spend the rest of the night walking there by a circuitous route.

It spoke. "What?" I asked, forcing myself to lean closer, and the head whispered: "He never repaid me."

I guessed he meant Chalcedor, and it shocked me that he could still be capable of resentment. I suppose we expect only wisdom from the dead because they can no longer display the pettier side of their humanity, and Meinaries, through no fault of his own, was denied this advantage.

"Consider your rescue from the necromancer as repayment," I said.

"Don't you have some money?"

I bit back an oath and abandoned this conversation. Considering all he had suffered, it would be no wonder if he were stark mad.

The moon had set, and I reconsidered my plan as I peered into the blackness below. Negotiating the slope as I remembered it would have been difficult in broad daylight, and now I could see nothing. I stepped back hastily at a loud rustling from below, as of something determinedly rushing upward. At the same time Meinaries' hateful teeth began to chatter frantically. I turned toward his cage in time to see something explode from the darkness. I thought it might be a pale bird taking flight, it came up so swiftly, but it seized the cage and pulled it back, like the hand of a preternaturally swift and sure climber. A louder scrambling and rustling receded into the depths, accompanied by a cry of terror so thin that I may have imagined it.

*

I found Prince Fandiel at breakfast, as I hoped I would, and outlined my discoveries after my plate had been sufficiently laden. "So if you really want to enlist a ghoul into the police force, round up young Polliard," I concluded, "or behead Squirmodon and have Weymael Vendren interrogate the head. And then, if you want my further advice, burn them all at the stake."

"Haw!" The prince had an odd habit: he had never learned to laugh properly, so he signified high spirits by barking and rapping on a convenient surface, in this case, the table. My irony must have amused him greatly, for the plates danced and a tumbler smashed on the floor.

"The position of our cousin —" he meant the Empress —"is so tenuous that I can't burn Vendrens at the stake, even minor ones, much as they might need it. Nor should anyone indulge too freely in accusations of ghoulism and necromancy. The Cluddites would love that. They'd fall into the spirit of the thing and treat us to an uncontrollable bloodbath. We'd have to kick them out of the city, and they are of great value to Her Imperial Majesty as a counterbalance to Death's Dildos." He meant the regiment known as Death's Darlings, virtually a private Vendren army.

"Then Squirmodon —"

"Is an academic question, unfortunately. Without legs or arms, and with the anchor-chain from a galley around his neck, he managed to burrow out of his dungeon. He was famous for staging such feats, and his guards believed in this one to their dying breaths. It's more likely that someone burrowed in, although the collapsed state of the tunnel makes it hard to tell. It's likeliest of all that the guards were bribed to let him go and start a bogus tunnel to confuse us. It's not dissimilar to the case of that fellow, you know, in history, who supposedly escaped from somewhere or other."

"You have a gift for lending depth to any subject, dear, with your wealth of cultural allusions, just like what's-his-name, the poet," Nyssa said mischievously, and to me: "I have a surprise for you, brother."

"You didn't tell anyone that we had Squirmodon in custody, did you, Doctor?" the prince asked. "I thought I made it clear that was a secret."

"What sort of surprise?" I asked, turning my full attention to my sister.

*

She refused to tell me, and it surely was a surprise when I later opened the door that should have led to my office and found myself standing bewildered in a strange room, huge and full of light. I thought at first I had climbed the wrong tower, but then my eye fell on the myriad bottles and jars that contained my own anatomical specimens. They had been dusted and polished and, as never before, arranged on shelves.

An intruder, a lank, gawky fellow, was even now polishing skulls. I shouted, "You, there, Sir! What are you?"

"Your servant, Doctor."

"Yes, yes, yes, and I yours, but who are you, and what do you think you're doing?"

"My name is Feshard, Sir. Lady Fandyssa has directed me to serve you."

I recognized this impudent rogue from Nyssa's household and recalled her boast that he was one servant I would never be able to bully. I would see about that! "Go and tell Lady Fandyssa that you are not required here. Get out!"

"I've been instructed to obey you in all things, Doctor, except that one."

I stalked heavily to one of the tall windows, meaning to open it and throw him out. I was about to warn him of this, but I was distracted by the broken latch of the casements. It struck me that Weymael Vendren's servant had yesterday made a show of securing this very latch.

Leaning out to examine the eaves that had so interested him, I noted a pair of stout hooks driven into the beams a few feet apart. They seemed new, not at all weathered or rusted, and a pulley hung from one of them.

"I don't suppose you have anything to do with this, do you?" When he hesitated to lean out the window, I grabbed him and shoved him halfway through. "Look, Sir, look! What do you make of that?"

"Someone was lifting something to the window?"

"Or lowering it," I said, letting him go. He squeaked distractingly as he struggled to fall back inside the room.

I believed I knew what would be missing. The box containing the bones of the presumptive ghoul was nowhere to be found. Feshard insisted he had seen no such box while ransacking my belongings.

I stamped down the stairs, wondering where I could borrow a sword before presenting myself at Weymael's palace to demand the return of my skeleton. Halfway across the quadrangle it occurred to me that my righteous outrage was compromised: I had, after all, stolen his skull. Worse, I had lost it. A moment's reflection persuaded me that this was not the sort of argument one should start with a necromancer. I decided reluctantly not to press my claim.

I had stolen his map, too, and I still had it in a pocket of my cloak.

*

A very large man should avoid taverns like Gourdfoot's, in Emerald Street, for small drunkards will see his mere existence as a challenge to be met head-on. At least two such began to bristle when I stooped to enter a room where midnight prevailed at high noon, but as soon as I began asking the innkeeper about the cellar, they returned their attention to racing cockroaches at their table.

"I sell junk from cellar, yes, when wall fall down and men come fix, but nothing more down there now no more." Without being asked, Gourdfoot poured me a glass of *pflune,* a searing liquor popular only with Ignudos, our willfully unenlightened aborigines; and with criminals on their way to the scaffold, who want a strong anesthetic with no regard to consequences. As my eyes grew more accustomed to the dark, I saw it was the only drink he sold, and that he and his customers were Ignudos.

"It was once the cellar of a warehouse, wasn't it?"

"Something like that, I guess maybe. Whole block, all buildings, share same cellar, so we keep door locked. They say you can walk through all Blackberry Bank without once seeing light of day —"

"No, what they say is, if you try it you never see daylight again," one of the cockroach-racers put in, to general merriment.

"—but I don't know if that true."

Gourdfoot passed me a vial of ammonia, which one is supposed to sniff after drinking *pflune* to counteract the taste. It was not effective.

"May I have a look at it?"

"What, the *cellar?*" He was stunned, but his commercial instinct stayed intact: "It cost you many silver fillies."

"Why?"

"For all trouble of unlock cellar door, then lock after you. And remember, it my cellar. I keep anything you find."

"Not anything, Gourdfoot," the humorist shouted, but he was overridden by another one: "No, no, Gourdfoot get to keep *anything* he find. Maybe dogface wizard find *glybdi* slut to work back room."

The second comic had misjudged his audience. A sudden, nervous silence fell. *Glybdi* is the Ignudo word for ghoul.

I parted with a ridiculous sum for the privilege of touring the cellar, then learned that this did not include the lantern I had to buy. After he had undone a redundancy of bolts and bars, some of them so solidly mated with the floor that they required the help of his customers and their bargemen's hooks, he heaved up the trapdoor on a dank abyss. He lowered a ladder for me, but as soon as I stood in water to my ankles at the bottom, he retrieved it.

"Wait —"

"When you want come up again, you go someplace else," Gourdfoot said, dropping the lid. A flurry of grunting and hammering followed as they struggled to secure the door.

I began to entertain doubts about the wisdom of this adventure. I had been goaded to it by Weymael's insults —fatuous, posturing, masturbating humbug, indeed! If that catamiting Vendren popinjay could sit back and collect one priceless manuscript by tormenting the helpless dead, I would use Fand enterprise and courage to bring back ten of them. Perhaps I should have reflected, as I did now, that in the master's tales similar motives always lead a hero to his doom.

Poor Meinaries told Weymael he had stored six boxes in the warehouse, and only one of them had recently come to light, according to the auctioneer who obtained it. Neither the auctioneer nor the necromancer had investigated this site personally, perhaps because they were quite sensibly unwilling to venture among the Ignudos.

The savages' fear of their own cellar, however, and its association with "glybdi," cast sinister light on Weymael's note that Emerald Street was "hopelessly dangerous." Those red lines on the map that ran here from Dreamers' Hill: could they be *tunnels?* And could the entrances — one of them at this very spot — signify junctions between the world of men and the underworld of the ghouls?

I sighed ruefully and unshuttered the lantern, which revealed a cavern not unlike Weymael's home. Two centuries of rubbish had not completely hidden massive bales of once-rich fabrics, now thoroughly rotted, and scorched beams fallen from the original warehouse. My vision of a singlehanded search seemed even more foolish: a mining operation by a horde of workmen was required.

I waded to a cleared space where the foundation had been hastily patched with new bricks. The priceless box might have been found among the trash and building-rubble shoved aside for this work, but the bales and baskets and broken barrels had been jammed together to form an almost solid wall, and none of its components looked promising.

Some of it yielded to the poking and prying of my staff, so I put aside my cloak and attacked it more vigorously. I redoubled my efforts when an interlocked jumble of crates was revealed. Feverishly levered out, these proved to contain nothing but old clothes and broken dishes. A box of papers made my heart leap, but these were the ledgers of a long-dead purveyor of bone-meal and horse-manure.

I took no note of time until I realized that my limbs trembled with fatigue and my hands were bloody from tearing crates open without tools. I had spent hours of unaccustomed, physical labor, all of it for no purpose than to convert junk to wreckage and rearrange it. I was not ready to give up, but I was more than ready to leave and rethink my plan, preferably over a hearty meal. I would even be willing to settle for the sort of dinner I might get upstairs, pigfeet with cabbage and a bottle of *pflune.*

Bending to retrieve my lantern, I tripped and fell against a jam of rubbish I had not yet disturbed. I ended on the floor, soaked with foul water and dazed from a painful knock on the head. When I raised my light, I saw that I had revealed an unsuspected doorway.

A dry and relatively clear passage led upward, perhaps all the way to street-level by another route. I decided to explore this for a short way in preference to pounding on the trapdoor with my staff until I overcame the Ignudos' fears or died of exhaustion. I was soon shivering, both from my soggy clothes and from contact with an ancient city of cobwebs and its madly scrambling citizens. I spent more time cursing and pounding spiders from my limbs than I did looking where I was going, with the result that I tripped again.

I must have knocked my head again, too, this time more seriously, for I had passed from the real world into that of Chalcedor's tale about the young man who stumbles upon the magic words that open a thieves' cave. I stood in a room where a wealth of jewels and coins, gold statuettes and silver dinnerware lay tumbled. The locked chests of gold-chased ebony and sandalwood hinted at even more wealth than the thief had troubled himself to count.

The thief himself lay scattered on a floor of uneven stones that he had stained with his blood. Nothing about his skeletal remains suggested his identify, except that the legs and arms were missing; but the iron collar and massive chain — not the anchor-chain of a galley, but I had suspected that Prince Fandiel exaggerated — persuaded me that these were the relics of the unfortunate Squirmodon.

His loot had been treated with slovenly indifference. I discovered a painting by Lutria of Ashtralorn lying face-down on the floor of the mouldy cellar. An instinct for the fitness of things prompted me to dust it off and prop it upright. It was hard to imagine a thief so stupid or uncaring that he would do less; and from what little I knew of Squirmodon, he had been both intelligent and discriminating. Alive or dead, he must have been dragged here from his dungeon and eaten by a ghoul. His treasure had then been retrieved by a second thief.

Nothing was arranged for private gloating, except one object, but this exception disclosed the very heart of that second thief as a cesspool of depravity, mockery, blasphemy and treason. A bust of Sleithreethra, carved from obsidian and rendered even more hideous with ruby eyes, had been placed neatly on a plain wooden pedestal; the latter not part of the loot, obviously, but dragged from some other part of the cellars for the specific purpose of honoring the abomination. About its neck hung a string of progressively larger emeralds, the lower ones large as hen's eggs, with a massive gold pendant representing the Dragon of Fand.

I had seen this necklace last year — and there could be no other like it — when a new wing at the Anatomical Institute had been dedicated by the lady who had worn it, Empress Fillitrella. Although contact with the bust made me retch, I muttered a hasty prayer to Polliel, made a protective sign, and took the necklace. I put it around my own neck for safekeeping and fastened my shirt over it.

A second room led off this one. I stiffened my resolve and stepped forward, but I immediately faltered, nearly overcome by an urgent desire to scramble back and pound desperately on Gourdfoot's trapdoor. What almost unmanned me was an odor I could never forget, the stench of the ghoul that had assaulted me in the graveyard. I made very sure the room was empty before I tiptoed in.

The most intentionally frightful object here left me unmoved. It was a throne made of bones, mostly human, although I noted some tusks that might have come from wild boars. Yellowed and broken, patched with bits of wood and wire, its effect was less terrifying than childish. The phrase "King of the Ghouls" came unbidden to my mind.

This small, dank space hardly seemed a fit throne-room for even a king like that. By one wall lay a compressed heap of papers and rags, partly covered by a fabulous carpet of Phyringian workmanship. Aside from that carpet, probably loot from the next room, it looked like the sort of mattress favored by derelicts. It even held the hard-packed imprint of a large body. Perhaps the king was only storing his throne in this, his shabby bedchamber.

I pulled back the carpet for a closer look and was repelled by a staggering concentration of the stench that had frightened me. The old and crusted stains in various shades of brown and yellow conjured up the image of a creature worse than any animal, one that would lie in its own filth over and over again.

I gripped the carpet, meaning to fling it back on this mass of putridity, and I wish I had, but I was stopped by a glimpse that broke my heart. The oddments that the monster had torn and crumpled and wadded down for its comfort included a scrap of parchment bearing an unmistakable fragment of Chalcedor's marginalia: a tiny, winged fairy alighting on the tip of a monstrous phallus.

Poking and peeling a bit deeper, I came upon more scraps: some containing a word or a phrase in his hand, others a fragment of a drawing that might have been his. But I reached the point where I simply could not bear to root deeper into foulness, not without long-handled tongs, plugs for my nose and a bucket to puke in now and then. I had uncovered enough to know that the King of the Ghouls had found my missing boxes and used their precious contents, rat-like, to fashion his foul nest.

I slipped the scraps I had found into my pocket and sat back on my heels as I tried to sort out my anger and grief. That I had found Squirmodon's loot and solved the puzzle of his disappearance paled to insignificance beside this disaster, but I knew others would think my findings important. Much as I might hunger to track down the King and wring his neck — damned unlikely, of course, but that was my desire — I owed it to those others to bring back the truth.

My thoughts were interrupted by an ordinary sound, but surely the last one I ever expected in this place, and therefore all the more horrifying: a woman's voice in ordinary, animated conversation: "And *did* you?"

What answered might have been a voice, although it sounded at once like scraping metal, boorish flatulence and brutish growls. I could make out no clear words.

I got up hastily and raised my lantern. I had not noticed the other doorway to this room, a smaller one that gave onto stone stairs leading downward. The voices were ascending those stairs, and they were close. I hurried back to the treasure-room and shut the lantern completely; but in the utter blackness of the cellar, the light leaking from the seams was caught by every polished gem and gold surface to produce an effect worthy of an Imperial ball. Unwilling to put out my only light, I muffled the device in my cloak and put it aside. I snatched up Squirmodon's chain, the nearest thing to an iron weapon at hand, and held it ready.

" . . . expected of you," the woman was saying.

"Expected by whom? By *what*, I should say, by the sort of scum whose parents should have been drowned in a rain-barrel at birth? Vomikron Noxis, King of the Ghouls, indeed! The ghouls laugh at this — yes, yes, of course, they laugh at everything, but they laugh at this most of all — for I am ruler only to a festering of human perverts and malcontents, people I would have murdered for presuming to lick the dirt from between my toes when I was mortal, people who want to become ghouls, people who want me to eat their grandmother's nose so I can tell them where she lost her diamond ring, people who merely want to *seem* dangerous and wicked. This throne of ebony and crystal from the tomb of King Ash-clamith is too good for them, of course — skinning alive with twigs would be too good for them — but it pleased me to use it."

I heard a resounding thud. I assumed he had set down the piece of furniture he described. They had entered the room, but they had brought no light with them. They could see in the dark. How would I know if they spotted me? Near the door I hugged the wall of the treasure room with my back, willing my flesh to seep into the pores of the stone.

"Whatever you might think of them, they are your subjects, your only access to power in the world above. They've adored the Throne of Bones ever since your father had it made to his specifications."

"My grandfather was a drooling idiot, and nothing proves it more than that stupid throne."

"Your *father!*" she shrieked, and I believe she slapped him. "Does it make you feel less guilty about murdering him, calling him your grand-father?"

He paid her back for the slap somehow, because she screamed, and that unforgettable sound confirmed her identity as Lady Glypht.

"Father, grandfather, great-grandfather, too — if I had all three of him here, I'd kill him again. And laugh." He demonstrated his laugh. I prayed fervently that he would not do it again. "I don't know why I don't kill you."

"Because you love me. Because I am the only woman who could ever understand you. Because I didn't just give birth to you, I *created* you by concentrating the superhuman blood of the Glyphts in your veins."

"By making me a monster, you incestuous whore. The only thing I ever had to be proud of — even in this hideous state — was that my father was a Fand. And you would take even that little away from me with your disgusting stories, which are probably lies. If you love me so much, stop protecting that horrible boy and give him to me."

"Perhaps, Glyphtard, if you stop calling me names and ask me nicely, if you —"

She began to scream again. She mentioned her arm, so I guessed he was twisting it, but his own roars suggested she was getting back at him. It would be the ideal time to steal away, but I wanted to hear more, even though all the lies and family history made my head swim. I had thought at first this must be the son she never spoke of, but he had probably never existed beyond the lie she told me. This could only be Lord Glyphtard, who had somehow escaped death at the hands of Never-Vanquished.

The scuffle continued with much grunting and screaming and ghoulish laughter. I wondered how, considering his superhuman strength, such a fight could go on for so long. It struck me only by slow degrees of escalating nausea, compounded by my memory of embracing this despicable woman, that Lord Glyphtard and his mother were now vigorously pursuing an activity quite different from fighting.

"What's that smell?" he demanded.

"Smell? You mean you can smell something besides this filthy bed? How many times when you were a boy did I tell you — "

"Shut *up*, mother! Something's burning —"

"Yes, yes, and only you — unnhh! — can quench it —"

He was right. My cloak, draped over the lantern, was smoking. Even as I turned to look, a tongue of flame pierced the cloth.

I was lost. They might be distracted by the fire for a moment while I fled, but where would I flee? I never would have believed that Prince Fandiel could have told me a single worthwhile thing, but I now remembered a rule he had told me about combat: when caught unprepared by the enemy, it does no good to hide or run; the only choice is to attack with speed and ferocity.

I silently thanked Lady Glypht for mentioning that abominable bed. That was where they had to be. Snatching up the burning bundle without a thought for the pain, I dashed into the room and flung it at the bed. I gave Squirmodon's heavy chain a preliminary swing to build up speed and brought the massive collar down where I thought the ghoul-king's head might be. It connected solidly. I heard, and through the chain I even felt, the gratifying crunch of a well-broken skull. But by the light of the now furiously burning mattress, I saw that I had miscalculated: Lady Glypht had been on top.

The ghoul roared in a way I had never even imagined possible as he thrashed this way and that to fling his mother's bleeding body aside. The sound threatened not just my hearing but even my consciousness. Stunned and disoriented, I staggered to the stairs they had mounted and fell all the way down.

Attack was impossible now. My burning bundle was gone, my chain was gone, I had lost my staff along the way. Sobbing in mindless panic, I fled blindly down a slimy earthen tunnel that seemed to lead into the bowels of the earth. I knew that safety could not lie in this direction, that I was descending deeper into the king's own kingdom, but the elephantine trumpets of rage and grief at my heels drove me faster.

Soon I was splashing in cold water, and before I could even consider this fact, I was forcing my way forward in water to my knees, my hips, my chest. I had hesitated for just a fraction of a moment to take a deep breath when a hand as big and hard as a shovel-blade, tipped with claws like spikes, engulfed my shoulder as easily my own hand might have engulfed a pastry.

A nest of furious vipers, but no human throat, could have hissed the words that exploded against my ear in a blast of ghoulish breath: "My *mother!*"

I wrenched myself forward, oblivious to the tearing of my flesh, and got a blinding clout on the forehead from the roof of the tunnel. Nothing but water lay ahead, but I dived into it and hauled myself forward. My ankle was pierced by a claw, but I was able to rip it free.

On Weymael's map, the red lines had ended in the Miraga. But I could not be at all sure that those lines were accurate, or that this particular tunnel was even represented on that map. I might be swimming deeper into a pool with no exit. As the walls on either side expanded away from me, I no longer knew which way I was swimming.

The ceiling rose, too, but so did the water, and I could find no air at the top, only a confusion of waterlogged beams that might entangle me. I dived a little deeper, still pulling forward.

I had swum constantly in the Miraga as a boy. My playmates had been the sons and daughters of Ignudo bargemen, and I had often outdone their feats of underwater swimming. That was a long, long time ago, but I remembered the technique, and I remembered the insane determination that had pushed me beyond the excruciating pain of burning lungs and a throbbing head.

I could go on no longer, though. Death would be a blessing. I kicked myself upward. If I found no air at the top this time I would just have to breathe water, no matter the consequences. But the top was now a long way off. I did more twisting and thrashing than purposeful swimming as I tried to escape the overwhelming need to breathe.

I thought for a moment I was beholding the pure light of Cludd that his Sons are forever prattling about, but it was the sun of an autumn afternoon. I whooped in as much cold water as I did air in my first breaths, laughing in triumph even as I scanned the river around me for some sign of the pursuing ghoul. But he had not pursued. Perhaps some aspect of his disease made him shun water, as his smell had certainly attested.

I grew aware of a great commotion above me and saw that I had very nearly been run down by some noble's bloated pleasure-barge. The sailors threw down a rope with a loop that I managed to secure under my arms, and they hauled me on deck. Only when they began exclaiming over my wounds did I realize that I had indeed been badly wounded. I might have collapsed then if it had not been necessary to drop to one knee as gracefully as possible. I was face to face with the Empress herself.

Amazingly, she asked: "You are Dr. Porfat?"

"Er, yes. How — ?"

It became clear how she knew when I saw Prince Fandiel and my sister, Princess Fandyssa, among the glittering entourage at her heels. Nyssa was plainly struggling against an urge to throw herself on me, which probably would have been a breech of courtly decorum, while her husband looked oddly sheepish.

"What on earth have you been doing this time?" the Empress asked with a little laugh. "Fandiel has told us so many delightful Porfat stories — how you went to a lecture without your breeches, how you had to be rescued from the roof of the Institute after you wandered there while lost in thought — and I can't wait to hear what prompted you to take a swim in the Miraga with your clothes on."

I shot the prince a glare that he avoided as I struggled with the rope still around my chest. The pain in my right shoulder rendered that hand useless, but I thrust my left into my shirt and undid the clasp of the necklace.

I tried to perfect the gesture by rising to my feet, but I found that I could not. "Madame, I believe this is yours," I said, extending the emerald necklace to Her Imperial Majesty.

I'm sure I would have relished the look on my brother-in-law's face, but that pleasure was denied me as I lost consciousness.

*

Delirious with fever for a time, I enjoyed several peculiar conversations with the skeleton of the alleged ghoul that Weymael had stolen from my office. She reminded me that I had acquired her from an innkeeper named Dodont, who had put out her eyes for blaspheming the Sun God. It was the skeleton's contention that she had been praying, and that her prayer had moved the god to restore her human form after her death. This sounded plausible; the gods love to bestow useless gifts.

As soon as I came to myself — in the Empress's own cabin, no less, and nursed by her own hand — and gave a coherent account of my discoveries, Prince Fandiel was dispatched to recover Squirmodon's loot and exterminate the ghouls. Unhappily for both these missions, the fire that started in my cloak had burned down Gourdfoot's tavern and a dozen buildings around it, burying the former warehouse-cellar in a second layer of debris and blocking access to the treasure and the tunnels.

Amid the universal acclaim I enjoyed, nobody mentioned — not in my hearing, but it may have provided another "Porfat story" to amuse the court — that I had probably destroyed most of the stolen goods I found. The remainder would most likely be carried deeper into the Underworld by the King of the Ghouls before human workmen could reach it.

The workmen may find proof that Lady Glypht is dead, too; unless, of course, her son assuaged his grief by eating her corpse.

I declined Her Majesty's offer to recuperate in the palace under the care of her physicians, reminding her that I was no mean physician myself, and I was permitted to go home and nurse my wounds in private. Or so I thought. But that Feshard person had installed himself in my lodgings, having given them the same intolerable "tidying" he had given my office, and I was too weak to kill him.

Prince Fandiel, whose advice had saved my life, continued to demonstrate that he might not be a complete imbecile. Although still officially maintaining that Weymael Vendren's connections put him beyond the reach of the law, he had his men kick down the door of the palace and ransack the premises. There they uncovered enough evidence to have the necromancer burned ten times over; but the prince permitted himself to be bribed with the original manuscript of *Nights in the Gardens of Sythiphore*, which he then delivered to me.

That same day a bailiff appeared at my door to inform me that Gourdfoot was suing me for burning down his tavern.

V
How Zara Lost Her Way in the Graveyard

When Vendriel the Insidiator lay dead on the field at Lilaret, a ghoul ate the king's corpse and took his place among the living. After a time the mimic tried to shed his borrowed guise, but found that he could not. The Insidiator, although exhibiting some alarming new quirks, lived his life as if he had never died; the ghoul that had eaten him was seen no more.

> Moral: Eat no corpse whose spirit is stronger than your own.
> —Mopsard, *Fables for the Fabulous.*

Dolton Bose hadn't looked Sythiphorian, but his mother more than made up for it, a fish-faced witch who phlegmily gargled her speech.

"Thou hast fed long enough off the living," she spat at Zara by Dolton's waiting grave, where only they, a Cluddite preacher and some unhopeful creditors stood by, "now go feed off the dead! And may Gluttriel consume thee, whore!"

"Mother!" the preacher cried, uneasy from the first to find himself among such people and now thoroughly shocked.

Zara ran, trying to rub the tears from her eyes without smearing her paint. Mourning or not, she had to earn her supper. There was nothing to eat at their rooms in Potash Alley, and Dolton's mother surely wouldn't invite her home.

Worst of all, the horrible woman was probably right. Dolton had died from a catastrophic attack of the botch. She knew he was unfaithful, he was a swine, but she had most likely brought him the disease. Women often showed no symptoms.

She gasped, faltering. Perhaps running had brought on those symptoms. She was ill. She had never felt worse. She fell in the tall grass, retching, curling into a ball against the fire in her stomach.

Before the world folded in upon itself and fled down a long, dark tunnel, she had time to reflect that this was like no symptom of the botch she knew. It was more like a hunger that blotted out all thought, all feeling, that blotted out awareness itself, a hunger that could never be satisfied, not in a hundred years, nor two hundred.

*

A sweating moon hung over her. It looked deeply concerned, even frightened.

A fist pounded continuously on a door.

"Stop it, stop it, stop it!" the moon screamed.

"I'm not well, am I?" Zara whispered.

The moon withdrew, became the twitching face of a man. "Oh, *you're* all right. You look healthy enough."

His glance bounced over her naked body. She felt an urge to scrub herself, for suffering his shifty gaze was like being pelted with mouse-droppings. He, in turn, seemed appalled by the sight of her. When she sat up, however, she saw nothing to appall a normal man.

The pounding resumed.

"Cover yourself," he said.

"Why? I'm not cold."

"The boy. He's not used to nude women."

She laughed. "I thought they were a boy's constant study."

"I forgot. Things were different — *are* a bit different where you come from."

"Where am I?"

"In Crotalorn."

"Are you mad? I was born in this city. I live here."

"Forgive me, I'm not myself." She thought that he had been stricken by a mortal attack of asthma. It took her a moment to understand that he was laughing. When at last he could speak, he said, "You're not yourself, either."

"I must leave." She slid hastily off a bed that was rather splendid, although the bedding was frayed. The room might have been elegant without the dust and cobwebs. A massive statuette overlooking the bed, a cowled owl or an owlish priest, seemed oddly familiar.

"No, no, no," he said, pushing her back on the bed. Zara was taller than he, and strong, but she allowed herself to be pushed.

He asked, "What are you laughing at?"

"I just thought up a fine epitaph for myself."

"It's a bit late for that." The cryptic remark chilled her laughter. Before she could demand an explanation, he screamed: "Stop hammering! All in good time!"

"I want to see my mother!" a muffled voice wailed.

"His mother?"

"Yes. Explanations are difficult. You've been ill, very ill, perhaps more ill than anyone has ever been before. Rest now. We'll talk later."

"I don't want to rest. I want to go home." This was true. She crackled with life and energy. Even that terrible hunger, the last thing she remembered, had vanished. "Let me go. My patron, Dolton Bose, will pay you well for nursing me."

His mouth fell open. "I don't . . . Dolton *Bose?*"

"Yes. Why do you stare?"

"It's an unusual name. A unique name, I had thought. A Cluddite from Sythiphore?"

"His father's ancestors came from there a long time ago. His horrible mother was a recent import. But his father had been a Son of Cludd and gave him a Cluddite name. He never liked it."

"This is fantastic!" He suffered another long siege of giggles. "And he wrote, didn't he . . . under a different name?"

"You know him? He calls himself Chalcedor."

"I know something about him. You are that same Zara who stuck with him for so long?"

"It's strange enough you should ever have heard of *him*!" She wondered why he should gawk at her as if she had announced her true identity as Queen of the Frothoin.

"You were with him when he wrote *Nights in the Gardens of Sythiphore,*" he stated. "Do you know what happened to a tale he may have written for that book, 'The Abstemious Necrophage?'"

"That? It was horrible! I made him burn it. Where on earth did you hear about it?"

His pallor grew ghastly, his twitches more disruptive. "I owned the manuscript of the book once, but it was stolen. I still don't have it, even though the thief has paid dearly indeed." Although that seemed to amuse him, his voice grew suddenly cold as he demanded: "Did you persuade him to burn anything else?"

When her captor's eyes were not flitting here and there, when they bored into her with black intensity, she realized that he could be menacing. Dolton had no devoted following. His manic secretiveness would prompt him to tell any lie rather than admit he had slept well last night or planned to go for a walk this afternoon. Only a wizard might have known the details of his career and of their life together. She was forced to admit that this man, who had seemed only an absurd nuisance at first, looked like one.

"I persuaded him not to use my name in all his stories." She smiled wryly. "He used everything else, though."

He studied her deliberately from head to toe and back again. She was not unused to such evaluations, but this one made her flesh crawl, it was so thorough and so cold. She wouldn't have been surprised if he had produced one of Dolton's books and compared the written description with its subject.

It surprised her to learn, as it sometimes did when she was nervous, that she was still talking: " . . . and I would draw in the margins of his manuscripts to tease him, he said it was embarrassing to bring them to the bookseller with all the silly pictures cluttering —"

False concern throbbed in his voice as he interrupted, "I'm sorry to tell you, he's dead."

"Yes, I know. He couldn't have paid you anything, either. I really do want to leave, that's all. Please"

Slowly, like one instructing a child, he said, "He's been dead a long time."

"This morning. . . . May I —"

She meant to ask for a mirror, but the need for one was too urgent, and she had noted a pier-glass by the door. She sprang from the bed and dashed to it.

"That won't tell you much," he said.

"It tells me you're lying!" she laughed. Her hair was thick and lustrous, her eyes were undimmed, no unfamiliar lines marked her face. She knew she was thirty, and she looked no older. "So much for long-dead Dolton! So much for giving birth to some boy without remembering it! Forgive my bluntness, Sir, but you are a lunatic, and I must leave you to gibber alone."

"Wait —"

But she had unbolted the door and yanked it open. Her heart leaped. Impulsively, she cried, "Poll—!"

Perhaps she had meant to invoke the Sun God, for this golden boy was so like a vision of Polliel. His eyes yearned to her. She almost reached out to him. Then his face crumpled. Oddly, his obvious pain evoked no sympathy. It was the pain of a demon; she sensed that he meant to pass it on.

"This is not my mother!" he screamed. "This is a *woman!*"

She thought the man's impressive wealth of tics had been exhausted, but now he began to hum and do a little dance-step as he mumbled, "Yes, well —"

"You fool!" the boy screamed. "I'll kill you!"

"*Two* gibbering lunatics!" Zara said. "Forgive me, I must —"

As no child should have been able to do, the boy seized her and hurled her back into the room, where she landed hard on her rump.

His face softened, but she could no longer confuse that face with any sort of god's. Seeming to look not just into her eyes but through them, to some other person behind her, he said, "Don't worry, Mama. I'll put things right again."

*

It was odd that Weymael Vendren's ward should be called Polliard. Did she know him, and had his name been on the tip of her tongue? She had felt a certain warmth toward him then; but the more she tried to pin it down, the more it faded. His strength was unnatural, his coarse expression hinted of vice, he was a brat: she could never feel anything for such a creature but distaste. She knew that wizards could plant suggestions in one's mind, even control one's thoughts and actions with casual words, and perhaps Polliard, an apprentice wizard, had attempted that by calling her "Mother."

When Weymael left, she heard him conferring with another man, but the door was too solid for eavesdropping. She heard a bar sliding home — three of them, in fact —and this was confirmed when she found the door shut tight.

The six windows of the room were unlocked, but it was a long drop to the cracked flagstones. A tree had taken root among them and grew within reach of one window, but it was like a giant, limber weed that might not bear her weight. The wall itself, carved with fanciful designs, might offer purchase to the toes and fingers of a desperate woman, but it looked ready to crumble rottenly in places. She wasn't yet entirely desperate, but at least she had alternatives, however slim, to jumping out a window and trusting in Cludd.

Looking beyond the derelict garden and its wall to the surrounding slum, she wondered if Weymael had told the truth. Crotalorn was a big city, she hadn't seen every corner of it, but she knew of no *old* palaces of stone within its limits. The surrounding hills were abundantly forested, and until recently the nobles had contented themselves with mansions of wood, but with the accession of a Vendren king to the throne in Frothirot, that Tribe had succumbed everywhere to a passion for marble architecture. An old marble palace in the city of her birth was an anachronism; any kind of palace for a Vendren like Weymael, whose badges and tattoos were those of a minor knight, was an absurdity.

Wherever the palace stood (and she suspected Fandragord, ancient home of Vendren wickedness), it was ghastly, at least the garden was, and the ghastliest thing about it were the pale statues that no one had troubled to paint for uncounted years. They looked like ghouls; or, with their broken limbs and missing heads, like corpses gnawed by ghouls.

"Gluttriel consume them!" she whispered, as the pious should when even thinking of a ghoul. She felt the oddest twinge, but it passed.

Moving to a window at the front, she saw a group of statuary that shocked her at first and then delighted her. Wait until she saw Crespard Vulnavon and told him she knew that he had copied his celebrated *Hours* from the work of an ancient master! He would give her some lofty rigmarole about homage to the past, but Zara knew theft when she saw it. Most of the figures were fallen or dismembered, but their attitudes and arrangement were the same as those of the beautiful statuary ornamenting a marble pool in Princess Liame's garden. These sorry relics disported themselves around a sinkhole crusted with dead leaves.

She looked for the Hour she had posed for, Midnight, since Crespard had professed to see something dark and witch-like about her. What he had really seen about her, of course, was something moist and furry, which he had explored to the limits of his ability. Midnight had been broken off at the ankles in this older sculpture. She glimpsed something white in the weeds that could have been the rest of it. She was curious to see how the model from antiquity would compare with her face as Crespard had carved it, a very good likeness.

In fact the sculptor would be a good man to look up, and she might even forego the pleasure of calling him a thief. Dolton had been old enough to be her father, and Crespard was old enough to be Dolton's father. He was gnarled and bent from his work, often dusty and smelly from it, but rich from it, too. He wouldn't urge her to lie with other men, to be exhaustively quizzed later while he took notes, as Dolton professed his literary endeavors demanded. He wouldn't ask her to pay the landlord or the grocer or the barkeep with her body, either.

She had loved Dolton. He had taken her in when her family disowned her for killing her uncle — a stupid accident, really, but would they listen? — and he was always gentle and even-tempered when he was sober. Even when drunk, he could speak like a god as he paid the most elaborate but heartfelt compliments to her beauty, her wit and her discernment. He had never asked her to make love to anyone who repelled her.

She began to weep for him again, but she was distracted from her grief by an odd memory. She ran back to the window overlooking the original of Crespard's sculpture. His work had decorated the garden of a Vendren princess who evoked the word *cadaverous* from many who saw her. Zara thought her lean and beautiful as a rapier. "I didn't say she wasn't beautiful," Dolton said, "I just said she looked cadaverous, that's all."

At the party given to unveil Crespard's masterpiece, the cadaverous but beautiful princess ignored everyone else to lavish courtesy and attention on Zara. Skin stretched tight as a drumhead over the bone gave some justification to her unhappy epithet, but it was the fairest, most translucent skin Zara had ever seen; nor had any skull ever boasted such a living glory of auburn hair.

"You shouldn't let them call you such names, dear," Liame said.

Zara started guiltily, for she was thinking of the name so often applied to the princess, but she asked, "Who?"

"That jumped-up stonecutter-person with the freakish hands and forearms," she said, thus dismissing the foremost sculptor of the age, as Crespard assured everyone he was. "He called you the jolliest whore in Crotalorn, and you laughed."

"Well, that proves I'm jolly! What's wrong with that?"

"Even the noblest ladies offer their affections for money at the temple of Filloweela. Anyone who dared call them whores would be bundled off to the Lord Collector of Tears."

"Those ladies give the proceeds of their efforts to the Goddess," Zara said, "and I give them to Dolton Bose. It's a fine but very real distinction."

"You've been associating with artists and intellectuals for far too long," Liame sighed. All the while she kneaded Zara's thigh with a bony hand in a way that was not at all unpleasant. "You should insist on being called a courtesan, at least."

She whooped with laughter. Among the eyes drawn by this outburst — jolly was indeed an accurate word, for her humor was exuberant — were those of her patron, who smiled benignly on the progress of the princess's fingers.

"A *courtesan* would never lie with the likes of our landlord, Princess."

"Well, there you are! Don't you realize that a name is *everything*? Do you suppose anyone would want to read your precious Chalcedor's tales if he called himself Flubbard Gloob, or whatever his real name is? Call yourself a courtesan and you'll win the love of princes. Or at very least —" Zara was pleased to accept the tender kiss she offered — "of princesses."

"But how much do you suppose a prince — or a princess, for that matter — would pay such a courtesan?"

"You certainly have been spending too much time with those people. All artists ever think about is money. That's what separates them from the aristocracy, who never think of such matters, and so can free their minds for truly deep and beautiful thoughts. Poetry, painting, sculpture — all would be infinitely better if only the best people had the time to waste on such trifles."

Zara gently pushed Liame's hand back to her thigh. "If I may distract you for a moment from your deep and beautiful thoughts, how much would a princess pay?"

Liame laughed. "I love you!" she cried, kissing her again. "You're such a whore!"

"I adore you, Princess, and I'd almost be willing to do it for nothing but the pleasure and the honor. Almost."

"I have a certain special requirement," Liame said, withdrawing her hands and clasping them together, lowering her eyes as modestly as a girl in a temple less lively than Filloweela's. "It involves no real risk, it doesn't hurt much, but some find it repugnant. So I would be willing to pay very well."

"It doesn't hurt *much?*"

"Hardly at all. I would want to open — just the tiniest slit, nothing serious — a little vein in your wrist, perhaps, or in your ankle, and drink some of your blood."

Liame was right, a name was everything, and Zara remembered that this woman's name was Liame, Princess of the House of Vendren, Beloved of Death's Darlings, Mistress of Tigers, Initiate of Sleithreethra, to cite only its short version: a name to make intractable maniacs quail. And this woman was proposing a deed that witches, most of whom were Vendrens, did; that ghouls — may Gluttriel consume them! —did; that revenants and marticoras and other black agents of the night did, a deed that might destroy Zara's spirit or bind it in thrall.

"No!" she cried, springing to her feet. "Never!"

"Oh, don't be such a baby. How do you know you won't like it —"

"*No,* what?" Dolton asked, coming up to slip his arm about Zara's waist. "*Never,* what?"

She was proud of him for standing up for her so boldly. But, as was the case with so many of Dolton's proud moments, it swiftly degenerated. He was drunk, and he launched a tirade against aristocrats, against sexual deviants, against any number of grievances that had nothing to do with the present situation. He was thrown off the grounds, spared a beating only by Zara's intercession. She was asked to stay, but she left, too.

She never told Dolton, but after the encounter had preyed on her mind for several days, she returned to Liame's fine palace on Vendren Hill. She paused by the fountain, wondering if she really looked anything like the magnificent figure of Midnight frozen with the others in the complex steps of a never-ending dance.

"It's you," the princess said, gliding up beside her unnoticed. "I come out and pray to you every night at that hour."

"I don't think I should do it for money." Zara was careful in articulating her long thoughts on the subject. "I want to do it because I love you, and to give you pleasure. It must be only once. It should be special."

"It is."

"And I want you to promise that you won't use it to bewitch me or enslave me to your will."

"As you have me?" Liame said, but saw that her flippancy displeased. "No, of course not. I need it, you see, to draw strength, because of an illness I have. A chronic condition, actually, not at all dangerous to anyone else, but it's the only thing that gives me relief and refreshment. You won't suffer for it in any way."

"And don't ever say a word to Dolton."

"That is by far the easiest of your conditions."

As Liame had promised, the drawing of blood hardly hurt at all. It was only a very small part of the experience, though it gave the princess great pleasure. Toward morning, when Zara concluded that it had all been fun but, generally speaking, she would rather make love to a man, Liame began slowly to construct an elaborate masterpiece of the senses that ended with Zara's transfiguration.

Having squandered the rhetoric of rapture on her paying customers, Zara could only murmur, "Oh, my."

"Listen to me," the Vendren princess said. She had been sucking at Zara's ankle again, and she paused to wipe the blood from her mouth and lick her fingers. "Contrary to your fears, I am yours now. If you ever need me, you have only to call me, for I am bound to you forever. Do you understand?"

"Yes," she lied. She silently congratulated herself on not asking the one question that had been uppermost on her mind all night: *Are you really alive?*

She could have sworn she hadn't spoken aloud, but Liame said, "Only insofar as you make me so."

*

Gazing down at the ruined fountain, she made a disturbing discovery. Weymael's garden, if one could give that name to this rubbish-heap, was laid out exactly as Liame's had been. The fountain and its pool stood in the same relation to the palace. From what she could see of this decayed building, it seemed to duplicate that palace. If she leaned out the window, she would see the spot corresponding to the one where she had held her conversation with the princess on a stone bench.

She leaned out the window. A stone bench stood far beneath it. By willing it, she could almost see the figures of two women, one alive and one perhaps not, engaged in mutual seduction.

"And who's alive now, I wonder!" she cried, and she laughed until the sound of her laughter began to frighten her.

She cast her eyes wildly over the ramshackle buildings huddled beyond the wall. It was much too easy to discern the shape of Vendren Hill beneath the jumble, to replace the tenements with stately homes and temples.

But those homes could have fallen, the garden could have grown, the palace could have decayed, only if the Hours had pursued their dance around the fountain a thousand times, ten thousand times, ten times ten thousand times —

"No!" she screamed.

*

Zara believed she had dozed off for only a moment, and she reached out to reassure herself that the princess still lay beside her. She was eager to share her scary dream about a far-future age when the palace on Vendren Hill would house a lunatic-asylum.

Liame was gone, but Zara's sense of her presence was strong. When she fumbled among the bedclothes, thinking the princess might be playing a game with her, she stirred a mouldy smell from threadbare cloth. She was still trapped in that nightmare.

Now that feeble moonlight concealed its dirt and decay, she knew that the room was the same one where she had visited Liame. She recognized the staring, stylized owl that had overlooked the princess's bed. Perhaps its looming presence helped to account for the powerful impression that she was not alone.

"Gluttoria," a voice whispered, and she screamed, clenching herself into a quaking ball at the head of the bed. The voice continued, "Can't you see me?"

It was the voice of the boy, not the man, but that was no comfort: he was strong enough to overpower her, old enough and strange enough to harbor any of those foul urges of which she had been warned by women grown old in the service of pleasure.

"Of course I can't see you! What did you say? What did you call me?"

"Gluttoria." He seemed to choke on the name, as well he should have. It was an absurdity derived from the name of the God of Death, at once an insult to her and a blasphemy to the god.

"That's as foolish as naming someone 'Polliard,' and even more offensive," she said

"It once suited your sense of humor." Did he have an odd laugh, like his patron? Or could it be that the brat was repressing sobs?

"I never had a *ghoulish* sense of humor." She added hastily, "Gluttriel consume them!"

He yelped. Perhaps her surprise at this and the shrillness of his cry accounted for the sudden queasiness that she herself felt.

"Mama —" he began.

"Don't call me that! That's far worse. Once and for all, I am not your mother." Unaccountable tears welled up when she thus disowned him. Why should it pain her to be honest with this demonic child? She summoned up her coldest voice and said, "Go away!"

She screamed when he scrambled out of the shadows and onto the bed beside her. She tried to pull away, but his embrace was unbreakable as he babbled urgently in her ear: "Mama, Vomikron Noxis wants to kill me.

He hates me for taking you away from him, but he hates me even more for my human appearance, and you're the only one who can intercede for me. Lady Glypht pretends to be my protector, she tells everyone she's my grandmother, but she only does that to annoy him, and Weymael Vendren is an ass. Please, Mama, I need your help!"

This was spoken most plaintively, and she had the unpleasant feeling that it would all make perfect sense if she allowed her grip on the real world to falter. She hardened her heart against him.

"Go away, I said! Better still, let me go. I don't know any of you people, I don't know what you're talking about, and I don't want to know you. I want to go home!"

"Unlikely," he sighed, releasing her and sagging back on the bed. With one of the jarring changes of tone that characterized these mad people, he said casually, "You must be hungry. Shall I call for the servant?"

She supposed she was, but that was a minor concern. The servant would bring light with the food, allowing her to locate a suitably solid candlestick or fire-iron. Life had taught her that the best defense is an unexpected blow from behind.

"Phylphot!" Polliard called.

The door opened and a darker shadow entered. Squeaks and rattles suggested the wheeling of a decrepit cart. That all this should take place without any light hinted of some abnormality beyond madness, but she kept the fear from her voice as she demanded, "Am I supposed to eat in the dark?"

"It once pleased you well enough. Phylphot, bring light."

The servant fetched candles that revealed him for a shaggy-haired tatterdemalion whose appearance would have blunted her appetite even if his smell hadn't. As he fussed with the setting, he destroyed her desire for food completely by thrusting his free hand inside his breeches, the better to scratch himself.

She averted her eyes to Polliard, who positively leered at the table, who advanced toward it by hesitant steps as if struggling against an irresistible hunger.

"This is a very special meal. This will set everything right, Mama. Please — *please* eat before I. . . ."

"I can't remember when I've so much enjoyed getting the fixings for you, Master Polliard," Phylphot said. "That arrogant buffoon —"

"Enough! *Eat*, Mama!"

The candlesticks were too delicate to serve as weapons, but she might use a knife from the table. She smiled at the servant as she uncurled herself from the bed. Disgusting he might be, but he was the first male here who had looked at her with anything like normal appreciation. He blushed and giggled, distracted, as she had hoped, from whatever she decided to do.

"You'll love the brains, I'm sure," he said, and he sidled close enough to let her know that he was not the source of the worst odor in the room. Could it be the food itself? "*He* certainly thought they were the best part."

"Eat," Polliard whispered, creeping closer.

The ornate, silver cover of a tray might be her best weapon. If she hit Polliard square between the eyes with the edge, then turned and struck the servant, she might get a running start down the stairs.

Weymael Vendren appeared at the door, blocking her exit, and said as if criticizing her plan, "I don't think it's going to work."

"What do you know about it?" Polliard cried.

"I? What do I know? I'm only the one who found your precious bones in the first place, who planned and executed their theft, who assembled all the graveyard earth and shit and semen and other filthy ingredients, the unborn child and the blood of a Pollian priestess, the rare weeds that no one ever heard of, who calculated the exact moments for fetching them and putting them together, who had the courage to speak those words from the scroll I found beyond Cephalune and achieved — look, damn you, look at her! — a perfect result —"

She doubled over, retching. He must be talking about the stinking food they had tried to serve her in the dark.

"Now see what you've done?" Weymael demanded. "Her equilibrium is more delicate than a butterfly's wing —"

"Damn her equilibrium!" Polliard slobbered now, more like a ravenous dog than a human. "A filthy *woman* —doesn't know food when she smells it —"

The boy abandoned his fearful struggle for self-control and attacked the table. He ruined her plan by flinging the cover of the tray to the far end of the room with a resounding clang. The smell that he released was even worse than could be explained by the ingredients Weymael had cited, although the contents of the tray were different: the innards of a large animal, a raw heart and liver and intestines, all of it about to liquefy in greenish decay. Abnormally larger than any pig's or sheep's, a brain festered amid the foulness.

She had mastered her nausea because she had no choice. Before the boy could begin gobbling up this horror, she seized the laden tray and hurled it at Weymael. Reacting like a normal person for the first time, he screamed, furiously batting the filth from himself. Polliard fell on him, lapping and biting greedily at the mess on his face and clothing.

The way was clear. Weymael had blundered away from the door, flapping his hands and jittering aimlessly. His face was already clean, although it now bled from the incidental bites his ward had inflicted. As for Polliard, he squatted in the spillage from the tray, stuffing it with both hands into his deceptively capacious mouth.

She hurled herself toward the darkness beyond the door, but she had forgotten Phylphot. He tripped her, fell on her from behind and, with an economy of effort that testified to considerable practice, twisted her arm up behind her back while simultaneously shoving down his breeches. She screamed and tried awkwardly to claw his eyes with her free hand as she clenched her sphincter tightly against a searing intrusion.

"Damn you, damn you!" Weymael screamed, kicking his servant repeatedly without much effect. "Are you crazy? Don't you know what that is?"

"Yes," Phylphot grunted, savagely twisting a thick handful of her hair and wrenching her arm even higher. "It's my payment for butchering your fat fool, which you seem to have overlooked. It's the nicest bag of meat I've ever seen. It's a tight, dry hole, and I want to get into it! Leave me alone, you idiot!"

"Yet another worthy son of Quodomass Phuonsa!" Weymael cried cryptically to the ceiling. "Oh, if only I had never met that swine!"

He kicked Phylphot's ribs more viciously, but he only drooled more, grunted more, and thrust harder. The pain of the unnatural intrusion was worse than any that the degenerate could inflict on her arm or her hair, and Zara refused to stop bucking and twisting away from it, cursing all the while.

"Polliard!" she screamed in her ultimate desperation, but her self-styled son, crouching an arm's-length away, only added nervous giggles to the disgusting sounds he was making with his food. Remembering a promise that had once been made in this very room, she grasped at a straw that seemed so flimsy that she couldn't the muster the confidence for a proper scream and all but whispered: "Princess Liame! Help me!"

"You stupid bitch!" Weymael roared, and now he abandoned his assault on Phylphot to kick Zara in the ribs. "Do you have any idea of the hell I've gone through to keep that impossible woman out of my home? And now you've probably . . . oh, no."

The candles blazed up suddenly and then went out, but this phenomenon had no effect on anyone but Weymael, who stopped kicking her and kept perfectly still. Phylphot's ground on, Polliard ate with undiminished gusto.

"Your Highness," Weymael muttered. "I had no idea, really, if I had known —"

Phylphot screamed. This might have been his usual style, for the sound coincided with a pathetic dribble into her torn rectum, but it was also accompanied by a sharp, cracking noise behind her, as of a branch being snapped. The rapist began to jerk and flail wildly as he lost control of his bowels and bladder. He did not resist when she shoved him off and staggered to her feet. She could not at first imagine how the fallen man managed the incredible feat of simultaneously presenting both his slack face and beshitten breech to the moonlight.

Tears of rage and nausea oddly distorted the moonlight, rendering one patch paler than the rest. It was this patch that seemed to murmur with Liame's voice, "You should have called me sooner."

Unable to credit that a moonbeam was speaking to her, Zara wiped her eyes clear and tried vainly to find another source for the voice. She yearned to run into the arms of the princess and beg her to make everything right again. "Where are you?"

"Where, unhappily, I am adjured to cease from troubling," Liame sighed, her voice no more substantial than her shape. "You must run now, for I can stay no longer to protect you."

Phylphot was dead, she could get no satisfaction from him, but Weymael cowered on his knees, sobbing obsequiously to the phantom and citing the elaborate genealogy that connected them. She knew she should leave while she had the chance, but she wanted to hurt him first. If she could lift the owl by the bed, it would make a good club.

But another presence blocked her way. It had to be Polliard, because it squatted where he had, it scavenged among the filth as he had, but it was no longer a boy. Its pallid bulk seemed larger even than a man's. Unwilling to face any further horrors, she turned and fled the room without even thinking to thank Liame.

No one pursued her, luckily, as she picked her blind way through the junk-shop that had been Liame's palace. She decided she had time to wade through the dead leaves and scrub herself in the questionable waters of the fountain. Her eyes were drawn irresistibly to the fallen figure of Midnight in the weeds. Once, twice she started toward it, then thought better of the impulse.

She had almost worked up the courage necessary to examine the face when something lurched out the palace to the shadowed portico. It was the pale giant that had seemed to replace Polliard. She ran.

*

She no longer questioned that she had been wrenched into the future. The cold stones under her feet and the throbbing pain of Phylphot's legacy gave continuous assurance that this was no dream. She surprised herself with her calm acceptance of fate, but she saw no point in weeping. The addled wizard and his kept boy could not be typical of Crotalorn's new denizens; she would still have a trade. Until the gods revealed the reason for suspending their laws on her behalf, she would watch and listen.

"Hide thy shame, woman!"

Some things hadn't changed. The cheap, leather-and-bronze armor of this Cluddite were like those of the preacher at Dolton's grave. Even the mad, starved look, a scary mask with a bewildered boy behind it, was the same.

"I was walking up and down the streets in search of the wicked, and lo, it was granted unto me to find a woman flaunting her sinful enticements for all to see," he preached, more to the blank walls of the street than to her, and he alarmed her thoroughly by drawing his hand-me-down sword. "She shall lure no more into her pit of foulness, Father Cludd, for thy lowliest servant, Cluddax Umbren, will thrust into her bare body with holy iron, again and again, tearing out the sources of her shame and stamping —"

She had often wished that Dolton would not quote at extravagant length from *The Book of Cludd* when he was drunk, but now she thanked him for it. "'All thy worldly goods, save only thy sword, are on loan from the poor,'" she quoted sternly, and added: "So please give me back my cloak."

It was hard not to laugh as he goggled at her and said, "It doesn't *mean* that!"

"It *says* that. Either give me your cloak or take me to your reverend lord commander, that I may tell him how Cluddax Umbren quibbles with Scripture. That I may tell him how he refuses to clothe a naked woman so he can gawk at her. And put that up. 'Show not thy sword to the wretched and the hungry, lest I show thee My fist.'"

Confounded by a woman who could quote his Book, Cluddax tried to take off his cloak and sheathe his sword at the same time, dropping both. He tripped, but managed to gather up the rough woolen garment and extend it at extreme arm's length to a creature who probably alarmed him more than would a talking cat. She left him struggling manfully to pick up his sword, apparently unaware that he was standing on it.

*

She knew that she could find food and shelter at one of the temples on the other side of the Miraga, but her feet kept her on this side. They took her around Dreamers' Hill to Hound Square. The closer she got the more fearful she became, but she could put no name to her fear. She told herself that the square would be a good landmark for finding Potash Alley, where she had lived, and that was why she followed this route; but she could think of no good reason for going to Potash Alley, either.

The square was still dominated by a very ancient statue of a hound, crude by the standards of her day. Most people claimed it had been erected to honor a dog whose barking had saved the city from a surprise attack, but Dolton said it was really an idol that the Frothoin had worshipped before the true gods revealed themselves: Yelkeh, the Hound Goddess. The snarling beast seemed the center of the indefinable menace that filled the place, and she kept an uneasy eye on it as she crept around the edges of the square, still wondering why she had come here.

The buildings were different. As elsewhere, brick had largely replaced wood, and the facades seemed unduly austere without the fanciful carvings that had once rioted along the streets. Perhaps it was unfair to judge the people of this new world by their architecture, but it seemed fit for a race of lock-stepping blockheads.

She stayed off the new, brick-paved footway, keeping her feet on the familiar cobblestones, smoother now than they had been. They belonged to her world, and she willed them to convey some message through their feel or sight. But they were just cold stones, and not very pretty to look at.

Looking up, she gasped. She stood by a lamp-post, and it was this, not the statue, that concentrated the menace in Hound Square. She had the irrational fear that the post would seize her and drag her up, screaming, to hang from its cap. She couldn't breathe.

Turning to run, she collided with a very large man and knocked him down in the gutter. She fell sprawling on top of him.

"You!" she cried.

"Indeed it is, madame. What led you to that remarkable deduction?"

She scanned a face as familiar as Dolton's or Crespard's, but a face she could put no name to.

"I don't know," she said. "Weren't you kind to me once? Didn't you look after me during a long illness?"

Weymael had told her she'd been ill, but she'd had no memory of him at all by her bedside until today. She remembered this man gazing down at her with sympathy, talking to himself and . . . *picking up her head?* Oddly, this image held no fear. If it had happened — and of course it could not have happened — it had been unremarkable in its context. She must be recalling a bizarre dream.

"I'm sure I would have been kind to you," he said. Unsurprisingly, for he was a man, he had quickly discovered that she wore nothing under her cloak. She believed she had found the new protector she badly needed, and his words confirmed this: "May I do you any sort of kindness now? You seem to be in distress."

"I am. My patron was buried this morning, and I have no one. . . ." She tried to affect tears and found herself shedding real ones. The stranger left off caressing her to give her a reassuring hug. "I was kidnapped from the cemetery by a vile man, raped by his servant. I don't know where to begin."

"You don't need to. I had a peculiar experience myself today, but I won't burden you with it. I would be obliged, though, if you would let me get up."

Her heart sank when she got a better look at him. She had thought he was wearing the ceremonial gown of a priest or royal deputy, but he was draped in a piece of yellowed linen with tassels and fringes that might have been a tablecloth. His feet were bare, too. She had to laugh. She had run for protection into the arms of a deranged derelict.

"Pardon my appearance," he said a bit stiffly. "I hadn't known I would have the honor of meeting a female Son of Cludd."

She laughed even harder at the thought of how she herself must look, and it drew a smile from him. In the next instant he scared her by seizing her jaw in his hand and peering intently as he traced the outlines of her cheekbones and temples. She was again struck by the odd picture of this man picking up her head.

"Amazing," he said. "Oh. Forgive me. I'm a professor of anatomy, you see, a student of bones, and the structure of your skull bears an incredible resemblance —"

"There you are, you wretched boy! Bring her and come home with me now."

The stranger ignored this, unable to comprehend that anyone would address him this way, and in the next instant he was staggered by a blow from behind to his shoulder. His assailant, she saw, was Weymael Vendren. She set herself to run.

"You, Sir!" The stranger roared, his face flaming, his jowls puffing out with fury at the sight of Weymael, whom he seemed to know. "You dare to lay hands on me? To call me *boy?* If there be any shred of you left to burn for your crimes when I have done with you, I will arrange it."

This threat brought out the worst of Weymael's twitches, but he stood his ground and said, "Stop this nonsense and come home, you fool. And bring your damned mother with you."

"I'm not *his* mother, either," Zara cried. "And why you —"

"You don't know what you are, you stupid whore, or what he is, so just shut your auxiliary cunt —"

"I will thank you not to address a lady in that style, Sir," the stranger said to Weymael, who was now lying flat on his back with a bloody nose.

"*Who smites the Tyger?*" Weymael hissed, quoting the slogan of the Vendrens as he drew a sword from under his cloak.

"Smite? *Smite?* Smiting is for men, Sir, we Fands have a simpler way of dealing with obnoxious toads who hop from a privy!" the stranger cried, and he ignored the sword to deal Weymael a ferocious kick in the face. He then fell on him with one knee foremost, wrenched the sword from his hand and hurled it spinning across the square. He slapped his face forehand and back until Weymael screamed for mercy.

He let Weymael up, propelling him faster on his way with another kick. The man was neither young nor handsome, Zara reflected, but he was wonderful to behold with his gray hair frizzed out like a storm-cloud, a picture of godlike wrath as he shook his huge fist after the fleeing wizard.

"When at last I get a chance to kick that rascal down the street, I'm not wearing boots. Come into that tavern with me, we'll have something to eat and drink."

She thought they would immediately be thrown out the door of the Plume and Parchment in their ragamuffin costumes, but the innkeeper, alone in a dim room that looked as if it had recently been visited by a horde of enraged apes, knew her companion. "Dr. Porfat!"

His shock was mixed with pleasure. Hers was not when he moved into the light. She cried: "You!"

"Don't mind her, Dodont," the doctor said. "That's how she greets everyone."

Dodont eyed her suspiciously, but her attention had been seized by a bronze bust smiling wistfully on the room from behind the bar. She knew that face, too. If she had been brought into the future only this morning, how could she recognize so many people? Why did they not recognize her? She could make no sense of it. She wanted to flee, but her feet refused to move toward the door. Outside, she would be alone with the thin, sinister lamppost. She resisted the urge to peer through a window and verify her fear that it had crept closer to the inn.

"Have you spoken to the prince?" Dodont asked the doctor. "He's quite beside himself, and one of him is too many, if you'll forgive me, certainly too many for the peaceful conduct of my business. He tore the place apart."

"Why?"

"Because your bloody cloak was found in an alley nearby. You'd been in here earlier discussing the recovery of a stolen skeleton with a villain called Phylphot, a reputed grave-robber. Everyone assumed he'd murdered you."

"That name is not unfamiliar," Porfat said. He fingered one of his tassels. "He robbed me, perhaps. That must be why I'm wearing this thing."

"But that was *last week*," Dodont said. "Have you been running around the city in a tablecloth since then?"

"See here, Sir!" Zara and Dodont both jumped when the doctor slammed his sizable palm on the counter. "I came here for food and drink, not foolish prattle and vexing questions. Bring us *pflune*."

"Are you crazy? No, no, Doctor, forgive me, of course, you're not. *Pflune* it is." He clanked his way among bottles beneath the counter. "We don't get much call for that."

"I hope you don't mind," he said to Zara. "I acquired a taste for it from some Ignudo friends."

"I've drunk it," she said. In fact it was what Dolton Bose drank when he had no money for anything better, which was most of the time.

She wanted to ask him how he knew Phylphot and Weymael. She believed he could have explained some of their more obscurely unpleasant remarks. He might be able to determine how she knew Dodont and the man depicted in the bust over the bar; and how she knew him. But she was sure that none of the explanations would make her happy, and she shoved her questions forcibly aside as they talked of nothing in particular, settling at last on the subject of her price. Since he had no money with him, and she had to conceal her ignorance of its value, she trusted him far more than she would have liked.

*

She woke from a horrible dream of crawling in tunnels and feeding on the sort of filth Polliard had served her. She clutched desperately at the man beside her in bed, who turned out to be Dr. Porfat. He had apparently been lying awake.

"You seem to have dreamed you were a ghoul," he said when she had poured out a confused stream of terrible images.

"Gluttriel consume them!" she cried, and she was alarmed by the sudden spasm that racked him.

"I have long tried to make a study of ghouls — and please, my dear, don't use that superstitious archaism again, I think it must remind me unpleasantly of my demented grandmother — but I discovered that the only people who could give me first-hand information about them were people I couldn't stand. That's had a chilling effect on my life's work." He sighed heavily. "I keep having a strange dream, too, that I'm a boy trapped inside a mountainous prison of flesh. I can't convey the rage and terror I feel in this dream, over and over again. . . . Whenever it seems I am about to find the way out, I wake."

She laughed, her fingers encircling flesh that had, incredibly, risen once again. "That was no dream. In fact, I'm convinced you must be a boy in disguise."

"Believe me, it's no laughing matter," he laughed. "But it was only a dream."

VI
The Tale of the Zaxoin Siblings

My brother-in-law was lucky to have been born a prince. Whenever I felt the impulse to kick him down the stairs, I would recall the penalty for high treason.

"You've been studying all your life, Doctor," he said. "Isn't there a danger your skull will explode if you don't let some knowledge leak out for the benefit of others?"

He would rap the table when he barked at his own jokes, signaling everyone to join in. Everyone did, except my sister, Nyssa, who gave me a wry look; and the woman for whom he was dragooning my services, Zephreinia Sleith, who favored me with a smile that seemed sympathetic.

I didn't laugh, either. I said, "I allow some of it to *leak out* during my thrice-weekly lectures at the Anatomical Institute." I avoided Nyssa's eye as I said this, for she knew I had been neglecting my duties at the Institute for several months now while trying to recover from the queer mental effects of a would-be murderer's attack. I was able to face her again as I added truthfully: "Some leakage may also be perceived in the eight books and two-hundred-odd papers I've written."

"Oh, that." Prince Fandiel waved as if consigning my life's work to a bonfire, which I supposed he could do. "You study medicine to help people, Doctor, not to scribble about bones. How many bones are there? You must by now have written two or three papers for each one. You remind me of that story by what's-his-name, that writer, about the fellow who didn't do something because he was always doing something else." He rapped the table again in case anyone failed to hear his raucous guffaws.

"Forgive me for mentioning it," Zephreinia murmured in my ear.

She hadn't mentioned it to me, she'd mentioned it to my sister, who had then seated her beside me at dinner. I had nothing against examining her, especially since her Frothiran frock had allowed me to make a nearly complete visual examination already; but I objected to being seated next to a lovely young woman who batted her eyelashes at me while she hung on my every word, then to be advised by our host that she wanted medical advice. I objected to being conspired against.

Unfortunately for my principles, Zephreinia had captivated me. She came from Omphiliot, dreariest of provincial cities. She had told me early in our conversation that her husband remained at his post there as Inspector of Aqueducts. In Crotalorn no more than a month or so, she had adopted a fashion that would have earned her a day in the pillory back home. It revealed an adventurous spirit, to say nothing of splendid breasts.

"Oh, no, it's not your fault," I said, though of course it was, but it's hard to be stern while simpering. "It's just that I, I study, you see, I write — " Here she folded the fan that had provided her with a modicum of concealment and touched it to the sensuously intriguing pad of flesh beneath her lip in a pose of pert attentiveness. I forgot whatever else it was that I did with my dull life. "What I mean, a physician more experienced in your body — in examining the human body, I mean, not specifically *your* breasts —"

"But no other physician, however experienced he may be, has written Porfat's *Etiology of Ghoulism.*"

"You mean *Polliard's,*" I laughed, and then realized I had surpassed my embarrassing slip of the tongue with a truly idiotic blunder. I cast my eyes furtively at the prince, fearing he would soon be regaling everyone with the best "Porfat story" of all, that I had forgotten my own name, but he was absorbed in explaining religion to a priest.

Ignoring Zephreinia's bewilderment, I said, "You know of that work? But surely you don't think that you —"

"No, no, no." Her tone was uncommonly somber, but she remembered to laugh as she added: "No. But the book displays such a masterful intellect, such a firm grasp of provocative material — and above all, such nearly godlike sympathy for the poor creatures afflicted with so foul an ailment, that I know you can help. Please, Dr. Porfat."

I hadn't the heart to tell her that my godlike sympathy had withered since writing that book under the strain of actually encountering ghouls. I said, "Well, if you'd care to come —"

"Come to my place, please, in Sekris Square. Tomorrow at noon?"

The prince was rapping and barking again, but this time I hadn't even heard his joke, probably at my expense. I told her I'd be there.

*

Feshard was born a servant, so there was no good reason for not kicking him down the stairs, though I never did it. I sometimes wondered why not.

"Shall I go out and buy you a sword?" he asked.

"What? What are you babbling about now? Where have you hidden my bag?"

"Attractive women of thirty or less are the only exceptions to your rule against practicing medicine. Since it's unlikely that Princess Fandyssa would subject any young, unmarried woman to your company at dinner, the woman you sat next to, and who begged you to have a peek up her dress, must be married. In the unhappy event you'll have to fight a duel with her husband, you'll need a sword, and you don't have one. Shall I go buy one? Or, better still, shall I send your regrets to the lady and refer her to Dr. Beliphrast?"

"Be buggered with your sword and your regrets, Sir, you and Dr. Beliphrast both! What have you done with my bag, you insolent hound?"

"I put it in the sedan chair that's been waiting for you this past hour, as you instructed."

Not trusting myself to speak further, lest I should use harsh language, I stamped down the stairs to the street, where I discovered that I had forgotten my hat. As I trudged back, I met Feshard loitering down. He held out my hat with an outrageous display of patience.

"Trust me, Sir, you'll regret this," he said, and I broke my resolution against harsh language.

*

I tried to think when I had last been such a fool, and I had to admit it was the last time a pretty woman had taken any notice of me. Such insights are discomfiting to a man in his fifties, if he has the brains to know that few men improve with age. I had once looked forward to the day when the combination of a comely face, a trim figure and a kind word would not enfeeble my intellect and enslave me like a demon's energumen, but that day had yet to dawn.

Filloweela had not been kind to me. That Goddess is supposed to oversee the distribution of beauty, and she had omitted to send me any at all. And love, her other area of responsibility — I won't vex you with prattle about a particularly lovely look in a particularly lovely eye, or about the way the sun struck a certain shade of hair on a certain day in a certain place. I have had two great loves; one died and the other fled. Those sorrows in my early life determined me to get on with my work and put my dealings with the Goddess on a cash basis.

I turned my thoughts deliberately, as I seldom did, to Zara, whom I maintained in a cozy suite at the Plume and Parchment. She was a handsome woman with a keen intelligence and an exuberant sense of humor, who would do anything I wished and pretend to enjoy it. Some thought her eccentric for affecting the speech and manners of an earlier age, but I have been accused of the same quirk. She liked me well enough for myself and even boasted of me, her patron who wrote books.

Then why had Zephreinia's praise been so important, why did I crave her further approval, why did I want to look into her eyes when I could direct my chairmen to the tavern and gaze into Zara's, which were equally bright and equally blue? I didn't know, I would never know, I would go to the grave with some such futile question on my quivering lips and an equally futile tingle in my desiccated loins.

*

Sekris Square had been so renamed for one of the Lord Admiral's victories, but most Crotalorners thought the Lord Admiral was a homicidal halfwit and persisted in calling it Peartree Square. Because Zephreinia had used the new name, and because each word she had spoken was a delight I yearned to recapture, I directed the chairmen to Sekris Square. They consequently assumed I was a tourist and tried to charge me twice the usual fare when I alighted. This led to hard words.

"Dr. Porfat, what are you doing?" Zephreinia cried, running halfway down her stairs as words became blows. She diverted my attention fully, permitting one of the cowards to send me sprawling. "Zephryn, come quickly, help him!"

"I need no help, lady!" I called. Invigorated by her presence, I kicked one of them off his feet and regained my own. The other tried to attack me from behind, but I fell back to pin him against the fallen chair with my not inconsiderable bulk.

"No, please! Help me! Please, Sir, I'm sorry, don't crush me!" the chairman sobbed.

"Which one shall I help?" a young man asked Zephreinia. He spoke through his nose in the annoying way of Omphiliot, and I took a dislike to him even before he said: "The poor lout beneath the whale is getting the worst of it. Do you fancy him?" The first of the thieves, seeing the newcomer's naked sword, ran off, pausing to fling oaths and cobblestones. I kicked the other on his way.

As Zephreinia fretted and exclaimed over me and I dusted myself off, I covertly studied the young man with the sword. The shadows under his eyes and the slack-lipped sneer that seemed his habitual expression suggested unhealthy habits, as did his boneless, can't-be-bothered-to-stand-up slouch against the railing of the areaway. Worst of all, for I assumed he was Zephreinia's lover, he was more handsome than I had ever been. It consoled me slightly that his bones would pay for his idle posing, and that he would be a twisted wreck by the time he was my age, if drink or his loose tongue failed to kill him first.

"Doctor, this is my brother, Zephryn Phrein," Zephreinia said, and no words she had yet spoken gave me such unalloyed joy. They dote upon the Z-sound in the former kingdom of the Zaxoin, and I had not realized that the names of this brother and sister made the kind of match that parents of a whimsical bent find irresistible. I embraced and pummeled the young man as I gripped his hand. In my elation it took me a moment to grasp that he detested this.

We went in to a lunch where the sister flirted, the brother sulked and I beamed on both of them, although I regretted that Zephreinia had traded her bold fashion of the evening for modest daytime dress. Last year only a Frothiran or a faddist would have seated a naked guest at the dinner table, and now I met them at the palace of Prince Fandiel. That the world was going to hell, I reflected, might not be an unrelieved disaster.

Closer study suggested that Zephryn was her younger brother, perhaps no more than twenty, although he had seemed at first an older man. The immoderate quantity of wine he drank while cutting his food in bits and pushing it around his plate suggested one cause of his deterioration, but I thought there must have been others.

"Well," I said when food and conversation grew thin, "you wanted to consult me, lady? If we might retire to —"

"Doctor, not I! I thought I made that clear. It's my brother I want you to look at."

I wish I could have seen my face at that moment, for I felt it collapse. Actors wishing to portray a character whose fondest hopes have been dashed might have studied it with profit.

"*Look at?*" her brother echoed with his intolerable sneer. "He's been looking at me all through the meal, when he could spare a moment from thrusting his great red turnip of a nose down your bodice and peeking at your tits, dear sister."

"Sir!" I rejected the many words that might have offended Zephreinia and said only, "You try me!"

"Zephryn, please, you know you haven't been able to sleep for a week —"

"It's not that I can't sleep, I don't choose to sleep," he whined as he sprang to his feet and kicked his chair away. "And whatever I do, what have you or this prosing old jackass got to do with it?"

I gathered up my bag and prepared to retire, the sole course I could take that would not be irreversible, but Zephreinia clung to my arm. No matter how deceitfully she had used it on me, her charm still worked.

"Please, Dr. Porfat —"

"Porfat?" Her brother seemed astounded, as if in his arrogance or drunken confusion he had not heard my name before. In a tone that flew as far beyond respect as his earlier one fell short of it, and no more endearing, he said, "The famous ghoulologist?"

"I despise that name even more than your manners, Sir. Never speak it to me again."

He laughed. "*Porfat?* I completely agree. I might have enjoyed hearing what you have to say about ghouls, Doctor, if only as a relief from all the inanities you've blithered. Rather than suffer any more of your sententious nattering, I'll leave you to wallow in this bitch-infested hellhole and grub for my sister's twat under the table until chance takes pity on your failing memory and guides your fat fingers."

I might have struck him at last, but his parting shot so shamed me that he got away. It was true that I had patted Zephreinia's thigh from time to time in making a point, and I had taken no small pleasure from this. I must have been crude and obvious indeed.

"Forgive me," I said, disengaging my arm. "I've behaved inexcusably."

"You? Oh, Doctor, no! My brother has, certainly, but please don't abandon him. Sometimes his ways are abrasive, but he doesn't mean to offend."

"I don't know what's wrong with him," I said, "and he doesn't want me to know. There are physicians who can catch an elusive patient, they make it their business to know such tricks, but I don't. As I told you, my work is with books and bones."

"And with ghouls," she said. "Doctor, he prowls the dark, he haunts strange places, he has odd friends. Must I recite all the symptoms from your own book?"

I could not deny this. His sardonic manner and his lack of appetite were also consistent, though hardly conclusive. During my slow convalescence I had noted similar peculiarities in my own habits, and I was surely no ghoul. But if she had wanted to seize my interest, she might have done so more surely by telling me these things than by misleading me with her wiles. I wanted nothing further to do with either of them, and I told her so.

"At least give me something, Doctor, something to make him sleep. He's killing himself."

And good riddance, I thought, but I gave her a small bottle of the laudanum I had prepared to treat my own illness and advised her to consult Dr. Beliphrast. I tried, too, to give her some hope: "If he were afflicted with ghoulism, he wouldn't be running out into the daylight so eagerly at this stage."

"I know. But you wrote that nothing about the disease is certain." She smiled wanly. "I really did read your book."

*

Next day it rained, and I seized the excuse to relapse into my new habit of sulking at home. I could see that Feshard, as he dusted around me, itched to comment on the book I had chosen to idly peruse, my own *Etiology of Ghoulism,* but he sensibly restrained himself. Reading my work had soured my temper. As I remembered the book, my brilliance should have curled and ignited the pages as I turned them. It did not.

Experience had refuted my fatuous assertion that a graveyard miasma caused the disease. I had crawled through the tunnels of the ghouls; to my everlasting disgust, I had been clawed by one. If it were infectious, I would now be breakfasting on something quite different from pears and cheese and Fandragoran wine.

I was not ready to abandon the work of a lifetime and join the fools who ascribed the condition to diabolism. I now inclined to the theory that it was hereditary. Lady Glypht, a far greater authority than I had ever been, had claimed that she ensured her son's ghoulism by the incestuous concentration of her degenerate bloodline. Without intending to, I began making notes in the margins for a revised edition. The notes sprawled onto the backs of letters, to crumpled papers from the pockets of my robe, to blank pages of any other books that came to hand. When I called for a second bottle of wine, I was so absorbed that I neglected to study Feshard's manner for signs that he disapproved of the request.

"I said, a lady to see you, Sir."

"Oh. Well. Send her in."

I hardly noticed this exchange. If I had given it any thought, I would have supposed my caller to be Nyssa. Zara was the only other woman who visited me, but not unless I sent for her. It gradually penetrated my preoccupation that my caller sat opposite me without saying a word; neither my sister nor my mistress had ever so much as attempted that feat. I looked up to find myself staring at Zephreinia Sleith.

"No, don't stop! It's a thrill to watch a man of genius at work.

It was like Mopsard's tale about the woman who could fly: when someone told her she flew, she fell. The next time I tried to concentrate on my work, I would think of Zephreinia and her comment. I would be aware of myself as she had seen me. I might never be able to concentrate again, thanks to her. I kept such churlish thoughts to myself as I tried to put my notes in order.

She must have walked here. Her hair was darkened by the rain and clung to her head in a way that bared the structure of her face and clarified the crystal of her eyes. I had thought her pretty; she was in fact unbearably beautiful.

Instead of trying to express this, more like a hollow inside my chest than a thought, I said, "You're wet." Then I called, "Feshard! Lay a fire."

"You have one," Zephreinia said.

"Oh. Yes."

I stood, shedding loose notes and even a few books that had rested unnoticed in my lap. I wanted to embrace her; I wanted to pick up the fallen books. Doing neither, I struggled to keep my confused hands from flapping aimlessly.

I hesitate to set down the chief cause of my confusion, for Filloweela is a Goddess for the young. Until yesterday, I had not seen the inside of her temple for at least twenty years. But after leaving Zephreinia's house, I was compelled to go there — by nostalgia, perhaps, by bitterness, by the Goddess herself, who knows? I bought a white dove and asked the priestess to sacrifice it for my intention. Exactly what that intention was, I had not stated clearly even to myself, but my prayer had obviously been answered: and not in the quirky way of a god, but with the prompt obedience of an un-Feshard-like servant.

But if I raised her from her chair and kissed her as if she were a gift from the Goddess, and her visit were only a banal coincidence, Zephreinia might take offense; if I failed to carry her to my bed soon and gratefully, the Goddess might take offense. So I dithered.

"You have one, Sir," said Feshard, who had taken so long to get here that I forgot why I had called him. "A fire, Sir."

"Of course I have a fire, moron! Get out my sight, my hearing and my home until tomorrow! Go and visit those nieces you're forever rattling on about." I observed my guest's startlement and hastened to pat her hand. "Don't mind that, it's the only way to talk to that impossible man."

"Do you give him holidays that way so you won't be burdened with his gratitude?"

I disliked hearing my motives analyzed, even by her, so I said, "How is your brother?"

I had picked the worst alternative subject. She started to speak, then her lip quivered and her eyes brimmed. I raised her to her feet and held her. This was not quite as I had dreamed it, but it would do. She clung so totally, so trustingly that I think she would have fallen if I had let her go.

"How can I speak of it?" she sobbed. "You won't help him."

I wished she would use some of her analytical skill to explain how she could make me writhe on my back and wag my tail. I heard myself saying, "I'll help him. What can I do?"

She regained the strength to stand, to pull away, and then she sat, leaving me warmed with the imprint of her body. I resumed my seat, too, arranging my robe to conceal my state of excitement, though of course she had felt it. I tried hard to look wise. I doubt I succeeded.

"Doctor, my brother is no longer a boy, but he wishes he were."

"We all do," I said, sounding unintentionally flippant.

She smiled, her eyes lowered. "I see you don't follow me. It's difficult. As a boy he was beautiful, you have no idea, and happy. He rages against becoming a man, as you . . . so clearly . . . are. When he was a boy, he joined with others in exploring the new possibilities of his body, the wonders of the flesh, as I suppose all boys do. He yearns always to turn time backward and return to those golden moments. But he has the body of a man, you see, while his playmates are still boys. Where we come from, few circumstances arouse so much antipathy."

I was still grinning absurdly over her delightful "clearly" and secretly praising the name of the Goddess when her meaning pierced my euphoria. I said without pausing to think, "You mean to say, in addition to being a boor and a drunkard, the swine is a pederast?"

She recoiled as from a blow. "You're cruel! Yes, yes, he is, but I had hoped for some pity from a man who can spare it even for *ghouls!*"

I would withhold pity for her degenerate brother until he had been castrated and flogged, but I ground my teeth and held my peace.

"Doctor, he's looking for happiness, as are we all, he's trying to express the nature that the gods gave him. Do those human traits make him less than human?"

I still didn't trust myself to speak. I now seethed over her remark about "all boys," which suggested a low opinion indeed of my sex. I never did such things as a boy. I would have bloodied the nose of any boy who dared suggest such foulness; as, come to think of it, I once had.

At length I said, "And so you removed him from Omphiliot, where the Cluddites would have burned him alive if they'd caught him at his tricks, and brought him to Crotalorn, where he might get away with them?"

She nodded jerkily, biting her lip, unable to meet my eyes.

"Why didn't you take him to Frothirot, where they would have put him in charge of an orphanage?"

She let out a wail of pain that tore my heart. I admit it, I was too hard. It did her no discredit that she could love such a brother. I got up and made soothing noises as I patted her shoulder, leaning awkwardly over her chair, for this time she didn't rise to embrace me.

I remembered my earlier thought about the quirky ways of the gods in blessing us. Was I being tested? I had presumed to sacrifice to Filloweela; and whatever men and nations may choose to do, that Goddess condemns nothing. She is the fire, and we, however twisted and fantasticated our separate shapes may be, are all her lamps.

"Burn brightly," I muttered, quoting a hymn without thinking of it.

She caught the reference. She looked up joyously through her tears, seized my hand and pressed her wet cheek against it. "I knew you'd help him!"

"Some things are shocking, that's all, that's all there is to it," I grumbled, pacing. "What do you want me to do? What on earth *can* I do, if that's what he is? At least he slept last night, didn't he?"

"The medicine had no effect. I put it in his wine, as you said, but he went out before midnight and looked even ghastlier than usual when he woke this afternoon." As if to ease the pain of speaking, she picked up one of the books I had dropped and leafed through it. "He does that — he goes somewhere, I can't imagine where, and returns looking worse each time."

She paused to inspect an illustration from a different angle. "Would this book help him, do you suppose, by diverting his mind from his usual desires?"

I went to her side and saw to my chagrin that I had been scribbling my thoughts about ghoulism in the margins of Chalcedor's *Lives of the Wicked Apricants*, a justly notorious work. When I tried to take it from her, she gripped it and insisted on browsing the engravings. I knelt before her chair to guide her study of the book laid flat in her lap. The pictures made her smile, a welcome respite from all the tears I had caused. She even giggled.

"Have you ever tried this?" she asked, using her fingertip to decipher the parts of one tangled couple. Pretending not to notice what I did, she had allowed me to push her dress above her hips and ease her thighs apart.

"No," I lied.

"Let's." She put the cold, dry, odorless, colorless, hairless and tasteless picture from her lap. It had concealed a reality whose every attribute was precisely opposite.

I was right: the Goddess had sent a test with her gift, and I had passed it. I resolved to buy her a lamb. Not today, though.

*

Like all sensible people, Empress Fillitrella hated the former capital. As soon as decently possible, she had brought her crown home, resisting pleas and threats from the Council of Lords. They wanted to prop her up in Frothirot like a mummy in a silver mask, whispering in her ear those hieratic oracles a ruler was permitted to intone; she wanted to gad about Crotalorn or hunt in its surrounding hills, saying whatever she pleased. Unfortunately, Frothirot followed her. Strangers clogged our streets, mangled our language, and changed our ways.

Many a time had I crossed the Miraga on the Victory Street Bridge to be exhilarated by the panorama of broad river and many-spired city, but not on this drizzly evening, and perhaps never again. Space had grown so scarce in the city that on either margin of the bridge a congeries of sheds and stalls had risen fast as fungi, blocking the view and smothering the senses with the plucking hands of Frothiran merchants, their shrill gabble, their relentless bell-ringing and gong-banging, and the reek of their nauseous cookery.

I suppose I should have been grateful for their whirl and dazzle. It did more to conceal me than the black cloak and slouch hat I had thought suitable for trailing Zephryn Phrein, until queer looks had persuaded me otherwise. A helpful passer-by might have told the young man he was followed by a vengeful stalker from melodrama. He would never have spotted me on his own, for as he hurried onward he kept his eyes on the footway.

I regretted this errand more with every step, but Zephreinia had threatened to do it herself if I refused. I could never have stood by for that, since Zephryn was surely headed for some boy-brothel, and such dens festered in the vilest slums. A pretty woman unfamiliar with our city would likely be knocked on the head and shipped to Sythiphore with the next barge-load of hapless tourists.

If my suspicion was confirmed, and he entered such a place, what then? I took more notice of the boys who swooped and shrieked through the crowd than he did as I tried to puzzle my way into his mind. I could barely suffer to share the public street with the impudent, snot-nosed beasts. To share a bed with one would have been not just loathsome but ludicrous. Mere opinions, however, were unlikely to change his ways.

We passed through Hound Square, where habit almost turned my steps into the Plume and Parchment. Another example of universal decay: the inn had formerly called itself the Willing Lepress, but now it was dominated by the bust of a bad, dead poet and, if I picked the wrong night, by the vaporings of his all-too-worthy successors. It would be more sensible to go in out of the rain, as the drizzle had become, and consider Zephryn's problem over a bottle, perhaps with Zara's help as a woman of experience. But I had promised his sister, so I pressed on.

He took that exit from the square I feared he would, down a stepped alley and into the dismal tangle of Blackberry Bank. I, a lifelong resident with some taste for the odd, never ventured here at night. Lights and street-signs were rare, but the visitor from Omphiliot kept his head down like a man hurrying home.

He cut through the gates of gardens become refuse-heaps, refuse-heaps become rooming houses and rooming houses become fighting-pits. Alleys narrowed into tunnels only to widen into rooms where the most exotic foreigners cooked, lounged, gambled or primped their goats. I brushed past lately-cannibal Orocs and fish-faced Duzai, past savages from Tampoontam whose tattooing was so extensive they felt no need of other covering. If one of these had unexpectedly strolled through my parlor, I would at very least have stared at him, but they were more sophisticated: neither Zephryn nor I aroused the slightest interest.

The Bank squeezed between the river and Dreamers' Hill, and it was upward toward the necropolis that his steps tended. Somewhere near here I had endured a perilous venture into the tunnels of the ghouls. The entrance I found had been destroyed, and the map I once possessed had been lost. Although I had come back to search the neighborhood with some capable men from the prince's regiment, I never found another way in. Now I began to notice details — a yellow door, a snarling stone dog with one ear missing, a sign at a dank areaway that commanded, "EAT," in the angry calligraphy of a lunatic — that whispered of memories deliberately mislaid. I was treading perilously close to the border of the Underworld.

The way grew narrower and even darker as the high houses yearned to fall into one another's embrace. When the clutter of carved eaves and fanciful chimney-pots permitted a glimpse of the sky, it seemed that the enormous graveyard hill hung there, not before me but above me, and that the innumerable, pale blots that were its tombs might presently tumble down on my head with the rain.

When I saw a sign that read Potash Alley, each further step required a separate act of will. When Zephryn slipped into a black fissure marked Algol's Close, my will and my strength deserted me, for I recalled now from the lost map that an entrance to the catacombs of the corpse-eaters lay near. I longed for the sight, now friendly and familiar, of a scarred cutthroat or naked savage, but the street was empty. No light shone in any house.

It was ironic that Zephreinia had tried to pique my interest in her brother by hinting at ghoulism. I had dismissed the notion, but it was true. I doubted he had the disease, but he was likely one of those that itched to catch it. Believing ghouls to be masters of forbidden magic, such depraved nitwits sometimes sought me out as the prophet who might point them to their idols. They most often found themselves gifted with the magical power to fly, assisted by my foot.

I believed I could find my way back to this street in daylight. Prince Fandiel would again lend me some of his troopers, who had welcomed my last expedition as a humorous break in their routine. I was about to turn and leave when I heard footsteps approaching, and voices. I stepped back into a doorway.

Out of the darkness the elements of a crowd emerged to coalesce around the hole that had swallowed Zephryn. The conversations I overheard comprised banal complaints about the weather and the neighborhood, or tedious discussions of the latest dwelth-match. Except for the surrounding squalor, I might have been eavesdropping on fashionable theater-goers in Ashclamith Square.

Forced for the moment to remain, I weighed my impulse to run. A promise to Zephreinia was like a promise to the willful and whimsical Goddess who had sent her to me, and I had promised I would help her brother. My every instinct screamed that he needed help now, this minute, not whenever I chose to find my way back with armed men. However much I wanted to, I could not run away.

My costume was not out of place here, where everyone was shrouded in black. I tilted my hat lower, waited for a suitable break in the pedestrian stream, and stepped out as smartly as if I belonged. I regretted that I hadn't let Feshard buy me a sword, but I carried a sturdy staff.

The only light in Algol's Close struggled feebly to escape an open door. A man and woman passed through it ahead of me, joking about the ancient images of prostitutes that decorated the moldy walls of a derelict brothel. I followed, shaking in every limb, and no amount of silent scolding or measured breathing helped me. Odd: I didn't know I was terrified, but my body did.

Passing beyond the light of the single candle, I took note of an odor that had first hinted its presence at the outer door, the unmistakable smell of rotting flesh. It steadily thickened as I approached the door to the cellar. Although there are worse smells, none is fraught with more terrible associations for me but one. I smelled that one, too. My nose told me there was a ghoul in the cellar.

I waited until those ahead of me had picked their way down the decrepit stairs. This caused a pileup behind me, but no one objected when I raised my hand for patience. They continued to exchange the murmured commonplaces you would hear on any line. In such close quarters they must have noticed how badly I shook, but no one denounced me as a spy.

The way was clear. I had no further excuse to delay. The stairway creaked and swayed to my steps. It vibrated from my tremor with an alarming rattle, as if the rotting wood cackled at my fear.

The cellar room spread far beyond the house above it and even beyond the other buildings in the alley. How far I could not say, for my view was confused by the uncertain light of candles, by an underground forest of brick pillars, and by a multitude of men and women, not all of them living. In varying stages of putrefaction, the dead hung here and there by hooks through their ankles, less like a butcher's orderly stock than a casual display of trophies.

Some of the gathering had stripped naked as the corpses, although my hat and cloak were not out of place. Making my way toward the focus of attention was surprisingly easy, despite the thickness of the intervening crowd. However depraved these necrophiliacs might be, it was the rare one that denied a rotting corpse, with its attendant flies and maggots, ample space to dangle. I followed a route marked by these hanging carcasses, elbowing aside the living less often than the dead.

I strove for professional detachment as I covertly inspected the bodies, but my profession had never exposed me to such evidence of torture and mutilation. These wretches had been whipped, broken and branded; eyes and genitalia were missing, as were the breasts of the female corpses. Copious bloodstains suggested that the atrocities had been inflicted on living victims. Heads, hands, and chunks of muscular tissue had been bitten off later.

I still trembled, and now my stomach threatened to rebel, but the worst lay before me. Even in the fog of decay, I smelled the ghoul, and that smell was strongest where the greasy candles sputtered most thickly. When I saw it, I gripped the corpse before me for support; I turned my face for a moment against the slimy flesh of its buttocks to block a sight even more loathsome.

I had intruded upon a foul parody of some grand lord's audience. The ghoul lounged naked on a throne of bones that I recognized from my earlier visit to the underworld, toying shamelessly as might an idiot with his gigantic phallus. To describe this organ, which seemed in a permanent state of inflamed erection, would require a specialist in the maladies said to be inflicted by Filloweela on those who earn her hatred. The pimpled and knobbed and suppurating obscenity served the ghoul as a lord's scepter. One by one, suppliants were led forward to petition him by ushers, swathed and hooded in black. All were first required not just to humiliate themselves but to demonstrate their total contempt for cleanliness and decency by kissing this rod of office.

In some nightmare where I might have been called upon to play physician to the ghoul, the botch of Bebros and Lushirion's discharge would have seemed the least of his afflictions. His dead white skin was eaten by molds and fungi and verminous infestations, he bore the lesions of cancer and leprosy, his body was gaunt as any gibbeted felon's; and yet, consistent with nightmare, his manner was one of exuberant vigor. Feeding on the dead, he thrived on the ills that had carried them off.

His habitual expression was a smirk, which he varied with a leer when some cultist struck his fancy. He laughed almost constantly; though sometimes muted to a bass chuckle, his laughter often rose to a maniacal shriek. It stopped only when anger overcame him, and that was a fearful sight indeed, for whatever was vestigially human in his guise would then burn away. His chest swelled to twice its size, the bristles on his arms and shoulders erected, the hair of his head puffed out. His bell-shaped ears folded back, his globular eyes narrowed to yellow slits and the lines of his face ridged into a mask of fury as he bared all the teeth in his massive jaw and howled in the face of some sniveler. Certain toads and lizards achieve a metamorphosis no less complete in their displays of anger, but theirs is only show; his was no less convincing than the tiger's mask of wrath. Those who provoked this change were dragged screaming into the darker reaches of the cellar, perhaps to await fuller attention at his leisure.

This thing had been known in its human form as Lord Glyphtard, whom I had once seen from a distance, who now styled himself Vomikron Noxis, King of the Ghouls. The high, domed forehead was the same as the living man's, and the black hair; but the nose was absent and the eyes, ears and jaw were not human at all. It seemed less a caricature of his former appearance than a logical development, as if the human face he had presented to the world for twenty-some years had been the unformed embryo of this horror.

My own courage, or more likely my bemusement, alarmed me when I found myself virtually in the front rank of his servants. All of these were naked, waiting their turns to abase themselves, and my clothing at last made me stand out. To retreat from this point would only draw further attention. But this ghoul would recognize me the instant his eyes chanced to fall on me. I had to withdraw.

At that moment a man edged in front of me: Zephryn Phrein. All his sneering assurance had deserted him. Without his clothing, he seemed awkward and more youthful, even pathetically boyish. I had lost my tremor somewhere along the way, but he shook worse than I had. I found myself wanting to help the poor lout for his own sake. In the presence of real evil it struck me forcibly that his errors were those of youthful bewilderment. Whatever he might be, he was human.

I stepped forward and reached for his elbow. If he objected, I would rap him on the head with my staff, throw him over my shoulder, and bull my way to the stairs. Once I build up speed, I am hard to stop.

As I reached for his left arm, an usher took his right. He was drawn forward to kneel, and I was left standing alone in the lurid glare of the candles, directly in front of the ghoul. A murmur rippled near me. I had been noticed at last: not yet as an intruder, perhaps, but as a bumptious petitioner.

Having made his obscene obeisance, Zephryn said: "O King, I don't have the boy."

"I see that. Zephryn — " no human throat could have formed the name as the ghoul's did, like the buzz of an angry wasp that rose to a shriek of claws on glass — "we chose you for your talent to dupe boys. Have you failed us?"

The smirk was dissolving into the wrathful mask. I eased forward, clutching my staff more firmly.

"Majesty, I haunted the necromancer's palace for a week, I even crept inside to search. I saw no boy. At last I approached Weymael Vendren and confessed the sort of interest in his ward that he understood. He claims Polliard died from eating tainted food. I believed him, for he wept as he told me."

"Polliard Phuonsa was a ghoul, you dunce! There was nothing he couldn't eat . . . unless he was subsumed by what he consumed."

"I don't understand."

"It is for the King of the Ghouls to understand, and for you to obey!" The bristling unexpectedly subsided. The fangs retreated behind the thin lips, only to re-emerge in the ghastly leer. This seemed to exhaust the creature's stock of facial expressions. "If you can't bring us the boy, Zephrynnnn —" the way he said that name hurt my teeth — "you may bring us your sister."

My heart leaped out to the youth, for he tottered awkwardly to his feet with the battle-cry of a free man on his lips: "No!"

I was already moving quickly, and before the ghoul could deal with his contumacious slave, I said: "No, Sir, you shall not have her!" I swung my staff with both hands and all my strength against the thing's left ear.

It was a solid blow, mashing cartilage and perhaps cracking bone, and it toppled the King of the Ghouls, throne and all, in a most unkingly heap.

"It's the ghoulologist!" someone screamed.

I tried to pull Zephryn away with me, but he shoved me back with unexpected strength. "Go!" he shouted. "Warn her! Guard Zephreinia! Get out of here, you fat fool, while you still can!"

I saw through his impertinence to the sense in this. Even so, I might have stayed to argue with him, but Vomikron Noxis had staggered upright to pump forth trumpets of rage. Hands plucked at my cloak, blows fell almost unnoticed on my head and shoulders as his followers mobbed me. Before the ghoul could attack, Zephryn grappled with him. Many of the king's courtiers dashed in to restrain the youth, blocking my way. It would have been harder to go forward than to go back to the stairs.

I went back. But I went back in a rage. I hated myself even more than I hated these scum, for it seemed I had failed Zephryn and his sister, but it was the ghoul's toadies who suffered for my bad conscience. I plied my staff with a will, pausing to strike a second blow whenever the first failed to satisfy me. I pursued a few who tried to get out of my way, men, women, it made no difference. As a physician, I can judge the sound and feel of a broken skull. I broke a few skulls that night, and I doubt that all of their owners are laughing about it today.

I thought I had done with horrors. Nothing seemed left now but ordinary fear and extraordinary anger. But what had gone before seemed almost commonplace when I discovered that not all of my opponents were human. Some of the draped ushers that I had casually pushed past earlier were ghouls. Worse, some were humans well on their way to that status. Not even the unveiled spectacle of their king had unnerved me so much as the sight of a human face, perhaps one hinting of former beauty, marred by bulbous eyes or porcine tusks. Them I hit the hardest, and so much for my pretensions as a healer.

A curious order of battle prevailed. The true ghouls, for all their fangs and claws and coffin-cracking strength, contented themselves to gibber and shriek in the background. The intermediate cases were only slightly less timid. It was the humans who most boldly blocked my way, who weighed me down by clinging to my legs or my cloak.

I wondered why none of them had thought to use a blade on me. Men of a certain class — mine, but I am an oddity — feel naked without a sword, and no one goes without a knife. Except here. I had seen no one armed, not even in the midst of this fight. Superstition gave me the answer: ghouls fear iron. The king was so uncertain of his subjects that he allowed no iron in his court.

Just as I was hailing a triumph of superstition, I felt the unique and unmistakable pain, the momentary paralysis of mind and body, that attends the sudden and unexpected piercing of one's hide. I had been stabbed in the back. My attacker still clung to me. I twisted to see him. My theory about iron had not been refuted, but I took small consolation from that, for a ghoul had buried his fangs in my shoulder. I could not swing the staff handily, but I jabbed the butt into his great yellow eye, which burst and spattered me with jellified foulness. He released his grip and dropped writhing to the floor with a scream that matched his king's.

The knot of ghouls that had formed behind me, waiting to join in the attack if their braver comrade succeeded, fell away to scream insults at a distance. I almost pursued them, I was so sick by this time of being called "ghoulologist" in their skull-scraping ululations.

I had a certain advantage over this mob. While Zephryn fought their king, and the noise from that quarter told me he still did, they had no leader, and they were the sort that needed one. They didn't fight well. They did nothing well, and that was why they longed to command magical powers, even if it meant eating corpses. They could have crushed me in their numbers, but so could an equal mass of worms. As long as I kept my head and controlled my nausea, I had a chance.

I was within sight of the door to the stairway, and no one had thought to block it or even close it. If I took many more steps in that direction, it would dawn on even the stupidest to seize and defend that door. I feinted to the right, kicking a ghoul who had sneaked up on that side, clubbing a human, and swinging one of the pendulous corpses behind me to block pursuit for a moment. I stirred up a filthy swarm of flies that momentarily blinded me and clogged my nostrils.

"Zephryn!" I shouted, turning back toward the king's throne. "This way!"

I regretted that ruse. I had no real hope to offer him, no help to give him. I had used his name merely as a diversion, and it worked, for some of my attackers wavered uncertainly toward the throne. But I regretted it even more when the intolerable rasp of Vomikron Noxis replied: "He's not going with you, Dr. Porfat. He's chosen to wait here till his sister joins us."

I suppose he wanted me to attack him, and I was tempted, but no one now stood between me and the door. I dived for it, slammed it behind me, and had pounded halfway up the stairs before I saw my error. The framework bent, the tortured wood screamed louder than my pursuers. But it was too late to be cautious. I scrambled the last few steps on my hands and knees and clawed my way into the upper room as the stairs collapsed under the added weight of pursuit. My own blowing and wheezing seemed louder in my ears than the dismayed screams or the splintering crash of the staircase.

I lay still for a moment, bleeding from the bite in my shoulder and a score of lesser wounds I hadn't noticed. I knew it was no place to rest, however, and I had started to rise when Vomikron Noxis, so strong and agile that the missing stairway posed no barrier, bounded through the door after me.

I believed that my death had come, that it towered above me in this animated cesspool of human ills and fears and sins, but it was a death that would give me no rest, no peace, no clean and irreparable snipping of the fragile thread. This thing would eat me, and then it would prowl the world in my form for a span, thinking my thoughts and speaking my words as it polluted and destroyed everyone I cared for: foolish Fandiel, jolly Zara, my own, dear little sister, Nyssa. . . . My shame is so great that I must wedge my fist against my mouth now to keep from screaming as I recall it, but I pleaded with the ghoul in the most abject way, I begged him to spare me.

His leer faded. He did have a third facial expression, no less fearful, but what it meant, I have no idea. I screamed. For an instant I seemed to be in peril of physically slipping off the world and falling into the great yellow globes of his eyes. He saw deep into me.

"I *know* you!" he said, and his voice roused me from my sick trance of passivity. Yes, he knew me, he had pawed and fondled my secrets, my most precious dreams and my most miserable shames. He had stirred filth to the surface that even I could not recognize, except to know that it must be mine. Even if he never laid his claws on me, he had mauled me and crippled me forever by wrenching my perception of myself into a sickening shape, by altering the very thing that had always said, "I."

And then he threw back his horrible head and *laughed*! "Now," the King of the Ghouls howled, "now, boy, at long last, it's your turn to kiss my — "

"With pleasure, Sir! Here's a kiss for you!" I cried, and I thrust the gnarled head of my staff at the very part his subjects had so honored. He clutched his battered member, doubled over, and fell back into the pit, shrieking all the while in a voice to make a statue cringe.

I hurled myself out into the prickling fog that had succeeded the rain. When I stumbled over unknown obstacles in Algol's Close and the alley beyond it, I didn't pause to pick myself up, I just crawled or thrashed or rolled until I was running again. But how far must I run before I reached the limit of that enormous cellar, and the limits of the burrows that might join it to other cellars? In my terror, it seemed that the solid cobblestones were but a thin shell between me and the Underworld, and that the ghoul could track me as surely as iron filings track a magnet through paper. I dared not stop to test my conviction that the echoing clatter of my footsteps masked the noise of subterranean pursuit. Every blot of deeper blackness in the night seemed a hole from which Vomikron Noxis might burst.

At last I fell and could not rise, even though I was nearing an intersection where a dim glow stained the fog from a mass that might have been a tavern. The stones beneath my ear were cold and wet, but I pressed it harder against them to listen. I heard only the roar of my own blood.

I knew I must get up and push on, but the will to try had drained from me. Sleep promised a respite from the wretched spell the ghoul had cast. That spell denied me any good reason to live, but the mere habit of life was strong enough to raise my weary body to its hands and knees.

I heard a cry of distress that chilled me: "Doctor! Dr. Porfat, where are you?"

Although it was Zephryn's voice, I didn't answer. He was probably dead. The king must have assumed his likeness. Fighting against the human impulse to reply, I got up and staggered away from the voice as quickly and quietly as pain and despair and vertigo would allow.

"Doctor!" The cry was closer, more anguished, and now I heard more than one set of running footsteps. "Help me!"

I sagged into a dark doorway and waited. Zephryn stumbled past, still calling out, though his failing breath and abraded throat could now produce little more than a pitiable whisper.

The man — or thing — had been wounded. His twisted left arm hung useless, and he lurched on an injured leg. Blood clothed his pale body in dark lace. Old wives' tales, my sole source of knowledge about such matters, told me that a dead man personated by a ghoul always appears to be whole and sound.

While I dallied with metaphysics — and perhaps I was merely looking for any excuse to keep my head down and save my skin — the hunters overtook him. He managed one last, full-throated scream when a club struck him across the shoulders and drove him to his knees, but he could only groan as they kicked and stamped him into submission.

Three of his pursuers were men. When they had finished punishing Zephryn, they dispersed to peer into likely refuse-heaps and alleys and doorways. I thought the black figure that grabbed him by the ankles and began dragging him back into the darkness was a man, too, until I noticed its clawed and malformed hands. I very nearly screamed aloud until I glimpsed its face and saw that it was not the king. My encounter with him had been so dreadful that *ordinary* ghouls could no longer impress me.

Could his subjects have battered their disguised ruler as they had the apparent man? If they knew I was watching, would they put on a show to trap me when they could attack me directly? It seemed clear that this was truly Zephryn Phrein who was being reclaimed by the underground. Still I hesitated. I had no idea how a ghoul thought; I had no idea of their real powers.

Others were not paralyzed by doubt. As I did nothing but watch, men who had heard Zephryn's last cry burst from the tavern and pelted down the street, shouting heathen gibberish. They appeared to be Ignudos. Never had I imagined how pleased I might be to meet their like in a dark alley!

They were enough to frighten the ghoul, who faded into the shadows, but the three men abandoned their search for me and lifted their captive. Hearing the sound of rescue, Zephryn came to life and struggled. He succeeded in breaking their hold, but he was dropped on the pavement for his trouble.

"Clear off, you scum!" one of the men shouted at the rescuers. "This is Frothoin business."

"Our business break your head, dogface!" an Ignudo cried, his epithet being a slur on our facial hair.

"Mine, too!" I shouted, at last pushing myself out of the doorway with my staff at the ready. "Help us, friends!"

Zephryn was on his feet again, trading blows with his attackers when I waded in. They were outnumbered by the savages alone, some of whom were armed with their short, curved swords, but still they didn't flee. This suggested that Vomikron Noxis had given dire orders; it seemed to confirm that Zephryn was no impostor.

More of my doubt vanished when the young man seized a sword from an Ignudo and used the iron weapon to cut an opponent's throat. This delighted the savages, who grinned like sharks and trilled in their peculiar way. Having subdued the other two, they thrust one toward Zephryn with an eager pantomime of throat-cutting, and he obliged them. Mimicking the dead man's gargling cry, some of them fell down laughing and rolled in the street. Others pushed the last one forward, yanking back his head by the hair to present his throat most conveniently.

"Wait — " I began.

"It's a ghoul! That's not a living man, you fools!" the last of the condemned men screamed. "Tell them, Porfat, it's Vomikron —"

"Noxis," Zephryn finished, for his victim no longer could.

"Lots, lots *glybdi* walk round around here," said an Ignudo, using his word for ghouls. "No like dogface-tooth."

The last phrase was his jargon for a sword, and it seemed a strong endorsement from a disinterested party. Zephryn might not be a ghoul. But as he laughed through his bloody mask and embraced me warmly with his good arm, the sword dripping on my back, I reflected that he might not be much of a man, either.

*

We accepted the hospitality of the bargemen at their tavern and suffered the attentions of a witch-doctor, or perhaps he was merely a surgeon, whom they extracted forcibly from a hempen torpor. All the while Zephryn never stopped yammering and posturing. He relived, over and over again, our pursuit by three rogues who had set upon us in a whorehouse with — to explain our stranger wounds — their savage dog. He judged his audience well. They never tired of hearing the tale, even with new and contradictory embellishments. He seemed well on his way to becoming an honorary Ignudo.

I found it impossible to forget that he had formerly been an honorary ghoul. That unspeakable king's commendation of his "ability to dupe boys" stuck in my mind. What plots had he hatched, what perversions had he wallowed in, what murders had he done? I tried to hold the memory of his last, ringing refusal to serve the ghoul, so much finer than my own groveling, but other memories superseded it. His skill in slitting the throats of three unarmed men suggested diligent practice.

A cat never studied a bird more closely than I did Zephryn Phrein. I analyzed each word, each accent, each gesticulation for a whiff of something less than human. All I found, in a toss of his head, a sidelong look, a way of wrinkling his nose, were unwelcome and disturbing echoes of Zephreinia. His existence colored her image; I would never be able to see her or think of her again without his intolerable taint.

Rested, fed on questionable dishes, clothed in a bizarre farrago of bargemen's castoffs and slightly drunk, we found our way to civilization and a chair that Zephryn directed to Peartree Square.

I said to the chairmen, "That's at the foot of the hill with the temple of — which temple is that, Zephryn?"

Without the slightest hesitancy or suspicion, he replied, "Polliel," a name that ghouls supposedly may not pronounce.

When I asked him how he had made his escape, he told me in a straightforward way, with none of the japes and mummery he had thought suitable for Ignudos. By calling his name when I had, I had saved him. Believing him finished, Vomikron Noxis had turned to taunt me, and Zephryn had seized on that moment of inattention to flee to the end of the cellar and a tunnel that led to the street. It sounded plausible.

The Miraga had exhaled an enormous white ghost of itself to haunt its course through the city. Those waiting atop Temple Hill rejoiced to see the sun and proclaimed that the God had granted us a fine day. Only because their shouts echoed down to the bottom of the ghostly river where we drifted, and because the bricks and leaves of Peartree Square ignited with color beneath their wet gloss, did I know that it was dawn. Zephryn showed no more discomfort at the light than I myself felt, owing no doubt to my exhaustion.

"Doctor," he said, when we had reached our destination, "I know you dislike me, and my ill-considered words have given you more than enough cause. I know you helped me only for my sister's sake, but I owe you my life. Believe me, I will pay you back."

"Ill-considered words are the least of your errors, Sir. You can mend some of the worst ones, and pay me back fully, by accompanying me to Prince Fandiel this afternoon and telling him all you know about that loathsome cult."

"How ever could I have called you a mouthing moron!"

"I don't recall that you did."

"You're too kind. But I shall go with you, of course, and cleanse myself completely." As he limped out, he turned with an unpleasant little smile and said, "Give yourself credit for a miraculous cure, Doctor. My unhealthy obsession led me to that hell. I plan to fight against it, and to begin my research into the female sex . . . immediately."

There was no getting around it: I would dislike this young man no matter what he did, said, or became. But I managed some kind of a smile and said, "Get some rest first."

His laughter followed me across the square.

*

I wanted nothing but to sleep. I was unable to tolerate Zephryn's company one minute longer, nor did he invite me in. For those reasons I was eager to go home, and for one reason that weighed more than the others combined: I was afraid to test my new perception that Zephreinia was too like her brother.

Whenever I tried to conjure up her delightful voice, I heard a feminine version of his provincial whine. I had treasured all the words she had spoken to me as if they were rare spices, but when I took them out to savor them, I found Zephryn's accents crawling on them like weevils.

I realized that I was drifting back into the illness that had kept recurring since I was nearly killed by a wretch called Phylphot Phuonsa. The first symptom of a relapse was a sick state of mind in which words became things, noisy, obsessive objects that cluttered my mind so densely that my surroundings faded. The words would be repeated, again and again, until I heard them shrieked in the voices of ghouls. I would soon sink into delirious visions of capering with those ghouls and feasting on the corpses of all I had ever loved. Lucid intervals would fill me with terror that I had fallen victim to ghoulism, the disease I had studied for so long and to so little profit.

As the chairmen trotted me joltingly home, I heard Zephreinia's voice, or perhaps it was Zephryn's, repeating the words, "Peartree Square." The taste of pears touched my tongue, but it abruptly degenerated to something unspeakably foul as inhuman voices cackled and gabbled the words.

"Stop!" I screamed.

"Sir?" I was screaming at the voices, but the chairmen came to an abrupt halt. I heaved myself out of the chair, tumbling onto the pavement, cursing and shoving the men aside when they tried to help me rise.

"Where did that young man direct you?" I demanded.

"You mean, Peartree Square, where we left him?"

"Yes, but what did he call it? What name did he use? The old one, or did he call it *Sekris?*"

They consulted together, scratched their heads, tried not to look at me as if I were crazy while I mumbled a Pollian prayer to override the chattering inside my skull. At last they concluded that Zephryn had called it *Peartree,* as no tourist from Omphiliot would do, but as Lord Glyphtard, born and bred in Crotalorn, would surely do.

I thanked them volubly, thrust money at them, hurried back on foot the way they had brought me. I walked with my head down, for the light hurt my eyes and disordered my thoughts, all the while praying to drown out the evil words in my head: *.20.20. mouthing moron .20.20. my research into the female sex .20.20. immediately.20.20.20.*

Another word that recurred as a rasping undertone was *Phuonsa,* Polliard *Phuonsa,* a foul libel that the ghoul-king had spoken, for Polliard's surname was *Glypht,* and he had subsequently been enrolled in the Tribe of Vendren by Weymael. Why this grievance of a depraved child who had died from eating tainted meat should trouble me, I had no idea, but I felt the pain of that slur as if it were my own, and it made me pray all the louder. Those pedestrians I blundered into were less inclined to expostulate with me than to flee.

The door of the house in Peartree Square hung ajar, which seemed ominous. I dithered at the threshold, struggling to master my confusion and the cold waves of nausea that threatened to overcome me. I felt that Zephreinia was in danger, but what good would it do her if I walked in the door and fainted? Worse, what if I opened my mouth and began babbling the nonsense now shrieking in my head? Perhaps I could pull myself together if I escaped the light and noise of the street for a moment, where porters and fishmongers and fruiterers were starting the day with their inharmonious cries of "Phuonsa, Phuonsa, Phuonsa!" I slipped inside and shut the door behind me.

Contrary to all that has been alleged since, I never saw any servants, alive or dead. Zephryn must have killed them before I arrived. If they were sprawled bloodily in the atrium, as they were later found, I failed to notice them in my peculiar state.

All my concentration was focused on Zephreinia's voice. She wasn't screaming, but her voice was loud, firm and full of outrage as she said, "No, stop it! Zephryn, no! Get away!"

It seemed clear to me that he was honoring his promise to begin his research into the female sex by raping his sister. But of course she wasn't his sister. Zephryn Phrein had died bravely in that cellar, a far braver man than I had proved to be, and it was Vomikron Noxis who was assaulting Zephreinia in the next room. What I did then is almost too painful to write: I fell to my knees and pressed my hands to my ears in an effort to shut out her cries. But you must understand, this was the King of the Ghouls, and what could a mere boy do against him? If only my mother —

I was going mad. He had called me a boy, my ghoulish voices were screaming the word, and I had somehow come to believe that it was true, that I was not a very large and capable man who had already bested the ghoul-king once. I staggered to my feet and forced myself to enter the room where Zephreinia was fighting him off.

*

Now you would think that one who rescues a woman from being raped by her brother, even putting aside the fact that this brother is in fact a personating ghoul, would be forgiven almost any excess due to the necessity of the moment and the righteous fury such a situation would provoke. You might even think that this savior would be accorded a certain measure of honor. I fear you would be wrong, for I write this in a dungeon under sentence of death.

Whatever good I may have done was counteracted, in the view of the magistrates, by the fact that I had ripped out Zephryn's throat with my teeth and appeared to be eating him when passersby, drawn by his sister's screams, burst into the house and tore me from my victim.

The woman's testimony is no help. I know what I heard and what I saw, but she swears that they were grappling half-playfully as she blocked her brother's way to the liquor-cabinet. He already reeked of *pflune,* she said, pressed on him by the wicked old man — myself — who had enticed him to some low den for a night of debauchery. She insists on these lies to protect her brother's reputation, even though that has been thoroughly destroyed, and even though the story has put my neck beneath the ax. Degenerate Zaxoin yokels, they were probably lovers all along!

My noble connections. . . . I can hardly bear to write what follows, but I must. My brother-in-law professes the greatest affection and respect for me as he hammers me with his daily, repetitive questions, but no one else in the government is imbecile enough to concoct the theory that I conspired with Weymael Vendren, Lady Glypht, Squirmodon, Zephryn Phrein and certain Ignudos to commit murders, burglaries, grave-robbings, cannibalism and arson. Weymael's discovery of Chalcedor's lost classic and my scholarly work in preparing it for the press have prompted a further charge of distributing pornography, while Weymael and Zephryn's vice has damned us all with the charge of procuring boys and murdering those, like the missing Polliard Phuonsa, who might have accused us. Since there are no witnesses against us, we must have killed them all and probably — given my study of ghoulism and my alleged treatment of Zephryn — eaten their bodies.

To perfect this ghastly charade, I have been convicted of murdering *Phylphot* Phuonsa. I cannot explain the reasoning of the magistrates, I can only retail it: he was last seen with me, my bloody cloak was later found in an alley, I cannot account for my activities during the following week, and no one can now find him; therefore, obviously, I killed and ate him.

I had thought the Empress might intercede for me, since I did recover her necklace, but even that good deed is twisted against me. I was able to retrieve the necklace because I had stolen it. I burned down Gourdfoot's tavern so no one could disprove my wild tale of a ghoul's treasure-room beneath it.

At least she has spared me from torture, and I must thank Her Imperial Majesty for that. Weymael has not been spared, however, and the Lord Collector of Tears has extracted from him a detailed confession that names me as mastermind of the conspiracy.

*

I was very deeply confused when I came here, and I had not yet learned that one must say nothing at all out of the ordinary, not even to those one loves. I asked Nyssa if my warning had been heeded, if Zephryn's body had been exposed to sunlight for a full day; preferably in Hound Square, where the statue of an ancient goddess is said to have power over ghouls.

"Why would they want to do that, Brother?"

"Because," I said slowly and with great forbearance, "that was not Zephryn Phrein. He was personated by Vomikron Noxis, King of Ghouls. Do you suppose I would have attacked a man — a wounded man — with such fury? It was a desperate struggle against a superhuman creature, and I used every means at my command. Didn't they do as I asked?"

She averted her eyes. "No. He was sewn in a shroud and buried in the common pit reserved for criminals. Fandiel has assigned some Cluddites to watch the pit, so —"

"So he'll have a hearty breakfast when he resumes his terrible form!" I laughed.

"Please, Brother, please! You should be setting your mind at ease, composing yourself for. . . ."

"Death?" I kept laughing. I couldn't seem to stop. "If they didn't expose Vomikron's body to the sun and the goddess, they won't expose mine, either. So I'm not going to die, I'm going on a journey. I'm glad that dear Vomikron will be there to receive me. At last we'll see who's fit to be King of the Ghouls!"

I don't know what I meant. I raved on in that style until she clapped her hands to her ears and screamed to be let out of the cell. Even when the guards were kicking and clubbing me, I found it hard to stop laughing.

I have since learned to keep my own counsel, and I have tried to resign myself to my fate, although the most bizarre thoughts and images will burst into my mind at odd moments and it is hard not to speak them or write them down.

*

I just noticed something funny about my hand. It's not mine. No longer huge and veined and hairy.

No, I take that back, it *is* mine. It's not old, that's all, it's not Porfat's hand. It's mine!

EPILOGUE

To Fillitrella, Empress of All Seelura and the Outer Islands, Scourge of the Thallasshoi, Torch to the Argyroi, Hammer of Gastayne and Beloved of the Fairies, from Fandiel, Prince of the House of Fand, Cmdr., Never-Vanquished, most humble Greetings:

The guards who permitted the regrettable escape of Dr. Porfat maintained that they rushed to his cell when they heard someone other than the doctor laughing. There they found a boy alone in the cell, they said, attempting to destroy the enclosed manuscript by eating it.

If I may direct Your Imperial Majesty's attention to the most salient fact of this otherwise absurd narrative, it is that Dr. Porfat denies none of the charges brought against him. On the contrary, under the guise of irony intended to delude an "imbecile," he says outright: "I was able to retrieve the necklace because I had stolen it. I burned down Gourdfoot's tavern so no one could disprove my wild tale of a ghoul's treasure-room beneath it."

This, and the other memoir recovered by Feshard, the agent I inserted into the criminal's home, do indeed comprise a wild tale, one that is a match for any of the wild tales concocted by that author from antiquity, whose name eludes me at the moment.

The purpose is of course to distract us from a conspiracy of real-life cutthroats, thieves and pornographers. By writing the memoirs and substituting a boy for himself, the doctor hoped to convince us that he was dead, murdered by a henchman of Weymael Vendren; that this boy was an untypical ghoul who normally retained a human form; that the ghoul had, after eating the doctor's body, successfully personated him for several months; and that he miraculously reverted to his youthful form just in time to escape punishment for the doctor's crimes.

Having observed Porfat during the time of the alleged "personation," and having known him for years, I can confidently assert that this is nonsense, regardless of whatever my distraught wife, his sister, may say about it. My view is supported by Dr. Beliphrast, now our foremost ghoulologist, who has examined the boy and pronounced him normal in every respect.

The condemned necromancer, Weymael Vendren, attempted to delude us with similar lies, but recanted them under repeated interrogation and admitted that Porfat had concocted the plot in order to discourage pursuit. Needless to say he is being actively hunted, and an arrest may be expected soon.

Although only such tortures as are deemed suitable for children were employed, the boy confirmed that Weymael Vendren arranged to free Dr. Porfat and insinuate him into the cell with the help of the guards, who were summarily executed. The boy has been identified as Polliard Phuonsa, the necromancer's missing "ward," although he insists that he should be called by the noble name of Glypht or Vendren. Since he was apparently duped and bullied into his acts by the real criminals, he was provisionally released in the custody of his mother.

This mother, a common whore called Zara (although she also claims membership, as yet unverified, in the Tribe of Glypht) at first denied kinship with the boy. Only after a private interview with Polliard, from which she emerged notably pale and shaken, did she own up to her son. She identified his father as one Quodomass Phuonsa, deceased. Her knowledge of these events seems slight, and whatever value she might have had as a witness would have been vitiated by her marked peculiarities of speech and demeanor, to say nothing of her ill repute.

I regret to report that the mother and son are not available at this time for further questioning. They were followed after leaving the prison, but they eluded surveillance somewhere in the necropolis of Dreamers' Hill. The agents who bungled the assignment, Dodont and Feshard, were summarily executed.

Although the escape of the doctor is unfortunate, it is to be hoped that the executions of Weymael Vendren and a score of peripheral malefactors have demonstrated to the Sons of Cludd that Your Imperial Majesty will not tolerate the activities of necromancers, pornographers, pedophiles, arsonists, cannibals, etc., etc.

I would respectfully submit once again that the way of containing Cluddite fanaticism is to direct it toward projects with the least potential for public inconvenience. To this end, I dispatched a contingent of them to guard the pit where Zephryn Phrein was buried. Please accept the following terse and rather curious report:

To Fandiel, called Prince: The ghoul emerged at midnight. Sore beset by the abomination, we were unable to slay it. I thank you for setting us in the path to the Everlasting Light of Cludd, which five of my men achieved. I remain yr. obdt. servt. for the glory of Cludd, Dolton Zogg, Rev. Lord Cmdr., Cludd's Whirlwind.

I doubt that the ghoul they encountered had anything to do with

Zephryn Phrein, but this is purely my opinion, since it proved impossible, owing to the normal process of dissolution and the activities of scavengers, to find and identify his body.

The Vendren Worm

Wake, Worm!
A mighty hero is coming
To try his strength against yours.

Richard Wagner: *Siegfried*

Penetrating the depths of the Municipal Palace in Crotalorn is not easy. Those who descend from the lobby must stop at the gate of the detention center, where guards will either redirect or welcome them. Only by slipping through an unmarked door at the rear of the tax office can one bypass the dungeons and enter the equally gloomy warren of the maintenance department.

At this point it seems unlikely that a misdirected visitor could go deeper without meeting a malingering sweep or sulking carpenter, since I must grumble through a clutter of them on my way to work each day. It seems even less likely that one of these civil servants would miss a chance to magnify himself by chasing a stray back into the clutches of the clerks who lord it over the upper floors.

Why anyone who escapes their notice would persevere in opening unmarked doors, daring treacherous steps and blundering through lightless corridors until he at last stumbles into the archives of the Inspector of Moats and Trenches is a puzzle to me, but they keep doing it, interrupting my work with questions so inapt that I sometimes wonder if the world above me has not gone mad.

"I have come to inquire," said a woman who intruded on me a few months ago, after she had made her excuses for misting me with sneezes provoked by tripping over a pile of ancient scrolls and clouding the room with dust, "if, contrary to law and common decency, human sacrifice is still practiced in Sythiphore."

I don't know what they do in Sythiphore, and I don't care, but I said: "Unfortunately, you are not qualified. Virginity is not essential, but a memory of that state, however dimmed by the passage of time and the reception of multitudes, is. Nor are beauty and intelligence necessary, but one must at least approximate the lowest degrees consonant with being human. No, dear lady, they would spurn you in Sythiphore. I suggest that you go home and hang yourself, offering up this sacrifice to whatever God might be persuaded to accept it."

"You dog!" she cried, and she added, as if it were both a mortal insult and a clever discovery, even though my black garments and the heraldic tigers of my badges and tattoos clearly announce it, "You are a *Vendren*. What name do you go by, that I may report you to my dear friend, Lord Vendrard?"

"Six Lord Vendrards grace the ruling council of my Tribe," I said, "but none of them is influential or even sane. I, however, am the only Vendren who bears the name Asteriel."

"Murderer! You murdered your dear wife . . . *twice!* Help!" Raising further billows of dust and mold, she screamed her way out of the archives and into the dank maze. For some time after this, her cries of "Help!" and "Murder!", swelling or fading, announced the contorted path of her underground adventures. At long last I heard no more. She had either found her way out or broken her neck. I resumed my writing.

As interruptions to my work go, it was a very long one, but not without diversion.

*

Yes, I am Asteriel Vendren, but I never had a wife. If I'd had one, I probably would not have killed her for taking lovers, for I am a gentle and forgiving man. It is even less probable that I could have raised her from the dead with nostalgic coition, or that I would have killed her a second time when she took up her old ways in her new life. Yet that stupid woman had believed it all.

Neither did I, as a youth, toss a cloth soiled by solitary pleasure into a pit behind a slaughterhouse, ignorant that the body of a murdered woman lay buried in the animal refuse; nor did my seed impregnate the morass of corruption to produce a monstrous son who haunts me in hope of a father's blessing. Other unwelcome guests have fled my office in the mortal fear that this son hulks in the shadows.

The fault is not mine. It lies with those too literal-minded to grasp that I have breathed new life into the popular tale by making it the storyteller's own.

Some day the world will catch up with my genius. In the meantime I must be screamed at by fools, and all because idle pranksters, whenever demented strays ask them for directions, send them straight to me. They resent my being paid as Inspector of Moats and Trenches, when the moats have been dry these two centuries, and the trenches are overgrown lanes.

They deny it, of course. One doesn't play jokes on a Vendren, even on a mild one who spends his time writing stories in a cellar; and I'm sure that those morons upstairs believe that I, if I knew who was responsible, would set my son on them.

In spite of the tales I write and the name I bear, I thought I was the most ordinary and harmless fellow you would ever want to meet, apart from two embarrassing defects. One, whose symptoms I had described to physicians, seemed to be a variant of Frothard's Debility: a disruption of consciousness, characterized in other sufferers by flailing of the limbs and foaming at the mouth.

Victims often know when an attack is imminent. They speak of flashing lights, anomalies of smell or hearing, a drastic narrowing of vision. Many accounts show similarities, but no attack I ever heard of was exactly like mine. My first hint would be a vile smell, not unlike a freshly opened grave, not unlike the approach of that son of mine. (Yes, I draw on personal experiences, artfully rearranged, for all my tales. That one is a record of my illness, masked in fable.) I would notice a pattern of glistening cobwebs on the ground, in the air, or even on my person.

Oddly, my ability to see the strands was determined by the intensity and direction of light when the attack came on. This curiosity puzzled physicians, and some of them, their opinion reinforced by their misunderstanding of my work, tacitly concluded that I was mad. The cobwebs were a product of my mind, they told me, and I should be able to see them in pitch darkness, but I did not. Light should not affect their visibility, but it did.

I was not totally honest with the doctors, but I must be in this memoir, or it will be worthless. I never revealed that I sometimes saw the strands when no attack threatened. They were visible if the light was strong enough and angled correctly, but so tenuously, so translucently, that I often convinced myself I imagined them. Rather than look closely, I would seek a shadier place. My office, with its thick shadows and real cobwebs, let me ignore them completely.

Here is the greatest oddity of all: others saw them. No other victim of Frothard's Debility is warned of an attack when bystanders sense strange sounds, sights or smells, but I have been. When I was a boy, before I learned to shun the light, people would try to brush "lint" from my little black tunic, never succeeding, and it made them most uneasy. Some recoiled from the touch.

The true warning sounded when I could not ignore the strands. They thickened, they swelled, they reddened, they pulsated — they sickened me! Gagging and shuddering, I began to see double, but in ways so weird that I feared I was dying or losing my mind. Meanwhile the rancid odor congealed, suffocated. The grave was open, and I tumbled into it.

What happened then, when the light went out? I never knew. Illness, Mother tried to teach me, is not evil, and sick people must not be condemned, but she had always seemed a finer person than I am. The afflicted disgust me, and I am not alone. My own foaming and mewling, my — Sleithreethra knows what! Whatever it is I did, whoever saw it shunned me forever after. My first seizure gripped me in the presence of my father, and I have not seen him since.

My mother, too, was present, but her love for me did not falter. She seemed, as I said, a fine person, but she could have schooled foxes in evasion. She never told me what I did that first time, as I watched them in their bed and felt myself losing control.

My illness was not an unmixed curse. Not even my Uncle Vendriel (Lord Vendriel the Implacable of Fandragord, not to be confused with those piffling Vendrards who infest our House) could get me a commission in Death's Darlings, the traditional family regiment. My appointment as Inspector of Moats and Trenches at Crotalorn was the best he could do. He has since avoided me, living proof that his power has limits, but I never cease from blessing his name. The job was made for me.

*

I spoke of two defects, and the second is more embarrassing. I did not choose to throw fits, but I do choose to spy. *Choose*. . .perhaps I am too hard on myself. Does a drunkard choose to drink? Yes, I suppose he does, as a thief chooses to steal, as a bad poet chooses to write, as an inveterate duelist chooses to kill: from all these spring exhilaration and a release from pain that the addict craves. Jam a pillow over my face, and I can't help myself, I will crave breath.

Oh, they know it's wrong, they lecture themselves, they set down rules to avoid temptation, but they always find excuses to drink, to write, to steal, to kill, to spy . . . to breathe.

I have known for quite some time what naked women look like. I have memorized the details. If I could draw, I could draw you one without reference to a model. And if I forgot some aspect, I could run up to the lobby and refresh my memory with the statue of Empress Fillitrella that adorns the central fountain. Were marble not enough, I could travel to Frothirot and buy a ticket to the baths; or to Sythiphore, and stroll through the streets. But in the baths at Frothirot, they do not sell tickets to let you conceal yourself; in Sythiphore, they would laugh if you hid behind a palm-tree to watch the women promenade the beaches. I love to watch, but watching without secrecy and danger blights my love.

*

I seldom give readings anymore. I am sick of women who scream or faint, men who grumble, "Barbarous!" or "Obscene!", sick of the self-right-eous show they make of stamping out before I finish. And half of those who remain, of course, will approach me to ask if I really skinned my mistress to preserve her exquisite tattoos, and might they not call on me to examine the artwork? When invited to read, I usually send a slave to recite.

It would have been impolitic to send a slave to Lord Nefandiel's palace on the Feast of the Assassination. As head of the city government, he has the power to expel me from my cozy office. It was the sort of gathering I most loathe, though, a swarming of the shallowest illiterates, whose holiday costumes and drunkenness would give them license to abuse me and my work even more than usual. Many would never have heard of me, and some would try hard to persuade me that I had written their favorite story, the tale of the Vendren Worm that my Tribe could invoke with unpredictable results in time of need: an ancient fairy tale, I believed, probably an allegory of our erratic relations with the dragon-bannered House of Fand.

After the banquet, after the dancers and clowns and sword-fighters had done their turns, the lights were lowered, and I walked to the center of the hall. No one applauded, but I was gratified by the hush that fell over the revelers, followed by a riffle of unease. My appearance, the lord had told me, was to be a surprise, his homage to the tradition of scaring people on this holiday. He had surprised them — shocked them, even. It remained for me to scare them.

I always feel that the tale I have just written is my best, and that was so now. I was blinded by enthusiasm. It seemed ideally suited for a public reading, since no one could confuse me with the narrator, dead for two hundred years, a Fomorian Guard called Pathrach Shornhand. He tells of the Great Plague that claimed the beloved Fillitrella, and the gruesome comedy attending the disposal of her remains.

Except for her return as a walking corpse who devours infants, the tale was grounded in historical fact. I was well pleased with myself, and far into the reading, before it occurred to me that Fillitrella was indeed beloved, as none of our rulers before or since. Even the Sons of Cludd, who despise the secular nobility and have no use for women, revere her as a saint; and a reverend lord commander of that order (unless the man's uniform was meant as a festival costume, but I doubted it) was sitting squarely and sourly in the front of my audience. The Fomorian Guards still glory in the title "Fillitrella's Own;" and the fishbelly-white redhead lounging behind him, a man so large and muscular that he could have, after a few brisk twists, used me to clean his ears, was obviously one of those merciless shock-troopers, even if he was costumed as a butterfly.

But more to the point, a point I stuck into myself more intimately with each word I read, was that Fillitrella was a Fand, which Tribe my host ornamented. My hungry corpse was his grandmother, several times re-moved.

Halfway through the story, Lord Nefandiel turned even whiter than the Fomor, who had himself begun experimenting with ever-darker shades of red. No one cried "Shame!" or "Treason!" They were stunned. No one screamed, but four persons did faint, not all of them women. The reverend lord commander's hand seemed glued to his sword, which revealed itself from the scabbard by slow but steady increments. I doubt that the plague-pit of my story could have displayed so many slack jaws and fixed stares as faced me now.

I thought of editing my work, but that was impossible. Once a story is finished, I can no more take out a word than I can take out my own liver. I considered adding an idiotic epilogue in the manner of Feshard Thooz — "But it was all a dream!" — but an artist would rather die first.

And, as my host whitened, as the barbarian reddened, as more steel gleamed in the Cluddite's lap, it appeared that I might indeed die. I began inching backward, intending to turn and run when I had read the last word, throwing the manuscript down with the hope that they would vent some of their fury on the scroll before pursuing its author.

The last word was read, and I could not but look up to see their reactions. We were frozen, the rabbit ringed by wolves, none of us able to move in an eternal moment of suspense. Then Lord Nefandiel began to applaud, and so did they all, even the Fomor and the Cluddite.

"I never knew all that about my illustrious ancestor," my host told me when I went to accept his congratulations. "Imagine that!"

"You don't look at all like a Fomor," Lady Fandrissa said. "And you seem so young to have been alive then!"

"Your friend hasn't eaten, has he? We could have something brought out," Lord Nefandiel said.

*

Yes, the Feast of the Assassination, when you scare people: and my host had just scared me more than he had during my reading.

I should have said that I have *three* defects, and the worst may be my talent for attracting supernumeraries. In any crowd like this, there will be one who cannot be accounted for, and everybody will assume that he came with me. I am a singularly single man, a haunter of the dark, an outsider, and yet I always have the sense of being followed, because I always am.

Walking home in the small hours down Potash Alley, a soiled wrinkle in the street-map that is never busy even at noon, I have many times turned to confront unlikely followers, each of them different, each with a plausible excuse for being there, but each following me, no matter what he might say.

I had never before seen the one that Lord Nefandiel indicated, a short, bald man with a demonic mask. I might have gone to demand who he was if, at that moment, a wall had not fallen on my back.

"You think like Fomor," said the giant butterfly, who had amiably mangled my shoulder with his paw. "How you do that?"

In twenty years of unappreciated writing, this was the most astute question I had ever heard, and I addressed it seriously while Akilleus Bloodglutter nodded and growled. I have no idea if he understood me, but he seemed pleased and vowed to send me the head of the very next prisoner he took.

Meanwhile, the man with the demon mask had vanished.

*

Whenever I read, I look for one attentive face and ignore the others. Ignoring that mob had been impossible, but I found someone who seemed sympathetic, and I did my best to read only to her. The wonder in her wide eyes, the parting of her pink lips, the flush of excitement that tinged her cheeks like the first light of dawn on apple-blossoms, suggested a child enthralled by a bedtime story, but she was no child. Dressed, or nearly so, as a nymph, she wore a coronet of yellow flowers on her artfully disordered hair.

I saw her again and angled through the crowd. I believe in the redemptive power of love. I had always hoped that one or more of my defects might be cured by the love of a good woman, or at least by the tolerance of an attractive one. I began to feel awkward as a boy, my head light, my extremities tingling. My store of words flounced away like a jealous mistress, and I knew that when I spoke, I would sound less urbane than Akilleus Bloodglutter, but I kept sliding toward her as if the room had tilted to abase itself at her pretty feet.

The man who faced me in her knot of admirers, the same Cluddite officer who had so intimidated me, began to shrug and grimace. Failing to read his signals, she continued: " . . . worse than I expected, a skinny, twitching gawk, as if some inept taxidermist tried to stuff a raven, then hid his mistake away in a damp cellar for years. Do you suppose the cobwebs on his clothes are part of his act, or does he sleep in a tomb?"

The Cluddite turned red as the pile of bricks he resembled, and he cleared his throat like a man choking on a fishbone, but she was oblivious to his distress. I should have fled, but even in that moment of despair I was hypnotized by the swells and planes of her mostly bared back. All colors but its rose and gold and cream had been deleted from the universe.

"That horrible son of his — have you read that vile story? Well, I'm sure his son would be much less of a monster —" here she laughed, a delicate tinkle of chimes in a torture chamber — "if he had taken more after his *mother!*"

One of her companions, more direct than the Cluddite, said: "He's standing behind you."

She turned, and I had to admire her: eyes flashing, chin thrusting, she attacked. "Your stories are garbage, sir. If the Sons of Cludd had their way, they would be burned, and you along with them."

Take this for proof of the brutal honesty of this memoir, that I am willing to reveal myself as a worse fool than anyone else. I said: "If the Sons of Cludd had their way, lady, they would make you cover your porcine rump in public."

One doesn't strike a Vendren, at least that is what Vendrens always say, parroting our motto: *Who Smites the Tyger?* Her response to that boast rang through the hall. It was such a shock that I stood and gaped, examining the pain of her slap with more curiosity about a new sensation than the outrage I should have felt, as she swirled away. I had once more become the center of attention in a silent throng.

The reverend lord commander gripped my arm. Dueling is forbidden to the Holy Soldiers, but so is attending parties like this one, and I thought he meant to lead me outside. Humiliation gave way to terror.

"'Of making many books there is no end,'" he quoted from his *Book of Cludd*, "'but there one day will be.'" Inappropriate as that quotation was, I think he meant it to comfort me. Perhaps it was the only one relating to literature that he could think of; and perhaps he felt only the concern that one feels for a marked victim. He gave my arm a comradely squeeze and walked away.

*

Except for a few sidelong glances and snickers, my disgrace was forgotten as the company gaily organized itself for the candlelight procession to the graveyard, where, on this night, one traditionally sees demons, posthumes and ghouls who may be questioned about the future. These would be mummers, of course, hired by Lord Nefandiel to titillate his guests. I overheard the cruel nymph plead a headache to our host, excusing herself from this romp. I hurried to bribe a servant, who told me her name, Vulnaveila Vogg, and the location of her room. Planning nothing, guided by my feet, I sped upstairs and concealed myself in her wardrobe.

The itch had mastered me, you see, the irresistible need to breathe. I wanted to pay her back for shaming me, too. She would never know I had examined her as thoroughly as I might examine a slave offered for sale while commanding one of her intimate garments to fondle me, but I would know. She might wonder, if I met her again, how I could meet her eyes and perhaps even smile into them as I savored my secret revenge. You need not tell me how sordid this seems, for my own spirit cringed from me as I crouched among her scented silks and furs.

I felt much as I had the first time, spying on my parents as they conjured up a beast with two backs: one whose hateful but fascinating existence I had never suspected, the beast with feet at either end. My first attack struck me then; and now I saw my cobwebs in the dimness of the wardrobe. O Gods! The woman I had wanted, who had reduced me to a child in front of the company, would witness my further reduction to a puling infant when she entered her room. Never mind the shame and the loss of my cozy office: for this abuse of his hospitality, Lord Nefandiel would have me racked and gutted, and my quaking remains diced.

I should have known better. The thrill of spying often provoked a fit. My previous targets had been mostly sluts, who would not raise an outcry upon discovering a man of the sword-bearing class twitching and drooling outside their windows. For whatever reason, I had never been denounced as a criminal pervert. I would always regain consciousness on my way home, never dogged by municipal guards, solicitous strangers or angry lovers. I had been very lucky. But a driven man cannot choose his doom, and I had been driven to possess Vulnaveila with my eyes.

I had just begun to creep from concealment when the door to the hall opened. I had no choice but to hide again.

She hesitated at the threshold, scanning the room in disquiet. I thought at first that I had left some trace, that I was about to be discovered. No: her nose wrinkled prettily. She *smelled* it, that graveyard odor of my coming attack. She knelt to look under the bed. She examined the chamber-pot and was puzzled to find it clean. The odor still bothered her. A proud woman, as I knew she was, would go straight to her host and demand another room, and I prayed that she would do so before I lost control. No, the silly creature flung open the casements! I jammed her silks into my mouth to muffle my cries; I knotted them clumsily around my arms and legs to restrain my thrashing. I wept, for this was going so wrong, so terribly wrong. She shed her costume as easily as one passing from shadow to sunlight, and for a moment I forgot my danger. She was perfect, achingly perfect. Her nipples were like bold bosses on the shields of conquering heroes. For calling her rump *porcine*, I could have torn out my tongue and ground it under my heel.

Now I felt like a carpenter whose hammer conceives the notion of beating him to death. Irony is the hammer of my craft, and it turned on me and savaged me as she picked up a book from the bedside table and snuggled down with a smile of anticipation to resume reading it. It was a volume of my own tales.

She did not trouble to cover herself against the unseasonably warm breeze from the windows. Staring at the fur-cradled center of her secrets was like staring at the sun, so my eyes lowered for a moment to the carpet. It held a confusing pattern of red and yellow strands. One of the red strands twitched, betraying its slimy thickness. The final alarm had sounded. The vileness of the odor redoubled, and I retched against my gag.

The door to the hall opened.

"Who are you? Leave at once!"

Blinking away my tears, I saw that my companion — or so Lord Nefandiel had thought him — had entered the room in his demon's mask. Was it a mask? If so, it was most cunningly made. Cobwebs on his garment writhed, they seemed connected to those in the rug, just as mine were. I had never before seen these strands on one of my supernumeraries. But I had never retained consciousness for so long, either, not after all the usual warnings, perhaps because I was struggling so hard to contain myself.

That a man in my position should try to rescue a woman from an intruder was ludicrous. That I might learn anything from him, when I was about to fall down in convulsions, was stupid. These motives nevertheless drove me to step out of the wardrobe.

At that moment my double vision assaulted me. Superimposed upon the door to the hallway was the open door to the wardrobe. I saw Vulnaveila's beauty from two angles at once, and you might think this was a spy's dream come true, but it frightened and sickened me. I saw myself through the intruder's eyes, and him through my own, at the same time.

Vulnaveila hurled my book, and her aim was good, it struck squarely between the eyes, but the result was nightmarish. The head split and melted aside as a monstrous growth erected. The neck metamorphosed into a tubular creature, a pale worm, whose red mouth sucked and slurped at the air as it writhed.

I shrugged out of my makeshift bonds, but she and I could only watch as the prodigy elaborated itself. The neck swelled, subsuming the man beneath it, and his garments, too: black and orange swirls on the pale hide suggested his clothing, a distorted eye and a cluster of unformed fingers recalled the man on the upright worm. It bloated to impossible size, arching, its bristly hump brushing the ceiling and its mouth poised over her head. Tendrils squirmed in that edentulous maw, their obscene red shading to an even viler purple.

Crystals of drool spattered her perfect body, and this broke the spell. As she tried to scrub them from her flesh, she screamed.

I have witnessed executions that I would hesitate to describe in one of my tales, botched executions whose cruelty and duration exceeded anything envisioned by law. Living as I do in an unfashionable section of the city, I sometimes hear citizens assaulted by thieves, degenerates, or religious fanatics. I am not unfamiliar with screams of pain and terror. Never have I heard a scream quite like Vulnaveila Vogg's. It was not loud, it was muted by her rising gorge, but her gagging cry conveyed more fear than a full-throated shriek.

Weakling and pervert though I be, I am still a Vendren, heir to the Insidiator, and I had my sword. What a happy tale this could have been: my quirk justified, the monster slain, the woman mine. Oh, for the pen of Feshard Thooz! But my trade is in that foulest of wares, truth. I am no sworder, whose weapon is part of his hand; my tiger-hilted rapier is only a social ornament; and with my eyes locked on the unfolding horror, I failed to find it when I groped for it.

In that moment of unforgivable clumsiness the worm struck: the mouth descended, capping her head and shoulders, while the tendrils clutched and probed her in unspeakable ways. Kicking and squirming, she was lifted from the bed.

The monster contracted itself to a fat barrel as it held her, flailing legs up, and swallowed her by steady degrees, through a loathsome alternation of stretches and compressions. The shape of her body remained visible, as in a crude rendering of wet clay. Abrupt bulges and dimplings in the flexible monstrosity suggested that her struggles never ceased. The sucking and squelching were intolerable.

I was helpless. Her splendid feet had vanished, and with their disappearance an immovable weight fell on my soul. If the worm had attacked me next, I could not have moved. Not fear, but a conviction of total futility, immobilized me. The fit came on me at last. My next memory is of striding through darkness toward my home.

*

I buried myself in my office and my work. The servant I had bribed would talk, his testimony would link me to the missing woman — but nothing happened as two weeks passed, then three. I had just begun to breathe more easily when a young officer from Never-Vanquished appeared at my door. His expression alarmed me until I realized that a scar had set his mouth in a permanent sneer.

Then I looked into his cold eyes, and my alarm returned.

The usual visitors sent me by the jokers upstairs are silly matrons, doddering simpletons, callow youths. I knew that this capable young man with his hand on his sword had not come to chat with me about ghosts, fairies or flying ships.

Over the centuries, my office has become the final resting place for rubbish from the floors above: tax forms, trial records, thumbscrews and gibbet-irons. Bracketed on the wall was one of the two-hand swords that Death's Darlings wield, or at least wear, called a manqueller. I doubted that anyone could actually use such a large and heavy weapon. I nevertheless rose from my writing desk and drifted toward it, knowing that I stood no chance against him with rapiers.

"Sir, I want to ask you about my betrothed, Vulnaveila Vogg," he said.

I knew him. He had changed his appearance, as he always did, and was no longer short and old, or bald. His hair was long and wild, like hers, like the woman he had devoured. He was my nemesis, he was the worm.

I pulled the manqueller from the wall with a great scraping clang and spun with it, nearly overbalancing. Contrary to my belief, it could be used, and with great effect. It split him right down to the wishbone. No worm burst out, foiled by my cleverness: only an explosion of the distasteful fluids and solids one would expect from a split man.

After cleaning my office as well as I could and dragging my victim to a niche where no one would ever think to look, I rode all night and half the next day. *Mother!* She knew, and I would make her tell. The inn where I first stopped had no fresh horse immediately available, so I drank myself senseless. I needed to forget the peddlar who trailed me.

The green mountains around Crotalorn gave way to farmlands, flatlands. I remembered horses, carriages, ferries, and I remembered mountebanks and pilgrims and mercenaries who seemed to follow me, but none of them clearly. I think I killed another man on my journey, a mendicant monk whose persistence grew suspect.

I rode at last in dark streets cut from the black rock of the underlying hill. "Witch-cursed," Feshard Thooz would call it, "demon-haunted" Fandragord, and he would be right. When the Sons of Cludd occupied the city, it is said, you could not see your hand before your face at noontime for the greasy smoke of burning sinners, and I suppose many of them cursed it as they burned. As for the demons, they are the Vendrens and Fands, not at all like the polite folk you meet elsewhere, but always ready to avenge a long-cherished insult against their great-great-grandfathers with a riot or a murder. It is a dismal and dangerous place, and I had rejoiced to be free of it, but I was home.

"Astri!" my mother shrieked with delight, which moderated as she took a second look. "What on earth have you been doing to yourself? And what is that for?"

The manqueller was strapped to my back. It is terribly heavy, yes, but effective.

"I am a Vendren, am I not?"

She accepted that answer with a wry smile as she drew me into the great hall. Pale servants and slaves drifted along with us, attentively lurking. I scanned them, wondering which one she would pick as "my companion," but I could not tell.

"Am I not?" I repeated with heavy emphasis.

She studied me quizzically. The gray streaks in her hair suggested a young woman's whim, effected with dye. Instead of answering, she batted her eyelashes and giggled, but I had steeled myself against her usual stratagems.

"Years ago — " My prepared speech was interrupted by her calls for food and drink, a bustling of underlings, my fussy placement at the head of the table.

"Years ago, I spied on you and father —"

"Oh, Astri, that's forgotten."

"Fangs of the Goddess! I have not forgotten it. It was wrong, I regret it, but it happened, and my father left us. Why? Where is he? Did *something* kill him?"

"Something?"

Imagine my difficulty. I wanted to say: "When I lost consciousness, did someone enter the room, transform himself into a giant worm, and eat my father?" Fandragord boasts one of the largest and least enlightened lunatic asylums on earth. She used to take me there on holidays as a child. Although deploring the popular sport of throwing refuse at the inmates, she had been unable to resist hurling a few eggs at a common madman who claimed to be our grandest ancestor, Vendriel the Insidiator. Would she come and throw rotten eggs at me?

I hit upon a saner but perhaps even more pointed question: "When I was a child, why did you never tell me the old fairy tale that every other child knows, the one about the Vendren Worm?"

"I never told you any such stories, Astri. Don't you remember how they frightened you, when a playmate or a foolish nurse told them?"

The hall was full of cobwebs, most of them real. But some of them were mine. And some of them — that glistening strand on her left breast — were hers.

"Mother!" I cried. "Tell me. . . ."

"Do you have the feeling that you are not alone, Astri?"

I sprang to my feet and kicked back my chair. Her pale servants had grouped around us like a fairy-ring, so symmetrical, so neatly spaced; and as she spoke, each of them simultaneously spoke her words.

The foul worm writhed forth — but a different worm from the one that had eaten Vulnaveila. Can a monster be elegant, a horror beautiful? They can, for I marveled at these qualities in its swaying posture and in the complex pattern and colors of its verminous hide. I drew my manqueller, but I could not strike, for the creature squirmed from the dissolving body of my mother.

"What are you?" I screamed. "And what am I?"

"I am your mother," the pallid chorus around me said in duplications of her tender voice, "and you are my beloved son, who goes by the name of Asteriel Vendren among the apish flocks we tend. Cast off that ugly guise, cast off your false knowledge of the world, and embrace me at last as —"

I remember these words now, I can read them on the stone of my heart, but at the time I felt them only as the bites of the stone-cutter's chisel. They were meaningless, they pelted me like hail, these words in the voice that had once crooned me to sleep, and would you blame a man in a hailstorm for shielding his head with his hands? The same sort of un-thinking impulse sent the manqueller in a great whirring arc that began at my heels and ended deep in the wood of the table. Midway through that arc swayed the lovely abomination: swayed, then tumbled in two segments.

What had I done? I think I asked this question aloud, and it instantly received more answers than I could grasp. The chorus of attendants jittered in erratic circles, their skin blackening and bubbling, their voices a discord of wheezes and whistles. The halved worm tried to transform itself into my mother, but failed in increasingly more ghastly ways. Her face, bloated beyond human proportion, would be split by the feeler-crawling maw of the worm; the legs would knot and coil; the breasts would swell and burst, spattering a vile fluid before reforming and swelling again. Its death agonies sucked up flooring-blocks that ten men could not have lifted and crushed them to gravel. Ancient armor, which no sword ever dented, racketed through the hall in tinkling shards as it was splintered by a flailing worm-tail or a giant mother-hand.

I could not flee. I was surrounded by a heaving ring of pustulence that had been the bodies of the servants. Pimples constantly rose in the mass, bursting into holes that vented unspeakable odors. It seemed no less dangerous than the worm, and I could not bring myself to wade through it. Instead I struggled to wrench the manqueller free from the table and strike again.

It was hopeless. Perhaps I should have been a soldier, for my strength had driven the sword into the massive table beyond extrication. I was about to reach for my rapier, as useful against the monster as a pin against a whale, when swells that resembled enormous buttocks, but patterned like the skin of the worm, gripped the table in their cleft and crushed it to powder.

The manqueller was free, and I used it with a will.

Toward the very end of my orgy of slashing and hacking, a bit of the worm metamorphosed into a perfect replica of my mother's head. Sobbing, I picked it up in my stained hands with some vague thought of giving it funeral honors, but it spat in my face before melting into a foul jelly that slipped through my fingers.

*

The barrier of former servants had shrunken and dried. I could pass through it to tear down torches and cast them into the twitching horror. Much of the hall was made of wood. It would burn well. With luck, the stone walls would collapse upon themselves and leave no clue for the curious.

Everyone, but him so fortunate as to die first, loses his mother. It is a hard fact that unites me with every idiot who ever wandered into my office, with men so different from me as Akilleus Bloodglutter and Reverend Lord Commander Cluddax Umbren. You can imagine some of my feelings. I daresay you cannot imagine them all.

What had she meant, that I should shed *my* ugly guise? The worm dwelled in others, in that demon-masked intruder, in the strangers who followed me.

It dwelled within the man I now saw fleeing before me as I staggered from the burning home of my childhood.

All of my grief and anger and frustration condensed to a murderous core. He was the one who hounded me. He was the extension that held my hereditary evil, the Vendren Worm.

The chase continued on foot, on stolen horses. The questions that tumbled through my head were enough to drive me mad, and perhaps they already had. What was I? Was I a sensory organ of the worm, a tentacle-tip sent out in the guise of a man to find victims through my habit of lurking and spying? Had I, through my dedication to art, created a self more powerful than the monster's own?

Out in the thorny desert of Hogman's Plain that surrounds Fandragord, his mount snagged its hoof and collapsed.

"Die, worm!" I cried, hoisting the manqueller athwart the rotting face of Ashtareeta, our moon-mother.

"It is a wise hero," he said, with a suggestion of a smirk, "who knows the worm from himself."

This gave me pause. While I pondered, I hardly noticed the transformation that came over me, no more difficult or memorable than peeling off a glove; or than shedding silk bonds, as I had seemed to do in Vulnaveila's room. Thinking back on that moment of double vision, I realized that the man who became the worm had worn the black garments and heraldic symbols of the Vendrens. The other, the masked intruder, had not been so dressed. What I witnessed had been my own change, through the eyes of the shadow-self who followed me.

As my abstraction continued I devoured him, and both our horses.

*

Since then he has come back, or someone like him, and is with me always. He no longer trails me at a distance. Whenever rage overcomes me and I turn on him and eat him, he returns as a closer shadow. I try to restrain myself, but now he stands at my side.

When I grow older and stronger, I suppose I shall be surrounded by a ring of such creatures, as was my mother. Were they mindless organs in human form, or did they embody aspects of herself that she could not contain? Whatever they were, she seemed able to control them, and I have no power over mine. Not just for sentimental reasons, I often wish that I had not killed her.

The discovery that I am not human, you might think, would be shattering, but it brings consolations. I understand now why I feel so different from the common run of men, a difference that used to trouble me. I no longer lose consciousness during my transformations, I no longer fret about Frothard's Debility: whatever I am, I am not ill.

One of my hopes has been blighted. I cannot win the love of a good woman, which might heal me, when a man is always beside me. Everyone assumes he is my lover.

I tell them that he is my son.

Meryphillia

"For a ghoul is a ghoul, and at best an unpleasant companion for man."

— H.P. Lovecraft, *The Dream Quest of Unknown Kadath*

Meryphillia was the least typical ghoul in the graveyard. No man would ever have called her a beauty, but her emaciation was less extreme, her pallor less ghastly, and her gait less grotesque than those of her sisters.

Untypically tender-hearted, she would sometimes shed a tear for a dead infant that her nature compelled her to devour. She was considerate of her fellows, too, and her feeding habits were all but mannerly. Least typical of all, for ghouls love to laugh, was her inextinguishable sorrow for the world of sunlight and human warmth she had lost.

*

Traditional wisdom holds that ghouls bring their condition upon themselves by indulging morbid interests in adolescence. Gluttriel, God of Death, takes note of such youngsters and offers them the knowledge of the corpses they will eat in return for their lives.

Others assert that ghoulism is a disease, called Porfat's distemper after the physician who described it, and who later vanished under circumstances of suggestive peculiarity. Before the transformation becomes obvious to those grieving at the sickbed, their grief compounded by the loved one's growing taste for perverse wit and unseemly laughter, a hunger for dead flesh impels the victim to the nearest burial ground. The first meal induces physical changes that destroy all hope of return to human society.

Either explanation might apply in Meryphillia's case. As a girl nearing womanhood in Crotalorn, she knew the necropolis called Dreamers' Hill better than the malls and ballrooms where her peers flocked. She wandered among the tombs of the rich and the ditches of the poor in all weathers. Her clothing, lacking style to begin with, suffered from these rambles, and it never quite fit: perhaps because a pocket would always be weighted down with a volume of Asteriel Vendren's tales, malign carbuncles of that madman's diseased fancy.

Perched on some collapsed slab that might well have capped a ghoul-pit, innocently ascribing the scratches and titters she heard to the creak of trees and rustle of weeds, she would play an air of Umbriel Fronn on her recorder, a cherished gift from her late mother. Often she would pause to ponder questions that the healthy young person is well advised to leave to priests and philosophers.

Her father strove to cure her moping and put some meat on her bones in the hope of marrying her into one of the Great Houses. He would regularly purge her library, castigating her preference for tales of terror to worthwhile literature, for Umbriel's cerebral nocturnes to the cheery ditties of the day. He would pinch her cheeks into smiles as he bellowed for food, wine and happy tunes. Unfortunately his business as a timber-merchant kept him often from the city and their home on Hound Square, and Meryphillia would resume her unhealthy habits as soon as he had breezed out the door.

When he held up her stepmother as an example to emulate in his absence, she would only hang her head and mumble. A giddy Frotherine not much older than the girl herself, she filled the house with robust athletes and ditty-strummers in what she claimed was an effort to cheer her daughter up. She never seemed to notice when Meryphillia fled to the nearby cemetery to escape their din and their importunities.

Whether she fled into the arms of Gluttriel, or whether vapors of the corpse-crammed and claw-mined earth afflicted her with Porfat's distemper, the result was the same: shortly before her eighteenth birthday, she vanished irretrievably into the burrows of the ghouls.

*

For all their laughter, ghouls are a dull lot. Hunger is the fire in which they burn, and it burns hotter than the hunger for power over men or for knowledge of the gods in a crazed mortal. It vaporizes delicacy and leaves behind only a slag of anger and lust. They see their fellows as impediments to feeding, to be mauled and shrieked at when the mourners go home. They are seldom alone, not through love of one another's company, but because a lone ghoul is suspected of concealing food. Their copulation is so hasty that distinctions of sex and identity are often ignored.

Just as she had once yearned to know the secrets of the grave, Meryphillia now longed to penetrate the mysteries of friendship and love. Mostly she wanted to know about love. She believed that it must transcend her bony collisions with Arthrax, least unfeeling of all the male ghouls, whom she untypically clove to.

"Why are you crying?" he once asked while their coupling rattled the slats of a newly emptied coffin.

"It's nothing. Dust in my eyes."

"That happens."

His question and comment were the nearest a ghoul could come to sympathy, but it fell so far short of the standard she imagined to be human that she wept all the more.

*

She sought answers from the dead, for the ghoul acquires the memories of what it feeds upon, but her strength was no match for the giants of the underground in the battle for mnemonic bits. Studying human experience from the scraps she got was like learning about painting by spinning on her toes through a museum. She hugged vivid glimpses: the smell of orange spice-cake and a childish song that evoked a long-gone celebration of Polliel's Birthday; the creaking leather and muscular embrace of someone's beloved brother, home safe at last from a forgotten war; a shrine ablaze with stolen candles, a wan face among borrowed blankets, the words, "The fever has broken."

Others did far better. Feeding lustily, they would recall great chunks of lives. For a while they would assume a likeness to their meal and give those satiric impersonations of human beings that are a favorite entertainment of their kind. Even Meryphillia screamed with laughter when Lupox and Glottard disputed which of them was Zuleriel Vogg, the notorious grave-robber, whose execution the ghouls had cheered only less gleefully than the disposal of his pieces in an unguarded pit.

Scroffard once wolfed down an old beggar woman so completely that his performance lost its satirical edge. He alternately whined for spare coins, complained of the dark and damp and smell, and quavered, "Who is that? Who's there?" at every furtive patter and stifled giggle.

Most shunned the mock woman, hoping that Scroffard, when he recovered and found no one else on whom to exercise his temper, would tear off his own head for a change; but Meryphillia, who would formerly have crossed the street to avoid such a wretch, was drawn to caress the fragile face. She seemed beautiful, not least of all for her intensely feeling eyes.

Handicapped with human vision, Scroffard was at first unable to make out the young ghoul by the glow of the niter-crusted tunnel. When he saw what pawed his human face, he screamed his way to the surface, where he was battered about the head by the shovels of two grave-robbers. To their dismay, for they thought they were dealing with the routine nuisance of a prematurely buried hag, the beating restored the most irascible of ghouls to his roaring self. He wrenched from the luckless men the vengeance he might otherwise have wrested from Meryphillia.

*

She treasured what happy moments she could retrieve, but murder, disease and madness were the staples of her diet, with the manifold agonies of death for dessert. The fond memories of the rich were locked away in tombs of marble and bronze, while souvenirs of poverty and despair lay everywhere for the taking. The very poorest corpses, unloved, unmourned, unwanted by either medical students or necrophiliacs, were thrown directly into a riddled pit that the gravediggers called Gluttriel's Lunch-Bucket. No matter how full the hole was filled by nightfall, by morning its rocky bottom would be licked clean as a dutiful child's porridge-bowl.

One day word chattered through the mines that a man of substance, sleek as a pig and skewered cleanly in a duel, had just been laid in a plain grave. His widow, no native of Crotalorn, had conceived the notion that its ghouls were a myth. As the box dropped into the earth of an unfashionable quarter, she was overheard to assure the attentive victor in the duel that bronze-bound tombs of stone were vulgar.

No ghoul resumed his sleep that day. The ground of the thrilling burial was too quaggy for tunneling; the meat must be extracted from above. Digging should begin at the first blink of darkness, before human thieves could cheat the underground of its due. As the watchmen would still be reasonably sober, as mourners might be dawdling, the daring of the raiders would set new limits for legend. Debate over tactics grew so heated that the crows of the necropolis took wing and blackened the dome of Ashtareeta's temple, which was seen as a fearful omen by her clergy, and cause for an emergency collection.

Meryphillia knew the debate was a farce. Plans would be trampled in a general stampede for the grave. Her own best hope was to creep out at twilight and work her way among the hedges and headstones until she had found a hiding place near the target. Her intention was not to get there first: whoever claimed that honor would be run over by a monster like Glottard or Lupox. She would wait for one of them to make his dash and cling to the bristles of his dorsal ridge while he punished the early starters. Sticking close as the warts on his rump, she would snatch what scraps she could.

When the moment came, Clamythia, wiliest of ghouls, usurped the shadow of Lupox. It pained Meryphillia to trip her sister and emboss the mud with her venerable muzzle, but protocol had foundered in howling chaos. Lupox savaged the first arrivals like a fighting-dog set on rats, uncaring that two of the obstructions he flung from his path were human watchmen. Whimpering mindlessly, they left their broken bills where they lay and staggered to the safety of their lodge.

The grave erupted in a fountain of dirt, pumped pluming into the twilight by a frenzy of ghoulish talons. The geyser soon began to spray crushed flowers, splinters of wood, then tattered silk and trinkets of gold that a robber would have wept to see so treated. Without undue effort, Meryphillia found herself hugging a whole quarter of a head, with the coveted eye adhering.

This was the ghoulish equivalent to a delicacy that a banquet-guest would have exclaimed over before daintily sampling; but Meryphillia, with claws scraping her back, elbows gouging her ribs and jaws stretching over her shoulder to seize her prize, could only stuff it into her mouth, grind it hastily, and gulp it down.

Hunched between Lupox's gnarly knees, she then beheld the strangest vision: of herself, standing up straight, as her father had so often told her to; with her hair pushed out of her eyes, as he had so often pushed it; and with an unlikely smile dimpling cheeks not nearly so gaunt as they had been. The vision glowed with love, tinged only slightly by the acid of vexation and fixed forever beneath a glaze of sorrow.

She realized whose grave she crouched in, but, being what she was, could only scrabble for more and leave her feelings to sort themselves out. Her next find was a hand, one that held a far clearer imprint of her stepmother's buttocks. It proved a timely antidote to the first course.

*

In her preoccupation with life, Meryphillia relapsed into her solitary ways. She was allowed to. No one suspected her of hiding food. The ghouls thought her as odd as humans once had. Like them, her new companions were grateful for a respite from her brooding silences, her inappropriate observations and her reluctance to join in a good laugh.

Lurching one night along a path she used to glide with her recorder, she nearly stumbled over a man who had come neither to loot tombs nor kill himself. He was declaiming verses to the full moon with such rapt fervor that he failed to notice her slip hastily into the tent of a willow's branches.

This was the poet Fragador, which she learned from his own lips, for he gave himself credit for each poem as if afraid the moon would confuse him with someone else: "*On the Hands of Therissa Sleith*, a sonnet by Fragador of Fandragord," he would announce, or, "*For Therissa Sleith on Her Birthday*, an ode by Fragador, poet and tragedian, lately of Fandragord."

It would be an inconstant moon indeed, she thought, that would forget his name. He was the most beautiful man she had ever seen; but she viewed him with the eyes of a ghoul, unaware that many people thought him ghoulishly pale and thin. Her heart, so still even before her present state, startled her like a hammering visitor at her breast.

His subject pleased less than his voice. Therissa Sleith was the darling of Crotalorn, and had often been held up to her as an example of what she was not. Fragador desired her as ardently, though perhaps not quite so hopelessly, as Meryphillia desired him.

He visited the graveyard as often as she used to, and always with a new batch of poems praising the wit, grace and beauty of the same unsuitable person. When the moon had other obligations, he would recite his verses to a statue of Filloweela that reclined complaisantly on one of her cleric's tombs, unaware that the lavish form of the Goddess hid a quivering horror that yearned to give him everything Therissa withheld.

How she loathed that name! It figured in every verse he wrote, and his voice would falter and throb on its snaky nastiness. She learned to anticipate its occurrence, and she would whisper her own name just loudly enough to bar the syllables from her ears, even though this lamed his elegant scansion. Sometimes she would speak too vehemently, and he would clear his throat, clean his ear, or peer uneasily into the shadows.

His heart heard her name, however imperfectly, for one night he thrilled her by declaiming a poem to "Morthylla," whom his poetic intuition identified as a lurking spirit of night and death, and whose help he invoked in softening Therissa before her lithe limbs should go to feed the ghouls. Meryphillia would recite the lines to herself while wishing that those limbs were in fact within reach of her coffin-cracking jaws.

They were so alike, or had been, she and Fragador, with their delight in horror, their flirtation with death, their love of shadow and solitude. If only she had met him — but she withered her wish: even if she had stood up straight and combed her hair, even if she had twittered pleasantries and smiled now and then, no man drawn to the pert face and nubile form of Therissa Sleith would have spared her a glance.

His verses swerved into delirium when the cruel ninny was betrothed to another. The corruption that had always festered beneath his sunniest images tore off its mask as he raved of murder and suicide. Not just a beautiful man, not just a gifted poet, he was a genius, Meryphillia avowed, one who gazed even more deeply into the abyss than had Asteriel Vendren. She loved him, she worshipped him, and now that the incongruous object of his desire had shown herself an even worse fool than had been obvious, she timidly hoped for him. She hardly ate, she never slept, she grew so listless that rats began to eye her with an impudent surmise. She pictured her brain as crawling with busy ants, each ant a notion for declaring her love, until she could have smashed her skull to exterminate them.

The full moon returned, but the poet did not. She fretted, pacing from the favored statue to the willow and back again. At last she broke the circle and loped to the main gate, to the very fringe of life and light. Springing atop the wall, she peered up and down Citron Street, then leaned perilously far to scan Hound Square, descrying no one but unremarkable stragglers and lurkers. So great was her concern for her beloved that the sight of her festively lit home, the first she had had of it since her transformation, gave her no slightest pang.

The first note of a shriek told her she had been seen, but she slipped into the darkness so swiftly that it lost conviction and ended as an embarrassed laugh.

She feared that Fragador had made good the threat of his latest poem and killed himself, but her fear was superseded by fearful desire. She had longed for union with him. What union could be more complete than to be the man himself?

His grumbled asides had told her that he would be granted no impregnable crypt. She would raid his grave at high noon to beat the greater ghouls to his dear relics. Watchmen be damned! What finer way to end her existence than in the form of her love, to remember the pain of his death even as she saw her own coming, and saw it coming with his very eyes? No passion had ever been so fully consummated. It would cry out in vain for the immortalizing pen of Fragador.

Fatigued, distraught, but now ever so dimly cheered, she found her way to his favorite tomb and lay down in the moon-shadow of the Goddess of Love, where she slept.

She was woken by sobbing so bitter that she thought it must be her own. The fat and ruddy moon had decayed to a ghoulish disc above her. Rubbing her eyes, she felt no tears, but the sobs continued. It was he, and her joy nearly drove her to dash forth and embrace him before she thought what effect this might produce.

"Ghouls!" he suddenly screamed. "Fiends and demons of the dark, attend me! Morthylla, come to me!"

Before others could respond, she rose.

"By Cludd!" he gagged, and half his sword appeared like silver lightning from its scabbard. In a like flash, she saw herself in his loathing grimace. A wheel revolved ponderously inside her, leaving something crushed. She crossed her hands to her shoulders and hung her head in supplication.

"I did call you," he said after a long silence. "Your promptness startled me."

"Forgive me."

"Offense and forgiveness have no meaning, for meaning itself is nonsense. Therissa Sleith is no more."

"I'm sorry," she lied.

"You would be, of course. Not even a ghoul's dream could penetrate the sepulcher of the Sleiths."

She looked up to protest this misunderstanding, but his face silenced and melted her. Something like wonder had crossed it when he saw her eyes. Her father had always praised them as her best feature, and now they were the most vividly yellow globes in the underground.

"Are you really. . . ?" he began. "No, it would be mad to ask if you are a symptom of my madness."

"You are the sanest man since Asteriel Vendren."

"Sleithreethra spare us from literate ghouls!"

She shuddered. Not even a ghoul would speak the name of that Goddess in a graveyard at midnight, and certainly not with a laugh. He was indeed mad, and it thrilled her. No more to be held than a sob or a last breath, it burst out: "I love you!"

He stepped forward boldly. "Come down from the tomb, then, Morthylla, and let us speak of love."

Her claws clicked with their shaking until they rested in his firm clasp. She whispered, "Don't mock me." She added, "And it's *Meryphillia*."

Correction seemed to irk him, but he took it. "I have heard that a ghoul who eats the heart and brain of a person becomes that person."

"I have seen it."

"I mean no offense, but this restoration would have no added characteristics? No redundancy of teeth, no odor, no urge to laugh at odd moments?"

She averted her misting eyes. "The personation is perfect." She flared. "My odor offends you?"

She was instantly sorry, having forgotten that her new face and voice translated petulance as demoniacal fury.

"Please," he said when he could speak again. "I meant nothing like that. A dead body, you know. You have an inner beauty, Meryphillia. I see it through your eyes."

"Really?"

"Please don't laugh, I'm unused to it." She was unaware that she had laughed. He thrilled her by taking her hand in both of his. "Dear ghoul, I have acquired the key to the tomb of the Sleiths, where Therissa will be interred tomorrow. I wish you to do with her as we said."

"But that's monstrous!"

His look clearly told her that the word was inappropriate on her nominal lips, but she pressed on: "She would be just as she was in life. If she denied you then — "

"Her parents denied me, her position denied me, her name denied me; never her heart. If she had but one hour, she might listen to her heart. If I could have a word with her, a look — dare I hope for a kiss?"

A perverse impulse to refuse seized her. She desired him as she had never desired anyone, but the price he demanded, to transform herself into the sort of person her father and stepmother had wanted her to be, was too high.

"Please, Meryphillia," he murmured, and he shocked her by touching his lips to her cheek. She took the key he pressed into her callused palm.

*

Near the hour of the tryst, she crept through the flowering precincts of the richest tombs with ghoulish stealth, which makes the hovering owl seem rowdy. Her ears were extended to gather the whispers of moths and the mutter of coffin-worms. Her nasal pits gaped to the fullest, so that each encrypted corpse around her, however desiccated by ages uncounted, announced its discrete presence: none more brightly than that of Therissa Sleith, its decay just a sigh beneath the salt tears and scented soaps of the servants who had primped her for the last time.

No other ghouls blighted the air with their rancid breath, nor watchmen with their wine, but she crept nonetheless, horrified by a vision of the underground host bursting over her to fill the tomb of the Sleiths, ransacking bones inviolate for a thousand years and scattering Therissa's shreds into a thousand greedy gullets. If that happened, she could never face Fragador. No, she would creep up from behind, fight down her distaste for unripe flesh, and eat him. Denied the looks and sighs and touches of his love, she would at least know him from the inside of his being.

She rose to her full height only in the shadow of the doorway, where the terrible motto of Therissa's tribe was incised beneath an image of Sleithreethra: WHO TOYS WITH US, SHE SHALL FONDLE. The brass key that Fragador had given her slipped from quivering fingers to clatter as loudly, it seemed, as the head of a watchman's bill, nor could her scrabbling claws at once fit themselves to the human device. She was sobbing with frustration by the time she succeeded in juggling it up to the keyhole and jamming it in.

The bronze leaves swung inward on oiled hinges. The chain to a gong in the tower had been cut by a watchman with a taste for Fragador's verse and an even greater gusto for opium, who had been persuaded that the poet contemplated no unusual indecencies with the dead darling of Crotalorn.

She was lovely, Meryphillia had to admit when she had ripped the massive lid from the sarcophagus, especially now that the pink tinge of her skin had been replaced with hints of violet. The fatal twist of her head had been all but straightened; she could have been a sleeper who would wake with nothing to complain of but a stiff neck.

She paused for a moment to admire the elfin nose, so unlike the assertive one she had worn, before biting it off. Uncoiling her razorish tongue, she slipped it in to shred the brain into manageable morsels. Dainty swirls of her smallest claw served to scoop out the eyes. She savored them with restrained whimpers of pleasure before proceeding to the large and tasty breasts.

Therissa heard her sisters chattering as they returned from the regimental review of Cludd's Whirlwind. It was their custom to tease the Holy Soldiers with inviting smiles and restless wiggles. The celibate warriors were charged to be on their sternest behavior, and the girls' object was to make one drop his pike or, worse, raise his staff, offenses that earned the culprit a flogging and a night spent kneeling on pebbles. Why had Meryphillia never had such fun, never even thought of it? She almost wept for her wasted life before recalling that she had done it, as Therissa Sleith.

Ripping down to bare ribs, she opened them like a book: the Book of

Love. She gobbled the tough, lean heart.

How that heart had leaped when, whirling at the head of the stairs to show off her bridal gown, Therissa had felt the hem snag her heel! The floor tilted, the ceiling spun, but she was spared from terror by the knowledge that this could never happen to her. Even if it did (and there could be no doubt now that she was plunging headlong down the stairs) she would suffer only inconvenient bruises. She pitied the chorus of screamers. She wanted to assure them that she was Therissa Sleith, whose youth and beauty were invulnerable . . .

. . .but who was dead.

Meryphillia raged at the unfairness, the tiresome untimeliness. Most of all she regretted the graceless exit she had made, and right in front of her sisters, of all people. Examining these thoughts, she knew that the moment was upon her, and she rushed her meal. She had hardly started on the tangy kidneys when she glanced at her hand and was shaken by that mixture of emotions few other creatures can know.

The sight of her own hand sickened her, its tiny, maggot-plump fingers so unlike the talons she had grown used to. At the same time Therissa gagged with loathing to see what her dainty hand clutched, what smeared her arm to the elbow.

It took more than a moment to calm themselves. Therissa accepted her death more gracefully than Meryphillia did the alien will that made her wash in the wine and oil provided for a differently envisioned afterlife. Drying herself on an unsullied corner of her gown, Therissa scolded her for not having taken better care of it, for now they had nothing to wear. The ghoul was reminded of her stepmother.

Therissa unwound the clattering bones of an ancient Sleith from their wrapping and swirled it around her. She succeeded in looking more stylish than Meryphillia once would have in her newest clothes.

"I believe in making do," Therissa said. "Even if I were a filthy ghoul, I'd make the best of it. And I don't want to spend my brief resurrection moping in a smelly tomb, so let's go, shall we?"

Part of her wanted to linger over her unfinished remains, but another part refused even to look into the sarcophagus, and both were parts of the same person: who called herself, in her inmost thoughts, Therissa Sleith, but who felt an almost uncontrollable urge to laugh when she did.

*

Fragador had sacrificed for it and fully expected it, but Therissa's emergence from the tomb shocked him speechless. She tossed her hair in exactly that heart-stopping way of hers and gazed around the cemetery before spotting him in the shadow of a stone demon. When her face lit up, his heart woke like a sunrise choir of birds.

"You're not dead!" He laughed wildly. "I knew they had to be wrong, you . . . ."

The pity in her eyes stopped him even before she said, "No, they were right. Nor am I entirely as I seem."

"Morella?"

"Please get her name right. Her love for you makes mine seem shallow."

Love had brought him here, yes, but anger, too, anger with her for slavishly heeding the rules of society; anger with himself for breaking those rules by being poor, and a poet. She had planned to marry a man who had won a contract to build public conveniences for the city.

"You can't wear sonnets or eat odes," she had said, "but you can build a fragrant palace from urinals."

In his maddest moments, he had wanted to resurrect her so he could strangle her. At very least he had meant to ask her, with a suitable flourish at the moon-blazing marble of her tomb, what she thought of her fragrant palace now. In the presence of wonder, however, spite was impossible.

And there was that other to consider, that monstrous but magical being that animated her. In a strange part of himself, he loved her even more than Therissa. Unlike Therissa, she appreciated his art. She had even compared him to Asteriel Vendren, whom the dear, dead dunce had never heard of.

"Meryphillia," he enunciated clearly as he took her into his arms.

*

Now that she had known the soft sighs and shouted transports of human love, Meryphillia lamented more bitterly than ever her exile to the underground.

"Why are you crying?" Fragador asked tenderly.

"Nothing. Dust in my eyes."

"That happens," he said from the depth of his human wisdom and sympathy, and she wept all the more.

"What if I was vain and frivolous by your absurd standards?" said the voice in her head. "I knew life and love and happiness. Now I shall know peace. Will you ever say such things?"

She was unsure whether these were the words of the fast-fading Therissa or the words she would have put into her mouth. Whatever they were, they bit like truth.

She rose before the transformation could become complete, unwilling to show her true form again to the poet and blight his memory of love. Turning for one last look, she found herself staring into the grinning face of Arthrax.

"Now I can write poems for you," he said. "*We shall know what the darkness discovers* — how's that for a start?"

The sight of him had speeded Therissa's evaporation. Meryphillia scanned the necropolis with all her senses for Fragador, but he, too, had vanished. She demanded, "What have you done with him? Where is he?"

"He contracted with two of us," Arthrax said. "You, last night. Me, tonight, just before he drank poison." He grimaced so horribly that even she retreated.

She had learned from Therissa. No longer inclined to weep, she turned and smiled at the gaping, unguarded sepulcher of the Great House of Sleith. Far off she heard the cackling of creatures like herself born on the night wind, and for the first time she held back nothing as she joined in their laughter.

Reunion in Cephalune

There is some truth in the folk-tale that the Cephalune Hills hide the way to the Land of the Dead. Over several thousands of years, an ancient race pocked the cliffs with tombs for its better-class corpses. Only the faded ghosts of murals linger to whisper of obscure triumphs, and the tombs are thinly peopled by grave-robbers who cherish the delusion that the richest burial-chambers have yet to be found, including that of Queen Cunymphilia, whose mention elicits smirks from responsible historians. Those who seek the Land of the Dead could find few guides more eager than the misfits of Cephalune to speed them on their way.

It was here that the necromancer, Mobrid Sleith, fled when he had achieved such infamy that not even the folk of Fandragord could stomach him. The elders of his own Tribe were divided only on whether Mobrid could be more discreetly hidden away in a lunatic asylum or poisoned.

Some would argue that restoring a semblance of life to the dead can enlighten the perplexed and comfort the bereaved, but even such liberal thinkers boggled at Mobrid's practice of killing people for no better reason than to revive them as his slaves. His theory that a cadaver can be made livelier by stoking its ashy lust was universally rejected, too, for the dead are by definition tireless, and some of the hired harlots and volunteer voluptuaries who helped further his research were injured or unhinged in orgies with ardent cadavers.

Even more detested than either his theories or his practices, perhaps, was a vat of feculent slime whose sluggish bubbles popped and siffled in a dim corner of his studio. He boasted that this was a plasma of his own design, replenished with the waste products of his art, which could make the most grossly mangled corpse look better than new. This muck disappeared with Mobrid, and fanciful persons claimed that it transformed itself into a conveyance for his narrow escape: a pallid toad, some said, that he rode like a hopping pony, while others swore they saw him lofted above the city walls by an octopoid bat.

In prosaic contrast to these tales, Mobrid fled under heaps of books and household furnishings in a plain mule-cart attended by his protégés. Although their manner was odd and their dress dictated by the necromancer's fetishes, they passed unchallenged. This was, after all, Fandragord, and a cartload of rubbish accompanied by immodestly dressed and apparently drug-dazed whores and catamites was just more froth on the passing stream. In streets where garbage vied with dung and beggars to ravish the nose, only a nymph newly whisked from her pristine glade might have sniffed out their odor of graveyard disgorgement.

Even for one steeped to his grizzled locks in horrors, as Mobrid surely was, the tramp through the thorny waste of Hogman's Plain became a nightmare. Carrion crows and hyenas were not so easily fooled as the watchmen and busybodies of Fandragord. After a few tentative nibbles, they mounted a running attack on the corpse-herd's flock.

He could never relax his watch, for the dead cannot deal with anything new. When overtaken by disaster, a corpse can but try to match it to confused memories of life. Thus Mobrid, stupefied with exhaustion, ignored a dead woman's cry, "The bacon is burning!" Recalling too late her mental limitations, he turned to see her torn to pieces by a herd of feral swine. A youth who fretted that he was "late for work" was staggering under the weight of a vulture on his shoulders as it gobbled his eyeballs. The necromancer was kept dashing from crisis to crisis with naked sword; but, having determined the nature of his companions, the impudent scavengers began to scrutinize his own credentials as a living man with the time-honored right to cow them.

To his further chagrin, he learned that feathers and trinkets and leather straps are poor attire for desert travel, and that death grants no immunity from sunburn. It tore his heart to see his favorites redden and blister, while their cosmetic plasma jellified in the cruel rays and sloughed off to reveal missing parts, moldy wounds and bare bones. He saw himself as the toy of an ironic demon: cursing and beating the mule on its reluctant way, waving off rot-crazed flies and slashing at bumptious vultures in the remorseless sun, while his remaining slaves took their ease under books and blankets in the back of the cart. As this close confinement accelerated their ripening, even his zest for their aroma faltered.

The Cephalune Hills bulked black against a feverish boil of a sunset when the exile at last stood at the foot of the cliffs. While he scanned the furtive hearthfires for a tomb that would suit his domestic tastes, an old corpse dropped from the heights to land before him with a crackling thud. He took this for the best of all conceivable omens.

*

Angobard the Fomor believed that he might die among the tombs, but he would do it in comfort. He chose a dry and spacious chamber near the top of a cliff and spent the afternoon casting out the debris of earlier squatters and sweeping the dust of centuries with a besom of briers. He believed the job well done, and was brewing an infusion of hallucinatory tubers to while away the evening, when a persistent notion that he was not alone made him bound up the three steps to the massive sarcophagus that dominated his new home. It vexed him to find it occupied by the leathery body of a hermit. Knowing his end was upon him, he had combed his hair, modestly arranged his greasy goat-skins, and laid himself out in a posture of regal composure.

Angobard would have left this dead wit in peace, but he wished neither to share the tomb nor to search the dangerous cliffs in darkness for another. Already the red wolves of the hills were tuning up a chilling antiphony, so over the side went the desiccated lich, but not without a brief prayer to Uaal for its eternal rest.

Cleansing his nostrils with the steam rising from his tea, he turned his thoughts to Paridolia. Mere memories wearied him. He had taken to grinding his teeth and snarling when they returned to plague him. A drug-induced vision, fresh and vivid and speaking new words, would be almost as good as his lost love herself; or so he hoped.

"Love," he laughed. Love was for boys, for poets, for fools; and although he was quite young, had been known to scribble verses, and had risked his life against seasoned killers in the fighting-pits, he would have excluded himself from those categories.

Well, fool, perhaps. No one else would have jumped at the chance to earn a few silver fillies by fighting at a private party, where spectators always demanded more than the grunting and clanging, climaxed by a splash of chicken's blood and a groveling surrender, that satisfied the public. That it was to be a wedding-party should have warned him off. Only the most frivolous and decayed aristocrats would pollute a sacrament with the deaths of men like himself.

Second thoughts came only when he awaited his turn to perform, sharing an anteroom jammed with lunatics passing for clowns, Ignudo snake-baiters, and acrobatic eroticists from Sythiphore. To the pain of such companions was added the torture of advanced music from the banquet hall, where it sounded as if a giant bronze statue were shrieking and stamping its hollow feet under the assault of chanting imps armed with drills and chisels. He was almost grateful to his chosen opponent, a cannibal from Orocrondel, for tracing the connection between effeminacy and red hair like Angobard's, and recommending to the other entertainers the gustatory delights, which he soon expected to savor, of caponized white meat. Such gibes focused generalized irritation into a specific itch to braid love-knot's from one man's bones.

At last it was their turn to burst into the room, the Oroc mouthing some gabble and savaging the air with his spear while Angobard whirled his sword into a blurry disk that hovered about him like a guardian spirit. From drunken boredom, the wedding guests bayed for blood; the groom, a lump with bulging eyes and a moist, drooping underlip, too drunk or lazy to bay, impatiently wriggled.

Angobard sprang, meaning to sever the haft of his opponent's spear and then his head with a pair of strokes, but the haft was colliding with his chin, or so he supposed it must have been as he goggled from his supine position at the man about to kill him.

The Fomor came to himself and rolled aside just in time to avoid the spear-head as it struck the floor with a strangely hollow ring. The frenzied howling of the spectators, not bored at all now, seemed to echo down a well. He slashed at the Oroc's legs, but the savage avoided the strokes as nimbly as a child skipping rope while trying to set himself for a fatal thrust. Fully restored at last, Angobard scuttled away crabwise and was about to regain his feet when a kick to the groin undid him.

Given his injury, he almost accepted the feminine shriek that pierced the universal roar like a bell as his own, but it couldn't have been, for he was unable to breathe, much less scream. The voice was so clear, so pure that he was compelled to turn his eyes even from the toothy grin of his own doom. Just as he had heard one voice in the din, so he saw one face in the crowd: in which the formless desires of his youth found form. She might have been a silver statue in an ape-cage.

"Don't kill him!" she cried to the pile that was the bridegroom. He gave a half-wave, as if his wrist were unbearably heavy. If this was a signal for mercy, it came too late. Angobard saw his death-blow arrive. Gallant to the end, as Fomors are expected to be, he offered the goddess an ironic smile and mouthed, "Had I lived. . . ."

*

He didn't die, but that was not at all apparent to him when he woke. Not even the questionable vintages that he was wont to pour down his throat by the two-handled urnful after a night's fighting had ever scoured the brains from his skull and replaced them with a bundle of spikes that threatened to burst through his forehead if he dared to move. The enormous throbbing in his groin suggested that he would henceforth need a bag to contain the pulp of his manly parts. He had heard gossip lately about the cantrips of a foul necromancer, and he suspected that his corpse had been imperfectly revived by that villain.

"How do you feel?" the goddess from the ape-cage said at his bedside, and he promptly answered, "Fine!"

She laughed: a stylized, birdlike laugh that noblewomen were taught to perfect. However much it enchanted him, he was unable to keep from wincing as its crystal shards abraded his vertebrae.

Blinking back tears, he forgot the pain. The thin, straight nose, the strong jaw, the downward-sloping eyes, the slim delicacy of a figure that was yet voluptuous: these so plainly asserted her place in the grandest aristocracy of the Frothoin that the tattoo overflowing her left breast, the dragon of the Great House of Fand, was superfluous. Her every gesture and inflection resonated with a thousand years of culture, of privilege, of fabulous loves and legendary deeds; and, a small voice tried to warn him, with an equally ancient heritage of monstrous atrocities.

*

It didn't surprise him that Lady Paridolia was the bride whose nuptials he had helped enliven, nor that the heap of ordure who had spared him was her husband, Lord Phormiphex. A dozen times a day his brain was replaced by dizzying gas, just because he happened to see her husband whisper in her ear or touch her hand. The cure for his malady was obvious, and he tried again and again to take it. "I must go," he would say, and she would say, "Please, don't go," and her words would bind him to their palace with another golden chain.

Having recovered from his beating, he fell into a lackey's role. His duties included shoving common people out of her way when she visited the shops, sparing her the effort of carrying the flowers she picked and applauding when, with endearing ineptitude, she fingered the clavier.

He tried hard not to picture the couple making love, but his unruly mind frisked toward that filth like a puppy. Convinced that most positions would prove impossible for his patron, he was tortured by a persistent vision of Paridolia's lithe body bouncing astride the tiny apex of rigidity on a rippling, gurgling mass of amorphous pallor. He wondered how much it would hurt, and for how long, to fall on his sword.

*

As she did every night, Paridolia crept into his bed. Even though he was dreaming, Angobard knew that she would soon become a wad of bedclothes, and that he would wake in solitary besmirchment. This was strange knowledge to have in a dream, and he took advantage of it by racing with brutal haste against his banishment to the real world.

"Oh!" she cried. "You hurt me!"

"I hurt myself," he gasped.

None of this made sense. He should feel no pain in a dream, nor pleasure: either sensation would normally have woken him, but he dreamed on. Neither did it make sense that Paridolia, the loveliest woman that had ever enchanted the earth with the imprint of her pretty feet, should have remained untouched, even by so sodden a husband, after two months.

"It doesn't really hurt all that much," she said. "You don't have to stop on my account. You may proceed. Go on. Please?"

He braced himself up and stared at her, shining in the moonbeam that fell through his window. The black pools of her dark-adapted eyes gave her beauty a touch of the weird, but this was no dream.

"Enu!" he cried, not as an idle oath but a heartfelt prayer of thanks to his Goddess, who in turn reminded him to be gentle and granted him the self-control to persevere for a few more precious strokes.

Even so, it was over too quickly. "If I had known — "

"I didn't know, myself. My husband — "

Conjured by that vile word, the ogre himself squeezed from behind an arras like a colorless maggot from a shroud.

"Well done, my boy!" His chuckle had never so closely resembled the eructations of a clogged drain. "Get off now, please, and let me have my turn."

All the pain and rage and shame came later. At the moment, the Fomor coolly pondered which one to kill first. Since it was Paridolia who had so cruelly betrayed him, she should suffer her terror longer. But in the time it took to wring the fat man's neck, no time at all, he had relented. Killing her might provoke the wrath of Enu, who had formed her so perfectly, but who had neglected to grant her the decency of a reptile.

"I loved you, you stinking whore!"

"You don't understand — "

"I understand. Oh, I understand! A show for your husband."

He snatched up his sword. He meant to run, and his sword was the only possession a Fomor valued. Misunderstanding his intention, she screamed, and she was still screaming when he leaped onto the bed beside her and through the window.

*

And so Angobard sat alone in a derelict tomb, courting a vision of the love that still obsessed him. When a bony hand fumbled out of the darkness to grip the threshold, and the hermit's corpse that he had heaved out of his new home pulled itself into the light and staggered toward him, he merely glared at it.

The drinker of moonspite-root who would avoid such horrific visitations must fast and purify himself, and this he had omitted. He had taken the drug in haste and selfishness. Its tutelary demon was exacting payment.

"Go away," he said, dashing the hot drink at the hallucination.

Now this was odd: instead of flying through the vision, the tea splashed to a stop in its face and ran glistening over its cracked lips. A blackened hook that might once have been a tongue creaked out to scrape the droplets. The corpse cast a convincing shadow across him, and its odor was persuasive. Even before his mind could sort the evidence, Angobard's body knew that he faced a real threat, for the fine hair of his head rose weightlessly. He sprang to his feet and swung his sword.

Among the Fomors a few sworders are fabled to have mastered the Thunder of Ar, purported to divide an opponent in eight pieces before the first of them hits the ground. Angobard had never imagined he commanded this skill. He was astounded to realize that he had destroyed the revenant with a flawless demonstration.

Instead of bloody sections, it exploded into flakes of parchment and scraps of bone, but mostly into a cloud of yellowish dust that hung in the air for a moment, during which moment Angobard could have sworn he heard a ghostly sneeze and a thin complaint about a draft. He paid no mind to this, for other shapes were hauling themselves through his door.

He feared that the Tribe of Fand had tracked him down to avenge the murdered lord, but now he saw that the border guards from the Land of the Dead had come to welcome him. That they were mostly females, primped and painted in ghastly seductiveness, suggested the fearful explanation that he had fallen victim to the wrath of Enu. He had called his love a stinking whore, which she was surely not, and the Goddess had undertaken to show him precisely what those words meant.

"Ar! Ho! Uual!" he roared, calling on the masculine side of his pantheon to counter his female damnation, as he attacked in a frenzy of terror and despair.

His blows were prodigious, they would have hewn armor, but they were unnecessary: he was carving meat that shed its bones as if it had simmered all week in a stock-pot. But he was too frightened to be cautious, and his sword whipped through his opponents to clang and spark against stone walls until his arms passed beyond agony to numbness.

Worst of all was the way these corpses took their dismemberment. An epicene cadaver that he had bisected and bifurcated and blasted with his wheel of steel lisped that it had thrown its back out. A severed head complained that it had slaved all day over its hair, "And now look what you've done!" What could he do with such foes?

His sword shattered against the sarcophagus, and with it all his courage. Whimpering and shrieking, he clawed the walls for an exit that he knew did not exist. He could only sob when a squirming weight of filth heaped him. The mass bore him down until his splintering ribs pierced his lungs. As a final indignity, he was neither torn nor bitten, he was fondled, caressed and loathsomely penetrated. He was forced to take a last kiss from lips that worms had pricked.

*

Anyone who might have rejoiced in Mobrid's exile to the wilderness would have been annoyed to see how well he took it. Allowing for the complexity of his wickedness, he was a simple man. A cave in the Cephalune hills was as much home to him as his palace in Fandragord, as long as he had a few choice books, some obedient corpses and his degenerate imagination. When he bothered to look at the blank blue sky or the crystalline profusion of stars framed by the door of the tomb, they pleased him neither more nor less than the clutter of chimney-pots he would have seen from the window of his studio back home.

He was unknown here, too, and for the first few days fellow expatriates would come calling. Later these callers might be seen fetching water for his bath, gathering sticks for his fire or lying in wait with preternatural patience to welcome new company.

Mobrid was an artist, and such impromptu homicides and resurrections meant no more to him than an out-to-lunch sign, hastily scrawled for the door of his studio, would have meant to a master-painter like Omphiliard. He reserved his genius for the restoration of his two masterpieces, a female pit-fighter known as Aryana Axkiller and a beautiful youth called Syssylys.

The latter had been the favorite of the Apricant of Fandragord. That princeling-priest had decreed, after his ward's mysterious death, that all statues of the Sun God have their heads sawn off and replaced with likenesses of his late incarnation. The decree provoked a minor religious war that ended with the restoration of the statues' heads and the removal of the grieving priest's. The monstrously extravagant sepulcher of the youth remained a shrine for heretical pilgrims, however, who would have been outraged to learn that his adored corpse had for some years been lounging about Mobrid's palace, communing with a looking-glass and complaining of boredom.

Aryana's original death had disordered her leonine body, and Mobrid's repairs had dissolved in the desert sun, but as a better fighter dead than Angobard alive, she had suffered little from her posthumous scuffle. Syssylys's death, effected by discharge of subtle poison from the golden dildo that Mobrid anonymously sent him, had left no blemish; he had spent the trip to the hills in a box to avoid recognition; but then he had pranced guilelessly into the Thunder of Ar. His hands had later twitched through the tomb in search of a looking-glass until Mobrid nailed them down, and his head had whined of boredom until the exasperated necromancer submerged it in a jar of honey, which persevered in bubbling pettishly.

Mobrid envisioned a third masterpiece in the Fomor who had so inconvenienced him. As a dead man, he couldn't be made to suffer, but Mobrid would wrench as much pleasure from him as possible when he had been revived. He could set him to fight the ferocious Aryana every night and spend every day repairing him. He had never determined how extensively a corpse could be patched with his plasma and retain a glimmer of life, but Angobard might provide the answer.

Perhaps to the future distress of Fandragord, he had dumped most of his plasma down a sewer, retaining only a bottle of mothery slime. With the addition of pure spring water, the blood and bones of the now-super-fluous mule, and the remains of his least prepossessing visitors, he soon had a new batch brewing in the sarcophagus.

His work went well enough, but the weather of his soul suffered a shift. He slept hardly at all, misliking the swarm of phantom faces that waited to rush the breach between waking and sleep. He caught himself listening for intelligible words, and very nearly hearing them, in the piping of the wind among the vermiculated cliffs, in the flatulence of his plasma, in the shuffle of dead feet about the floor of the tomb. Even the howling of the wolves quavered on the brink of articulate speech, although it threat-ened to become the speech of apocalyptists.

He resisted the obvious but profoundly embarrassing explanation, that he had ignored the elementary step of purging his workshop before practicing his art. In raising the recent dead, he might have evoked unwanted spirits from dust that had drifted here for centuries: even the dust, perhaps, of the legendary witch-queen Cunymphilia, said to have illuminated her revels with necromancers soaked in pitch.

At last he gave in to his fears and devoted a full night to leaping, stamping and shouting through the figures of the most potent exorcisms. A waning moon seemed to mock his powers, if not to oppose them, by squeezing fingers of shadow across the desert toward his tomb.

*

"Sir, please! I'm grateful your servant rescued me, but he can let me go now. Please, tell him."

"Gabble and foolery," Mobrid grumbled, not lifting his eyes from the rent he was caulking in Aryana's magnificent thigh. The dead could prattle interminably to no purpose; the pit-fighter, for instance, had been com-plaining that her sandals were strapped too tightly ever since he began surgery on her leg.

"Sir, if you please!"

An unfamiliar spark of animation and arrogance in that voice forced his eyes toward the door. A living woman struggled in the grip of a new servant called Squazzo, formerly a passionate amateur of archeology.

"It is she, I tell you!" Squazzo rasped. "This is the mummy of Queen Cunymphilia, found precisely where my calculations — "

"Let her go!" Mobrid commanded. When he was obeyed, the girl fell on her face.

He ran to her side and tore aside her rags, his breath catching at the beauty of the unlooked-for gift. Her emaciation and dehydration would pass in a few days, her burnt and lacerated skin would repair itself. Killed cleanly after she healed, she would need no patching at all to become the crown of his collection.

"What do you think you're doing, you horrible old man? Stop that at once!" she croaked, batting his hands aside.

"Don't worry, I'm a doctor."

"A doctor should know that I need water far more than I need having my breasts squeezed, assuming the latter procedure is even necessary."

"Aryana! Bring water."

"My sandals are too tight."

His visitor stared at the blond giantess for a moment before whispering, "She's not wearing any."

"Most of my patients — " Mobrid believed he had made his flock presentable by now, but he furtively scanned the room to make sure no especially horrific sights were displayed — "are sick in their souls."

She sat up and tried to pull her tattered clothing together as she gave him and his protégés a closer scrutiny. "I can believe that," she said. "But surely no one can cure lunatics!"

"I was driven from Fandragord for insisting that I can." He composed his features in a look of martyrdom that he had perfected in his youth.

"It's a shame you left before you saw my husband." She snatched the cup from Aryana and drank greedily until Mobrid wrested it away. He shoved his minion aside before the girl could notice the maggots squirming in her fissured thigh.

"We don't want you dying just yet," he said with a twinkle as he dispensed the water a little at a time.

She slept, and she remained asleep for all that day and the following night while the necromancer tidied up his tomb. He finished his work on Aryana, who no longer complained of tight sandals when the maggots had been scraped out. The body of the Fomor he shrouded in a niche where one might expect to find a corpse.

With time on his hands, he made an exhaustive study of the treasure that had fallen into his lap, nor could he discover one detail to displease him. As she slept the sleep of youth and exhaustion, he denied himself only the most intrusive indecencies.

*

"Did you know that this honey is *fermenting?*" *Lady Paridolia asked. She sniffed at the bubbling crock before slathering some on a shingle of the unleavened bread baked by Mobrid's servants. "That must be why it tastes so odd."*

"You began to tell me," he said as he sidled in to cover the crock that held the severed head of Syssylys and ease her away from it, "why you came here."

"That's easy enough. My husband was a vile degenerate, if not actually mad." She paused to survey the glassy-eyed servants. "Do you suppose, on top of being crazy, your patients could be drunk? From the honey?"

"What you observe are the effects of my therapeutic potions. Go on, please."

"He told me he could play the husband only if he first watched me embrace another man, a guest in our home. I reasoned, I pleaded, I threatened to return to my mother. This was an empty threat, unhappily, since he had bought me from an impoverished branch of our glorious Tribe."

"How much . . . that is, how much of this could a noblewoman of your spirit endure?"

"Not much, let me tell you, especially since the man he was forcing on me, in contrast to himself, was neither old nor fat nor a slobbering deviant. But I would never perform with him for the delectation of Lord Phormiphex. I went to the man's room without telling my husband. But he understood me better than I did myself. He had known just how to thrust me into another's arms, and he was waiting. When he made his presence known, panting like a dog in a queue, my lover strangled him and fled to these very hills, or so everyone believes."

"Surely with your late husband's wealth, you could have hired an army to find him."

Paridolia's wry smile tore at his heart by recalling a girl he had loved in the dim days when he had fancied himself lovable. He hoped fervently that he could train her corpse to smile like that.

"I never saw my husband's wealth. I was arrested as the instigator of his murder. I am free only because Lord Fandastard the Shy thought it would set a bad precedent to allow a relative of his, however humble, to be burnt at the stake. He stormed the prison to free me, and he believes I've gone to Frothirot."

*

Days passed. Paridolia healed, then bloomed. Golden now, her skin flaunted the texture of the orchid, her hair the drifting grace of the willow, her eyes the color of the lilac. She was a garden in the desert, where Mobrid found tranquility. She was a live thing among the dead, with whom he found companionship.

The dead, too, were charmed. She had the patience to listen, as Mobrid never did, to Aryana's recital of the horrors she had inflicted on her opponents. When the fighter described her own death, Paridolia humored her. Among the rubbish the necromancer had flung together in his cart for a hasty departure, she found a looking-glass for Syssylys, who had been repaired while she slept, and she tried to persuade him that boredom and life are incompatible.

"But I'm dead, my dear," he droned. "Boringly defunct."

"Nonsense! You just need fresh air. Go outside and pick some lovely flowers, and then tell me you're bored."

"O Queen, live forever: where is your treasure?"

"Squazzo, you have to *look. Would it be any fun if I just told you?*"

Mobrid found himself actually listening to such chatter and smiling fondly into the book he pretended to read. She stirred the itch that served him for lust, but he felt none of his usual glee at the thought of quenching it on her cold corpse. For once it was the flame that obsessed him, not the exquisite molding of the candle that bore it.

He oiled his locks, curled his beard, arrayed himself in his finest robe, whereon the most potent stars and planets and symbols of necromantic import were embroidered in silver and prinked out with opals and amethysts. He arrogated Syssylys's looking-glass, the better to practice smiles he imagined to be seductive. But with the predictability of a corpse's conversation, Paridolia's talk turned to her lover.

"His smile, Mobrid! Can you imagine? He turned to smile at me as if death were no more than a new cloak he was being fitted for."

He had long since identified her lover, whom she never tired of describing in repulsive detail. His presence on a nearby shelf had become an embarrassment to the necromancer; but it was the sort of embarrassment he was used to.

"How foolish!" he said, and she let him take her hand and caress it as if his touch meant nothing. "He smiled, did he? It proved he was a fool. Would you have loved him even more if he had crossed his eyes and stuck his tongue out?" He made a funny face, something he hadn't done in decades. He was rewarded by a giggle that emboldened him to writhe closer. "If the idiot can grin at death, he can laugh at separation from a girl so lovely. He's run home to live in a tree and breed apes."

"He's near, I know it. He's here, Mobrid, in these cliffs, I can feel him as clearly as — as your hand, which I would adjure you to remove at once!"

"Lady, I cannot, your beauty has maddened me, I — "

A cold voice told him that he was a greater fool than the Fomor had ever been, to force kisses on her that she so obviously loathed, but that voice roused him to a fury of denial. He fought his own chilly cynicism as vigorously as he fought her teeth and knees and elbows, and she could fling no worse accusations than he flung against himself: "You disgusting old pervert! You foul, horrible, stinking charnel-house worm!"

"O Queen, live forever!" Squazzo declaimed in hollow tones. "Behold your treasure!"

Paridolia screamed as the servant pulled the shrouded corpse from the niche and unrolled it on the floor, limbs flopping and head lolling. Preserved by necromantic arts, the large young man might have died yesterday.

Cursing and tearing at his newly curled beard, Mobrid let her evade his clutch to fall on the cadaver. At length he gathered his grand robe about him and stood looking down at the pair of them. It was odd, he thought, that the sight of her lavishing kisses on a corpse should so disgust him, when he himself had done that so often.

"One last look!" she cried. "One last kiss, one last touch, one last word — "

"And what would you give for them?"

"My life, you toad!" she choked through her sobs.

"Done."

He slipped a lancet that had given him much good service from his sleeve and jammed it into the base of her skull. A few deft flicks of the wrist shredded her brain like a cabbage, but when the blade was withdrawn, only one pure drop of red glittered beneath her hair until he licked it away. Her ragged breathing and convulsive jerks lasted long enough to help him pretend he was raping the living woman.

Unaware that he had picked thorns and grasses and ill-smelling monk's-rut, Syssylys returned from his mission and gazed at the three naked bodies on the floor. Only the least attractive one moved. The weeds trickled unnoticed from his fingers.

"Too boring," he said.

*

Now that his collection boasted a new pair of masterpieces, Mobrid regretted his exile. He acknowledged no peers whose opinion he valued, but even fawning idiots and censorious fools would have pleased him more than the vast silence of the desert and the indifference of the stars. Not as in Fandragord, where colorless pinpricks dotted the thief's hood the city donned at night, stars in this clear air burned red and blue and green. They began just out of reach of his fingertips and ran beyond the writ of the gods. From one side to the other of that void, two wolves exchanged demoniac rants.

He turned from his disturbing door on the night and back to the orgy in the firelit tomb. Urging his creatures on, he switched one here and the other there, adding a fourth to this group and a fifth to that. He slapped chilly buttocks and squeezed breasts that felt like toadstools, where never a hint of sweat or other fluid greased the scraping and rustling of his orgiastic music.

He wallowed among them, probing and prodding, kissing and stroking, accepting the touch of whichever cold finger or dry tongue came close, but he was beyond true participation. The orgy had endured for two days and almost two nights now, and live flesh had its limits. Like the immortal Gallardiel, who defers the longed-for duet to the very end of his operas, he had contrived to keep Angobard and Paridolia apart. To his annoyance, they had exchanged looks, they had brushed fingers, but always he had paired them with others. They had always obeyed. Of course they had! How could they not?

He believed that the time had come, however, and the formation of this thought provoked a tingle he had thought impossible. He bent over her wriggling back and crooned in her ear, drawing the syllables out, "Par-i-do-li-aaah."

"This filthy clavier needs tuning," she muttered.

"It's time," he whispered, "for your tryst with Angobard."

Obedience, respect, even concupiscence — his creatures always displayed these qualities, but alacrity? That was unheard of, and his surprise helped dump him on the floor when she sprang from her present involvement and flung herself on the Fomor.

Mobrid paid close attention to the prickle of the hairs on his neck. Perhaps having found each other, the two lost, mad wolves had ceased to howl. The dry wind whispered in the chinks of the walls, but it fell silent when he tuned his ears to it.

"Live forever, O Queen!" Squazzo groaned.

"Cut out your tongue!" Mobrid shrieked. "This is *not her tomb, I did not accidentally raise her dust. . . .*"

The orgy had stopped. With the exception of Angobard and Paridolia, rocking in the most fervent copulation he had ever beheld in corpses, his flock stood about him in loose array.

"Are you planning treachery?"

"That would be too boring."

"The poor fool thought she had me, once my ax slipped out of my bloody grasp, but when she strutted in for the final thrust, I killed her with one blow of my fist. It hammered her nose-bone into the middle of her brain; my knuckles were sore for a week."

The dead hand that had done that deed now weighed down Mobrid's shoulder.

Shivering, he shrugged it off and went to the side of the mutually absorbed couple. Tears — impossible! — streaked their sunken cheeks.

"Stop it," he shouted. "Stop it!"

Unthinkably, he was ignored. He leaped over the lovers like a hurdler and sprinted beyond the royal sarcophagus to the rear of the tomb, where his books crammed shelves stained by melted knights and dissolved ladies. His books held all the answers, they had always held all the answers, but none of the volumes he wrenched down and tumbled aside, none of pages he ripped in his babbling haste, held an answer to the many-footed question that shuffled after him and blocked all exit.

"Oh, oh, oh," the dead deceitful lovers sighed over his ransacking researches, and, "Ah, ah, ah."

" . . . and then there was the time a pallid, puling, puking pretense of a man tried to force his way with me," he heard Aryana say as her long monologue came again within earshot and she gripped his biceps as a millstone grips grain. "I took a handful between his legs — no, I'm a liar, it was no handful at all — and twisted it off the way a girl might twist a rosebud off a bush."

"No!" Mobrid screamed, crouching to shield his crotch, but the warrior merely maintained her grip on his arm and propelled him toward his plasma.

"O Queen, live forever!" said Squazzo. "Your bath is drawn."

"I commanded you to cut out your —"

Gripping Mobrid by the ankles, Squazzo upended him into the seething slime. He held his wildly kicking shanks aloft to keep him from raising his torso.

"There's a bug in my soup," Aryana said, ignoring the necromancer's bone-deep bites to hold his head beneath the muck.

"Boring . . . boring . . . boring," said Syssylys with each thrust of Mobrid's own sword into his convulsing body.

*

Denied the guidance of their mentor, the dead strayed into the wilds on dreamlike promptings from their former lives. Denizens of the Cephalune Hills were no longer set upon by corpses, but they continued to shun the tomb that Mobrid Sleith had usurped. Those who dared creep close enough descried a curiously domestic scene on its portico: a young man and woman who sat very still as they observed, day after day, the interplay of light and shadow across the desert.

It was generally believed that they were dead, although they persistently refused to decay. After several months, it was remarked that the man's right hand had moved. Formerly holding the woman's hand, it now rested on her belly; which, some insisted, was swelling.

The Art of Tiphytsorn Glocque

It's not easy to cause a stir in Sythiphore, where people go naked in the streets and make love in plain view, likely as not with close relatives, but Tiphytsorn Glocque did.

Gossip had flurried when his parents died horribly after gorging themselves on a dish sauced with the poisonous ovaries of blowfish. His father was a wealthy fish-merchant who had started in life with his own net, who knew more about fish than the squid he resembled in his inky secretiveness and grasping nature, if not in his personal odor, and for such an expert this was surely an unlikely end.

"Glocque! Glocque!" the empurpling merchant gurgled, clutching his throat with one hand and flapping the other as urgently as the fin of a speared shark, according to the most oft-repeated and scurrilous version. "*Glocque!*"

"Yes, yes, I'll drink to that!" Tiphytsorn is purported to have cried with a maniacal laugh. "To our glorious family, you silly old pervert! *Glocque*, indeed, Glocque forever! *Tiphytsorn* Glocque!"

"And Phitithia," his sister supposedly murmured as she scraped the sauce from her portion and dug in.

However virulent, the gossip then was brief. The real stir came later, when the young heir began to disport himself in public as an eccentric hobbyist — or, as he would have it, an artist.

Disdaining clothing, fashionable Sythiphorans satisfy their urge to make a splash, and even their convoluted notion of decency, with body-painting. They have themselves decorated by cosmeticians who vie savagely with one another to ride the crest of the latest fad. Grandiloquence comes easily to these rump-daubers, but Tiphytsorn outstripped their wildest flights when he took up their craft and called it Art.

He made his debut in Leviathan Square at high noon on the Feast of Valvanilla, local goddess of oysters and pearls, who is also fancied to have jurisdiction over impotence, frigidity and unsavory defluxions. The square was packed. Body-paint was confined to minimal enhancement of skin-tones. In fact the better sort of people were draped almost modestly, out of respect to the Goddess whose nude image towered over them.

Leviathan Square fronts the bay, and a dripping boy, believed to be a virgin, hoisted himself onto the esplanade and ran to the altar with the oyster he had chosen: a remarkable specimen, big as a human skull, knobby and massive as some barbarian helmet. Its weight very nearly caused him to stumble, a fearful omen, so the crowd heaved a vast sigh when he recovered himself and passed the mollusc to an acolyte, who passed it to the high priest.

Silence fell as the priest raised his knife to the Goddess. If the oyster contained a pearl, the year would bring potency, warmth and continence to the faithful. If it smelled strange or looked odd, if the priest's knife chipped the shell, if he failed to open it deftly — but some fears are best left unformed.

First lovers gazing into each other's eyes, or victims staring up at their murderers: their looks might have seemed uninvolved, compared to the intensity of so many eyes in Leviathan Square that day. But at the height of the yearning silence, at the moment when all attention should have been focused on the priest and the knife, the oyster and the Goddess, a buzz rose from the rear of the crowd.

This was sacrilege. What were those idiots chattering about? Idle heads turned. Marginally faithful heads turned. Then even the faithful swayed and revolved like kelp in a random current. The wet boy who was believed to be a virgin pointed and cried something that was variously interpreted. Unthinkably, the priest himself turned to look.

What they saw was a file of four naked women that slipped forward with the swift sureness and organic cohesion of an eel through mud. Totally hairless, they were painted in those shades of green and pink that are especially sacred to Valvanilla.

No drill sergeant could have faulted the synchronization of their barefoot steps. They were of equal height, their painted faces looked alike. Observant lechers later averred that their most intimate details were exactly the same. Were they some enigmatic message from the Goddess?

A fat young man, out of step and out of breath, wallowed in the wake of this lovely crocodile. He was unpainted, but his streamers of pink and green gauze suggested a connection with the women. He was none other than that notorious parenticide, that son of a fishmonger, it was — and here the thousands of Sythiphoran tongues, as only they could do, produced an echoing chorus of phlegmy gurgles and glottal clicks that were the young man's name. At this first taste of universal recognition he puffed up like — as some malicious tongues would have it — a blowfish.

The women at last stood in a perfect line before the altar. Their escort said to the priest, who had been watching the parade in consternation, "I am Tiphytsorn Glocque, and I have come to pay homage to the Goddess with my Art."

Instead of denouncing this fat fool, instead of merely ignoring him in the first place, the priest stared at the painted women a moment longer, nodded distractedly and said, "Oh," before proceeding with his duties.

His stroke with the knife was sure. The oyster proved sweet and plump. It contained a pearl large as a walnut, though black. The priest announced that this rarity was a marvelously auspicious sign.

Others interpreted the omen differently.

*

Never devout, Phitithia had not attended the ceremony. She was as shocked as anyone when her brother led his creations into her quarters at their palace.

"You painted them yourself? These slaves? How absurd!"

"No, it's a statement —"

She demanded: "Who shaved them for you?"

"I did. To trust another with any part of my statement —"

"Oh, ugh! Get your tainted hands off me! You actually lathered them and put the razor to their — *ugh*!"

"How is that worse than kissing them, fondling them, or —"

"It is, believe me, it's different! It's disgusting! It's demeaning, it's unhealthy, it's sick! *Shaving slaves!*"

Anger always emphasized his sister's bulging eyes, thin lips and weak chin. These are not uncommon traits in Sythiphore, but she wobbled perilously close to ethnic caricature. Her knobby shoulders always curved forward as if to hide her vestigial breasts. When the hue of nausea tinged her tallowy skin, not even the most doting brother would have called her pretty. Unable to control her stomach any longer, she dashed from the room.

She was only trying to vex him, he knew. It had been their father's fondest hope to marry her into a noble house, but she had conceived an absurd passion for a sponge-diver called Dildosh. Their father instructed ruffians to discourage this unsuitable young man. Dildosh somehow survived with his good looks nearly intact, though he had indeed been discouraged; but once Tiphytsorn was head of the household, his sister assumed that she would be free to indulge her imbecilic lust.

The heir believed that the least he could do for his father would be to honor his wishes in this respect, and he had forbidden Phitithia to see the sponge-diver. Love may be blind, but there was nothing wrong with Dildosh's ears, and he surely heard the chiming of gold and silver with each one of her wayward, knock-kneed steps. Refusing to understand this, but unable to openly defy a brother who controlled the family fortune, Phitithia bedeviled him in every way she could. He knew that her show of vomiting at his artwork fell short of honest criticism.

He sighed and brooded on his creatures, who stood with demurely downcast eyes and blank expressions. He tried to explore the pain felt by abused and misunderstood artists, but he discovered that he was far too well pleased with himself and his work.

He pulled the nearest slave down on the cushions with him for some fun. No arrogant painter or sculptor, he reflected, could claim that his creation, however grand, was nearly so *useful*.

*

The artist felt something very like pain, but even more like blind rage, when commercial salons began to claim that their inept smearing was done "according to the Glocque technique." His anger boiled over one day when his litter was borne past a mean stall in some squalid quarter where a scoundrel displayed a sign reading, "Be Painted by Glocque Himself!" A garish poster depicted a woman painted in the same color-scheme, allowing for its degenerate crudity, that Tiphytsorn himself had created for the Feast of Valvanilla.

"I'll paint you!" he roared, pouring out of the litter and bursting into the stall like a turbulent wave of quivering jowls and pectorals that sprayed spittle before it. "I'll paint you with acid, I'll trowel you and scrape you and rub you out!"

"May I help you, Sir?" asked the graceful little man who intercepted him, grinning and fawning and clasping his paint-stained hands together like a fly gloating in a privy.

"You speck, you hole, you waster of skin and paint, you offspring of a masturbating monkey and a slut's menstrual rag, know that I am Glocque! Glocque, you thief!"

"As am I, Sir, as am I!" The fawning smile faltered for never an instant. "Thoozard Glocque, your most humble and obedient servant."

Tiphytsorn recoiled before an impregnable defense. His was the commonest surname in Sythiphore, though perhaps the oldest. When he was a child, his father had shown him how a gurnard belches the name when it is drawn up in a net, and he had adduced this as proof of the family's honorable descent from fish. There was no way he could protect his name from infringement. Any rogue who claimed his work was "just like Glocque's" could point to this wretch, or to a dozen others.

Tiphytsorn bellowed a laugh and clapped the rascal on a narrow shoulder. "Be Glocque, then, with my blessing! I'll outdo you. I'll go where none may follow."

"Best of luck, Sir. May Valvanilla never forget you."

*

Tiphytsorn found his promise hard to keep. Meticulously detailed, weird flowers and vines would run riot over his subjects, they would be embraced by plants and creatures unknown to any human eye; but as soon as they were observed and copied, any human eye capable of looking down at its attendant skin would know them.

For a while he vowed to keep his Art to himself. Lavishing long hours of toil over his beautiful slaves, bathing them and shaving them, priming them with saliva, semen, urine, or a few brisk strokes of the lash, and then easing oily pigments into their skin should be reward enough for any artist. Since his eye was the only one that could appreciate his work, his eye alone should view it.

His slaves came from the island of Parasundar, where everyone looks alike to Sythiphoran eyes, and where inscrutability to Sythiphorans is the ultimate virtue. Painting perfected these qualities. Not even Tiphytsorn, who fancied he could normally tell them apart, could say which was Butaphuda and which was Phutabuda, nor had he the slightest clue what they thought of the masterpieces he made of them. But he persuaded himself that they pined for the pleasure of striking wonder into the people, and no sooner had he created a design that he had intended to keep to himself than he was parading them once again before the public.

And no sooner had he paraded them than his design was copied by mercenary apes.

@Bullet = *

The artist was a creature of the city. Great gulfs of sea and sky disturbed him. Having himself rowed to the eastern horn of the Bay of Sythiphore, a trip of less than an hour in a hired skiff, was like a voyage to the edge of the world.

Food and wine for a banquet had been stowed aboard, select slaves had been taken to divert him with songs asserting the powers and pleasures of wealth, and a pair of inflated goat-bladders had been strapped securely to his shoulders in case of accident; but none of these was a defense against the violent expansion of the sky as his boat leaped forward. The city behind him and the ships at anchor shrank to toylike insignificance. He was an insect, exposed and helpless on an endless floor. Memories of his father's early efforts to teach him the fishing-business, when he had hidden belowdecks, puking and gibbering, sprang back with ferocious clarity.

"He'll probably grow up to be a poet," he heard his father saying, just before dumping a fresh-caught netful of wet, flopping, slimy things onto his screaming head, "or an artist."

This memory so bemused him that he forgot to be frightened. His father, the rudest oaf that ever oppressed the earth with his flat feet, had for once been dead right.

He felt like an accomplished seaman by the time the skiff docked at the decayed village of Mereswine Point, and he hauled himself onto the rickety wharf without help. Having ordered Captain Calamard to wait for him, he squared his shoulders and rolled toward the skewed huddle of sand-scoured shacks with the swagger of a pirate just back from the cannibal coast of Tampoontam.

"Your water-wings, Sir!" the captain called after him.

His face burning, Tiphytsorn fidgeted and fumed while the captain puzzled his way through the redundant fastenings of the goat-bladders. He was sure that all the fisher-folk watched and snickered from the edges of their narrow windows while he

suffered this like a child being fussed over by his mother. They got an even bigger treat when one of the bladders burst and he lurched forward with a shriek, knocking the captain off the dock and into the bay.

He swept the skiff with his eyes, planning to flog any slave who smirked, but they all seemed soberly intent on retrieving Captain Calamard. The artist ripped off the remaining fastenings and threw the water-wings aside as he plodded heavily into the village.

Odd people lived here, clam-diggers, winkle-pickers and witches. He believed that the presumptuous Dildosh came from Mereswine Point. He saw none of them on his brief walk through its alleys, whose leaning walls were festooned with drying nets and decorated with the whitened bones of monstrous sea-beasts. The only life was a flock of gulls who quarreled over a mountain of shells beyond the last of the driftwood hovels. He shied a rock at them, and was alarmed at the volume of shrieks, the thunder of wings. He raised his arms over his head protectively, but the birds only rose and circled, screaming, until he passed on.

Wearing a wide straw hat and a loose robe against the cruel sun, he slogged over dunes. His spirits revived as he contemplated his own fortitude and intrepidity. He laughed at the lesser men who would have demanded a litter for this heroic journey, or even a guide. The hiss and slap of the surf, displaying none of the rhythmic regularity that poets ascribe to it, guided him to the sea.

At last he stood atop a dune and saw it, stretching to a horizon that seemed unaccountably higher than the point where he stood. Before his fear of the enormous space could creep up on him, his eyes were opened to the splendor of its colors. Seven different shades of green shone in the sea, not counting various shoals of weed and the mosses on certain wet rocks, and the wooded hills to his left displayed at least four others. Only the laziest eye would have said that the sky was a uniform blue from its pellucid horizon to the height of its blazing dome. A shell that he picked up contained a pastel rainbow. His palette held none of these exact hues.

He scanned the beach below him, where stone blocks peeked through the sand like the ground-down teeth of giant jawbones, tracing dim outlines of former streets and plazas. Symmetrical depressions might have marked the sites of grand temples and palaces; or they might merely have been symmetrical depressions. No one knew for sure who had built the Old City, or when the sea had reclaimed it, but it had inspired many unpleasant fables. Its ruins were shunned by all but antiquarians, students of dubious disciplines and eccentrics: in one or more of which classes, Tiphytsorn admitted, his own sister might be numbered.

He had come here to find her, but his heart sank as he recognized her awkward figure lurching through the foam. He could hear nothing from the dune, but she spoke and gesticulated with great animation as she traced a zigzag course along the beach. Another observer — fortunately there was none — might have said that she was casting spells or praying to strange gods. Her brother assumed she was talking to herself.

He scrambled down the slope to put himself in her path. She had twined her hair with seaweed and draped herself with strands of shells and questionable wrack. Her face was twisted with the intensity of her senseless monologue. He wondered, not for the first time, if he shouldn't confine her at home. But she was ingenious, unfortunately, and he had no doubt that she would break loose and get even by revealing any number of family secrets.

She looked not at all surprised to see him, merely annoyed. She made to pass, but he caught her arm.

"Go away. Can't you see I'm busy?"

He resisted an impulse to mock this nonsense and said, "I need your help with my Art."

"Your *Art*? Ha! Why should I help a *slave-shaver*?"

A wave burst over his feet and soaked the hem of his robe. The sand crumbled under his heels as the wave pulled out, making him stumble. It was as if attenuated tendrils of the sea fumbled for a grip on his ankles. He drew Phitithia onto dry sand, keeping one wary eye on the water.

"You have a special knowledge of the sea. You know certain secret properties of its plants and creatures — to cite one example purely at random, the poisonous nature of blowfish ovaries."

"Whom do you want poisoned now?"

He scanned the beach nervously, but it was empty. The sea took advantage of his inattention to assault him again, drenching him to the knees and making him cry aloud. He dragged his sister higher, suspecting she had something to do with this. Allowing for her depraved cast of features, her expression was altogether too innocent.

"I don't want to hurt anyone, I want to benefit everyone with my Art —" he pressed on through her bray of laughter — "by using pigments that no one else can copy."

"Again, why? Why should I help you?"

"Dear Sister, you know I don't prostitute my Art with private clients. When Lady Dwelphisteena herself begged me to create a design for her birthday, I refused. But you — here, look at you, you're not wearing a smudge of paint today, you're not only unfashionable, you're immodest. I could make you the envy of all Sythiphore."

"With those same fingers that probe loathsome sluts from Parasundar? You'll never again lay a filthy hand on me!" As an afterthought, she jerked her arm out of his grip and brushed it with sand until it blushed red.

He was fond of his sister, but anyone who could spurn his Art like that had to be a prodigy of malice and ignorance. He struggled to keep his hands at his sides as he roared, "Then what is it you want from me, you impossible bitch?"

Instead of responding in the same style, as she normally would, she turned sickeningly coy. With lowered eyes she murmured, "There is a certain young man named Dildosh. . . . If you would get word to him that he need no longer fear our family and hide from me. . . ."

He studied her dispassionately. Marrying this gawky grotesque into a noble house, or into any kind of house at all, seemed an impossible hope. He doubted it was fear of him that kept the odious sponge-diver in hiding. "Done. Help me as I wish, and you can marry the beast. I'll be proud to call myself uncle to mouthing sub-humans with webbed feet."

"Brother!" she cried, and forgetting all her reservations about his unwholesome habits, she flung herself into his arms and kissed him with a passion he had almost forgotten.

*

Captain Calamard had been a trusted henchman of Tiphytsorn's father. When they returned to the city, the young man took him aside to a wine-shop, ostensibly to make amends for knocking him into the bay.

"Do you know a sponge-diver called Dildosh?" Tiphytsorn asked.

The older man flexed a gnarly hand whose broken knuckles had knit badly before he replied, "I think of him often."

The artist put gold coins on the table. "Do you suppose you could drown him?"

The captain laughed. "You're not the sly old devil your father was." The coins vanished into his misshapen claw. "Sponge-diving is a hazardous job. He could drown tomorrow."

Tiphytsorn pondered. He needed his sister's help first. He said, "It would be better if he drowned next week."

"Have you ever noticed that the horizon goes up at the edges? The world is neither round nor flat, it is a bowl on a table where demons feast. Any one of us can be snatched up today, tomorrow, next week."

"Tell your demons that next week is best."

*

The artist was engrossed in shaving the stubble from Dubaphuta's pudendum when his sister burst unannounced into his studio, but she cheerfully omitted to feign shock or disgust. Shedding dried kelp and sand on his floor of glassy-clean marble, she set down a smeary array of earthenware jars. They smelled rankly of the sea, but perhaps it was Phitithia herself who bore the odor.

He studied the pots. They all seemed to contain the same green muck, like various shades of puréed spinach, although far less appetizing. "How — ?"

"You must experiment." She rummaged among his own paint-pots, selected a pale yellow and smeared some on her palm. She dipped a finger in one of her pots and blended her potion with the pigment, then traced a childish line down Dubaphuta's splendid thigh.

Tiphytsorn gasped. The color of a perfect daffodil exploded before his eyes. This was no painted line on his slave's skin, it was a profound chasm that revealed the essence of Yellow.

"It tickles!" the girl giggled, not happily, but the artist had trained himself to ignore their comments.

*

A festival unique to Sythiphore is Morons' Day, when everyone masquerades as the stupidest person of his or her acquaintance. Servants ape their masters, husbands mimic their wives, wives mock their lovers. Phitithia padded herself with flesh-colored pillows, traced a pitiful attempt at a mustache on the corners of her mouth, tied a dead sprat to her loins, and paraded four tottering hags through the streets, all of them blotched with crude designs in clashing colors.

Everyone knew of her brother, and they loved the joke. To her astonishment the people demanded that she be crowned Queen of Morons at the riotous noonday ceremony before the Municipal Palace, and the mayor — whose impersonators had won this title for three years running — was delighted to oblige. The crowd went wild when Phitithia's overstuffed caricature accepted a kiss from a striking young man who was disguised as a lumpish old sailor, although very few could say who he was or whom he was made up to resemble.

No one could take her triumph away from her, but her brother deflated it when he made his own appearance that afternoon. He wore no costume. He had forgotten the holiday in his absorption with his work, he had not slept for a day and a night, and the mummers who capered through the streets nearly panicked him with fears for his sanity.

He soon caught on, and no one noticed that he had been cringing in terror from the fantastical mob. He was ignored as they gaped in wonder at his artwork. He had risen to the challenge of his new colors, and never before had he created such bold designs. Some observers strangely insisted that they saw no painted women at all, and that the artist was preceded by an indescribable creature of pure light whose hues and patterns shifted as it floated above the pavement; but then Morons' Day is traditionally celebrated with every sort of intoxicant.

The artist accumulated a train of admirers, while others raced ahead to spread the news of his masterpiece. Holding court on the palace steps, Phitithia was chagrined to find herself abandoned by her subjects; and much more so when she learned the cause. No one wanted to laugh at her brother. They had all gone to worship him.

"Morons' Day, indeed!" she snarled.

"But we have each other, my Queen," Dildosh murmured as he undid the fastenings of her padded costume and prepared to observe the holiday in true Sythiphoran style.

*

It is a fine thing to feel like a god, as Tiphytsorn often had in the frenzy of creation. Even finer it is for the whole world to hail you as one, and this pleasure he now savored. No one tried to imitate him anymore. No one could. People loitered outside his gates in the hope of getting the first look at his next sensation; but failing that, they seemed happy enough to see the artist himself, to cheer him, to buffet one another for the privilege of kissing his hand or even touching his litter. Poems were dedicated to him. Songs were sung about him, and only a few of them were satirical.

He grew lazy. He rose late, stayed long at table, played idly with his slaves, napped, then went out to show himself to the public and grace the salons of noble admirers. His pots of paint congealed and crusted.

He told himself that his life was unrelieved ecstasy, but he knew that he lied. Alone in the small hours the fear gnawed him that he would never be able to equal his last work. And everyone expected him not just to equal it but to vault beyond it to some new universe of color and design whose nature he couldn't even begin to imagine. He would viciously interrupt anyone who began a sentence with, "When —?"

Long before he intended to rise, Phithia shook him awake one morning. "Try these," she said.

"What?"

"You're looking for something new, aren't you? Isn't that why you're moping like a whale in a pond?"

"Moping? Ordinary men may *mope*, dear Sister, but artists rest and restore themselves for heroic new efforts, they digest experience, they ponder and weigh and plan —"

"When you stop moping, try these," she said. "The forgotten craft of the Old City itself has been distilled into these pigments. No living eye has seen such colors."

"How did you get them?" he asked, stifling a yawn as he cast a listless eye on more pots of green muck.

"It wasn't easy. But it's the least I can do for you. The very least." She flounced out.

Perhaps he had been neglecting her, he thought as he disentangled his limbs from those of his slaves and lurched off to wash. That might explain her brusque manner. He had been far too preoccupied with worries about his Art to pay heed to her psittacine nugacities.

Studying the new array of pots, he suffered a pang of regret. Angry with him or not, she had taken pains to assemble the very gift he needed. He wondered how to show his gratitude. There was always Dildosh: he could rescind his death-sentence. He couldn't tell Phithia of this generous act, of course. He still must do something to soothe her apparently hurt feelings.

An even worse pang struck him. He rummaged through the disorder of his studio until he found a calendar. By his best calculation, rechecked twice over, he had ordered Captain Calamard to drown the sponge-diver three weeks ago. It wasn't his fault that he'd forgotten about it. An artist couldn't be expected to trouble his head with trivia.

It must be grief, then, not anger that afflicted his sister. If she suspected him, she would surely have accused him. More likely she would have tried to claw his eyes out. Remorse grew sharper. Instead of finding her a gift, he ought to find her a new and even handsomer sponge-diver whose standards of beauty were as flexible as Dildosh's.

He admitted that affection for his sister seemed to be warping his judgment, so he shelved the idea until he could consider it dispassionately. He opened a new pot of green paint and mixed it with some of Phithia's new batch of slime. The result was a sickly gray with a markedly foul odor.

Except for the lazy Tuphaduba, whose purring snore rose from his disordered cushions, the slaves had gone off to primp themselves. He hauled the sleepy creature blinking and grumbling into the sunlight and stood her before his stool. He prodded her into bending to grip her knees and present him with a pristine surface that would have made an artist limited to such rubbishy media as wood, canvas or parchment weep with envy. The texture of her skin was doughy from sleep, but the artist soon slapped it taut.

"What?" Tiphytsorn cried, unable to believe his ears.

Tuphaduba hastily explained: "Sir, in my contemptible homeland of Parasundar, that would be a respectful salutation. It alludes to the noble tiger, whose uncountable splendors are enhanced by its rich aroma."

"Oh. Very nice. But what about the rest of it?"

"As the testicles are the repository of all virtue, Lord, as they are the source of courage and honor and potency, we treasure those of the tiger and grant them to a favored few."

"So that you meant to compliment me in your heathenish way?"

"Indeed, Sir, that was my pathetic intention. Forgive me if the highest accolade that my people can grant offends you."

He might have pursued this inquiry further, but he had just smeared some of the gray slime on her skin, and he tumbled into an abyss. No longer gray, it glowed and vibrated with a green brilliance he had never beheld. To say that it resembled any known shade of green would be like saying that a sunset resembled a skillet. It was not just the color, it was a new way of seeing it. The streak on Tuphaduba's buttocks was the gateway to another world.

He labored all that day and through the night on his subjects, painting over, erasing, blending, revising. The slightest variation on one slave threw the four-fold composition into a dizzying new perspective. Each design seemed more wonderful than the last. He rejected dozens of them, any one of which would have stunned and dazzled the world.

Licking his fingers to thin the paints, he learned that they had flavors that exactly matched their colors. He was astounded to discover that he could identify not just the taste of blue but the sound of yellow and the feel of red. Indeed, he must have been creating his compositions by the distinctive sounds and touches and flavors of his new palette, because he only now realized that he had forgotten to strike a light when darkness fell.

Sunrise painted the city with the unheard-of colors that his sister's potions had revealed to him, and with their sounds as well. The whining and grumbling of his slaves, begging him to let them sleep, added new flavors to the banquet of light, new themes to the symphony of color he had made of them. Ignoring the vivid orange of their protests, he hustled them out into the street, even though the only people he could stupefy with his genius would be early-rising workers and late-retiring carousers.

He acquired a considerable crowd of both, who followed him in silent awe. He grinned and nodded at them in a singularly red way, inviting their indigo praise. He tried to explain what he had done, since they were so obviously puzzled, but ordinary words wouldn't serve. He spoke new words that suited his colors and made strange gestures that evoked their music.

To his astonishment, the fools mocked and gibed. He might have borne this with the dignity of misunderstood genius if their jeers and laughter hadn't altered his composition by adding to it a hideous, foul-tasting shade that hurt his ears.

"I'll teach you not to fuchsia my Art, you browns!" he shrieked, attacking them with teeth, fists and feet. "I'll mauve you!"

*

It's not easy to cause a stir in Sythiphore, and it's even harder in that most tolerant of cities to be deemed a lunatic. By the time he was haled before a magistrate, Tiphytsorn had learned to keep his secret wisdom to himself. How could anyone understand his Art when they couldn't even see it? The fools insisted that he had herded a stumbling flock of badly-abused slaves through the streets, not painted at all, but so leeched of all color that they looked like drowned corpses. The only nervous symptom he exhibited, and it could have been a harmless tic, was to wince whenever the magistrate made his teeth ache with one of his high-pitched, magenta gestures.

A horrifying pattern, a purple conspiracy began to emerge as witnesses to other acts came forward to testify: commercial painters he had abused, lords and ladies he had offended by refusing to paint them. Every sensible thing he'd ever said or done was put forward as a symptom of madness.

He was about to heave a sigh of relief when Phitithia appeared, fortunately not trailing seaweed but painted decorously in cloying shades of pink and yellow. Even if she had chosen to have herself decorated by some tasteless nitwit, she would set everyone straight. But he nearly strangled on his sigh when he recognized the copper-painted figure beside her as the ineffable Dildosh, who should have been drowned by Captain Calamard.

"Who is Captain Calamard?" the magistrate asked, repeating the name that Tiphytsorn had foolishly blurted out in his shock.

Phitithia said, "My Lord, I spared my poor, deranged brother the pain of the news that his dear friend, the captain, perished heroically while rescuing my fiancé from drowning. But perhaps he heard of it elsewhere, and this was what drove him completely mad."

"My Lord!" the artist cried, rising and planning to demonstrate his sanity with a speech of the purest and most translucent violet. "As they say in Parasundar when paying homage to their greatest men, I'll cut your balls off and eat them, you stinking beast."

He got no further before the magistrate ordered him gagged.

A Scholar from Sythiphore

Yodeo Globb came from Sythiphore, which typed him so handily that the people of Fandragord neglected to look too closely at the man himself. To anyone's eye, he matched the type: plump, jolly and energetic, never failing to amuse when agitation thickened his accent and thinned his syntax.

If he kept odd hours, that was only to be expected, for any Sythiphoran behavior that cannot be classed as funny or disgusting is agreed to be inscrutable. If he sometimes smelled worse than hard work and a limited wardrobe could explain, it was ascribed to a lifetime of eating fish, and perhaps putting them to even less wholesome uses.

He said that he was an antiquary, an unworldly career for the hard-bargaining "melonhead" of folklore, but everyone agreed he had come to the right place. Fandragord was first built on the level of Hogman's Plain, according to the story children are told, but the giants stepped on it. A new city rose on the site, but they stepped on that, too, and so on, until the present city was built on a heap of ruins too tall for them to stamp down.

Grownups who tell this story know that the "giants" who destroyed the city more than once were the feuding Houses of Fand and Vendren, not mentioned by name because so many of them are still around, and still as touchy as ever, but any sharp-eyed child who spends an afternoon scuffing through the rubbish can find enough broken weapons, regimental badges, charred bones and cracked skulls to decorate a packing-crate castle.

Since Yodeo Globb was no intellectual, even by whatever absurd standard prevailed in his native city, his pursuits were seen as similarly childish. Mention of "the scholar from Sythiphore" never failed to raise a laugh at the cheap inn where he lodged, and no one laughed more merrily than the stranger himself. Taproom idlers would be encouraged to go on to such questions as, "How's your sister, melonhead?", alluding to the infamously close bonds of Sythiphoran families, and he would laugh all the harder. The jokes obscured his true interest: unearthing more recent artifacts, such as gold teeth, silver spectacle-frames, and the coins traditionally placed on the eyes of corpses.

Although Yodeo's window overlooked a brothel whose inmates were lax in drawing their blinds, he found his eyes more often raised to the distance and the mound that overshadowed the intervening expanse of Hogman's Plain. This was only the closest of several such symmetrical hills in the wasteland, popularly known as the Giants' Graves; and like so many other ruins and natural sites in or near the witch-cursed city, it was generally avoided.

Yodeo was not a fanciful man, but little imagination was needed to see the rough shape of a supine figure in the mound, a fancy lewdly enhanced by the lone oak-tree rising from its groin. For the first time in his career, he was tempted to step over the line that separates the grave-robber from the true antiquary. He had no faith in giants, but he did believe in ancient warlords with giant purses.

He had struck up acquaintances among the sluts across the courtyard, who had time and inclination to gossip of such news as the fatal accident to Tubok, the rich grocer, or the funeral arrangements for poor Lady Roxilla. He would often bring them extravagant bunches of flowers or odds and ends of junk jewelry, charming them with his gallantry and his queerly old-fashioned taste.

"They never was giants," he told a pair of them one day. "They's foot-bones would break when they do walk."

"That's why he's lying down, probably," said Poppy, the pert one. "Maybe he wasn't a giant all his life."

Orchid, the somber one, said, "Like all men, only more so, the giants were swine. So my mother told me. When the gods at last get sick of all this garbage — " her gesture included the courtyard, the whorehouse, the ancient city of Fandragord, and everything else under the sun — "they'll be roused from their graves to root it out."

"Orchid can't wait," Poppy said, pointing to the absurdly placed oak.

Yodeo distracted the women from the scuffle that ensued by telling them about whales, a species they believed in no more than he did in giants; but they agreed to go upstairs and examine the proof of his claim that he, like all Sythiphorans, was descended from these prodigious mammals.

*

One morning he set out through the thorny desert of witchgrit and monk's-rut that separated the mound from the city, soon regretting the economy and skepticism that had kept him from renting a mule to carry his tools and fetch back his loot. The path had been made by goats no more eager than humans to visit the mound. Fighting his way directly through the brambles soon frayed his clothes, his skin and his temper, and often led him into unexpected pockets where he could see neither the city nor his goal. He was forced again and again to wriggle his way out of dead ends and start over.

The vertical sun found him less than halfway to the Giant's Grave. He had brought only enough crusty bread, goat-cheese and the ghastly local wine for one meal, but he saved half for later. He did not neglect a libation to Thululriel, although the offering to his sea-god had never seemed more futile than in this dusty waste.

"New deaders more better, I says," he grumbled. "Leave old bones for dogs, that kisses my ears less whelk-sarding stupidly."

An unplanned nap over the acid vintage did nothing to improve his temper or his timetable, and the sun had set behind the barrow before he reached it. The top was still washed with golden light, and the ascent was easy, for the witchgrit seemed reluctant to take root in the slope.

That it was a human earthwork was now evident, but he doubted that the figure depicted was human. Apart from being three city blocks long, it was taller than a four-story building at its enormous chest, and the sculpted arms and legs showed certain anatomical anomalies. It was impossible at close range to determine whatever features might have remained on the eroded head, but it was definitely broader than human proportion would dictate, and quite neckless.

At the head, which seemed as likely a place as any for the warlord's crypt, he began prodding the earth with a stiff wire. His spirits revived; he could be seen by anyone who might be watching from the city, and it amused him to practice his craft in plain view for once, a feat worthy of the legendary Zuleriel Vogg. Perhaps it was his destiny to be a great tomb-robber like Zuleriel, and not a pilferer of trinkets that mourners thought not worth retrieving from their loved ones; or to become the antiquary he claimed to be, donating his less negotiable finds to the City of Fandragord. The local elders might reward his philanthropy with a title and the right to wear a sword.

"Which would make them snippets think once before laughing on the way I speaks," he muttered. "Fluting bunch of eel-riggers!"

The sun had set, and a wiser course might have been to repair to the shelter of the oak, resuming work in daylight, but just then his probe hit a smooth substructure at a depth of four feet. It could have been marble. It could have been the burial chamber.

His probing grew frenzied as he scurried to find an entrance, and he was soon rewarded by the unmistakable clink of metal. He took up his shovel by the light of a pregnant moon and began slicing the tough earth.

Laboring like the melonhead of popular myth, who smiles while digging ditches or laying bricks all day without growing tired or thin, Yodeo at last uncovered an object that wiped the smile off his face. A smile is inadequate for a man who finds riches beyond imperial greed. He hooted maniacally and, though he had never known he was capable of dancing, danced on the panel of solid gold.

Having collapsed on it, having kissed it and stroked it and whispered endearments to it, he began scraping earth from its limits. It was round, some three feet across, suggesting a trapdoor that would give access to the crypt. And if the mere door was gold, what riches lay beneath?

Oblique moonlight and his scurrying fingertips enabled him to a make out a face embossed on the lid. It flaunted a portcullis of grotesque teeth that might have been the visor of a barbaric helmet. The perimeter bore a raised inscription whose characters defied his linguistic knowledge, admittedly limited. Nevertheless he was struck by a disquieting familiarity, not with the specific image or the letters, but with their arrangement on the disk.

Yodeo Globb had always been cautious, but a painful hike in the sun, more than an hour of digging, a growling stomach and a galloping heart, all combined to break the lifelong habit. He took a crowbar and, while standing on one edge of the trapdoor, tried to raise the other. His screamed curses cited his own stupidity when the lid pivoted to drop him into black emptiness.

He woke to pain and the most vile smell he had ever encountered in a career not characterized by sweet odors. He ejected the meager contents of his stomach, but this made him feel no better. In trying to raise his torso from a smooth, cold surface, he discovered that the impossibly heavy gold lid had fallen into the pit with him, crushing and pinning his legs.

"Oh, mother!" he groaned. "Why for came your Yodi to this wicked, witchy city?"

The answer was obvious, and it only increased his chagrin. Centuries of feuds and persecutions had taught Fandragorans to be the least inquisitive folk on earth. For that reason, it had seemed a likely place to ply his trade in peace; but for the same reason, no one would come looking for him. His only friends were drawn from a profession where memories are proverbially short.

The cold moon shone directly into the pit. Reflected dimly by tarnished gold and the dead-white walls of his prison, it allowed him to examine the dome above. He saw a second irregular hole, still stoppered with a gold lid, on a line with the one through which he had fallen.

Again he was struck by a horrid familiarity, but only when he had traced a third hole, below and between them, and beyond that a rack of tusks that beggared the aspirations of elephants, did he realize that he was lying inside a monstrous skull; and that the gold trapdoor that would hold him here forever was nothing but one of the coins traditionally placed on the eyelids of a corpse.

Vendriel and Vendreela

Lord Vendriel had descended to the crypt to bid farewell, in that wicked man's singular way, to his beloved mother: to bid her farewell for the last time, for even though he could evoke in her a glowworm-glint of life's memory, her skin had begun to slip from her flesh and her flesh from her bones like a fowl's, too long boiled.

*

Many of the House of Vendren have ruled our land, and almost as many were called Vendriel, so they took epithets to mark one from another. That one called the Insidiator, when our island was beset on three coasts by the Thallashoi, struck each army in a separate stroke, hacked each into chips and cracked each chip to splinters. Some named Vendriel did well; none was good.

But the Vendriel Vendren of whom I write was called the Good: so called with no hint of irony by anyone who prized his fortune, his sanity and his life; addressed as "Good Lord Vendriel" with no twitch of the lip or shift of the eye by anyone who feared the devastation of his household, down to his meanest slave's unhatched nits.

It was this Vendriel who built the New Palace, shunned since the ultimate metamorphosis of his great-granddaughter, Lady Lereela, although its construction is ascribed to her reign by historians less scrupulous than I. So black is the shadow cast by that Lady, last of the Vendren rulers, that it has leeched the blackness from the names of her ancestors. It is to restore the foul name of Vendriel the Good to its full foulness that I write.

*

Ascending from the crypt to the gloom of the New Palace, where the heat and light of our city dare not intrude, Vendriel was embraced by his consort, Lady Ailissa. She quickly broke the embrace.

"Good my lord, forgive me, but you smell . . . odd."

Absently chinking a pair of teeth in his palm, he stared at her. She quaked to recall her thoughtless words.

"My lady, you are dreaming."

She laughed and clapped her hands. The First Lady perceived that her husband, the New Palace and all within it, her parents and children and friends, the geography of our land, the history of our race, the wisdom of our philosophers and the folly of our fools, all the works of the gods, and indeed, the gods themselves, were products of her extraordinary imagination.

"How complex!" (I think I am safe in saying that she was the only person who ever tweaked Lord Vendriel's nose.) "How vivid!"

She followed the subsequent elaboration of her dream with interest and, for a while, detachment. She could even congratulate herself — for she, too, was a Vendren — on the exquisite perversity of her fancy. But at last she willed to wake, she prayed to wake. When her screamed prayers ascended to a pitch and constancy that troubled Vendriel's ears, ever sensitive, he woke her.

*

The lady woke to know that she was a rat who had dreamed of being human. At a change of light and shadow, the flirt of a palm-frond, the fall of a pebble in a distant stone-clock, she would dash headlong for a hole, most often inadequate. If she remained conscious, she would bite anyone who offered help, how courtly and decorous soever his approach. Her successes with noble toadies emboldened her. She became a deadly menace in the kitchens.

After she had savaged his concubine of the moment in a dispute over a plum pastry, Lord Vendriel ordered her confined to a bamboo cage. He patiently taught her to take nuts, drupes and bits of cheese from his hand without biting it. She even grew affectionate, but her constant chittering and nose-twitching became tiresome, so he directed that she be freed in a section of the dungeons antedating the palace: where, he said, among the cisterns, oubliettes and heaps of ancient bones, she would find congenial companions. She was seen no more.

When the First Lord had been dead for five years and his enemies felt reasonably safe in whispering against him behind locked doors, they hinted that he had set out poisoned baits in those remote catacombs; which he had. But Lady Ailissa's story has a curious sequel, and I shall relate it in due time.

*

Having persuaded himself that any woman he loved would end by offending either his senses or his dignity, Vendriel the Good set out to create one who would be both incorruptible and uncritical. He was a master of the Lesser Art, the casting of enchantments. He sought now to master the Great Art, the unweaving and reweaving of the world's web. At great peril he consulted with the spirits of earth and air, of fire and water. He knew something; he learned more.

What price Lord Vendriel paid to gratify his desire, only a third-degree initiate into the worship of Sleithreethra, Goddess of Evil, could begin to understand. I, Squandriel Vogg, a mere sifter of facts, and one who would not set foot inside her Temple of Thought for all the gold skilliglees in Frothann, do not know the price; nor, I daresay, did the First Lord understand it.

*

As Lord Vendriel's studies progressed, an unknown distemper struck certain inmates of the New Palace. This or that courtling would wake to find that he had suffered a loss of weight, sometimes drastic or disabling, overnight.

Some did not at once perceive this as an evil. We Frothoin tend to plumpness. But as they did in so many things, the court of Vendriel the Good defied nature and decreed by fashion that men and women should be lean, even cadaverous. Some victims thought the ailment to be the blessing of a kindly divinity, but few survived.

As the afflicted sickened, however happily, and died, physicians were surprised to discover that the weight they had lost was not just fat, but muscle, bone and even vital organs.

A stalwart young hero named Crespard, of the regiment Never-Vanquished, having died in his sleep, it was determined that his heart was missing. It had not been cut out. It had vanished.

Istreela Fand, whose long legs had inspired sonnets, statues and suicides, leaped from her hammock one morning with characteristic zest to assure Polliel, the Sun God, that she still ornamented his view. Expecting the thud of her springy heels on the parquetry, she heard instead a thump, as of a load of wet washing flung down by a laundress. Thus she heard; what she felt is known now only to Oreema, Goddess of Pain. The bones of her perfect legs had been filched.

Stranger abstractions from the riches of the court were noted: she who had laughed as readily as wind-chimes grew dour; she whose hair was midnight on the sea in one light, slickenside coal in another, yet in whose blackness Polliel could smelt bronze and strike gold, went gray as a sunless fog; she whose skin was old ivory washed with honey and kissed by the shadow of a rose appeared one morning white as bone.

Fancies overwrought by these real horrors might have inspired reports of less tangible thefts. The critic Ailiel Fronn wrote that certain lines from Pesquidor's *Seeluriad*, those describing the emergence of Filloweela, Goddess of Love, had gone unaccountably flat. The words were the same but the music had fled. Others professed dismay at a hitherto unseen insipidity in the erotic paintings of Omphiliard and the sensuous sculptures of Melphidor.

Least credible of all, but believed to the point of general panic, was the assertion that the one perfect day of spring granted our capital city of Frothirot, when the steam of the rains has burned off but the parching of summer not yet ignited, that this perfect day, so beloved of poets and pubescents of the randier sort, and popularly known as Filloweela's Birthday, had absented itself from the calendar for the past several years.

*

The First Lord suffered with his subjects, although some said that his loss of weight and ravaged countenance were the natural result of neither eating nor sleeping. He kept to his chambers, tinkering with and muttering over an arrangement of crystal prisms, rods and balls that tended to fuddle anyone who gazed at it too long.

During the general rash of thefts, the skull of his beloved mother, Lostrilla the Thrice-Damned, disappeared from the crypt, but no one dared report this to Vendriel the Good. Also, the two human teeth that the First Lord wore in a gold setting on a chain about his neck were no longer seen, but no one remarked to him on this, either. The only person who had ever asked Vendriel to explain the provenance and significance of these teeth, a silly courtier named Siriel Fesh . . . but it would be unconscionable of me, in a work that may be studied by persons of tender years, even to hint at the doom of Siriel Fesh.

Any minister, messenger or maid admitted to those chambers where Vendriel the Good had become a virtual hermit would later whisper of an inner room where an object lay beneath saffron silk: an object that seemed to grow from one visit to the next. They talked, too, of smells and scurryings and clandestine titterings, of shadows that fell where no shadows should fall. Those who defended Vendriel the Good — and almost everyone felt a pressing need to do so — argued that ministers and maids alike are given to fanciful gossip, that messengers tend to be excited and fatigued.

*

Then Lady Vendreela appeared from nowhere, and all losses seemed restored. The lines of Pesquidor, the tints of Omphiliard, the curves of Melphidor, even the lithe legs of Istreela Fand: such losses lost meaning with the emergence of the enchantress. Men and women did not merely adore her or desire her, depending upon individual proclivity, they wept at the sight of her.

Birds fluttered from the trees, not to take tidbits from her hand, but to delight in its touch. The green asp, deadliest mite in creation, slithered up to her lap and begged to be fondled.

One day a tiger padded boldly through the Sassoin Gate and up the Avenue of Bruised Jasmine, emptying all adjacent streets. The party of hunters and soldiers organized to deal with the monster found it squirming on its back, purring and playing with its toes at the feet of Lady Vendreela, to whom it had come to pay its obeisances. She waved the mighty men away with a laugh that enslaved them forever and escorted her stripy admirer back to the jungle.

It was given out that Lady Vendreela came from Ashtralorn. Anything at all may come from that wild city in the northern hills, but few Vendrens are found there; yet she was said to be a daughter of that ancient and evil House. Those who argued that she was patently a Vendren, whose long head, slanted eyes and sharp canines recalled Lostrilla the Thrice-Damned to the very oldest courtiers, when she was a young girl and still known as Lostrilla the Parricide, were actively discouraged by Lord Vendriel from pressing this line of argument.

When the Elders of the House questioned the First Lord on her suitability as consort, he presented them with her genealogy in fifty scrolls, transcribed in the quirkish dialect and orthography of the north. The Elders gave conditional approval; but if any Vendrens be left unburned after the Cluddite Protectorate, they may still be trying to puzzle out those scrolls.

Lady Vendreela became First Lady of the Frothoin. She had so won the hearts of all the people, whatever might have been whispered of her origin, that joy, long confined during the reign of Vendriel the Good, burst upon the world like Filloweela's Birthday. Vendreela displayed, however, one odd habit. Years passed, during which she showed an equally odd reluctance to age, before it became a disabling quirk.

*

Never had Lord Vendriel heard the words, "I love you," spoken with such fervor as Lady Vendreela spoke them. The birds, the asp, the tiger — minor miracles, for she charmed that evil old man himself. He knew that it was he who had lived all his days in a dream, to be wakened at last to beauty and love everlasting. Neither asked nor commanded, she did what he required. As he was now quite old, he mostly required her to look beautiful, gaze adoringly and keep quiet. Yet flame sometimes sprouted in the ashes of his days, and her flesh was grass.

He would discuss affairs of state with her, marveling at her aptitude for arriving so promptly at his own, correct conclusions. One day he was explaining his policy for the pirates of Orocrondel, old allies grown irksome, when he detected an annoying harmonic in his voice; or more properly, perhaps, a false echo in his unreliable ears.

Over the days this phenomenon became an obsessive nuisance. He heard the overtone in no one else's voice, and no one would admit to hearing it in his. Like the panther of Mopsard's fable, who was cautioned by the goat that his left paw always struck first and who consequently was immobilized by self-consciousness, Vendriel hesitated to speak. He feared that his ears had at last failed, if not his mind. Laconic by nature, he grew virtually mute, and even more terrible to those forced to approach him.

As a master of the Lesser Art, he could have deluded himself that his faculties were unimpaired, but he had always prided himself on eschewing self-delusion. And he dared not cure himself by attempting the Great Art a second time.

He instead consulted the court physician, who advised him by slow degrees and with infinite tact that the fretful harmonic was the voice of Lady Vendreela. She had always echoed his opinions; now she spoke his very words even as they fell from his lips. In a single, fatal lapse from tact, the physician compared that lady, the sole candle in Vendriel's dark cosmos, to a very quick parrot. The First Lord spoke a few words. Flapping his arms and screaming nonsense, the physician hopped from the highest pinnacle of the New Palace, a very high pinnacle indeed.

*

Unwilling to test the diagnosis, Vendriel stared at Vendreela, who stared back adoringly. He thought a thought and she made it flesh. He wept at her beauty and ardor. He whispered, "I love you," and he knew the truth.

His first thought was to call for his apothecary to decant them both their deaths. As he was a Vendren, his second thought was to defy the gods and dupe his creature into the belief that she had a soul of her own.

"You have deluded yourself!" he cried; as did she.

The captain of Death's Darlings who dared creep into the First Lord's chamber on the following afternoon found his master dead, and in a state of decay more advanced than anyone would have thought natural. Beside the deliquescent corpse lay an indistinguishable welter of animal, mineral and vegetable matter.

A sometime poet, the captain swore that he also sensed a hint of our brief spring in the fetid air about him, but that it soon dissipated.

*

As I have said, the story of Lady Ailissa, Vendriel's first wife, had a curious sequel. The First Lord's son and heir, Vendrard the Demented, believed that he was a date-palm. His father, oddly enough, had nothing to do with this: Vendrard had conceived his delusion and earned his epithet on his own. The Elders of the House, while regretting the loss of his unique talent for standing through the longest and dullest ceremonies with the most lordly grace, deemed him unfit to rule and sent him to Fandragord, unhappy home of his especially wicked branch of the family.

Frothard Vendren, of the Frothirot branch, was given the rings of the First Lord. Ten years into his reign his son Forfax, a devoted student of fungi, was investigating that region of the catacombs where Lady Ailissa had been released from her cage when he was seized by enormous rats of anomalous appearance and borne screaming into the deeper depths.

The unfortunate lad's fellows on the field-trip described the beasts as relatively hairless; as somewhat ungainly in their four-footed gait, though very fast; and as having uncommonly dexterous forepaws. An exhaustive search resulted only in the mysterious loss of a dozen searchers. The fumigation of the pits with sulfur provoked nothing more than an irruption of perfectly ordinary rats into the New Palace. The older region of the underground was securely bricked off.

It was said that Lady Lereela, when she came to the capital from Fandragord some threescore years later, trafficked with these creatures of the abyss: who might have been her rather distant cousins.

The Retrograde Necromancer

By the ninth year of his infamous reign, Vendriel the Good believed that he had heard everything.

When he disclosed his plan for chastising the wayward city of Lilaret, his generals said, "We cannot — "

"We have heard that before," Lord Vendriel said and jumped aside, for his sword-bearer was very quick.

When the epic poet Phoqquidor had chanted only half the first line of his latest canto, Lord Vendriel said, "We have heard that before," and Phoqquidor's cheeks soon squeezed those of his peers on the iron spikes of Poets' Row.

The First Lord's sword-bearer was a bulgy-armed youth named Flindorn, who seemed to have neither time nor desire for anything but sharpening his manqueller and using it. He nevertheless found enough of both for a vigorous exchange of juices with Glittitia Fulnathooza, his master's favorite. Barely had the transfer been made than the chill of the First Lord's presence fell upon them with his shadow.

Although she had tried to deceive a necromancer fabled to disperse himself into the dust-motes eddying through the Vendren Palace, the better to spy on his court, Glittitia wasn't stupid. But against the cold iron of his rage, her intellect froze like a raindrop, and she blurted: "He forced me!"

"We have heard that — "

Flindorn then astounded them both by leaping from the hammock and Glittitia's embrace, snatching up his weapon, and beheading himself.

The moment that Lord Vendriel spent fingering his beard as he stared at the twitching body was time enough for the lady to recover her wits. She said, "I know something you've never heard."

He thought he had seen everything, too, but Flindorn had proved him wrong. He said, "Speak, corpse."

"No. Unless you promise to spare me, I'll never say. The secret will rot with my head on Concubines' Row."

"We can make those heads speak, you know," said the First Lord. Then he chucked her under the chin as he complained in a mode he thought playful, "I have to spare you, don't I? Thanks to you, I'm without a headsman."

Accepting this as the best mercy she could get, Glittitia said, "You've never heard the voice of the Archimage."

*

Pondering this truth, Vendriel neglected to order her execution for nearly a week. By then he had a long list of heads that more urgently required separation from their bodies, and no one to see to them properly. He had used up so many sword-bearers that few candidates were left with the flair and energy he demanded, and those few had fled the city after Flindorn tendered his imaginative resignation.

Glittitia Fulnathooza had in fact told the First Lord nothing new. In his youth he had conceived a fascination with the mysterious recluse whom other wizards resemble only as whirligigs resemble a tornado. Even in the dizzyingly ancient scrolls that he had filched from the shunned ruins of Crotalorn as a boy, guarded allusion was made to an immortal Archimage.

None of the scrolls revealed by what name his hypothetical mother had called him. To know that would be to wield power over the immortal, and so Vendriel had raised old bones and even older dust to learn it. The word "Archimage" was repeated to him in ever more barbarous accents by the shades of his sea-raider ancestors, who had come from Morbia at the dawn of history. The aboriginal inhabitants of the island had a similar word in their apish gabble, but none of them knew a proper name.

His informants grew less substantial as he sifted more ancient dust. A shaman of the sea raiders, vexed at being woken after thousands of oblivious years, was able to blacken Vendriel's eye with his thigh-bone rattle before being subdued, and even then he managed to cast an antique spell that afflicted the necromancer with the botch of Bebros. Earlier shades, however angry, could muster no such strength for their blows or their spells. The very oldest were little more than whiffs of fetid air that chattered and wavered for an eye-blink before subsiding forever.

From an urn found beneath the nethermost crypts of Fandragord, he at last evoked a shadow unlike any he had yet conjured, disturbingly unlike any sort of man or woman at all. In the problematical language of the Lomar Texts, it whispered words that would have set Vendriel's hair on end if he hadn't temporarily lost it to the botch. This dust was uniquely pleased to have been reconstituted and defied all attempts to lay it. Skipping from the restraints of Vendriel's pentacle as if it were a child's hopscotch diagram, it burst from the wizard's tower and capered through the dark labyrinth of Frothirot's Lower City for a week, leaving scores of victims in its wake whose weightless bodies would crackle and flake away like the husks of cicadas. It was last glimpsed flickering toward Fandragord, where all evil finds its home; but before departing it had disclosed a fragmentary name.

Afraid of nothing in those days, Vendriel used the fragment in an exploratory spell, a tentative extension of an insubstantial feeler toward his quarry. The most potent adepts would never have noticed the spell at all, or would have dismissed it as an irksome gnat. Not one of them could have traced it back through its deceptive route to the tower of the necromancer. But barely had Vendriel begun to hiss the snaky syllables than his robe burst into flames.

The stargazer Quisquillian Fesh was heaped with derision for describing the visitation that night of "a comet with a bald, pock-marked head that seemed nearly human," after he witnessed part of the flaming necromancer's arc from his high window into the crocodile-pond below. Although used to receiving screaming treats from that source, the crocodiles were momentarily put off by the flames, giving Vendriel time to evade their jaws with a hastily gargled spell.

Shamed and scared, Vendriel resolved to tempt the Archimage no further; but his lesson wasn't over. For the next three years, the future ruler of the Frothoin was plagued by an imp that would set fire when least expected to such unlikely inconveniences as his boots, his bathwater and his semen. The attendants charged with dressing, scrubbing and diverting him would run and hide when they were most wanted, and for years afterward he would scream if someone struck a light without warning in his presence.

When he at last devised a spell for liquefying human bones that his father, Vendriel the Kindly, was unable to counteract, Vendriel the Good acceded to the First Lord's rings. He hoped that his boyhood impertinence was forgotten, and he decided to invite the Archimage to his investiture. No such mission had been undertaken in living memory, and the ceremony was delayed for a week while he tried to find members of his dread household regiment, Death's Darlings, who would rather carry the message than drink poison.

The delegation of heroes trooped back with a large orange cat. They said the wizard's servants had assured them that this animal was none other than the Archimage, in the form it had pleased him to inhabit for the last several centuries, and that he was delighted to attend, as his hearty purring showed. Vendriel closely quizzed the cat, which yawned and licked its testicles. He was almost certain that it was a plain cat, meant as a slur on the heraldic tiger of the Vendrens, but he didn't dare interrogate it through wizardry or show it the slightest disrespect.

Lounging in a conspicuous place of honor on a velvet cushion, the cat watched him assume his father's robe and rings in the Temple of Polliel. Like several others it dozed off during his maiden speech as First Lord of the Frothoin, but it was the only one to do so with impunity.

The cat disappeared soon after, leaving Vendriel uncertain whether the Archimage had honored him above all previous rulers or made a complete fool of him. The people feared that he was even crazier than they had supposed, but he knew that such a fear was never a handicap to good government.

He had put the immortal out of his mind until Glittitia Fulnathooza rekindled his old temptation. He was no longer the overweening boy who had tried using the master's own craft to spy on him. He was no longer the novice ruler who had pestered him with inept diplomats. He was old, wise and powerful. He had seen and heard everything.

Except the Archimage.

*

The only persons known to visit the palace of the Archimage were the unspeakable childcatchers. One of these hairy brutes was seized at the First Lord's command, roughly scoured and scented, clubbed to a semblance of civility and kicked into his audience chamber.

"I didn't do it!" Zago the childcatcher screamed as he tumbled by accident into a properly prostrate mode.

"We've heard that — *no!*" Vendriel caught himself before Gnepox, latest aspirant to Flindorn's place, could swing his manqueller; but that young man, gazing into the polished shield of a conveniently immobile guardsman while knotting various combinations of his muscles, had missed his cue. Although Flindorn had by now rotted so long in a common pit that not even the most skilled cosmeticians and perfumers could have made him presentable, Vendriel was of half a mind to reunite his head with his body and give him back his job.

He bade Zago rise. When apprehended he had worn only the codpiece affected by the second-lowest sort of wretch, which those charged with sanitizing him had immediately burned. Disinclined to waste clothes on a dead man, as any ordinary person who attracted the First Lord's notice would likely soon become, they had thrust him naked into Vendriel's presence. His shrinking stance couldn't conceal a wolfish physique acquired from chasing urchins through the sewers and warrens of the Lower City, from battling rival childcatchers and the odd outraged parent.

Vendriel wondered if he were skilled with a headsman's sword, and Glittitia Fulnathooza was not the only courtling who marked an aspect of the nude ruffian that pleased her, or that might.

Vendriel the Good tried to put his subject at ease with one of his wan, terrifying smiles and said, "You have seen the Archimage, fellow?"

"No, Lord."

"You have heard his voice?"

"No, Lord."

"At his palace, have you seen — " Vendriel's pale gaze whipped the court like sleet as he searched for anything like a smirk — "have you seen . . . a cat? An orange cat?"

"Lord, I've never been inside his palace."

"Then how do you transact your business with him?"

"I don't, Lord. I scrape up unwanted spawn and shove them through the west gate of his garden. Those that survive come out the east gate as the sweetest-tempered things you'd ever want to see."

"Our grasp of commerce is limited, but shouldn't someone pay you to do this?"

"Yes, Lord, that's the Lord Protector of Redundant Subjects, and if you want to interrogate a criminal, he's the one you should go after, not — " The childcatcher correctly guessed why Vendriel's lips became suddenly paler than his white skin and returned to the subject: "At the east gate I collect the ones with my brand and turn them over to the Lord Protector. He pays me, lord, if you want to call it that, though any fair man would call it sucking out my heart's blood and spewing it in my face."

"And what does he get out of it, the Archimage?"

"He eats their souls. Or so it's said."

Vendriel knew more about these matters than Zago ever could; he had less interest in the answers than in the manner of the man who gave them. He could use a terrorized dupe who dealt with the wizard in a scheme involving his own unique talent for disincorporating himself. It was a dangerous skill that he used sparingly, for he would misplace some of his substance each time he did it, but it might let him hear and see the only one of his subjects who could still rouse in him the dimmest glimmer of curiosity.

Forgetting that he continued to stare as he shaped his plan, he failed to observe that he was melting the childcatcher to a sniveling accumulation of tics. Zago believed that the necromancer was trying to see if he, too, could eat a soul, and that he was succeeding brilliantly.

Noticing the long silence at last, Vendriel said, "Do you believe that he eats their souls?"

"I — " Zago could no longer speak. He saw many slaves at the periphery of the court, gray among the noble peacocks. Dully awaiting orders, they looked as spiritless as the ones he collected from the Archimage. He meant to point them out, to suggest that the First Lord see for himself, but he could only jerk and flail like an idiot.

Vendriel grasped his meaning. "No, we wouldn't keep *his* products about us. These are the honest dead."

As if the court were one gorgeous jellyfish, it shrank in all its parts from contact with the slaves. The courtlings knew what the slaves were, but they hated being reminded. Those who served Vendriel the Good too well, whom he couldn't bear to lose, could anticipate a dim sequel to their butterfly lives; those who served him poorly might earn the same reward sooner. Trying to strike the fine balance, as they told anyone who would listen, made their lives hell.

Vendriel raised his voice to address the court at large: "It was once the custom to send not only redundant children but also lazy servants and other criminals to be stultified. This custom fell into disuse under the Empire, when it was thought too lenient, and when the Archimage began to cloak himself more darkly in his private concerns. But that personage came forth in humble form to bask in the radiance of our coronation, suggesting a desire to take his place at our feet; and in the absence of any lenient punishments, justice lacks its most effective tool, the power to shock. We have therefore determined to renew the custom."

Zago had experimented with breathing again during what seemed a typically boring speech, but its meaning at last trickled to his heart and stopped it. "No, Lord, please! What have I done? Maybe I deserve death, but — "

"Not you, fool. You will have the honor of escorting the malefactor we select to the west gate of the Archimage's garden — "

"Thank you, Lord!"

" — and through that gate. We wish you to deliver the offender personally with our message, and to observe closely what happens to him. Or her."

Although Zago had bullied a wailing herd through that gate every week or so for a decade, each visit scared him more. To pass through the gate himself was a horror he faced only in nightmares, but this time he would not be able to scream himself awake.

Those urchins whose nightmares he himself haunted might have been gratified to see Zago faint.

*

The childcatcher was not alone in his terror that morning, for the least of the First Lord's skills was seeming to speak pointedly to each member of a crowd. Even some of the dead slaves had to be revived after he swirled his cloak about his lank frame and stalked from the hall. Every man knew he was the malefactor whose soul would be eaten; every woman deemed herself damned by his ictic addendum.

None believed this more strongly than Glittitia. Her lord's normal coolness had grown glacial. He had called for her only three times in the weeks since her lapse with Flindorn, and then only to assist a new favorite in the most demeaning ways. Worse, whenever his new sword-bearer bungled an execution in more than usually ludicrous style, Vendriel would slide exasperated glances her way while ranting at Gnepox, as if impatient to reach her name on his long list.

But she was delighted with the sentence that had appalled everyone else, for it held the first hope she had dared entertain. She was a native of Sythiphore, with the ivory skin, almond eyes, black hair and general cast of features that led the Frothoin to boast they couldn't tell one Sythiphoran from another. She was also an avid reader of Mopsard's tales, and particularly loved the one about the princess who persuades her executioner to substitute the heart of a swineherd's daughter for her own and bring it to her wicked stepmother. She chose not to dwell on the fate of the princess when she later meets the Three Vengeful Pigs of the tale's title.

Substituting another woman for a beheading would be impossible: the substitute would surely make some inapt comment before the blade fell. But one whose soul had been eaten would say only what she was told to say. If Vendriel noticed any difference in the one Zago brought back, he might ascribe it to the process of stultification. She would let them argue about it, for she would be long gone.

It remained to subvert Zago, and she thought of that as child's play until she tracked him down to the exercise room where he was coaching Gnepox in the use of the manqueller. Her heart sank when she observed how the childcatcher clung to the handsome youth while guiding his strokes, how his hand lingered in patting the novice headsman's muscular rump.

"Come to help us practice?" Gnepox said with a laugh when he saw her. "You're just what we need!"

Infuriatingly, Zago didn't even look up from his rapt kneading of the young man's shoulders, but Glittitia's eyes bored into him and willed him to notice her slinking forward in her artfully disordered gauze.

"Leave us," she ordered. "I require a word alone with this wretched creature."

Zago at last looked up with a cool insolence she hadn't thought he could command. "Go ahead and talk to him," he said. "I won't listen."

This tickled Gnepox, and the pair of them whooped like giddy boys while Glittitia raged. Her one word in Vendriel's ear could formerly have squashed a dozen Zagos, but she had thrown that power away. Forcing her eyes back to her goal, she swallowed her bile.

"Gnepox, please. Have I ever asked you a favor?"

He swung his big sword in a whickering wheel not far from her neck. "You soon will."

The slum-vermin parodied a lordly gesture of dismissal that he had probably observed for the first time that morning. This further amused Gnepox, who winked at his new friend and sauntered out. Zago stared at her even more insolently as he folded his sinewy arms and said, "Know, Lady, that I have no use for girls."

Glittitia let her nominal garment waft away and slid close. Her deft fingers woke fully what Gnepox had stirred.

"Then let me teach you one for a woman," she breathed.

To Zago, sex required no more preparation than spitting in someone's face or kicking his backside. It was accomplished almost as quickly, and the effect was often the same. But to Glittitia, who had never known such rude treatment, it was a perverse ecstasy. It was as if a step onto a low and familiar stool had been transfigured into a breathtaking flight to a cloud. She could have torn out her vocal chords for all the inanities they squealed in the span of ten fluttering heartbeats.

Preoccupied with a study of human parts he had never much noticed before, he failed to sense her disgust. She shifted away from his fumbling touch. His childish curiosity annoyed her as much as anything, and she tried to distract him.

"How does one become a — " the word was so distasteful that she feared it might offend him, too, but no euphemism existed — "a childcatcher?"

She breathed again when he stopped behaving like a suspicious house-wife at a poulterer's and addressed the question: "I was once a Ghost Rat. That's what we called ourselves, and it was a fine thing to be. We lived in a ruined palace, one of those half-sunken ones on the Canal of Six Delights. We shared what we stole and drowned anyone who tried to steal it back. I suppose I had a mother and father, but the Ghost Rats were all I ever knew. We stole children sometimes, so perhaps that's how I got there."

"Maybe you were stolen from a noble family," she said, perking up at the similarity to a romance by Porpolard Phurn. "Maybe you're the true heir to some fabulous estate. Is that a birthmark?"

"No, someone's boot did that yesterday. My mother was no doubt a whore and my father one of her clients."

It was impossible to connect this dull beast with the thrill he had inflicted on her. She recalled his unseemly conduct at the audience, his unsavory show with Gnepox. Once more she had to swallow her exasperation before it could spoil her plan. She urged him to tell her more.

"Many children of that class escape being rounded up," he said, "but when they reach puberty, there's no escape. They must go to the Archimage, and everyone turns them in. I shaved, I pretended my voice hadn't changed, but I was big and loud and couldn't hide well. If no one else did, the Ghost Rats would have betrayed me to earn special treatment. So I betrayed them first. I arranged an ambush for the whole lot. My reward was apprenticeship to a childcatcher."

Sythiphoran faces are notoriously hard to read, but he read hers. He said, "Yes, it was a bad thing to do, and I'm a wicked man, but I'm alive, and I've still got my soul, whatever that is."

"Oh, Zago!" Thinking of her own peril, she wept.

Unlike any man she had ever known, he ignored her tears. "Teach me more about the uses of women."

"No, Zago! No, I . . . oh, *very* well."

*

The childcatcher agreed to her plan, or pretended to, but that evening as she made ready to visit the Sythiphoran enclave to look for a double, she was seized and confined to

her rooms. No explanation was given.

*

Glittitia had pictured spending her last hour as a cogitant woman in bittersweet contemplation of Frothirot's airy spires while the million catches and dirges and ballads of its noisy citizens rang across the canals where her funeral boat glided. She would stand tall and proudly indifferent, a doomed empress of romance. No one would notice the tear that glittered on her cheek as she thought of her far-off home in Sythiphore, and of all that might have been.

She had never imagined these precious moments soiled by thoughts of how fine Zago looked with his hair and beard curled and his broad shoulders draped in the gray traveling-cloak of the household regiment. Nor had she imagined being distracted by the slaves who rowed the boat: not the dead ones that Vendriel the Good kept prudently close at home, but incogitants who smiled and bobbed their heads each time she glanced their way. They didn't know it, but she was going to be made just like them, and their brainless eagerness to please seemed cruelly ironic.

She gave in to a temptation that had nagged her since leaving the Vendren Palace and made to brush Zago's shoulders, but the captain of their escort batted her hand away.

"But he's *dusty!*" she protested. "You're a soldier, surely you can see that."

"Orders." The man was grimmer even than Death's Darlings were supposed to be, as if this were his own last voyage. She supposed he was outraged to see a childcatcher dishonoring his uniform.

"I was told that the First Lord put a protective spell on this cloak." Zago muttered with unmoving lips, like a fellow prisoner. "I'm not to disarrange it in any way."

"Let me wear it."

He squeezed her hand. She cursed herself for finding this not just comforting but thrilling. He kept the enchanted cloak, though.

The touch thrilled Zago, too, and he again caught himself stupidly counting the guards. They still numbered the total of three hands' fingers, each was bigger than he, each had the hilt of a manqueller angled high above his helmet. He might snatch one of those swords and surprise a few of the soldiers, but then numbers would tell. Glittitia might swim away, but he would sink straight to the bottom in his ironbound boots.

The only thing to do with sources of confusion, he had found, was to eliminate them quickly. Glittitia confused him more than anyone ever had, so he had quickly reported her dimwit escape-plan to Gnepox. Vendriel the Good had relayed him his eternal gratitude, for whatever that was worth. That should have settled the matter, but she still confused him. He prayed that he could see his mission through without doing something stupid, but suicidal plans for saving her hopped through his mind like a plague of toads.

The traffic of boats and barges thinned, then vanished completely as they entered the Canal of Swimming Shadows. Zago studied the oarsmen, who smiled at him and bowed. He couldn't say if he had caught any of these slaves as children. If so, they didn't hold it against him. Neither would Glittitia. Once her soul was wizard-food, she would sing *Hurrah for Zago!* the marching ditty he had composed for his flocks on their way from the Archimage's garden, if he told her to. Much as he loved that song, he doubted he would have the heart to hear her sing it.

They moored at the dock of the umber palace, where he guided the group up to Bruised Jasmine Street and the westgate. It was the most familiar place in his workaday life, but visiting it in this strange company, in such strange clothes, wrenched it into the world of unpleasantly vivid dreams. The door to his worst fears looked less menacing than shabby, grimed by the fists of childcatchers and by so many small fingers that had tried to find a last grip among its intricate carvings.

Completing the strangeness, a yoked troop of children rounded the corner and shuffled toward them. A brute whose strut proclaimed him to be either the Emperor of the Thallashoi or a complete lunatic brought up the rear, prodding them with a hooked bill. He stopped short and stared in bewilderment at the armed strangers. Obviously he didn't recognize Zago, but Zago knew him as a colleague called Plistard. They were not friends.

Glittitia gripped his hand with all her strength. Perhaps he saw with her eyes, perhaps he had become a different person, but he had never noticed how piteous the children looked, how utterly despairing. Though some of them sobbed, the tears had long dried on their dirty faces.

"Free those scum," Zago told the captain. "We don't want them cluttering up our mission, do we?"

"Free those other scum," the captain told his men.

Bellowing, Plistard laid into the meddlers with his bill. A soldier fell with a cracked head, swords flashed, loose children scrambled everywhere.

"Back to the canal!" Zago whispered, giving his prisoner a shove. "You can swim, can't you?"

"Are you insane? The Canal of Swimming Shadows?"

"Go, it's your only — "

"What are you doing?" The captain loomed over them.

"Comforting the prisoner."

"Comfort her inside. We have things under control," he said and gestured at Plistard's disconnected wreckage with his dripping sword. But he held Zago's sleeve before he could obey. "Listen: if you see the Archimage, don't mention his visit to our First Lord's coronation."

"Why should I?"

"Good fellow."

Drawing Glittitia with him, he pounded at the gate as he had done before. It opened as it had done before.

"I'm sorry," he said.

"You did what you could."

"You don't know."

As he had never done before, he passed through the gate. The garden was alarmingly tranquil. Among susurrant fountains and murmurous bees, the palace napped like a friendly brown beast. The only person in sight was a gardener with the face of an alert monkey under his wide hat.

"Welcome," he said. "We don't get many adult guests."

Zago felt Glittitia nudge him, but he didn't know why. He said, "We've come to see the Archimage."

"Ah. Well. He doesn't see many people, you know."

"We come from Lord Vendriel the Good, First Lord of the Frothoin, King of Sythiphore and the Outer Islands, Sword to the Gastayne, Scourge of the Thallashoi, Hammer to Morbia, Beloved of Sleithreethra, and Tiger of the House of Vendren," Zago recited as he had been intensively coached.

"That may impress him. Come along and let's see."

When the gardener had gone ahead, Zago whispered: "Why do you keep poking me?"

"It's *him*, don't you see? Pretending to be a servant. Wizards are always doing that. Haven't you read Porpolard Phurn?"

"I don't read," Zago said, "but I think he's only the gardener." He heard himself mutter, "I've never seen anyone so brave as you."

"Perhaps I should scream and weep, but I feel numb. Let's get it over with."

He held her and kissed her in his unskilled way. Then she wept.

*

The room they entered was vast, but its only other attribute that Zago immediately grasped was stupefying heat. The day was warm, yet a fire blazed in a hearth at the end of the closed and thickly draped room. Still the only soul in sight, the gardener pattered across a black plain of mirror-polished marble until his figure markedly shrank.

Zago crept forward, and Glittitia hung on his arm, preferring the comfort of his presence to the shadows behind them. He felt her gaze on him, though he preferred not to look and verify the feeling. No one had expected hope or help or anything else from him in a very long time, and he hated it.

He had almost accepted her silly notion about the gardener when an angular arrangement of drapery beside the hearth shifted to disclose a face. Glittitia shrieked. Zago might have, too, but a spasm locked his lungs.

Too far off to hear, the servant spoke while the face listened, or perhaps not. It was immobile as a mask of dark wood, and just as inhumanly dry, although the gardener gleamed with sweat from his few moments in the stifling heat. Zago was uncertain whether the Archimage sat in a chair whose covering echoed the muddy tones of his vestments, or if there were no chair, and he stood or squatted in robes that concealed a body of unlikely shape. This remained a puzzle even when they had edged close to the intolerable hearth.

"Zago," the Archimage whispered. "The children often speak of you."

The childcatcher tried to disregard this remark as he recited the rigamarole he had memorized about reviving old customs and making new friends. At least he believed he delivered the message, but when he had done speaking, he couldn't recall what he had just said. It was impossible to think of anything but the browless, lidless, lipless mask that confronted him. While staring into the yellow eyes, he was struck by the queasy fancy that the Archimage was neither sitting, standing nor squatting at all, but had arrayed himself in restless coils. The patterned vestments were perhaps nothing more than his unnatural skin.

"Yes, Vendriel the Good, I know of him. I should have liked to attend his coronation, but the men apparently sent to invite me conferred outside my gate for a while and left without knocking. They stole my cat." The Archimage brooded on this for a moment, but Zago couldn't say if he was angry or merely perplexed. "He found his way home, though, none the worse for his adventure."

Glittitia was surprised that she could laugh, if only bitterly, at Vendriel's blunder. She regretted the laugh when the mask swiveled in her direction and the voice said, "This is the subject you wish . . . treated?"

"No, I don't wish it," Zago said. "I spoke the First Lord's words. If I spoke my own, I would beg you — "

"You're uncommonly dusty, young man," the Archimage interrupted.

A heavy hand snaked out of the confusing folds to buffet Zago's cloak. He had placed little trust in Vendriel's protective spell, but it dismayed him that it should be sniffed out and disposed of so quickly. He now felt more naked than in the presence of the First Lord. His shoulders shivered and crawled long after the touch had been withdrawn.

"What is it you would beg of me, childcatcher?" Before he could answer this, the wizard gestured with distaste at the dust now defacing his immaculate floor and told his servant, "Fetch a broom. Now, you wish. . . ?"

"That you not eat her soul."

"Her soul?" The angular face was thrust unbearably close. Neither Zago nor Glittitia could say who was now holding the other upright. "She may still have one. What about you, Ghost Rat?"

Those words tore a hard rind from Zago's heart, and the pain of his boyhood treachery stabbed him as cruelly as it had on the night when he lay hiding outside the derelict palace of the Ghost Rats, grinding his fists into his ears to exclude the screams of children and thumps of clubs.

The pain almost at once gave way to an indescribable glow of pleasure. He didn't see the faces of his lost brothers and sisters, nor hear their laughter, nor feel their comforting touch; but a forgotten warmth swelled inside him, the emotion he had known when he was with them. The souls of the Ghost Rats frolicked in this empty room, forgiving him and welcoming him. Impossibly and at long last, he felt he had come home.

The feeling faded, leaving a hollow that not even terror of the Archimage could fill. He had thought it unlikely that he ever would, but he wept for the friends whose souls he had traded for his own. He was on the verge of pleading, "Make me one of them," but the Archimage forestalled him with the banal remark, "Ah, here's the broom," and the childcatcher found the strength to hold his tongue.

"*Take it!*" Glittitia whispered. "Do whatever he wants."

He saw that the servant was offering him the broom to clean up the dust lately buffeted from his cloak. It seemed a strange offer to make a guest, but the ways of the mighty, let alone mighty wizards, were a mystery to him.

"Into the fire, would you?" the Archimage said.

The task was improbably difficult. At first the dust clung to the floor with a will of its own. When he plied the broom with new briskness, it was not at all like sweeping dust, it was more like tumbling a cumbersome bundle before the broom, an object that wriggled to evade him and thrashed back vigorously. It might have been an invisible, angry man, crippled or otherwise constrained, that he shoved ahead of him. The dust fought back even more violently when he reached the hearth, and he had to wield the broom like a club.

The fire blossomed out to singe his beard when the dust hit it, then screamed upward through the chimney in a twisting column.

"I hadn't known what a filthy hole the Vendren Palace was," the Archimage observed. "If I were you, I'd fly from it as far as I could. It would be wise to start now."

Neither paused to question this or make their farewells. Zago reached the door first, but concern for his companion prompted him to leave it open as he sprinted through the garden.

When she found him cowering outside the east gate, Glittitia asked, "What happened to you in there? What did you see?"

"He doesn't eat their souls. He keeps them safe from the world," Zago said. "I almost asked him to take mine."

"It's a little late for yours, don't you think?"

"That's what stopped me."

*

After five decades of obscurity, Quisquillian Fesh looked back almost with nostalgia to his one moment in the blaze of universal scorn. Younger stargazers neglected to laugh when he introduced himself; laymen no longer said of a drunkard on a spree that he was "observing Quisquillian's Comet;" and no one even bothered to mock him anymore when he predicted, as he sometimes did, its imminent return.

He realized that his earlier predictions had deserved mockery when he at last produced an irrefragable calculation based on the numerological value of his name. This time he locked the figures away. When scientists swarmed to his door crying that they had seen his comet and lamenting what fools they had been, he would say, "I know," and produce the sealed prediction.

He stayed late in bed with earplugs and a sleeping-mask on the designated day, intending to be at his best for the midnight return of the unique star-traveler. This apparently caused him to miss a fire or massacre or other popular diversion, for when he emerged in the evening, the street outside his house pullulated with quidnuncs.

He tottered to accost a stranger, who babbled that the end of the world was at hand, for a manlike head with a fiery train had been seen to arc steeply through the sky at noonday. Some said it had fallen with a hissing column of steam into the Canal of Swimming Shadows, which was a pity, since nothing that fell into that canal was ever retrieved.

"That was mine!" the stargazer cackled. "That was Quisquillian's Comet! I predicted it! Come and see my calculations! They may be off by twelve hours, but — "

"Let me go, old man! You're crazy!" the stranger said, as did everyone else.

Whatever the prodigy had been, it was soon forgotten in a frenzy of speculation over the First Lord's absence from public functions.

Gossip only intensified with the reappearance a few days later of a much-diminished Vendriel the Good. Above a body that seemed thin to the point of incorporeality, only his pallid features moved, and only with the most apparently painful difficulty. His flowing white hair and beard were clearly false. Fanciful observers said that nothing remained of the necromancer but a head propped on a stick-figure in his black clothes.

During his long convalescence, he dictated a list of those he wished beheaded. It filled a scroll the length of a dwelth-field, and included all childcatchers, Sythiphorans, Death's Darlings and orange cats. Gnepox boasted of impressive progress on the cats before his mysterious disappearance.

As soon as Gnepox dropped from sight, Vendriel recovered more than fully. His pasty look had always brought dough to mind, and now his body filled out overnight like dough left to rise. He was seen to leap about like a man only one-third his age, though in much the clumsy style of his missing headsman.

*

Zago learned how tiresome it is to live with a person one has betrayed, even if the victim never knows. And Glittitia, begging scraps from strangers and suffering ecstasies from an oaf, watched herself turn sour and shrewish.

They made their way to Sythiphore, among whose ivory-skinned and black-haired mobs she easily gave him the slip. He struck up a friendship with a young pit-fighter whose general cast of features reminded him of Glittitia, and before long he forgot most of what she had taught him about women.

The Return of Liron Wolfbaiter

I

Young persons usually sleep soundly, but none slept with the fierce determination of Elyssa Fand. Calling her or shaking her were useless. She had to be tumbled about like a baker's dough, propped on her feet and shouted at. Even after she had grumbled that, yes, she was indeed awake, even after she had correctly given her name and named the day of the week, she had to be watched, or she would subside to the bed and to an even deeper slumber.

"That storm was enough to wake the dead!" her mother had cried, hastily making a sign to prevent some malicious god from taking her literally, one morning when Elyssa had peered out the window and asked why the ancient oak lay across the well, its roots clawing empty air.

Her mother had gone on to describe the continuous raging of thunder, lightning that turned night to noon, the sky that became a sea and broke over the house in waves. Elyssa was delighted. She hardly ever dreamed, and this troubled her, but her mother's words stirred a dim memory of dreaming about a man walking on the roof in heavy boots.

She had slept through the noise of that terrible night last spring, but the odor that assailed her now dragged her from a sleep even more profound. More than a simple stench, it was an atmosphere compounded of every foulness she could name, and of some that were nameless. Not just her nose was offended: it burned her eyes, soured her stomach and clogged her lungs. Each breath was a struggle, as if she sucked the air through folds of moldy wool.

As she wiped her stinging eyes, a fearful suspicion gripped her. It was winter, she recalled, but no coals glowed in the grate. Even on the darkest nights, she could dimly discern the rectangles of her bedroom windows. Darkness now was total.

"I'm blind!" she screamed. "I've gone blind!"

Although her screams sounded more like rasping croaks in a voice untuned by sleep, they were loud enough to have brought a slave running, perhaps even to have woken her mother. No one stirred. She thought of screaming again, but her first effort had drained her lungs of the foul air, and the noise of her breath was almost as unpleasant as the labor it cost to catch it. Equally disturbing was the absence of other sounds: no cries from the streets, no distant barking, only the ragged rustle of her own, unfamiliar breathing. She was almost never ill. She believed she was now very ill indeed.

"It's a dream," she muttered to herself. "In one night, I'm making up for all the bad dreams I never had . . . *but I don't like it!*"

She had screamed. Wheezing and gagging, she resolved not to do it again.

She groped for the tinderbox on her bedside table. It was gone: not just the box, but the table. Rolling to search with her right hand, she rolled off the bed and fell to the floor. Moaning curses as she rubbed her bruised knees and elbows, she could no longer doubt that she was awake.

The thick carpet of her room was missing. The floor was of stone, like those downstairs, but it was cold and damp, even slimy. She shivered with loathing when she raised her fingers to her nose and smelled a potent concentration of the stench that had woken her. She wiped her hand so hard on her linen nightdress that the cloth parted.

Rising, she groped for the surface where she had lain. It was not her bed. It was higher. More alarming, it was no bed at all, it was a bare slab.

She backed away, and something poked her shoulder. She recoiled again, then reached for it. It was not stone. Wood? Its surface was more like dry, cracked leather. She traced its protrusions. It was shaped like — no, it was in fact a human hand: a long-dead one.

She tried to thrust it away, but she had twined its fingers in hers. She shook it vigorously, and the hand and part of its arm fell rattling to the floor as separate bones. She kept her resolution not to scream, but she could do nothing to contain the dry sobs that racked her. She knew where she was. Her worst fear had come true.

Years ago, her great-great-grandfather, Umbriel Fand, had traveled to Frothirot for the investiture of Vendriel the Good as First Lord. The strain of suppressing the curses that he longed to howl snapped some vital connection, and he dropped dead in the crowd that pressed around the Spider Gate to view the progress of the abomination. Although he was unknown to the Frothirot Fands, his rank entitled him to be buried in their ancestral vaults, and so he was.

More than a week passed before the news reached Fandragord, where it was recalled that the old man had suffered in his youth from fits that mimicked death. A dreadful possibility suggested itself to his loved ones. His youngest son set out immediately and reached the capital in three days and nights of riding, a feat never since equalled. Explanations were offered in feverish haste, the tomb was opened, and Umbriel sprawled out as if he had been crouching with his ear to the door. The blood was still wet on his fingers, abraded to the bone by his efforts to claw through marble, and physicians estimated that death had truly touched him only hours before. He was nevertheless brought home and put to bed, where his family took turns defending him from flies and mice until his odor and appearance had so degenerated as to blight even the most sure and certain hope.

The story was retold frivolously at family gatherings. Her ancestor had become a figure of fun. If a kinsman passed out at a festive table, her father would tell the servants to "put Grandfather Umbriel to bed," provoking roars of mirth. They even laughed at the ultimate horror, which had forever disgraced her branch of the Tribe: Umbriel had survived his confinement only by feeding on a corpse that had preceded him into the tomb by a month. "Grandfather Umbriel's favorite," her father would cry when the holiday pig or goose was brought steaming from the kitchen, "Frothirot Fand!"

The tale had horrified Elyssa when she first heard it, and each retelling only deepened her horror. She concealed her feelings, for her loutish brothers would have pounced gleefully on such a weakness. She had trained herself to pluck their snakes from her bed and their toads from her shoes with no more than a sigh of impatience, and so she was able to laugh with the others when Umbriel's name came up. But in the privacy of her vivid imagination she had relived each and every one of the wretched man's last hours. She felt his terror, she agonized with him over the unthinkable alternative to starvation, she felt her own nails rip as he clawed the unyielding wall. She had struggled to fight off the notion that her deep slumbers were an echo of his illness, and that she would one day wake up in the very tomb where he had been finally buried, but the notion became an obsession; and now it was a fact. Perhaps the bones she had scattered on the floor belonged to the flesh-tearing, marble-torn claw of her ancestor.

She screamed now. She raved. She raged through the tomb, strewing bones in her wake, tearing limbs and heads from desiccated bodies. She hated the dead. She hated the living even more, those who had abandoned her and still breathed the open air. Most of all she hated Lereela Vendren, heiress to Vendriel the Good. Everyone in her family knew that Grandfather Umbriel's fatal fit, suffered after years of normal health, had not been naturally caused. The wizard-lord had sensed his unspoken thoughts in the crowd and swatted him with a casual spell. And now his great-granddaughter had done the same to her.

"Ah," Lereela had said when they were introduced as children, "the ghoul's granddaughter?"

Elyssa had flown at her with the intent of scratching out those absurdly crossed eyes, which silly men now professed to find attractive, but she unaccountably stumbled and broke her wrist before she could reach her target. She would never forget the chime of Lereela's laughter, audible even through her howls of pain and rage, as she was taken from her own birthday party.

"Be nice to Lereela," her mother later advised her. "No one can afford not to."

She took that advice, greeting the witch's vicious smirks with polite smiles, pretending to misinterpret her sly insults as compliments. But on the eve of Lereela's departure for Frothirot to be received at court, Elyssa had been unable to resist taking a jab.

"You have no idea how glad I am to see you go, Lereela," she said; and paused pointedly before continuing, "to take your place, of course, as the brightest star at court."

"And even if that should happen, dear sister," Lereela answered, pausing for precisely the same length of time, "I shall never, ever forget your words."

Elyssa's screaming rage subsided to cold fury, silent except for the paper-crumpling rattle of her struggling lungs. Lereela had left . . . a week ago? Her memory of events preceding her last sleep were hopelessly tangled.

She would survive, however, she would escape, because no hatred like hers could be held by mere walls. There were powers greater than Lereela's, and she would learn to command them if it took her fifty years. She was a Fand, of the Dragon-bannered Tribe that had battled the Vendrens as often with sorcery as with swords. She prayed to Sleithreethra, whom her parents had always timidly neglected. She promised Lereela to that Goddess, along with her own mother and father and brothers, too stupid or uncaring to see that they were burying a living girl.

Sorcery would be too impersonal for Zornard Glypht, and poison too indirect. She would grip in her own hand the dagger that cut out his heart, after she had used it to remove parts that were regrettably more familiar. He said he loved her, but where had he been when they sealed her tomb? Moping over his memory of Lereela Vendren, no doubt; he had once roused her fury by venturing that the cast of the witch's eyes was "not entirely disfiguring."

Absorbed in her vengeful devotions, she grew conscious of a draft, but it was some time before she recognized its significance. When she did, she brought her prayers to a hasty but scrupulously respectful end and crawled toward the source of the air-current.

One of the flat stones of the floor had subsided near the wall, leaving a gap just wide enough to insert her fingers. Beyond it she felt nothing, only empty space — and a sudden incision of teeth like chisels.

It hurt, but her shriek was one of rage. Instead of jerking her fingers back from the rat's teeth, as the old Elyssa would surely have done, she rammed her whole hand through the opening until she found a grip on its body. It squealed and clawed, but she squeezed it, giggling softly, until its bones cracked and its life shivered away. She offered it to the Goddess, who had obviously heard her prayers, as a token of greater gifts to come.

She heard chittering cries and a patter of claws beneath the slab. The rats had tunneled below the tomb to undermine this stone in a project that must have taken them generations. About to celebrate their triumph by feasting on Fands, they had been attacked from an unexpected quarter. She understood their terror and confusion. If she listened hard enough, she believed, she could have understood their very words.

She shrieked to frighten them away as she ripped up the stone and screwed her way into the narrow hole, but they were not easily frightened. Thick as mosquitoes in Frothirot, they gnawed her fingers, nipped her arms, scratched her face. Powered by fury and despair, she clawed and bit more savagely than the rats. She knew in a cold part of her mind that she had gone quite mad, but this part averted its gaze like a squeamish spectator at the baiting-pits and placed its wager on madness.

The overmatched rats fled, their chirping chorus fading in the hollow distance. She strained her eyes into the darkness, but all she could see were dim smears of phosphorescence that vanished when she stared at them directly. Her nose told her more than her eyes about the ordeal before her. Fouler than the acid dankness of clay unknown to the sun, the tunnel smelled of graves that had long since drained their liquefied tenants into these deeper depths. But the only alternative to going forward was to remain in the tomb forever. She began to crawl.

At times the earth seemed as tight around her as the skin of a sausage, but her wriggling progress never faltered. When the tunnel branched, as it often did, she always seemed to know which branch to take. Even when the path sloped away from the sun and air she yearned for, she obeyed her instinct and followed it. At one point a clutter of roots clawed her, and she took this for a hopeful reminder that she was close to wholesome trees that reached for the free sky. She realized that the objects were the withered limbs of corpses, that she was squeezing her way through a mass grave from some plague or persecution. Here the rats had tunneled through compacted bones rather than earth. Her groping hands crushed worms fat as her fingers, but they greased her way.

The tunnel entered an empty tomb, where at last she could stand erect, rejoicing to see cold moonlight slicing through a door that hung ajar on broken hinges. She stumbled forward and flung it wide on the cemetery, laughing at the vastness of the sky and the glory of the light. Night-birds and insects fell abruptly silent.

The clutter of Fandragord rose before her, but so strange from this angle and at this hour that she thought for a moment she had emerged into fairyland. A history scrawled in blood had dictated that its buildings face inward, presenting only grim walls to the streets. Viewed from the cemetery, a thousand normally unseen courtyards twinkled with torches and colored lanterns. By daylight, the breached walls and toppled towers were constant reminders of sorry decline, but moonlight and haze combined to veil the city's scars and restore its grandeur. And, while all the happy people she pictured laughed in their splendid city, she had fought rats and crawled through corpses. The tide of rage that had buoyed her thundered back.

She stood on an older slope of the graveyard, its ruts and stones concealed by an overgrowth of brambles, but a ribbon of road gleamed palely below her, and that seemed the shortest way out. By the time she had half-struggled and half-tumbled to the foot of the slope, the roadside ditch looked more inviting than her own soft bed at home. She would have fallen gladly into it if hunger and thirst had not clawed her innards so savagely. She prayed now for one scrap from all the cakes she had nibbled politely and set aside, one sip of the water she had once squandered merely to cool her temples.

Stumbling and weaving forward, she recalled with less distaste the rats she had recently killed and the bodies she had torn. Her thoughts alarmed her, but they fed her hatred for those who had warped her mind with the story of Grandfather Umbriel. Daggers and poison no longer figured in her images of revenge; her weapons would be her teeth. She hungered for the proud neck of Lereela, the faithless heart of Zornard.

When she heard the horse overtaking her, her thoughts were so twisted that she pictured it first as an animated collection of roasts and chops that could be singed hastily over a roadside fire, or even eaten raw. It took a moment for its true significance to register. A horse suggested a rider who might help her; or harm her.

She remembered that she was alone in a desolate spot, and that her garments had shredded away in her long crawl through the tunnels. But she doubted that any man on earth would find her attractive now, scratched and bruised and filthy, still scented with the odors of the tomb. Even as she took heart from her ugliness, instinct made her comb her hair with her fingers and brush the dirt from her face.

The rider approached at a walk, giving her time to entertain misgivings as she spied from the contorted shadow of a cypress. The horse was big and rawboned, but the man was so tall that he suggested an adult clowning with a child's pony. His great bulk was magnified by a leather coat with bronze scales, poor man's armor. He was obviously a mercenary, bearing all the tools of his last questionable employment to his next one: a deadly man who knew no god or master, the sort who made her tingle when she read of them in the romances of Porpolard Phurn, but who gave her quaking chills when she saw one on a lonely road at night. Worst of all, he was outlandishly bearded and braided, as if he had just waded ashore for an orgy of murder and rape. Even if he understood her speech, her name and rank might only fuel his lust.

He still had not seen her, and she had a chance to study his face. Oddly, his features were not those of a foreigner, nor did they seem particularly cruel. Despite his savage guise, he looked less warlike than worried, as if he had more serious matters on his mind than ravishing the helpless. He looked old as her father, too, and that gave dim encouragement.

She called out: "Sir! You won't believe what's happened to me — I don't believe it myself! — but I need your help, please, to return to the city and my home. My father is Lord Ruthrent, of the House of Fand, and he'll reward you well if — "

He started violently at her first word, and his horse reared. His eyes clung to her as he wrestled inelegantly with his mount, and his first expression of shock never left him. His eyes stared wider, his jaw hung slacker, the more she spoke. Had he never seen a naked woman before?

Her mad rage crested again. Everyone was against her, no one could be trusted, they had all conspired to bury her. She hid her feelings and forced herself to extend her hands in supplication, well aware how enticingly this displayed her much-admired breasts. She took a hesitant step forward, stopping in terror and confusion when he drew a battle-ax from over his shoulder.

"Please, sir, I'm Elyssa Fand! I was buried — "

"As well you should be!" he roared, spurring forward, the ax whirling at his side like a wheel of moonlight.

She screamed even before the ax bit through her shoulder and parted one rib after another faster than she could have snapped her fingers six times at a lazy slave. She was wrenched forward, colliding with the wildly neighing horse, when he tried to retrieve his embedded bit. He mashed her face with his boot to tear the ax free.

"Sleithreethra!" she screamed. "Help me!"

He followed as she staggered back and dealt her a second stroke. She screamed at the sight of her severed quarter, twitching and jerking in the dust before her. She felt no pain yet, but she had heard that this was not unusual to even the most gravely wounded. What puzzled her was her failure to die.

Since she still lived, since she had one hand, since she was a daughter of the Dragon, she rushed at him and gripped his cloak, hoping to unhorse him. She never saw the third blow coming, but the moon and the festive courtyards of the city tumbled crazily, and she knew, before losing consciousness at last, that he had chopped off her head.

II

Crondard Sleith glanced uneasily from one part of the cadaver to another until all three had stopped squirming. It seemed to be dead, but he had no wish to get down and verify this.

He permitted himself to breathe again, even to laugh. As he was still shaking, the laugh sounded far from hearty, and he cut it off.

Some of the corpse's flesh had eroded to reveal bones mottled with decay, but enough was left to classify it as a woman. Furred with moss and trailing streamers of skin, it had seemed at first to be a shaggy ape, shambling forward to intercept him with outstretched claws as it shrilled and gibbered. He had noted the blank holes of its eyes and nose at about the same time he had smelled it.

"Ar's balls!" he cried at the memory of his terror, and he flung his befouled ax away in a reflexive gesture of disgust that he instantly regretted. His swordsmanship was indifferent, as several dueling scars testified, but almost thirty years in the Fomorian Guards had taught him how to handle a battle-ax: twirling it flashily was part of their drill. He laughed again, struck by the irony that this first victim of his ax had been already dead.

He found it some distance up the road. Looking back to make sure that the dim mounds of rotting flesh remained still, he dismounted and scrubbed the filth from the blade with gritty dust. His captain would have thrown a screaming tantrum to see him thus marring the mirrorlike surface, but his captain had been the first victim of Crondard's sword. It had been a fair fight — more than fair, considering their relative skills as sworders, until Crondard had evened the odds by tripping the arrogant puppy with an upended chair, kicking him in the face when he tried to rise, and sticking the blade down his gullet while gripping his perfumed locks — but try telling that to the Lord Commander of the Fomorian Guards! Drawing on your captain, to say nothing of killing him, is punishable by torture and death. That the captain had ordered Crondard, as senior sergeant, to have every third man in the company flogged because someone had sketched his caricature in the latrine; and that he had spat in Crondard's face and hit him with an ink-pot when he protested the order, would be no defense. Nor would it help his case if investigation revealed Crondard himself as the offending artist.

He shook off sweet memories of the captain's last, plaintive gurgle and stared down the moonlit road. He could not swear to it, but the alignment of the three foul heaps seemed to have changed, as if they were creeping toward one another. He scrambled onto the nag and urged it to totter faster. He kept scanning the graveyard slope for other untimely strollers, but he resisted the impulse to look back at the one he had dispatched. If it yearned for its mockery of life fervently enough to reassemble itself, he wished it well. He was beyond reach of its faltering gait.

Welcome to Fandragord! He had heard about it all his life: scary tales for children are invariably set in that malefic city. "But of course," his mother would say as she tucked him in after the last story, "such things can't happen here."

"Here" was Ashtralorn, where descendants of the Fomors, imported centuries ago as mercenaries, pretended that they were still hardy and guileless barbarians, although they had so enthusiastically embraced the local customs and women that they were not much different from the Frothoin neighbors they were always quarreling with. Those big enough, like Crondard, or fair enough to resemble their foreign ancestors found their way to the capital for careers in the Fomorian Guard. That once-fearsome regiment was now little more than a marching museum, a costumed choir that sang bloodthirsty songs in a tongue its ranks but dimly understood.

Although the songs could bring a tear of misplaced nostalgia to his eye, although his back hairs sparked when tales of the real Fomors like Shornhand and Deathmaker were retold, he thought of himself as a citizen of Frothirot, even more cynical than the natives. Nothing in his experience, and certainly not childhood fairy tales, had prepared him for the reality of walking corpses.

Ironically, he owed his un-Fomorian name to an ancestor called Liron Wolfbaiter, who had tracked the notorious ghouls of Crotalorn to their underground dens and exterminated them after they had dared to desecrate the tomb of the Great House of Sleith; or so the story was told, one which Crondard scoffed at. For that service, or for whatever it was he had really done, Liron and his descendants had been adopted into the Sleiths. The city of Crotalorn was a plain of ashes, the Sleiths were no longer strong or numerous, but Crondard wore the tattoos of that ancient Tribe.

If he scoffed at stories of ghouls, why should he accept walking corpses? He had often amused himself by browsing among the disputing philosophers in the capital's Market Square, where he had been persuaded that even a young man's eyes and ears can lie more outrageously than merchants or lovers, and his own sight and hearing were beginning to show the effects of long use. As he pictured himself trying to relate his adventure to Mantissus the Epiplect, the most mordant of those savants, he began to suspect that someone had made a fool of him. Perhaps highwaymen had rigged the corpse with wires as a way of stopping travelers. Since no highwaymen had sprung out to take advantage of his shock, pranksters were to blame. He decided he had behaved well. He had spoiled not only their joke, but their corpse.

"Liron is here, ghouls!" he shouted at the crumbling tombs on the slope. "Do your worst!"

The hollow echoes of his voice chilled him. He tried to pretend that he had kicked Thunderer by accident, but he did nothing to discourage its brisker wobble.

*

Within the ruins of the city wall, the first inn he came to was called the Sow in Rut, but he had not expected elegance in the provinces. Shaking the gate of the adjacent mews and shouting did no good, so he went to hammer on the iron door of the inn itself. A panel shot back to give him a glimpse of light and the noise of a crowd, both unexpected behind a visored front in an empty street.

"What do you want?" The voice issued from an extravagantly eared head that blocked the light.

"What does anyone want from an inn? Food, drink, a bed, care for my horse."

Silence followed, as if such unprecedented requests had stunned the innkeeper. At length he said, "Who are you?"

"Liron Wolfbaiter." Crondard suppressed an ironic smile at his own, nearly automatic choice of an alias.

"A foreigner?"

"From Ashtralorn."

"A foreigner," the landlord stated as he shut the panel.

Before Crondard could pull his ax and demonstrate serious hammering, he heard a clatter of bolts and bars and chains. A boy emerged to take his horse to the mews, and the Fomor stooped through the door to a shadowed entryway, decorated with cracked and soiled frescoes of hunting scenes and the moldy heads of beasts. He paused to examine a mural depicting Vendriel the Good, whose surviving images were few. The sardonically-named lord seemed to be pursuing a whale with tentacles, although it could as easily have been a boar, for it was impossible to say where the artist's work ended and a water-stain began.

The passage led to a low but extensive room where every eye was fixed on him: not so much insolently as apprehensively. He wondered if he had not chanced upon a gang plotting treason.

"We have a lord and his retinue staying with us, Lord Nephreiniel of Omphiliot." With the snobbery that only commoners command, the innkeeper spoke the names with less engagement than a man flicking lint; a hairy vagrant from Ashtralorn should bless the luck that got him past the door. "Our best rooms are taken."

"We can haggle about that later. Wine, now."

Two tables near the door were vacant, and he made for the one in a dark corner, but a menace radiating from the darkness stopped him cold. As an amateur of philosophy, he would normally have defied the impulse to shun that corner, but his recent shock had earned him the right to indulge it.

"You don't want to sit there," someone called even as he turned to retreat.

The speaker grinned foolishly from a nearby table, where his companions tried to pretend they were thinking deeply about serious matters, though one of them sniggered his way into a coughing-fit. Crondard was tempted to flout the warning and take the corner table, probably the favorite of some locally notable brawler, but he resisted. A fight could entangle him with the police.

Ignoring the speaker and his friends, he took the table closer to the door and leaned his ax against the wall beside him. Chair and table had been designed for smaller men, and he knew that he cut an intimidating figure, but that hardly accounted for the pall he had thrown on the room. Some whispered behind their hands now, still staring. The landlord had promptly relocked the door. If this mob chose to rush him, he would never fumble his way through the unfamiliar bolts and bars in time to make a run for it.

Twenty years ago he might have taken on a dozen or so armed civilians, but the innumerable aches of his hard journey assured him that this was not twenty years ago. He vividly remembered all the trouble he had recently had trying to kill just one stunted pipsqueak of a captain. He glowered through shaggy eyebrows and bunched his wide shoulders. The gawkers pretended they never would have thought of staring at him.

"What's the matter with these people?" he asked the innkeeper when he returned to fill a mug from a stone jar.

"The matter?" He gazed around in amiable bewilderment, as if this crew normally behaved like demonolators caught in mid-sacrifice.

Crondard drank. The frightening stories about the local wine were true, too, but he was thirsty.

"Have I intruded — " he started to ask, but something nipped his arm. He stared in speechless outrage at the oaf who had previously spoken, who had now sneaked up and pinched him.

"I think he's real," the oaf said, and everyone laughed.

Forgetting how sore and tired he was, forgetting that this man was a native in a crowd of neighbors, the Fomor exploded from his chair and slammed him against the wall. Suspending him off his feet by a handful of his shirt and still shaking with fury, he had second thoughts. The grin persisting on his rubbery face declared that he was a genuine idiot. Crondard was acutely conscious that his back was now turned to the brighter cowards who had probably egged him on. He had no choice, though, but to hold his belligerent course.

"Have you never seen a Fomor?" he demanded loudly enough to be heard by all.

"No, but I have seen nightmares while waking."

Crondard turned with him and shoved him away. Pinwheeling his arms for balance, the fool swerved toward his companions and upset their table. Crondard took a step forward. They decided to laugh it off.

"This horse-piss must be better than it tastes," he said, grabbing up his mug and draining it. Now that he had turned the joke against the innkeeper, everyone laughed more easily.

He wondered how a Fandragoran idiot should know that the Fomors, in their own tongue, were called Children of Nightmare. Looking at him now — his companions were making a show of cuffing him, to prove he had acted on his own — Crondard thought it unlikely that he should know even his name from one day to the next.

"What did he mean by that?" he asked the innkeeper.

His question was quiet, but the man answered to the room at large: "Don't mind Fardel. As a boy, he fell in love with a cruel cow who repaid his devotion with a kick in the head."

Even Fardel, delighted by all the attention he was getting, laughed at this. Crondard had no wish to further the landlord's comedic ambitions, so he kept his questions to himself.

He dipped his thick forefinger in his mug and drew a line on the table to assist his meditations. Though perfectly straight, the line symbolized the ragged Zaxoin border. The bandits, religious lunatics and near-savages in the wild hills beyond it were subjects of the First Lord in Frothirot, but that was where fugitives generally fled to escape his long hand, or to die.

A cockroach scurried toward the line. He imagined it was Lord Frothiriel, Commander of the Fomorian Guard, hot on his trail. He took pleasure in squashing him with his fist. The innkeeper brushed the nobleman's remains to the floor without a thought when he set down the assortment of sausages and chops that Crondard had ordered.

Hungry though he was, he stopped chewing for a moment, arrested by his view of the departing landlord. The man's ears were so large that they nearly qualified him as a freak, and Crondard had avoided staring at them, but he was struck by the fancy that they had subtly changed in shape. Fardel was gaping at the innkeeper, as if he, too, saw something odd. That put his own notion in its proper perspective. He forgot the landlord and his ears.

A hammering at the iron door even more insistent than his own made him grab his ax, half believing that his idle game had magically summoned Lord Frothiriel. It took him a moment to grasp that the innkeeper knew the person he scolded through the panel as he undid the redundant fastenings.

His relief was short-lived, for the breathless arrival began babbling about a naked woman who had just been found dead. This had to be his walking corpse. These provincials would be too stupid to realize that she had been dead for a year or two. He might go to the block for chopping up a cadaver. Perhaps the prank had been more convoluted than he imagined.

"Where?" Crondard demanded.

Terrified to start with, the man recoiled and seemed about to faint at the question, barked in his face by an uncouth stranger, but he managed to stammer, "In Grabgroin Alley, behind the Temple of S-s-s—"

"Sleithreethra?"

The newcomer's head jerked assent as both he and the landlord made protective signs. Crondard returned to his seat and resumed mopping his plate with bread as others crowded around with questions. The places were unknown to him, but they had to be far from the lonely road where he had left the corpse.

The crowd thinned as drinkers rushed out to view the prodigy. As if his ill use at Crondard's hands had made them friends, a phenomenon not unfamiliar to the former sergeant, Fardel paused by his table to ask, "Don't you want to see the naked dead woman?"

"I prefer live ones." He gestured toward the women at the rear of the room.

No child would have giggled more delightedly at the sight of coupling dogs than the halfwit did at his reply, and he kept repeating garbled variants to his companions as they left.

The exodus had stranded a number of whores, some of whom eyed Crondard with listless surmise. For a place that was neither especially lively nor pretentious, the Sow in Rut boasted an unlikely wealth of flesh to let.

"Are they yours?" he asked when he was arranging for a room.

"They showed up to try their luck with Lord Nephreiniel and his hunting party," the landlord said, "but to their dismay, his lordship is a virtuous fellow, and the young men who fawn on him appear to be equally high-minded."

It dismayed him that he had picked an inn whose landlord enjoyed gossipy innuendoes, but it was too late to seek other quarters. He asked, "A hunting party?"

"I thought the boars of Hogman's Plain might have drawn even you yourself from far-off Ashtralorn," his host said. "I'm afraid I'll have to put you over his lordship's hounds."

"I'm weary enough to share their kennel. . . ." He forgot what he was saying as he happened to glance at the landlord. The furred ears of a jackass drooped to his shoulders, their junction with his head hidden by shaggy hair. If he was trying to get a laugh, his glum expression concealed it, nor was anyone laughing. To mention the ears, Crondard suspected, would make him the butt of some joke that the man regularly played on strangers. He deliberately ignored the bait as he continued, "Though maybe I can do a bit better."

The girls who lounged at the rear of the room seemed innocent only of clothing. Apart from a scattering of transparent veils, their bodies were covered only by tattoos where one could decipher their trade and shop for specialties among a riot of floral designs.

He strolled among them, exchanging lewd banter, accepting playful slaps and punches as he felt the merchandise, but his attention soon fixed on the only one who ignored him. She stood slightly apart, untypically draped in a plum cloak that clung to a slim but large-breasted figure. Under her hood he glimpsed a cheek of porcelain delicacy and a curl of bluish-black hair.

"What's your fee?" he asked, slapping her rump and liking what he felt, but recoiling in the next instant from a look that reflected not just anger, but concentrated hatred. At the same time he was almost awed by the aristocratic beauty of her face.

"Do you take me for a common whore?" she rasped in a high-born accent.

They had an audience of disgruntled sluts who resented her as an unknown intruder, probably a bored noblewoman playing at their trade. Crondard felt almost compelled to apologize, but for their benefit he said, "I don't happen to have one, but I'll take you for this," and he tossed a silver coin at her feet.

Trapped in the flash of her amber eyes, he set himself for the sport of fending off her claws. But she joined in the laughter, as if making a quick decision to step back into her role, and stooped to retrieve the coin.

"Filloweela grant you're not such a giant in every way," she said with a grin.

Crondard called for someone to show him to his room. This provoked only a heated but whispered discussion between the landlord and his servants. The maids, then the stableboy, and finally a cook fetched from the kitchens seemed to be protesting their ignorance of the floor-plan.

"Do you know of another inn close by, one with fewer mad people in it?" the Fomor asked his companion.

"This one suits me," she said.

"You're mad, too, are you?" he said, and she smiled without amusement.

Fardel reappeared, made pale and very nearly thoughtful by whatever he had seen, but he brightened when the landlord gave him a lamp and pressed him into service as a guide.

"She was naked, all right, but someone had torn away all the good parts," he told Crondard, who told him to shut up.

He risked a last glance at the innkeeper. Sagging against the bar, he fingered one of his ass's ears fearfully, looking less like a frustrated joker than a soldier palpating his final wound.

Fardel guided them through a musty warren that amazed and oppressed the Fomor. Adjoining buildings had been connected in different epochs by architects who had shared only their ineptitude. Corridors changed level or direction every half-dozen steps, and no two floors followed the same pattern. They passed stairways and passages that served no visible rooms before ending at blank walls, although their carpets were every bit as worn as the one they trod.

Crondard stopped at one intersection and peered in disbelief down a hallway that even the New Palace in Frothirot would have been hard put to contain. It was frugally lit by only a few sconces, and the illusion of length might have been produced by mirrors, but mirrors of the necessary size and quality would not normally have been found in a cheap inn. The girl dragged him on before he had satisfied his curiosity, as it seemed that their dim guide might leave them behind.

The progress of the uncertain lamp made the shadows leap and gambol through this geometer's delirium, and some of the stranger forms afflicted Crondard with the same unaccountable disquiet he had felt for the corner table in the taproom. He distracted himself by fondling his companion, who rubbed against him like a happy cat. She seemed not at all affected by the atmosphere he found so sinister.

They came to an irregular room that may have been the noisiest spot in Fandragord. Hounds barked and howled below, a lunatic diverted himself with a collection of pots and pans next door, while unfeminine oaths and unmanly shrieks racketed around the courtyard.

The room secreted a concentration of a moldy odor he had noticed throughout the inn, and he opened a door onto what he thought was a balcony. This proved to be a landing on a rickety stairway. Directly opposite at ground level, he saw a rear entrance to the taproom.

He turned to Fardel to demand why they had been led on a tour of Fandragord's dankest innards when they could simply have crossed the yard and climbed the stairs, but the idiot had left his lamp and fled; and Crondard forgot him completely as he watched the girl shed her cloak and plain linen dress. He had expected that her tattoos would not be those of a slut, nor were they, but he was shocked to see that they prominently featured the Dragon of Fand, symbol of one of the greatest of the Great Houses.

"Must I address you as 'my lady,' or do you require something grander?" he asked as he unbuckled his gear.

"Oh, this? I'm only a common girl called Fanda, and this is my whim."

That sort of whim, a green and gold dragon elaborately twined around her thighs and torso, could have led a common girl to the block. He smiled and said nothing.

In the next instant she outdid his reaction by starting violently at the image of Sleithreethra, symbol of the House of Sleith, on his chest.

"You don't like Sleiths?" he asked mildly.

"Everyone must be named something, I suppose," she said, her style confirming her status, "but they told me you were called Wolfdown Ratbane, or something similarly absurd."

He had no use for further conversation as he picked her up and carried her to the bed, but he reflected that what most people disliked was not the House of Sleith but its divine patron. Instead of making a protective sign and averting her eyes, as most would, she traced the image with her fingertips curiously, even fondly.

Of course Fandragord was the ancient center of the Goddess's cult, and he should not be alarmed to find worshippers here, especially among the Fands and the Vendrens; but he was disquieted as they lay on the bed by the way she kissed the image, as if finding it more to her taste than the man who wore it.

He reclaimed the initiative, tonguing the green and gold scales of her breasts and her belly, and then the pale ground of a thicket where the Dragon had not ventured.

"Let me taste you," she murmured, trying to draw him by his buttocks.

Something restrained him. He was not fully aroused yet, a condition unhappily not without precedent in recent years, but he ascribed it less to his own decline than to the doomful intimations that thronged around him. His passion for rationality had resisted them before, but that passion was hard to maintain with his head between a pretty girl's thighs, and forebodings crawled on him. Thin in his veins though it ran, the blood of demon-haunted barbarians screamed that he had blundered into a blackness deeper than the night beyond a northern hearth.

Fandragord was only the outer ring of the evil, the inn was a tighter circle, but he had fallen into the very center of the vortex . . . in this room?

No, the hairs on his neck and the galloping of his heart told him that it was even closer: that it was the woman trying to draw him to her mouth. He tried to ease away, but her claws dug deep, her legs clenched. He tore his head free, and a chunk of her thigh slipped loose with it. He saw maggots writhing in the wound as a strangling odor burst around him.

The fabric of the real world had parted as easily as an old corpse's shroud, dropping him into an unknown abyss, and he screamed like one falling as he thrust himself from the reeking heap in his bed. Her teeth missed their intended target, but they met through the flesh of his thigh. He drove his massive fist at her belly and felt it sink to the wrist in slime as even fouler stenches erupted.

He forgot his weapons in his dash to the outside door. He remembered only just in time that he was four flights above the stones of the courtyard. He tried to stop short, but his feet shot out from under him and beyond the landing. He grabbed the rail. It cracked, but it held. Balanced at the brink on the small of his back, clutching a flimsy and half-broken rail, he did not dare to move. Beneath him, the dogs went mad.

Sobbing shamelessly, he twisted his head to watch his pursuer. Slowly and unsteadily, but inexorably, it kept coming. It was still recognizable as a caricature of the girl called Fanda; and recognizable, too, by the unclosed lips of rents in its deliquescent flesh, as the thing he had chopped on the road.

"By all the Gods, why?" he cried. "What have I done to you?"

"Know, animal, that I am Elyssa Fand, buried alive by my cruel family in the full bloom of my youth. I lived, I escaped, I begged for your help, but you struck me down, and I swore by the Goddess you blaspheme with your impertinent tattoo that I would pay you back. How I still live after your murderous attack, none but the Goddess knows, but she restored me to life. . . ."

Her voice faltered, and then her steps. She held out her hand and seemed to be studying its rotting fingers with her runny eye-sockets. A sound such as Crondard had never heard, and hoped never to hear again, escaped her eroded mouth. He believed it was a sob.

"Elyssa — Lady Elyssa — you may have been buried alive, I don't know, but you were dead when I met you — long dead — and whatever it was I did to you, it would have been merciful if only I had been more thorough — "

"You lie!" she shrieked, and she lurched at him.

He lifted his legs and, against his expectations, managed to squeeze them under the rail. Rolling back on his shoulders, he kicked her with both feet. The impact flung her into the room, but she recovered and weaved toward him as he staggered upright. He could not summon the will to overcome his disgust and touch her again. Trapped in the corner farthest from the stairs, his back to the creaking rail, he had nowhere to retreat. When she hurled herself at him, he fell flat and covered his head with his arms.

Her foot mashed nauseously against his ribs, but she kept on going. He heard the rail splinter under her weight, heard a croaking scream, and then a wet slap on the stones below as if a baker had flung a great wad of dough from the roof.

The foot lay where it had snapped off. His belly convulsing, he shoved the twitching lump after the corpse before stumbling into his room and seizing his ax. He was mad with terror, but his terror threw him naked down the stairway in pursuit of the dead thing. He had to finish it this time, he had to destroy it utterly, for he would rather kill himself than live with the fear that Elyssa Fand might find him again.

She had fallen by the fence of the kennel, and its boards rattled and bowed at the onslaught of the savage boarhounds inside. They were driven beyond rage by the abnormality whose fall had disturbed them, that even now scrabbled and crawled its way to its knees, but he suspected they would settle for living flesh and blood if they broke free. He began swinging the ax in a way that would have made his arms-master weep, but the wild strokes worked.

He interrupted his hacking to heave a rotten leg over the fence, and the foot he had dropped separately. He hoped to quiet the dogs, but they fought even more noisily over the unexpected treats, and Elyssa shrieked with fury to see her parts so used. He himself howled as a bony hand gripped his ankle like taut wires and kept gripping even after he had severed the arm at the shoulder. He managed to wrench it loose, taking some of his skin with it, and hurled it into the kennel.

"Let's see you rise from the bellies of hounds, you whore from hell! Let's see you reconstitute yourself from dogshit!" he raved, but the horror that she just might do it silenced him.

The worst of it came when she began to plead, when she made promises and attempted wiles that would have aroused a statue when she lived. She was not fully convinced that she had become an abomination, and his loathing was mingled with pity. He strove to finish her as quickly as possible, striking with one hand and throwing with the other.

The head was last, and it gave him the most trouble, rolling this way and that to elude him as it mouthed airless curses. It bumped at last into a shadowed gutter. He believed that Liron Wolfbaiter, scourge of ghouls, would have thought twice about sticking his hand in after it, but he told himself that the secret was not to think at all, and he thrust his hand into the blackness with an oath that sounded more like a whimper to his ears. He gripped spongy flesh and flung her head to the dogs in the same motion, but not before it had left a perfect white tooth embedded in his thumb.

III

Crondard woke to a slimy kiss. The black face of a demon stared into his eyes and gagged him with its foul breath.

"You there, you Sleith person!" He was barely aware of the imperious voice, for a second black bulk had risen on his other side, at the edge of his vision. They surrounded his . . . bed? The rim he gripped was made of stone, and he thought that he had died and been laid out, however improbably, in an elegant sarcophagus, for he had dreamed of someone who had been buried alive. Then he realized that Elyssa Fand had been no dream. The undraped sun dazzled him, and his teeth chattered with cold, for the stone box was filled with water.

"Get that fool out of there. What does he think he's doing? Is he deaf? Are you deaf, fellow? Is that how you sleep in the Fomorian Guards?"

The demon kissed him again. The second one barked, freeing him from his fanciful terror but gripping him in a real one as two more of the ugliest dogs he had ever seen raised their demonic faces on bull necks to view him. He had never seen Zaxoin boarhounds this close, nor had he wished to.

"Don't be afraid of him, you silly person, get him out of there! I've never before seen you shy from a naked man."

The laughter suggested that he had a audience of five or six men, but only the haughty voice had spoken. It had never stopped. Crondard was unwilling to move even his eyes, but when the second hound licked his neck he was startled upright to face a youth who jumped back in even greater terror, though he did it gracefully.

"Please, sir, his horse-ship would like you to get out of the lords' trough," the youth quavered.

"Cludd!" the Fomor cried as blood began to flow through his numb body like acid.

"Very appropriate, but even the Sons of Cludd don't sleep in freezing water, only on stone floors, or so the dear little bigots would have us believe," the speaker prattled on. "Are you in training to join them, to show them what a really crazy fanatic can do? They don't take men with tattoos, and they might burn you at the stake for that Sleith horror."

Crondard remembered his last waking thought, to wash away the filth of his strange battle. Exhausted, he must have fallen asleep in the trough.

"I was . . . drunk," he managed to gasp as he dared to hoist himself out. He inadvertently splashed the dogs, who took this for a game, leaping away to shake themselves and then bouncing back to roar in his face before slobbering on him with passionate affection. Shivering with cold, he tried to fend them off as forcefully as he could without provoking the notorious anger of the breed; but they grew so exuberant, seizing his arms and legs and worrying them, that their anger could not have been much worse than their play.

"Look at that, would you!" The heraldic symbols on his hunting outfit identified the willowy master of these dogs and men as Lord Nephreiniel. "They would have torn most strangers apart by now. 'If your dogs love a man, clasp him to your bosom,' that was the only rational advice my father ever gave me, and I've followed it."

"Would you call them off, please, lord. I don't want to stand out here — "

"Oh, of course! Forgive me, their behavior quite bemused me." He flicked his hand, and the disappointed hounds were pulled away. Crondard hid his annoyance when he saw that they had been held on leads all this while, and that the handlers could have recalled them at any time. He returned to the trough to sluice the drool from his limbs.

"Do you hunt?" Nephreiniel asked.

At that moment a chambermaid passed them bearing a bucket to the dungheap beyond the stables, and she slyly inspected the naked Fomor. Favoring her with a wink he would not usually have given a woman so broad or plain, he replied, "Avidly."

"I believe you're making a joke, aren't you? How marvelous! Dogs love him, and he's droll, too. What is your name?"

His tattoos could be easily deciphered, but military life had taught him to stick with a story once chosen. He said, "I am known here as Liron Wolfbaiter."

"And so you shall be known to us, if that is your whim. Give him your cloak, Olycinth, before someone misreads his tattoos and calls him Crondard Sleith, or mistakes him for the senior sergeant of Company 'Ironhand'. Will you hunt with us today, Wolfbaiter?"

"My horse is not suited to the sport," he said as he draped himself with limited gratitude in a pink cloak, embroidered in a primrose pattern that was nothing less than exquisite.

"The gray drayhorse in the far stall?" When he had stopped laughing, Nephreiniel said, "You really do have a sense of humor! Don't worry, we'll lend you a hunter."

*

Crondard prayed that a brain addled with Fandragoran wine had transmuted a scuffle with an ordinary whore, but the condition of his room turned the prayers on his lips to bile. When he had regained control of his stomach, he forced himself to wad up Elyssa Fand's clothes with the bedding smeared by her decay. He heaved the bundle over the rail and hurried to dress.

Fortune had smiled on him, he reflected, in her quirky way. Lord Nephreiniel had been pleased to befriend him, and he saw no chance of ingratiating himself with any other Zaxoin noblemen who might give him employment as a bodyguard, huntsman, or even a dog-handler. Leriel Vendren might be First Lord of all the Frothoin, but it would take him a hundred years of litigation to retrieve a fugitive protected by a lesser lord.

He used a stick to thrust the bundle into the dungheap, catching himself at the last minute from doing the same with Olycinth's perfumed cloak. The lord's party was mounting, with much horn-blowing, spear-clattering and shrill boasts of feats to come, while recent sleepers bawled for quiet from a dozen windows. The hounds escalated the din when Crondard approached and they hailed him as their dearest friend, too long absent.

"I simply don't understand it," Nephreiniel said. "Have these horrid beasts been bewitched to lapdogs?"

"As your lordship's father knew, dogs trust a true and honest man," Crondard said with his most engaging grin, but he had no illusions about the motives of the hounds: they hoped he would feed them another corpse.

*

Hogman's Plain had been named by some fool viewing it from the comfort of a tower in the city, where the abrupt ridges and gulleys might seem only ripples in a blanket of witchgrit and monk's-rut. These weeds, Crondard's new friends assured him, flaunted a spectacular display of blossoms for one week in spring, but now in autumn they flourished only thorns like daggers and burrs like spiked flails in their tangles. Lacking the horsemanship of the others, he had reason to be glad of the armor he wore; but more reason for cursing the heavy cage of leather and bronze under a sun that disdained the calendar.

The dust he saw so much of, wallowing along at the tail of the party, mixed with his sweat and baked him in a red crust that made him look like a cannibal from the Outer Islands, as his cool and spotless companions never tired of observing whenever they let him catch up. Among the occupations he had thought of seeking with Lord Nephreiniel, he had not considered clown, but he believed he was proving himself qualified.

So far they had seen none of the wild hogs that grew more monstrous and fierce with each anecdote the huntsmen traded, but now the hounds they followed raised the pitch and intensity of their din. Horns brayed, spears flourished, and the dust in his face darkened as the pace quickened to a suicidal gallop. Sour a view though he had taken of this enterprise, he could not keep his heart from racing, nor did he restrain his equally excited mount from dashing headlong into the billowing cloud that whooped and thundered under a jittering glitter of spearheads. Disjointed lines and images from the Fomor epic, *The Hunting of the White Hart*, rang and racketed through a head emptied of both fear and thought.

A black shape plunged into the brush to his left, and he swerved to follow it as the others held their course. His mount hurtled down an almost vertical path, but he guided it with his heels as he juggled his spear into position with both hands: a feat he performed with less premeditation than if he were tossing back a drink, but one that would bathe him in cold sweat whenever he recalled it. His heart rose to his throat in the precipitous dive as he set himself to cast the spear at the bolting black mass. It seemed impossible that all the hounds and men could have failed to notice that the boar had cut away from them, but it had happened, and he would redeem his inept antics by having sole honor of the kill.

The spear was not his weapon, the back of a horse was not his home, but his arm was strong from years of sport and drill, and he made a mighty cast: the spear flew straight. Fortunately the dog, as he recognized his target to be an instant too late, swerved before the spear struck the spot where it would have been. He wrenched his mount to a halt, but the horse was much quicker to obey than Thunderer. It stopped short, and he flew over its head into a wall of witchgrit.

The horse hurried on its own way. The dog came back to fret over him, even though he cursed it by all the Gods of the Frothoin and the Fomors as he tried to free an arm from an interdependent puzzle of thorny vines. Only when he had done that could he begin to work on the even more complex trap that bound his hair and beard. The dog tried to encourage him by slobbering on his neck and whimpering. Crondard redoubled his efforts, ignoring torn flesh and uprooted hair as he looked forward to the moment when he would have the pleasure of skewering the animal on his boar-spear.

His anger had faded by the time he was free. The hound had probably abandoned the hunt to follow the scent of a wild bitch, and he could see himself doing the same. Remembering the boarhounds' perverse notion of play, he dealt this one a cuff that would have knocked some men flat. The dog bounced back with an inspired impersonation of demoniacal fury. Soon they were wrestling in the dust like old friends, more or less evenly matched. The Fomor conceded defeat when he found his throat enclosed gently but very firmly in a rumbling muzzle.

They sat companionably for a while, panting and listening to the racket of chirps and rattles and whirrs in the lively wasteland. The clatter and hooting of the hunt sounded like a remote war among tinsmiths. The dog snacked on bugs, his teeth snapping smartly. Crondard caught him a few in a hand once quick as lightning, but he had to admit the dog was better at the game. He was too old for it.

He confronted the hard fact that he had mistaken the dog for a boar because his sight had grown dim, and what use had Nephreiniel for a huntsman who speared his hounds, a bodyguard who slew his catamites, a courtier who doffed his cap with a grand flourish to statues? He lay now at the foot of a tall slope; he could discern individual vines, thorns, and flitting birds in the foreground, but then they washed into a brown and purple cloud. In the cruel blue sky at the top, sooty little creatures drifted slowly, more than he had ever noticed before. A follower of Sleithreethra would say those were the malign entities that constantly besiege us, but a physician had told him they were imperfections normal to aging eyes.

He rose, rebuked by his creaking knees and by the frisking of the young dog. It made no difference whether he trudged after the hunt or waited for it, but he might find distraction from his thoughts if he kept moving. He resolutely refused to lean on his spear as he picked his way up the brambly hill.

His ears were still good enough, and he was pleased to hear the hunt approaching. He might not have so long a walk. His pleasure wilted as he noted how rapidly it came. It flew at him like a whirlwind, just over the ridge, a pack of savage hounds, a dozen huge horses ridden by reckless men, and all of that unswerving tonnage hurtling behind a boar with tusks like scythes. The stupid dog beside him agitated the stump of its tail with glee.

He might climb a tree, ludicrous a figure as he would cut when they saw him, but the nearest tree lay a hundred yards away through thick underbrush. He might take cover behind a particularly thick clump of brush, and there was one near at hand, but the men might ride straight through it, nor would it stop their quarry. He could stand in plain sight, waving and shouting, but the boar might see him as a target. So might one of the men.

While he dithered over his choices in a way that Akilleus Bloodglutter of the old ballads never would have, the target of the storming horde topped the ridge, and its appearance stunned him: it was a naked boy, fleeing in terror and in the last stumbling gasp of exhaustion. The hound charged him with an exuberant roar.

"Hold!" Crondard thundered. To his surprise, the dog stopped short and stared back in disbelief. The boy altered his course and ran toward them.

He gripped the hound's collar, which bore the ideogram for its name: *Floss*. "That's no kind of name for an overgrown lout like you. Just stand here, that's a good boy, and I'll give you a proper name, like Corpse-cruncher, or Lord Frothiriel, maybe . . . ."

He talked on, taking no note of what he said, just trying to calm the dog. There was no calming him: he trembled and growled, yearning toward the boy as if his savage spirit would presently burst out of his skin to attack, leaving his body standing obediently behind.

Crondard risked a look at the boy and beckoned with his spear. He needed no encouragement. The hounds and horses had topped the ridge behind him, and he flew downhill with no trace of his former exhaustion. It took Crondard a moment to accept what he saw, but there was no denying it: the hunters were purposefully pursuing the boy. There was no boar. The hounds were at his heels, the riders glared at him with maniacal eagerness, some with spears already raised for a cast.

The boy himself defied explanation. His hair was copper, his eyes were blue, his skin was several shades paler than Crondard's own. He looked, in fact, like a pure Fomor, like the child Crondard himself might have produced with the very fairest woman in Ashtralorn, a child whose non-existence he sometimes bemoaned when he drank. But even if one accepted that the boy was a Fomor, and that he was here on Hogman's Plain, where no one lived, why was he not burned black by the sun or painted red by the dust?

Floss quivered even more tensely, and Crondard felt his own knees tremble. He could ignore his unanswerable questions for a moment, but he could not ignore the icy fingers that caressed his heart as he saw the way those sooty entities swarmed near the radiant child. When the boy smiled and opened his arms, running faster now that he was only a few yards away, Crondard's hairs crackled as if he stood in the path of a thunderbolt.

"Liron is here!" he shouted, and it was surely the first time he had ever used Wolfbaiter's war-cry without ironic intent as he fell to one knee and braced the butt of his spear against the earth. At the same time he released Floss, who launched himself at the boy like a bolt from a crossbow.

Even now Crondard had doubts. He screamed with horror as the child ran headlong onto the spear, as Floss clamped his throat in bone-crushing jaws. Blood sprayed over the white skin, the eyes widened in horror, but the spear bowed as if receiving a weight ten times heavier than the child. The mouth opened in a scream and kept opening impossibly wide, revealing teeth like sabers. Crondard was flung back as if he were the child, buried under the stinking weight of a humped swine half the size of a horse.

"Is that how you Fomors do it?" Lord Nephreiniel quivered with anger at being denied the kill, and so unconventionally. "No wonder there are so few of you."

Crondard was pinned beneath the boar, but he had no taste for asking help from the fluttering fops who ringed him. He craned his neck to stare down at the monster that still twitched and bled on him as Floss finished tearing out its throat.

More to himself than anyone else, he said, "Things are not what they seem lately."

"When were they ever?" Lord Nephreiniel said.

IV

The austere provincials insisted, to Crondard's chagrin, on segregating the sexes at the public baths, and he was required to scrub himself twice before enjoying a hot soak in the pool. Restored, though, and with his gear furbished while he bathed, he returned to the Sow in Rut with a spring in his step, but he lost it as soon as he entered. He thought he had blundered into the wrong inn.

He stepped outside, ignoring the crowd that jostled him, an inconvenient rock in its babbling eddies. By daylight, the sign over the door looked even more tasteless and crudely executed, but it clearly identified the place. It seemed unlikely, but he might have approached the inn from a different street last night. He remembered that street only as a silent array of shuttered facades, empty but for menace.

The shutters were open now, and sleazy wares overflowed onto the footway. Merchants bounced and bubbled as they chivvied passersby into bargains on candles that had been stored in hot attics or carpets retrieved from flooded cellars. All this jolly bustle confused the memory of his first impression, more suited to the evil fame of the city. Except for the pervasive black granite of the underlying hill, reshuffled and dealt into paving stones and building blocks, it could have been one of the seedier commercial streets in Frothirot.

He entered the tavern again: not into an oppressive passageway, but directly into the taproom. Unlike the room he remembered, its far end lay open to the courtyard. What he could see of the building around the court was smaller and tidier than the ramshackle sprawl he had seen last night. Patrons began drifting out of the room as he entered.

In his bewilderment he failed to note soon enough that three armed men were also moving to guard the exits. They wore the tower-and-thunderbolt emblem of the city on their helmets and breastplates. At least they had not come from Frothirot, but it was clear that they had come for him, and he drew his ax with a sigh of resignation. His condition had suffered an ironic reversal: their hooked bills would give them the advantage of hunters ringing a boar with spears.

Their officer, a puffed princock who vividly recalled his late captain, had no bill, nor did he deign to draw his sword as he strutted up to the glowering Fomor. He forestalled Crondard from splitting him with the amazing question, "Are you the murderous necromancer who calls himself Liron of Ashtralorn?"

"I am Liron Wolfbaiter," he said. He was chilled to recognize the plum cloak that the officer held at arm's length, but he went on: "I am a mercenary soldier on my way to Zaxann."

"On your way to a bonfire, more likely." The men got a laugh out of this, but Crondard's innards went hollow. "We burn necromancers here, you know. Do you deny that this garment belonged to a seamstress named Fanda, found dead and partly eaten last night near the temple where she was employed? Or that you were observed concealing it behind the stables this morning, along with her dress?" Drawing closer, growing more heated – the officer perhaps saw a future for himself as an examining magistrate, and was practicing his technique – he shouted: "Is it not true that you performed these heinous acts of murder and cannibalism as a diabolic ritual to revive certain bones, which you attempted to dispose of in the kennels?"

Crondard cursed the inept dogs, but he said, "Bones? What bones?"

Indulging a flair for melodrama, the officer flipped back the cloak to reveal the skull, now picked clean of flesh and missing its lower jaw, of Elyssa Fand. "Ha! See how he shies from it," he called to his men. "Remember that when the magistrate questions you."

The Fomor willed himself to wake from this nightmare to a world where the inn would be as he remembered it, a world where he would no longer be pursued by the irrepressible Elyssa Fand. Remembering how they had seemed to see, he could not tear his gaze from the empty holes of her eyes. The men with their bills edged closer.

"Wait! I know nothing of murder or necromancy. That cloak belongs to a whore who called herself Fanda, yes, whom I took to my room last night. The landlord. . . ." He glanced toward him and was startled to see that his ears were of quite normal size and shape. Even before he had played that trick with the ass's ears, they had looked freakish, but they had seemed to be his own.

The innkeeper said, "He was shopping for a whore, but I didn't see him pick one."

"And where did this Fanda go without the clothes that you were observed burying?" the officer asked. He jerked the skull at Crondard, making him jump. "And whose is this?"

The Fomor saw that he had let himself be surrounded. He was within reach of any of the bills leveled at him. As a frequenter of taverns, he was familiar with the techniques of law enforcement. The men would presently thrust out to hook his neck, an arm, and a leg, while the officer clubbed him into submission with his iron glove. If he struggled at that point, he could be torn limb from limb. His only chance lay in striking first.

"This temple where the seamstress worked, you say — which one was it?"

"The Temple of Sleithreethra, as you well know," the officer said, and he raised his hand to make the required sign that would fend off the attention of that Goddess.

"Liron is here!" Crondard roared in his face, and the man was arrested in mid-sign as the Fomor's ax splintered his skull. His helmet, containing the upper portion of his head, clanged on the ceiling and showered them with blood. The man to his right had kept both hands on his bill, so Crondard dealt with him next, driving his left eye deep into his brain with the butt of the ax-helve.

The remaining two, religious as their captain, were fumbling to regain a grip on their weapons when Crondard kicked one in the balls and demolished the other's face with the back of his ax. Though it was illogical, and he knew it at the time, he turned next to the thing that his screaming nerves insisted posed the worst threat of all. With a series of lightning-strokes, he smashed the skull that had rolled from the officer's hand. He scuffed the fragments with his boot to every corner of the room.

The man he had kicked was now struggling to rise, but Crondard beheaded him. Not thinking at all, impelled by some memory of the old ballads of Bloodglutter and Shornhand, he picked up the head by the hair, its face still twitching, and carried it with him as he strode out under the awning to the courtyard with his dripping ax over his shoulder.

His choices were limited. If he fled on the pathetic Thunderer, he would not get beyond the city wall before pursuit overtook him. The finest mounts were Lord Nephreiniel's, but if he stole one of those, he could hardly flee to Zaxann. Or would it be considered theft to take a man's horse and ride it to his home?

While he weighed these questions, his eye fell upon the trophy of that day's hunt, hanging from a hook at the far end of the courtyard. Its throat torn out, its breast opened by a spear, it was the body of a fair-skinned youth with coppery hair whose eyes now stared at him as the breeze idly stirred it. Closer examination revealed that its face was not just that of the son he might have had. Though slackened by death and crawling with flies, it was the face that he himself had worn as a boy.

He faltered backward and felt his skull explode: not so much with pain as with the paralyzing anticipation of pain to come. It was not the first time in his life he had been felled with a bung-starter, and he guessed as the stones of the courtyard rushed up to meet him that it was the landlord who had laid him low.

*

It was some time before he could spare sufficient attention from the pain in his head to wonder where he was, and then he faced a puzzle. He assumed that city policemen were taking him somewhere, and he was bound hand and foot, but unaccountably gagged. Lying on cushions in a dark enclosure, progressing feet first, he thought he might be in a coffin, and that they intended to take revenge for their comrades by burying him alive. The rhythmic jolting suggested that his pallbearers were trotting, though, and it was hard to accept that image.

He could hear their deep but easy breathing, and the slap of bare feet on stone, which he doubted he would have heard so clearly inside a coffin. Forcing his eyes a little wider, he saw that this box was larger. Openings on either side were covered with dark but not fully opaque curtains.

He breathed a little more easily. He was in a litter, it seemed, and being carried along by barefoot slaves, surely an odd way to be haled before a magistrate. He tried to sit up so he might look through the curtains, but he was tied to the frame, and so securely that he was unable to rap on the litter with his feet or elbows.

He told himself he should enjoy the unaccustomed ride and wait to see where it led, but he was unable to accept that advice. Being carried along on a pole, as intractable prisoners usually were, would have been less frightening than this mystery. He suspected he was being kidnapped. His desperate struggles only tightened his bonds.

What little light had sifted through the curtains now failed as the way led downward. The air grew cool, then positively dank. The slaves trotted less swiftly as their footfalls echoed in drafty spaces.

At last the litter was set down among odors of mold and dust. The slaves departed softly. He heard only water dripping; and, very distantly, a tinny clashing that might have been someone's notion of music. Footsteps approached, and one of the curtains was jerked aside.

The face of a man long dead, or so he had thought, looked down on him. Long and wolfishly lean, white as a tombstone by moonlight, and with eyes of pitiless topaz, it was the face of Vendriel the Good.

As if divining the nature of his captive's terror, this apparition was quick to say, "I am Lord Morphyrion," but this gave scant reassurance: he was grandson of the wizard-lord and head of the infamous Fandragoran branch of the House of Vendren.

With remarkable prescience, or perhaps merely with a sardonic glance at their family tree, his parents had named him for a notorious madman of antiquity.

He gestured with a hand so disproportionately large that it looked like an independent creature. Crondard was struck by the fancy that the lord's black garments contained only the wires necessary to manipulate his head and hands, for he was thin to the point of incorporeality.

Men in the black livery and tiger emblems of the Tribe obeyed the gesture and unbound him, but he was in no hurry to get out of the litter. He knew the search would be hopeless, and so it proved, but he felt about him for his weapons. Pulled forth roughly, he clenched his jaw against the pain of standing more or less erect.

"A Fomor." The lord studied him for a moment and frowned thoughtfully. "You *are* a Fomor? It is said that your folk can see through the veil of the material world."

So it was said, mostly by Fomors like his mother, who spent more time in conversation with ghosts, sprites, oracles and divine messengers than with real people. As a disciple of Mantissus the Epiplect, he had outgrown such nonsense, but he had entertained second thoughts since coming to Fandragord.

Feeling that it was expected of him, and dredging up a trace of the accent he had labored to lose thirty years ago, he answered, "That is the pride of my people, and their curse."

The Vendren lord nodded, seeming pleased. "I take it you are the same Crondard Sleith who recently fled the capital to escape the justice of my kinsman, Lord Leriel. Did you know my daughter, Lereela?"

The Fomor failed to repress a shudder at her name, but Morphyrion fortunately happened to be looking away as he spoke it. "We never met, but of course I know of the lady, whose beauty and grace — "

"Enough! I erred by failing to dash the wicked bitch's brains out as an infant, but I am not a complete fool. She takes after my grandfather, and you know it." He waited for a response, but Crondard was at a loss for a tactful one, so he went on: "You don't look well, young man. Please be seated."

He knew he was young only by the standard of Lord Morphyrion, whose marble face was cracked by a spiderweb of wrinkles, but the turn of phrase pleased him. The chair he chose creaked and listed beneath him. Like everything else in this huge room, it had once been magnificent. Now the tapestries rotted on the crumbling walls, and fine siftings of wood-dust lay about the furniture as testimony to the industry of termites and worms.

"In addition to possessing the natural talents of a seer," the lord said, sitting opposite and crossing legs like reeds, "you have made a name for yourself as a necromancer, no mean feat in Fandragord."

"That was a misunderstanding, one that I myself don't begin to understand —"

The explanation was waved away. "I heard some of the details, and I can imagine the rest. Lereela had many misguided admirers here, as she does in Frothirot. One of these was a young man named Zornard Glypht, who begged her, in a turn of phrase she found tiresome, to make his dreams come true." Sudden anger caused alarming red spots to glare in the lord's bony cheeks, and Crondard believed that the whole of his limited blood supply had been required for this effect. He spat: "And so the willful baggage *did it!*"

The Fomor looked away in embarrassment, which Morphyrion correctly interpreted: "No, no, no, I don't mean she took the moron to bed, that would have been refreshingly normal. Before leaving for the capital, as her vicious parting gift to him and to the city of her birth, she made his dreams come true. All of them.

"At first this was merely a nuisance, and mostly to Zornard himself. He dreamed in the darkest hours, when few others were inconvenienced. Streets would be rearranged in ways that defied logic, animals would develop the power of speech, heroic statues of the dreamer would grace our public squares.

"This palace, where he had so often pursued the inappropriate object of his desire, haunted the sleeper's mind, and so I suffered more than most from the suspension of nature's laws, especially as I sleep little and reserve the night for scholarly pursuits. Studying some ancient and irreplaceable volume, I would be vexed to find it transformed into a book of gibberish credited to Zornard Glypht, for the fool fancied himself a poet. The illusions were transient, though, and I could often will them away. Besides, my daughter was to blame for this annoyance, not him, and so I exercised forbearance . . . until his first nightmare."

Morphyrion's yellow eyes looked away, a relief to Crondard after some moments of suffering their concentrated intensity; but their fixed stare at empty space, like a cat's seeing ghosts, became almost equally disturbing as he muttered, "A living palace of pink, doughy flesh that caressed me, that sprouted wormlike offspring to pursue me, a palace that died and began to putrefy around me — this nightmare of his recurred, and more than once."

Crondard jumped when those horrid eyes flashed back to fix on him. "I am a merciful man," Morphyrion said, "one who would not kill another merely for dreaming. I had him brought here and attempted, by the most humane means, to keep him awake.

"This worked for a while, but more and more severe methods had to be used to restrain his inconsiderate wish for sleep. My servants continuously rattled pots and pans beside him, but after two weeks or so he had developed a facility for dreaming on his feet, and with his eyes open. All of his dreams became nightmares, and all of them centered on me.

"Only then did I resign myself sorrowfully to the necessity of pincers, hot irons and the rack as inducements to wakefulness. After just a few days and nights of this, his unexpectedly weak heart gave out. My own heart was heavy, as you may imagine, but after I had restored his corpse to the bosom of his family and paid them a reasonable indemnity, I tried to put the unfortunate episode behind me."

The lord's hair was full and long, like his monstrous ancestor's, and silver as rainwater. He tossed it back with a vain and oddly boyish gesture, as if demonstrating how he had put Zornard behind him.

"To my profound chagrin," he continued at length, "death did not stop his dreams. They wandered abroad at noon, and with even greater substance and malevolence. Tell me, Crondard Sleith, do I look familiar to you?"

Intent upon Morphyrion's monologue, and upon the lines of speculation it opened, Crondard answered the sudden question without weighing the consequences. "You look like Lord Vendriel the Good."

Crondard suspected that the lord's thin smile was a very bad sign, but his response was mild: "I don't, you know, not at all. My appearance was rather ordinary, though I always flattered myself that it reflected my kindly nature — until Zornard's dreams gave me the face and figure of my despised grandfather. I hardly dare go out by daylight anymore, weary of all the fainting and shrieking I now provoke from the little people who formerly worshipped the ground I trod."

Trying to give a suitable appearance of solemnity, Crondard counted the freckles on the backs of his hands. It was true that Morphyrion was no Vendriel, but in the capital he was rumored to have diverted himself in youth by sneaking around to strangle the weak and afflicted. He was probably the most powerful man Crondard had ever spoken to, as well as the craziest, and it would have been impolitic to laugh at the picture he painted of himself; but he was sorely tempted.

When the silence had stretched out uncomfortably, Crondard glanced up to confront that unsettling stare. At a loss for anything else to say, he blurted, "Why don't you do something about it?"

"Ah! Advice from so notorious a necromancer would be most welcome. What do you propose I do?"

"I meant — " Crondard wished he had kept silent — "why don't you reverse your daughter's spell? Or get her to do it?"

"My grandfather's natural talents have passed me over; my only skills are for scholarship and philanthropy. And my daughter, who inherited his abilities, has never done a single thing I asked her. You wouldn't believe how many charlatans and mountebanks lay claim to such powers, and how many of them I've employed. Zaggo, do we still have those people in the Rose Garden?" he turned to ask one of his attendants. "No? I fear I can't show them to you, Crondard Sleith, they all seem to have been buried. They all agreed, however, that this plague of dreams will stop only when Zornard Glypht's body has been found and destroyed."

"You said you restored it —"

"To his loved ones, yes, but it no longer lies in the family tomb, and they denied knowledge of its whereabouts with their dying breaths. Either it was moved, or the self-styled poet has dreamed himself somewhere else. I suggest you start your search in this palace, since it has always loomed so large in his nightmares."

V

Few things could please Crondard more than a dashing new uniform, but he had misgivings as he strode through the streets of Fandragord in the black regalia of Lord Morphyrion's guard. Any heraldic emblem, but most especially the Vendren Tiger, roused a certain uneasiness in one not born to wear it. He had only to glance down at his lacquered breastplate or the pommel of his new broadsword to be unnerved by the snarling mask of that beast.

He was nevertheless grateful for its magical power to clear a way through crowds, for he was in a hurry to return to the Sow in Rut and test his new sword on the innkeeper who had struck him down and handed him over to Morphyrion's men. After that he would get as far from the city as he could, losing the uniform on the way. In the lord's service he enjoyed immunity from the city authorities, but it was limited by the ability of the police to poison him, drag him into an alley or knife him in a crowd. If he remained in Fandragord, he could cut his throat either by appearing in public or by pretending to look for the corpse of Zornard Glypht in the palace of the Vendrens.

One long night of touring the palace, with the lunatic lord clinging like a bad smell and constantly inquiring if he felt any evil influences, had convinced him that would be the quicker route to suicide. He had counted sixteen fresh graves in the Rose Garden, presumably those of his predecessors in the quest for the elusive dreamer, and he might have missed a few by the uncertain torchlight. Never in his life had he been subjected to such a concentrated and prolonged assault by flesh-crawling terrors, but he was certain that their origin was entirely natural, insofar as that adjective could be twisted to describe Lord Morphyrion and his home. After a day of restless sleep, he had escaped the palace by prattling glibly of a dream that had inspired him to seek the corpse elsewhere. This assertion of his visionary powers had delighted Morphyrion.

Of course his troubles would be over if he found and destroyed the dreaming dead man. If he did, Morphyrion promised to shower him with riches and send him back to Frothirot in triumph: not just to be reconciled with the First Lord, but to assume the vacant captaincy of Company 'Ironhand' and eventually succeed to the leadership of the Fomorian Guard.

"Lord Commander Crondard Sleith" had a pleasant ring to it, but he might as well skip to the moon on a rainbow as seek the unquiet grave of Zornard Glypht. He had seen strange things in Fandragord, but could any student of Mantissus ascribe them to the nightmares of a corpse?

"Your own nightmares, more likely," he could hear that philosopher say. "A whore turned into a corpse and attacked you when you were drunk, eh? And after you fell off your horse and baked your crapulent head in the desert sun for an hour or so, you saw a boy instead of a boar, did you? You've certainly convinced me, Crondard, and now you must excuse me while I burn my misguided books and begin my new studies as a wizard."

He realized that he was talking to himself, which cleared his path even more quickly, and that his feet had led him to the inn. After loosening his sword in its scabbard and making sure his ax was not tangled in his elegant cape, he plunged through the door. His brisk advance faltered when he found himself in the phantom entryway he had seen on the first night.

"Liron Wolfbaiter!" the landlord cried from the taproom, distracting him from his study of the ghastly mural of Vendriel the Good. "Just the man I've been wishing to see."

"Enjoy the sight, you backstabbing bastard, for it will be your last." The room was quickly emptying again, but he saw no policemen. "Do you have a sword, or would you care to borrow one of mine? Or, if you have a spare bung-starter, I'll be pleased to demonstrate how a Fomor uses one."

"Would you have gone to Lord Morphyrion if I'd suggested it?" the landlord asked as he quickly shuffled tables into a makeshift barrier. "If the police had taken you, would the magistrate have given you a flashy new outfit and sent you on your way? Your own brother wouldn't have taken such care of your interests as I have, Wolfbaiter."

Stalking him around the growing island of tables, Crondard hurled a chair that shattered against the wall, a wall that had not been there yesterday. Forgetting his purpose for the moment, he went to the wall and struck it with the heel of his hand, cracking the plaster. It seemed real enough.

"This room was open to the courtyard before," he said, drawing his ax to give it a proper test.

"They knocked out the wall, but it keeps coming back." The speaker was Fardel, one of several patrons held in their seats by befuddlement or a taste for mayhem.

"Pay no mind to him, he's — "

"Telling the truth, probably," Crondard said, beginning to stalk the landlord again. He demonstrated how a Guardsman could spin a battle-ax in the air and catch it by the handle without looking. With two casual strokes, he narrowed the space between them by two tables.

"Lord Nephreiniel left you a handsome gift!" the innkeeper all but screamed. "Don't you want to see it? It's out in the courtyard, a truly splendid animal."

"He's gone, is he?" It had been his slim hope to accompany that lord to Zaxann and ask his protection against Morphyrion, though he doubted Nephreiniel's power to give it. If he betrayed the chief of the Fandragoran Vendrens by fleeing, he would have to travel farther than Omphiliot. But perhaps Nephreiniel had given him the means of fleeing far and fast. The splendid animal could only be one of his fine horses.

"I'll settle with you later," he told the landlord, although his thirst for revenge had been almost satisfied by throwing a scare into him and wrecking his furniture. Hesitating at the rear exit, he asked, "What's that damned music?"

The distant, tinny dissonance could hardly be called music, but he had heard it often since coming to Fandragord. It was probably a local craze, so commonly entangled with the noise of the city that natives were deaf to it, because the landlord and the others stared blankly. Fardel's stare was also blank, but the halfwit was tapping his foot to the jerky rhythm.

As on his first visit, a rickety structure surrounded the courtyard, looking even more slapdash now that he had time to study it. He knew nothing of carpentry, but it seemed improbable that such leaning and contorted walls could stand. He tried to find specific reasons for his disquiet by making a systematic survey, but it came to nothing.

Making his eye follow a straight line from base to roof or from one angle to another proved impossible: he would blink and lose his place, or his eye would be distracted by a flurry of motion behind a window. All those windows, when he looked at them directly, were empty.

The number of windows troubled him, too, for it seemed unlikely that the inn could hold so many rooms. He tried counting the windows of the first floor in one section, but the result fell short of his impression. Trying again, he got a different number. His third attempt produced a third answer. He was willing to admit that he was no mathematician, but he knew he should have done better than that. Trying a fourth time, he was nearly overcome by dizziness. His eyes told him that he was looking at a patched and crooked wall, but his stomach believed that he was gazing into an abyss.

He tore his eyes away from the courtyard. Far off, beyond the inn's crazy tangle of chimney-pots, the Vendren palace rose near the top of the hill. His recent tour had revealed it as a shabby ruin, but distance and a sunset worthy of the Last Day contrived to dress the palace in malign splendor. It was inseparable from the enormous clouds of blackest purple that hung behind it.

A credulous man might believe that he had wandered into the landscape of someone else's dream. Crondard tried hard not to believe this. His memory was beginning to betray him, that was all, just as his eyes and ears were. Once he escaped this malefic city, once he found a place where he could rest from flight, he would be his old, rational self. He hurried on to the stables.

He hesitated beside the fence of the kennel where he had disposed of Elyssa Fand. Something moved behind the fence, and then the boards burst outward in a shower of splinters. Whatever his logical mind believed, his instinctive cringe said that she had risen once more from the dead, and he screamed when a weight thrust him to the flagstones with a clang of his shiny new armor. He twisted toward his attacker, and his face got a thorough slobbering. Hammering Floss's solid skull with his fist staggered the dog for an instant, but he rebounded with all his lust for play awakened.

Floss having prevailed and run off to give the four corners of the courtyard a triumphant spraying, Crondard climbed wearily to his feet and trudged toward the stables. The only horse now quartered there was the absurd Thunderer, named for one of his viler habits, and Nephreiniel's "handsome gift" could only be that dimwitted hellhound. Had he remembered how to weep, he believed he would have done so.

Absently scratching Thunderer's ear, he recalled the landlord's prank with the ass's ears. One who believed Morphyrion's ravings might believe that the Sow in Rut had been as important to Zornard Glypht in his waking life as the Vendren palace.

"No dogs inside," the landlord said automatically. Glancing up to meet the Fomor's eye, he added, "Except, of course, yours."

"Wine for everyone," Crondard said. When his was poured, he pushed it back and watched the landlord take a sip from the mug before he picked it up. He ignored the cheers and thanks of the drinkers, and the landlord's muttering, as he watched Floss include the limits of the room in his territory. Approaching the farthest corner, near the front entrance, the dog stopped. He began to advance again, but paw by dainty paw, with fangs bared and fur crackling erect, his intense gaze fixed on an empty chair.

Crondard asked Fardel, "What's wrong with that corner?"

"It's a bit drafty — " the innkeeper started to say, but Crondard silenced him with a chopping gesture as Fardel said, "That's where the poet always sits."

"Sat, he means," one of the oaf's companions said. "The poet's been dead for a while."

Careful as the dog, but being less obvious about it, Crondard circled toward the empty table. A swarm of motes drifted against the pale wall. Drawing his ax and striking in the same motion, he shouted, "Liron is here!", and kept striking until the table and its four chairs had been demolished. Floss joined in, worrying the debris and flinging it around the room with scrabbling claws.

As if correcting him, Fardel said, "No one's there now."

"Do you know where the poet is?"

"I don't know. In his room?" Fardel had perfected nature's blunder with drink. He rolled his head around at unlikely angles, searched with unfocused eyes, and provoked a general rush for the doors by yelling, "Zornard!"

Crondard resisted the impulse to join the stampede and asked, "He has a favorite room, does he?"

"Oh, he's dead. He bought me drinks and never laughed at me, and so I never laughed at his poems."

Crondard went to the innkeeper, whose head was buried in his hands. Floss followed with a table-leg in his mouth for a souvenir.

The landlord looked up and anticipated his question. "He had a room, yes, but it was eliminated."

"Eliminated?"

"I burned the place down last year, or most of it, after things — " he gestured dismally at their surroundings and then sneaked his fingers to one of his ears, checking — "got out of hand. The inn was rebuilt . . . although you'd never know it, to look at it now . . . and that man's favorite room no longer exists. It shouldn't, anyway."

"Why didn't you do a thorough job, and move?"

"It's all I know, all I have. It belonged to my father, and his before him, and it used to be a jolly place when . . . that person you referred to was alive." He brightened ever so slightly, like a leper with a new hat, as he said, "You might not believe it, but our difficulties have attracted customers. Of a certain sort."

"Where was this room of his?"

While the landlord alternately scratched his head and chin to suggest perplexity, Fardel piped up: "It was next to the one I showed you the other night. The noisy one."

"It seems I have even more to thank you for than I thought, innkeeper."

"Well, you wanted a room, didn't you? Nobody who knows the place wanted that one. I told you, we were crowded."

"Your wine, at least, is an ordinary nightmare," Crondard growled. "Pour it."

Night had fallen by the time he persuaded himself to return to the courtyard. The peculiar inn was lit by a continuous flicker of pallid lightning. Beyond the Vendren palace, a full third of the sky was gripped by an electrical cataclysm. Dragons of flame writhed among three cloudy continents, whipped above them, exploded behind them. Not a whisper of thunder reached him, and a deformed moon drowsed overhead, but the breeze scurried this way and that in timid confusion. He tried to avert his mind from a curious fact: that the reflections flashing from the windows around him were not synchronized with the lightning. Only one of the many rooms showed an inner light. Directly above the kennels and beneath the roof, it was the one he had shared with Elyssa Fand.

The clatter he had taken for music grew louder as he approached the rickety stairway. He recognized it now as the relentless clatter of pots and pans he had heard from the room next to his. Zornard Glypht's torturers had made such a din in an effort to keep him awake. A disciple of Mantissus would spout some gabble about coincidence, but he now damned all philosophers to the kind of hell that Lord Morphyrion might preside over. His only hope was to succumb to the local madness that had obviously infected him, too, and seek out the dead dreamer. But if he found him, how would he kill him?

"Ar's clap," he muttered as he trudged upward. Halfway up the stairway, he appended an apology. This was not the time and place to offend any Gods.

No one had tidied the room. His knees trembled at a hint of decay in the close air. Floss searched eagerly for its source, perhaps remembering his feast, and found it in the stained mattress. He began to rip it apart. The lamp with its floating wick looked no different from the one Fardel had set on the table two nights ago, but still burning.

The crashing and banging of metal was even louder than Crondard remembered, and it burst upon his ears painfully when he flung wide the door to the hallway. The transverse passage was no longer outside the door, however; he stood at the entrance to the infinitely long corridor, lighted by dim sconces. He clutched the door, fighting the urge to run. He took heart from the courage of the hound, who trotted forward without hesitation to sniff the carpet.

He walked cautiously forward, wiping his sweating palms on his cape and taking a better grip on his ax. He planned to go only far enough to descry the end of this passage, but that proved impossible. The farthest lamps showed nothing of the hallway; they might have been stars hung in emptiness, and he grew convinced that they were exactly that. The passage led beyond the inn, beyond the city, beyond the earth itself: to the home of the Gods, as an unlettered Fomor would say, and of the dead.

The real lamp beside him died so suddenly that he reacted by striking at hazard with his ax. The blade sank into a yielding substance that was nothing like wood or plaster. Under the infernal racket of clashing metal, he heard a sob or a sigh from the wounded wall. Floss dashed forward eagerly and began to tear at it with his fangs and claws. He was eating the wall.

Crondard glanced back the way he had come, no more than a few steps, and his nerves screamed as he saw the appalling distance stretching to the door of the room. One by one, other lamps in the intervening space began to die. He grabbed the reluctant dog's collar and tried to run back, but the floor yielded queasily under each step. He could progress only at the halting gait of a man laboring through a swamp. The sighing walls wavered and seemed to melt. Right angles dissolved as the passage became a rounded tube, and he slogged his way up an increasingly steep incline. No longer resisting, Floss dragged him forward with his surer footing on a surface that had become decidedly slimy.

A sickly gurgling, punctuated by irregular slapping sounds, forced him against his better judgment to look back. Bulges in the wall heaved and shifted. Some of these would periodically succeed in detaching themselves from the parent mass and flop to the floor. Pink and shapeless, they crawled clumsily after him, recalling Morphyrion's account of his nightmare-plagued palace.

He tried to cling to the belief that this was an hallucination planted in his mind by the mad lord, but Morphyrion had said nothing about a shadowy figure that lurched behind the foul offspring of the living walls, a figure that Crondard was sure, if he dared to look for an instant longer, he would recognize as Elyssa Fand. Whimpering snatches of dimly remembered prayers and charms, mingled with curses against the philosophers who had stuffed his head with dangerous nonsense, he clawed and kicked his way upward in the steadily constricting passage.

Floss squeezed through the end of the tunnel first and turned to seize Crondard by the arm, dragging him out. The Fomor staggered to his feet to slam the door and bolt it, gagging at the muffled thuds and slitherings against the other side. After his ordeal in the corridor, he had never seen any sight more welcome than this hateful room and the nightmare-twisted inn beyond it, never breathed any air more sweet than that tainted by the lingering odor of Elyssa's corpse.

The jangling and crashing from the room next door had risen beyond the level of pain and noise to become a twisting auger inside his brain. He battered the wall with his fist.

"Wake up, Zornard! Wake up and die!" he roared in the parade-ground voice that had made recruits soil their kilts. "I had no quarrel with you, but you've tried to kill me once too often, and now a Child of Nightmare is upon you! I'll show you what a bad dream can be, you son of a bitch!"

Swinging his ax with the strength of both arms, he hewed through the flesh-like substance, here only a thin layer over real wood. Barking to match his master, Floss tore at the wall with his claws. Soon they had uncovered joists scaled with charcoal, and behind them a dark space smaller than an average closet, a corner boarded over during the rebuilding. As Crondard tore aside the beams to widen the opening, the metallic racket faltered and began to fade, though his ears still rang painfully.

Lightning filled the room with a flickering twilight, but it was night inside that hole. Crondard forgot to breathe as he strained to penetrate the darkness, and for once even Floss held back, growling. An intenser shadow in one corner could have been a bag of forgotten laundry, but now it stirred. A dim glitter resolved itself into a pair of eyes in a fire-blackened skull.

"My best dream yet," a voice rasped, and the dry rattle that followed might have been meant for a chuckle. "I never before dreamed of being a pathetic wreck with heroic delusions."

A fearful weakness gripped him, more than could be ascribed to desperate demands on an aging body. He felt less solid than the shadow in the corner. His mind refused to focus as his anger guttered like an empty lamp. This was what he had imagined death would be, when his fear of it dwindled. Even his memories began to fade; his life before the moment when he had encountered Elyssa Fand on the lonely road became faint and confused as dreams. He scrabbled for one clear image of Frothirot's cloud-piercing spires, for a memory of just one of the million songs he had heard ringing across her twisting canals, but they slipped away like minnows in a stream.

"From a nightmare, you have wakened me," that gritty voice continued, "and now, from that dream, you must . . . depart."

"Wish again, dead man," Crondard gasped, raising his ax with hands that seemed more than numb, that seemed hardly to exist, but that he knew he must trust in with more unquestioning faith than a Fomor woman squandered on Gods or ghosts. He could barely whisper, "Liron is here!"

A burst of light poured through the door and windows behind him, as if the noon sun had suddenly appeared in the western sky. It revealed the charred corpse, surrounded by a galaxy of swirling black motes; it cast the shadow of the hound against the wall behind Zornard's body; but it failed to cast Crondard's own shadow. Someone, some philosopher whose name escaped him, had taught him to doubt the evidence of his own eyes, and he refused to believe that he did not exist as he swung the ax in an arc that drove it through Zornard's skull, cracking it to a myriad flakes of charcoal. At the same time a sound like hell's roof collapsing seemed to lift him off his feet, a clap of thunder timed to his stroke.

Floss now felt brave enough to dash forward. His claws raked the ruin of the body in search of hidden bones, but he succeeded only in crushing the blackened scales to dust. Trembling, Crondard forced himself to look up. He could see his shadow now, cast by the dimming light behind him. He held up his gnarled and hairy forearm. Contrary to his expectations he saw it, and it felt solid to the touch of his other hand.

"The power of suggestion," he explained to the dog, for he was eager to hear his own voice. "He tried to kill me with it. When you've studied the works of Mantissus, you'll understand better what I'm talking about."

Floss gave him further reassurance that he existed by grinning slackly as he gazed up and wagged his stump. Crondard delighted in making as much noise as possible with his new boots as he strode to the door. The room was not the same. The bed and other furniture were neatly arranged, and it smelled no worse than what he would have expected from any sour hole at the Sow in Rut.

His survey was cut short as he looked up and saw the source of the light, much diminished, but still an impressive conflagration. Flames rose from the palace of the Vendrens, or what remained of it. To produce that ball of sun-like fire, its very stones must have ignited in one sudden burst.

He suspected that Zornard Glypht's ultimate dream had come true.

*

Crondard knew that this inn was no place to celebrate his triumph, but one round, one song and one story had led to another. It irked him that not everyone shared his high spirits; the landlord was gloomy as ever, brooding over all the breakage, and Fardel said he liked the inn better the way it used to be.

He was sitting in Zornard Glypht's old corner with a slut on either knee when a noisy party burst into the taproom. They were Fands, but he thought nothing of this until a large young man, red with drink and bloated with arrogance, swaggered over to inspect him.

Sneering at the Vendren emblem on Crondard's chest, he said, "I thought all the yellow pussies went into hiding when their master died." He called to his companions, "I've found one! What do you say we send it swimming in a sack?"

Crondard was not at his brightest. He said, "Who died?"

"Morphyrion, the foul wizard who fed you your daily mice. The Gods finally got around to striking him with lightning."

This talk of animals reminded Crondard of Floss, and he asked one of the sluts, "Where's my dog?"

"You tied him in the courtyard, remember? After he bit the innkeeper?"

"Did you call me a dog?" the Fand warrior bellowed, tugging clumsily at his sword.

"Shit," Crondard said as the news finally sank in. "I'm not going to be Lord Commander of the Fomorian Guards."

"A dead pussy with its yellow hide stretched on the door, that's what you're going to be!"

As the news sank in deeper, he realized that Lord Morphyrion could no longer protect him from the charge of desertion, the local charges of murder and necromancy, and the vengeance of the police; nor from Fands like this one, pining for an ancient feud. He had seen the palace burn, but it had not occurred to him that such a wicked old man could die. Instead of wasting time celebrating, he should have been fleeing for his life.

The young man's companions had been urging him all this while to rejoin them, but no one did anything to restrain him until he at last succeeded in disentangling his sword from his green and gold cloak. Then a woman dashed over to hang on his arm.

"No, Cousin Leodri! Come back and have a drink."

"Ar's crabs!" the Fomor cried, and the whores and the table tumbled to the floor as he sprang to his feet and fell back against the wall, groping for his ax. The woman was the one he had known as Fanda: the living Elyssa Fand.

Except for his quivering knees, he was frozen when she stared into his eyes. She seemed only slightly less shocked than he was.

"I know you . . . don't I?" she whispered.

"You can go to his funeral, then," her cousin growled, swinging her from side to side as he tried to free his arm. "We'll hold it tonight on the nearest dung-heap."

"You were dead!" Crondard managed to gasp.

"I'll teach you to insult Lady Elyssa!" Trying to break free, the swash-buckler fell on his back with a crash that shook the room. Two of his male companions came to hold him down while the girl took a hesitant step toward Crondard.

"Only in a dream," she said. In a transformation almost as unnerving as her previous ones, her face went haggard, her eyes darkened. "A terrible dream . . . I had forgotten. I was pursuing you. And you helped me, somehow, you helped me wake from it."

"I'm glad you're not dead," Crondard said, hugging the wall with his back as he edged away.

It seemed as if she really had forgotten. Her face brightened. She even smiled. "If you're looking for employment now, my father, Lord Ruthrent — "

"No!" Crondard said, adding: "Thank you. I have business in Zaxann. I must go, really."

"How unfortunate." She pouted. "It isn't every night I meet the man of my dreams."

"Yes," the Fomor said, nodding and grinning in what he knew was a sickly way. He turned and ran for the courtyard before she could recall her dreams more clearly.

"Flee, coward!" he heard Cousin Leodri bellowing as he untied Floss and hurried with him to Thunderer's stall. "Next time I see you, I'll make a torch of your tail!"

Elyssa Fand was beautiful. Even sober, he might have tried to overcome his memories and taken up her offer, if she had not smiled when she had. In Zornard Glypht's nightmare, the girl who called herself Fanda had smiled with a perfect set of teeth. But tonight, one of Elyssa's canine teeth was missing.

He believed it was the one she had left in his thumb when he threw her head to the dogs.

Afterword

When I read Brian McNaughton's "Meryphillia" in Lovecraft's Legacy, I found it a breath of fresh air; for it was not merely one of the two or three fine stories in an otherwise lackluster anthology, but it was perhaps the only story in the book that showed actual originality. Here, for once, was not a self-proclaimed "disciple" of Lovecraft paying dubious homage by merely writing a half-baked rip-off of one of his mentor's own tales. Reading that story again in this volume, in the company of its fellows (many of which are still finer specimens of horrific art), I come to wonder whether "Mery-phillia" was even conceived as a "Lovecraft pastiche," or a pastiche of any kind. For Brian McNaughton seems to have mastered one of the most difficult of literary arts: to draw upon the classics of the field without losing his own voice.

Like few modern writers in our realm, McNaughton has drunk deep in the well of literary horror and absorbed what he has read. To say that one can find echoes of Lovecraft, Clark Ashton Smith, Lord Dunsany, Robert E. Howard, and perhaps other writers in his work is not to say that he is in any way dependent upon them; rather, they seem merely to have provided him with suggestive hints on how to say the things he himself has to say.

Perhaps Clark Ashton Smith, with his delightful mixing of morbidity and humor and his evocative use of language, is the chief influence on McNaughton; but let me say bluntly that, in my humble opinion, McNaughton is a better prose writer than Smith. Smith's true greatness is as a poet. He is one of the great poets of our lamentable century, and would be so recognized if modern poets had not suffered a kind of collective insanity and decided that bad prose is superior to poetry. But what has been said of Smith's prose fiction certainly brings to mind the principal qualities of McNaughton's. Recall Ray Bradbury: "Take one step across the threshold of his stories, and you plunge into color, sound, taste, smell, and texture — into language." Or remember the precocious Donald Wandrei, who in his teens wrote what may still be one of the finest appreciations of Smith in "The Emperor of Dreams" (*Overland Monthly*, December 1926). Wandrei was of course writing about Smith's poetry, since Smith had not yet begun the extensive writing of fiction; but his words uncannily anticipate the fiction of both Smith and McNaughton:

He has constructed entire worlds of his own and filled them with creations of his own fancy. And his beauty has thus crossed the boundary between that which is mortal and that which is immortal, and has become the beauty of strange stars and distant lands, of jewels and cypresses and moons, of flaming suns and comets, of marble palaces, of fabled realms and wonders, of gods, and daemons, and sorcery.

The world that McNaughton has created in this book is the world of the ghoul; and who knows but that The Throne of Bones will become the standard textbook for the care and feeding of ghouls just as Dracula has become that for vampires? The ghoul entered Western literature chiefly through William Beckford's Arabian extravaganza, Vathek (1786); and it was the learned Samuel Henley who — aside from pilfering Beckford's French original and sneaking into print an English version a year before the French edition emerged — wrote highly learned notes to Vathek that H. P. Lovecraft absorbed when writing of ghouls himself in "The Hound" and other tales. Here is Henley on ghouls:

Goul or ghul, in Arabic, signifies any terrifying object which deprives people of the use of their senses; hence it became the appellative of that species of monster which was supposed to haunt forests, cemeteries, and other lonely places, and believed not only to tear in pieces the living, but to dig up and devour the dead.

From this nucleus, and from elaborations upon it in Bierce, Lovecraft, Smith, and others, McNaughton has built up an entire ghoulish universe — a universe, to be sure, full of danger and terror, but one that we perhaps wistfully wish we occupied rather than this prosy sphere of ours where the only ghouls are pathetic specimens of the Jeffrey Dahmer type.

But McNaughton has drawn upon far more than merely the master-works of horror for his conceptions. As I read this book I was startled to note how easily I could have imagined myself in the classical world — perhaps that long twilight of the Roman Empire, with barbarians at the gates, whose twisted decadence is so perfectly captured in Petronius' Satyricon. The influence of Graeco-Roman antiquity upon McNaughton would make an interesting essay. Those "Fomorian Guards" he speaks of: how can we not recall the Praetorian Guards, that cohort which began as members of the staff of Roman generals during the Republic but which later became the Emperor's private army and caused much mischief in the later Empire? When we read the name of Akilleus Bloodglutter, how many of us know that Akilleus is nothing more than a literal transcription from the Greek of that hero of the Iliad whom most of us know more familiarly under the name of Achilles? And perhaps it also takes a classicist not to be fazed by McNaughton's casual tossing in of recondite words like "psittacine nugacities," a charming Graeco-Latin hybrid (from psittakos, parrot, and nugae, trivialities).

An essay, indeed, ought to be written on the general influence of classicism on weird writers. It was Lord Dunsany who, in speaking of his failed attempts to learn Greek and the possible influence of that experience upon the creation of his worlds of fantasy, wrote that it left me with a curious longing for the mighty lore of the Greeks, of which I had had glimpses like a child seeing wonderful flowers through the shut gates of a garden; and it may have been the retirement of the Greek gods from my vision after I left Eton that eventually drove me to satisfy some such longing by making gods unto myself. . . .

Lovecraft read far more widely in ancient literature than Dunsany (although he too was very deficient in Greek, as his thoroughly botched derivation of the word Necronomicon attests), but he goes on to say that he himself derived his myth-pattern — what we now call the "Cthulhu Mythos" — chiefly from Dunsany. In other words, he too sensed that Dunsany's pantheon of gods in Pegana draw upon classical myth, and his own myth- cycle would do the same. Clark Ashton Smith's knowledge of the classics — not to mention his knowledge of such classically influenced poets as Shelley, Keats, and Swinburne — is evident on every page of both his fiction and his poetry. I have no doubt that McNaughton has his share of classical learning as well, whether gained directly from the ancients or from their modern disciples.

Then there are McNaughton's names. They are a wonder, for, bizarre as many of them are, they all seem uncannily right for the universe he has created. Lovecraft remarked of Dunsany: "His system of original personal and place names, with roots drawn from classical, Oriental, and other sources, is a marvel of versatile inventiveness and poetic discrimination"; and I can think of no better description of McNaughton's nomenclature. Sythiphore, Chalcedor, Paridolia, Zephryn Phrein, Lord Nephreiniel of Omphiliot — these names seem not so much invented as found in some remote corner of the collective imagination to which only McNaughton has had access. They are not the products of whim, but are logically formed on the basis of a language as rigidly governed by the rules of grammar and syntax as the classical tongues themselves.

But beyond the surface glitter of McNaughton's work — its controlled exoticism of language, its many nods to distinguished predecessors in the field, its flamboyant mixture of sex, satire, and morbidity — there is the incessant rumination on that most inexhaustible theme in the human imagination: Death and that "undiscovered country" that may lie beyond.

And it is here that McNaughton draws upon that immemorial classic of our field, Edgar Poe, who knew more than he or any man should have known of Death:

Out — out are the lights — out all!
    And, over each quivering form,
The curtain, a funeral pall,
    Comes down with the rush of a storm.
While the angels, all pallid and wan,
    Uprising, unveiling, affirm
That the play is the tragedy, "Man,"
    And its hero the Conqueror Worm.

It is that Worm that is the true hero of *The Throne of Bones*.
                                            — S. T. Joshi

Printed in the USA
CPSIA information can be obtained
at www.ICGtesting.com
LVHW051216170324
774667LV00001B/42